PRAISE FOR N

"Smart, emotionally intelligent,
and full of surprises—page-turning time travel,
with a twist you won't see coming."
—Nicholas Sansbury Smith, *New York Times* bestselling
author, on *And Then She Vanished*

"Jones brings time travel alive by getting
all the little details right—the sounds, smells,
colors, and textures . . . leaving the reader wishing
they could climb on board for the next jump.
Fast-paced and engrossing."
—David Pedreira, author of *Gunpowder Moon*,
on *The Observer Effect*

"Smart and fun . . . It's easy to become
engrossed in this fascinating plot which culminates
in a thrilling climax. Fortunately, Nick Jones has
left the way open for Joe to engage in more
time-traveling adventures."
—*Mystery & Suspense* on *The Observer Effect*

"Simply the best time-travel series out there."
Nick Pirog, Amazon bestselling author,
praise for the series

THE QUANTUM CHAIN

BOOKS BY NICK JONES

THE JOSEPH BRIDGEMAN SERIES

And Then She Vanished
The Shadows of London
The Observer Effect
The Quantum Chain

THE
QUANTUM
CHAIN

NICK JONES

**BLACK
STONE**
PUBLISHING

Printed in the United States of America
Originally published in hardcover by Blackstone Publishing in 2022

First paperback edition: 2023
ISBN 978-1-9826-9373-2
Fiction / Science Fiction / Time Travel

Version 1

Blackstone Publishing
31 Mistletoe Rd.
Ashland, OR 97520

www.BlackstonePublishing.com

PROLOGUE

As I climb the wooden steps of the beach house, I turn back, shielding my eyes against the glare of the midday sun. Pale sand stretches for miles. Gulls swoop and ride the thermals of a warm sky. Alexia is a dark silhouette, shin-deep in the ocean, surrounded and accentuated by a million sparkling diamonds that dance over the surf. She's throwing a ball for Jack, her dog—our dog now. He reaches the ball, and as he paddles his way back, she claps with joy. This holiday was her idea. Time away from everything and everyone. I soak in the moment, my heart swelling with love and appreciation.

I pad barefoot back to the beach house for lunch duty. The owners have tastefully decorated the place, a coastal theme with pale pastel colors and paintings of the local harbor. As I pass an impressive mirror framed in bleached driftwood, I pause and study my reflection. My skin is lightly tanned. I look healthy and happy. I'm a lucky man. For so long I thought I had lost Alexia. Now, our relationship feels written; finally, it can't be undone.

As if in reaction to these thoughts, my reflection breaks the rules. I don't move, but he glances toward the beach and then turns back to me. My eyes widen. My mouth falls open.

My doppelgänger doesn't follow suit.

He's speaking, but there's no sound. My mind flashes briefly back to Nils Petersen, trapped inside the void. Is that what's happening here?

"I can't hear you," I say, my voice already thin with shock and fear.

My silent ghost steps closer, sending my stomach into a crawling knot. He beckons me. Tentatively, I approach the mirror. Mouthing my words clearly, I ask, "What do you want?"

He places his right hand against the mirror, his expression urgent. He's asking me to do the same, for us to connect. Nervously, I scan the beach house. There are two realities. Which one is real? Can they both exist? I take a moment to consider how I got here. And that's when my fear really takes hold because I don't remember arriving, let alone packing a case, or saying goodbye to people at home. Nothing. This feels compartmentalized.

Am I dreaming? I hope so . . . But if I am, this is turning into a nightmare.

My reflection is insistent, his eyes pleading for me to place my hand against his. I can't just ignore him. That's when I notice that the beach house on his side of the mirror has begun to fade and darken, as though foreboding clouds are forming overhead. I place my hand against the cold glass, and the room beyond immediately brightens again.

My reflection exhales, clearly relieved. It appears that the crisis—whatever it was—has been averted. Our hands peel apart. I glance around, and a wave of shocked panic rushes over my body. The beach house on my side of the mirror has been replaced with an all-encompassing darkness. I call out but have no voice. My clone stands where I had just a few moments ago. He considers me, offers me a faint, apologetic smile, and then turns away. He's talking to someone, but I can't hear what they're saying. Alexia is in the room now. She walks over to him, and they embrace. She kisses the man who has just stolen my life. Our places have been switched. He tricked me.

The distant sound of an air-raid siren shocks me into action. The one thing I know about the void is that doorways are the only way out. The mirror. It's how I entered, perhaps I can exit the same way. But it's drifting away from me. I try to move, but my legs don't work. I'm rooted to the spot.

I need to warn Alexia, to tell her that the man she's with is an imposter. "Help me," I cry, my voice nonexistent. All I hear is the incongruous sound of that air-raid siren. The mirror starts to crack, splintering at the edges, and then explodes in a shower of brilliant light.

PART 1

1

The sound in my dream wrenches me awake.

"Huh, what?" I flail around in the dark until I find the cord of my bedside lamp. I switch on the light, whining, still trying to figure out where I am. The numbers on my digital clock inform me that this is a very unsociable hour. My heart is racing. The air-raid siren blares from my phone, which vibrates facedown on the side table. My anger builds. Suddenly, it all makes sense. Only one person would call me at this hour, the woman who earned this dramatic ringtone.

"Seriously? It's five a.m., Gabrielle! This better be important."

"I'm good, Golden Balls, thanks for asking." There's a boozy slur in her voice. "How *you* doin'?"

"Fine, thanks," Annoyingly, my British mental programming forces me to respond politely, which makes me even more irritable. The fact that she saved me from a guilt-ridden nightmare is beside the point.

Gabrielle Green is a touchy American time traveler who works for The Continuum, the organization based in the future that sends time travelers back to fix the past. I had the dubious pleasure of accompanying her on a mission to 1873 Paris a few weeks ago. I nearly died. Twice. She's pushy, annoying, and rude, and she always manages to brush me up the wrong way, but occasionally her cold black heart is in the right place.

I rub my face vigorously and swallow my annoyance. "OK. I'm awake now. What's up?"

"Oh, you know, making friends with a bottle of bubbly, minding my own business. Gimme a minute, will ya?" I hear muffled voices in the background, then raucous male laughter. She shouts, "What's your problem?" without moving her mouth away from the microphone. I yank the phone from my ear.

"Bridgeman? Are you there?"

"Yes, I'm here. Where are you?"

"I was over at Bruce's house the other night, and—"

"Who's Bruce?"

"Hang on, I need to get away from these guys." She breathes heavily, apparently walking, and then resumes. "He's a singer, you've heard of him. If I told you who he was, I would have to kill you, or at least drug you and leave you for dead in the Nevada desert. Anyway, I was at his place the other night, and we're on the wrong side of a bottle of scotch, and he's getting all teary-eyed. I'm thinking either he's going to make a move, or he's getting choked up about his latest divorce, or both, but no. Turns out Bruce was coerced into selling an antique from his personal collection."

"Right." I rub my hand wearily across my eyes, trying to figure out where this is going. "What did he sell?"

"One of his horses. He collects them—not real ones, obviously. Antiques. He sold it to a collector 'under duress,' his words. I'm like, Bruce! Why the hell did you sell it if you didn't want to? Anyway, he did. It was old. Chinese. Yang dynasty, I think."

"Tang dynasty?"

"That's what I said." She sighs heavily. "It's mega-ancient, apparently. Some kind of kimchi—no, wait, that's not right."

"*Mingqi.*" Now my interest is piqued. I've read about the objects the Chinese used to bury with their dead, but I've never actually handled one. I'd be afraid of dropping it too—some of them are worth a ton of cash. "Is it pottery?"

"Like I said, a pottery horse. Geez, Bridgeman, do you listen to anything I say?"

"I do actually, but what does this have to do with me?"

"Finally, the right question." Her voice drips sarcasm, but when she speaks again, she shows signs of the Gabrielle who turned the Paris mission around, the woman who's a legitimate asset to The Continuum. "Bruce didn't know what he had, obviously. He just loved the thing, but it turns out the horse is a focus object, a powerful one too. Its story involves union, one of the most powerful forces in the world and a massive multiplier on the Future Change Index, which means we need to get it back ASAP, before it gets sold and we lose it for good."

I've completed a couple of missions myself, which means I'm sort of part of this too. It's how I know about focus objects. They get charged up with the past, and when travelers touch them, they form a bond and create a portal back through time.

"What's the mission?" I ask.

"Oh, great, here we go."

"Er, are you talking to me?"

"Yes!" She growls, "I know what you're like, panicking already."

"I'm not panicking, I just want to know—"

"The horse links all the way back to ancient China. It's a love story, and those always have far-reaching outcomes, but listen, before you get all wound up. We don't need to actually *do* the mission, there's plenty of time for that. The problem is losing *track* of it. Bruce was supposed to keep a hold of that horse for at least another twenty years."

Visions of rock stars as time guardians for The Continuum fill my mind. "Hang on, are you saying that Bruce knows about time travel? That he takes care of focus objects?"

"Nooo." She says this like I'm being slow. "He doesn't know the horse is special in *that* way, but it was supposed to stay with him, to follow its correct and known path, nice and quiet, until we were ready. But in a massive case of Murphy's Law, the dummy sold it! Which means that now we have to get it back. Once we do, The Continuum can take it from there. Got it?"

"Er, yes, I think so."

"Good. So, are you in?"

I consider this carefully. Gabrielle prefers to work alone, has made it clear numerous times, so she wouldn't ask me to join her for the fun of it. There's more to this. "Obviously. I want to help, but I'm trying to figure out why you need me."

"I don't."

"OK, so why don't you go and buy it back yourself."

"So annoying." She tuts. "All right, listen. I'm in the middle of a mission, and my next jump is coming up any day. I could travel now, while we're on this call. Who knows?" I guess that makes sense—if it's true. Once you are bonded to a mission via an object, time decides when to throw you back. "And the dealer who bought Mister Ed from Bruce is super picky about who he'll work with. I tried, but he runs his whole setup face-to-face and won't talk to anyone who's not in the biz. So, I thought, who do I know who's into boring antiques and has nothing better to do? I'm not asking you to head over there on your own. I'll come with you, but like I said, I don't know when my mission might drag me away, and we can't run the risk of missing our chance to get this focus object back."

I'm actually quite excited about getting my hands on such an ancient object, but I'm not going to let Gabrielle get off so lightly. "So what you *should've* said, when I answered the phone, was 'Hey Joe, we lost a really expensive, very important focus object and need to get it back, but I'm clueless about antiques, so I need your help to secure it, pretty please, cherry on top, etc.' Does that about sum it up?"

"Whatever," she says sulkily. "Listen, my champagne is getting warm and my guys are getting cold, what's it gonna be?" I hear her take a slurp. "It's a really special piece, eighth century, I think Bruce said. Just your bag, right? Come on! How often do you get your clammy paws on stuff that old?"

She's right. I do want to get my clammy paws on it.

"Anyway," she continues, "you'd better say yes because I already booked you a flight."

"A flight?" I'd assumed it must be in the UK, since she was asking me to join her. That will teach me.

"Yep. Leaving tomorrow, three p.m. I've checked you in already."

"Where to?"

"Amsterdam."

"Gabrielle!"

"What?" I can imagine the face she's pulling, the picture of innocence. "It's only an hour's flight from Heathrow. I'll meet you there tomorrow night, presuming I don't time travel on the plane, although I guess I could go hide in the bathroom. Wouldn't be the first time I've gone pop in the middle of a flight, if you know what I'm saying."

"Gross."

Gabrielle laughs gleefully. "You're just jealous. Anyway, see you at the hotel tomorrow. I'll text you the deets. Ciao, Chosen One." She hangs up.

I put my phone back on the bedside table and stretch, breaking into a yawn. It's 5:10 a.m. I consider trying to get some more sleep, but my heart is racing, and my brain's in overdrive. I have to say, despite the short notice and sideways manner of her invitation, Gabrielle's call at least interrupted one of the most bizarre and uncomfortable dreams I've ever had, and that's saying something, given my viewings. Her call also got my antiques juices flowing.

I grab a nearby antiques magazine. I sometimes read them at night to help me drop off to sleep. Did she call me boring? I'm searching for a particular article . . . there it is. The headline reads: Chinese Grave Goods Back in Fashion. Maybe that's why this dealer bought the horse, wanting to cash in on this year's fad. There's plenty of money in this business if you play it right.

It's funny. None of the other focus objects I've come across have been worth anything, other than sentimental value. The radio, the metronome. Hugely valuable to a time traveler, of course, but it's interesting that some focus objects can be worth a financial fortune too.

My phone vibrates. It's a text from Gabrielle. I skim through it. She writes like she speaks, in partial sentences and with no additional information. I'm to meet her at the City Hotel, Amsterdam, at 5 p.m. local time.

If it weren't for the fact that I'm traveling with the red-haired hand grenade, I'd be excited about this trip. It's been a while since I've visited another country in my own time. I always find it good for the soul, for resetting my perspective. Whatever transpires, I know one thing for certain—visiting Amsterdam with Gabrielle Green will be anything but dull.

2

Heathrow Airport is heaving. A chirpy woman behind the check-in desk takes my passport, taps her keyboard, and says, "Good news, Mr. Bridgeman, you've been upgraded to business class, courtesy of Miss Mandalay."

"Miss who?"

She double-checks her screen. "Yes. I have a note on the system here, says to let you know the upgrade was paid for by . . . Anita Mandalay."

Anita Mandalay?

Oh God.

I need a man to lay.

Gabrielle is so immature, but also, kind of funny.

Stifling a grin, I take my boarding pass and for the first time in my life, I turn left as I enter the plane. It's been years since I've taken a flight, and I'm excited about leaving the UK. I'm not exactly basketball height—five foot eleven—but I always feel cramped in a plane. The wider seats in business class more than take care of that problem. The cabin crew hands out newspapers, drinks, and snacks, but before I can really enjoy the upgrade, the seat belt sign lights up, my ears pop, and we begin our descent into Schiphol Airport.

As soon as we land, I turn on my phone and receive a text.

> Yo. Meet me in the hotel bar.
> Anita x

I text back.

> Will do. Hugh Jardon x

An oldie but a goodie.

The taxi ride takes half an hour, an interesting journey along wide streets with tramlines down the middle and electrical wires overhead. People on bicycles everywhere, some with single riders, some with kids on the back or dogs in their baskets. A woman balances a plant across her lap and a shopping bag over the handlebars.

The City Hotel is in an upmarket part of town. Tall Dutch baroque buildings line either side of the street. The smoked glass doors open automatically, making me grin. One of Vinny's favorite things to do is pretend that he has magic powers and waft his hand as they open. I give it a go. It's fun.

The hotel is trendy and buzzing with activity. Guests in small groups chat around stylish coffee tables and low leather sofas. A man in a smart concierge uniform welcomes me into the foyer, and when I ask, he points me in the direction of the bar.

I pass through a kind of anteroom dotted with modern sculpture. The bar is busy but has a laid-back vibe. Cool music plays over the loudspeakers. Along one side of the room is a long bar, studded here and there with clusters of barstools. In the center, hanging above a forest of chairs and tables, is a mobile made up of full-size orchestral instruments.

I spot Gabrielle balanced on a barstool. She raises her hand. As I weave my way over to her, I'm surprised to see she's swapped out her usual, grungy attire for a green dress, jacket, and boots. She's even wearing normal-looking makeup.

"What?" she says, scowling at me.

"Nothing. You look . . . nice."

She growls.

We've hardly spoken since I got back from Paris. Gabrielle confuses me. I thought we had made some ground on that mission, but every time I meet her it feels like I'm starting from scratch.

She drains her cocktail and waves her little paper umbrella coquettishly at a young dark-haired man at one of the tables near the brasserie. He winks. She makes a slow throaty noise. "Well, that's my evening sorted."

"OK," I say awkwardly, wondering if I might need a drink.

"Before you start whining, let's talk about the plan. The dealer who coerced the horse from Bruce is called Johan Decker. He has a shop nearby. I checked, and his assistant said he was at his warehouse. So, we go there now, buy the horse back, and who knows, we might even have time to party."

"We just go to the warehouse and buy it back?"

"Yep." Her expression is pure innocence. *Butter wouldn't melt*, as Grandma Bridgeman used to say.

"And you really needed me to come all the way here for that?" I glare at her, arms folded. "Why do I get the feeling you aren't telling me the whole story?"

Her face scrunches into a scowl. "I told you when I called you yesterday. This Decker guy is particular about who he deals with. You're in the antiques business; you can talk about old stuff. Plus, I'm bonded to a mission already. Remember?" She pushes her phone into my face. On the screen is a photograph of a wonderful antique horse. It's impossible to guess the scale from this image, but the artistry and craftsmanship are exquisite. "What's it worth?" Gabrielle asks.

"Difficult to say. I won't know for sure until I see it, but only five percent of Tang horses have that blue cobalt glaze. It was more expensive than gold at the time, so that's going to push—"

"Ah, ah, ah. Let me stop you there." Gabrielle rolls a hand. "Let's fast-track this."

"OK, well. It's an impressive-looking piece. I've seen similar go for a million dollars, but it really depends on whether—"

"Bruce bought the horse a few years back for six hundred thousand dollars, said he couldn't really say no when Decker offered him nine hundred thousand."

"Wow. That's a lot of money." My brain catches up. "Hang on a minute. If we're going to buy it back, he's going to want more than that."

"There it is." Gabrielle claps sarcastically and hops off her stool. "Right, come on, Golden Balls, we're not just here to smoke weed and have sex with random people. Let's go spend some cash."

She sashays across the bar, ensuring that her future prey is watching. I follow behind and stick my tongue out at her back. A little boy at a nearby table giggles.

Outside, the late afternoon air is chilly, but Gabrielle hares along at speed, and I don't have time to feel the cold. We cross the street and walk along a footpath as cyclists zip past us. It's good to be soaking in the atmosphere of the Netherlands' capital. I read on the plane that Amsterdam is building a circular economy, and I think it's having an impact already. People smile in public here. It's the opposite of Cheltenham, where a happy face tends to make people suspicious.

I catch up to Gabrielle. "So, the horse is a focus object."

"Uh-huh."

"And The Continuum can see those? Sort of keep track of where they are?"

"Yeah."

This is how most of my conversations with Gabrielle play out. I do some guessing; she does some brief and occasionally sarcastic confirming. It's one way to learn, I suppose, like gaining crucial life skills from a grumpy but experienced teenager.

She groans. "I've just remembered what you're like. You're going to keep asking me questions, aren't you?"

"I'm trying to understand how this works. I understand why the horse is important, it's the link to a mission—"

"Not just any mission," she corrects me. "Union . . . love, baby. The kind of mission that can light the Index up."

"Sure, OK, but I don't know how you decide when to activate a mission. I don't know why we can't just wait and let the horse pass through different hands, maybe pick it up later."

She bobs her head and keeps walking. "Fair enough. I do forget sometimes that your training hasn't been exactly . . . extensive. All right, I can play teacher, briefly. Listen up, and pay attention. Focus objects emit energy that The Continuum can track. Initially, they're in a kind of stasis. Waiting. They can be like that for a long time, sometimes hundreds of years, waiting for activation, something we call 'priming.' The metronome we used in Paris? I primed that before you arrived at my hotel room. We get to choose when we do it. The horse has got at least fifty years left in it, but we're worried that we're going to lose it."

"Lose it? Why?"

"Objects have a normal path through time, but there's something . . . off about this one; it's not right."

"In what way?"

"Felix said the data appeared to be . . . unnatural. Objects have their correct place in time, a path they follow naturally.

Bruce wasn't *supposed* to sell it. Not yet anyway. And sometimes when that happens, objects can end up lost forever, or even worse, destroyed. It's like they get disrupted and then we lose the chance at the mission. So that's why we need to get it back and ensure it's safe." She checks her phone. "This way."

We turn onto a pretty street with a narrow canal to our left. Trees and old-fashioned streetlamps stand at intervals beside the water. It's the first canal I've seen since I arrived. Boats and barges pass by.

After a twenty-minute walk, we end up in a quiet part of town filled with low gray and white buildings with up-and-over-style garage doors, like aircraft hangars. The water in the harbor is dark brown and lackluster, and there are no plants or trees or people, just an odd abandoned truck and forklift. It's more than a little creepy. Instinctively I rotate my silver hunter pocket watch in my hand, its body reassuringly heavy.

Gabrielle's voice cuts through my thoughts. "Here we are. Cacaohaven—the cocoa port. That's Johan Decker's warehouse over there." She points to a hefty red hangar door, half-open. Light spills out onto the cobbled walkway.

"Aren't you coming in?" I ask her.

"Nah. Kind of burnt my bridges there."

Gabrielle's version of burning bridges plays out like a Vietnam movie in my head. "What did you do?"

"Let's just say it's best he doesn't see me."

Finally, we get to the truth. "This is why you wanted me here. You've already tried buying the horse back, but you messed up."

"Listen, Joe," she says, clearly annoyed. "The Continuum trusts us to track this object down." I love her tactical use of the word *us*. "When I pushed Decker, he slipped up and mentioned an auction, which he then fervently denied. If that's his plan, you need to snap the horse up before that auction happens."

"OK, so presuming Decker is here, and he has the horse with him, let's say that I persuade him to sell it to me. How am I supposed to pay for it?"

Gabrielle reaches into her handbag and hands me a jet-black credit card. I turn it in my hands. There's no writing on it—no raised characters, no chip—just a glistening, colorless gem in the middle of the face.

"That's a diamond, isn't it?" I ask.

"Yeah. You're authorized up to 2 million dollars. Try and get it for less if you can. I promised Iris we'd do our best to limit the damage."

Feeling a bit sweaty, I slip the card into my jacket pocket. I guess when you can see the past, money isn't really a problem. You can invest in whatever you like at pretty much any stage in history. I'm wondering how that kind of insider trading might work with resistance, the natural force that repels changes outside of time's plan, when Gabrielle jabs me in the ribs. "You know I mentioned that we prime objects when we are ready to bond and travel?"

"Yeah," I say, cautiously.

"Focus objects want to tell their story; they react when a time traveler is near. If the horse is in there, you need to be careful not to prime it."

"I have no idea *how* to prime it, so that's probably not going to happen, right?"

Nodding, she says, "Highly unlikely, but, so you know, it's all about intention. If a focus object thinks you're ready to hear its story, it'll want to pop its cork. And that would be a little . . . premature. I'm sure you know all about that."

I can't help but laugh. Gabrielle's acerbic wit is an acquired taste, but I'm learning to appreciate it. "OK, so worst-case scenario, I prime the focus object. What then?"

"Unless you want to waste a perfectly good mission, you have a few minutes to bond and then jump. You're still a rookie, so don't do that. It takes a lot to prime them. Just don't beg the horse to talk and you'll be fine." She hands me another card. Matte charcoal gray with embossed silver lettering: *James Theodore Blake. Fine Antiques.*

"Why didn't you use my real name?"

"This sounds more distinguished, and I figured it was safer." She gestures toward the warehouse door. "Good luck, Mr. Blake. Just get the horse, and we can go home."

The warehouse is cavernous, with floor-to-ceiling racks stacked with various crates and boxes. To my left is a desk with an old-fashioned lamp and an in tray neatly stacked with papers. There doesn't seem to be anybody around, so before I call out, I close my eyes and try to pick up any energy from the focus object. I'm shocked when I immediately hear a weak whisper, faint but undeniable. I don't mean the object is talking to me: the feelings, visions, or sounds that I pick up all come from my unique, psychometric connection. They are silent in the real world but powerfully evocative to me, a form of spooky action at a distance. It makes me think of the observer effect, how we influence and interact with the present and the past. Objects know when you're paying them attention, just like animals seem to know when they are being watched. There are senses and powers in this world that we don't fully understand.

"Can I help you?" says a loud voice behind me. I turn and face a tall, slender man in his midforties. His Dutch accent is strong, but I could easily have guessed his nationality by his stylish attire. He's dressed in a sharp blue suit, with a white shirt and an orange tie that matches the laces on his expensive cream-colored running shoes. His round glasses are thick and match his tie.

"Mr. Decker?" I venture.

He offers me a guarded smile, difficult to see beneath a sharply styled mustache. "And you are?"

"James Blake." I hand him my card, impressed that I remember to use my new alias. He studies the card and then looks up. "I have a shop in town. We mainly specialize in high-quality Dutch furniture and fine art, anything up to mid-twentieth century. If you want to drop by some time, I would be happy to show you around."

"Actually, I'm here about an item you recently bought from an acquaintance of mine."

He cocks an eyebrow. "Go on."

"It's an antique horse, Tang dynasty."

His displeasure is immediate. "For God's sake. Not this again. I don't appreciate the constant harassment."

"Harassment?"

He lets out a frustrated breath. "OK, I admit I lost my temper, but that woman—a colleague of yours, I presume—was extremely rude, not to mention persistent and annoying." He seems to have Gabrielle pretty well pegged. He steps toward me. "I will tell you what I told her. I run an honest and professional business. When I agree to a deal, it's between me and my client." He hands my card back. Clearly, I won't be joining his list of preferred customers. "As an antique dealer, you must understand. I bought that piece in good faith. What I paid was generous. As far as I'm concerned, that's the end of the matter. I don't appreciate the threats, the constant phone calls." He rubs his thumb and forefinger over his ample mustache. "You know, I can't remember the last time someone screamed down the phone at me. So unprofessional."

When Gabrielle burns her bridges, she doesn't mess around. With a calm, considerate tone, I say, "What you just said makes complete sense to me. I'm sorry about my colleague, but this is one of those times when the seller made a terrible mistake. The horse means a lot to him, has huge sentimental value. If you could see your way to returning it, I would make it worth your while."

He holds up a finger. "I'll save you the trouble. It doesn't matter what you're about to offer, it's too late. I already have a buyer. The horse is sold."

This might be true. Sometimes you can find a buyer before going to auction, and it's always nice to get a deal done, but the horse is nearby, which means there's still hope. I decide it's time to up the game.

"I can pay you 1.3 million dollars." A silly number, and I'm impressed that I'm able to say it without the words catching in my throat.

His brow narrows. "Are you serious?"

"Absolutely. I can pay you now."

For a few seconds, he is clearly tempted, but then he visibly deflates. "My reputation is worth more to me than anything else. It's been sold. I can't go back on that deal."

"One point five million," I announce confidently. Turns out that negotiating with someone else's money is more fun than I expected.

The frown is back. He lets out a small laugh, perhaps wondering if I'm joking.

"I'm serious. We can do the deal right now."

His demeanor shifts. He glances nervously around the warehouse, checks his watch, and says, "Listen, I'm closing up here. We're done, you need to go." His eyes flick back toward his desk, where I spot a metal case. For just a few seconds, the colors in the warehouse desaturate slightly. The lamp on his desk has a green shade, which blooms into a glowing jade orb. The effect is subtle, but it's the only clue I need. The horse is in that case.

I'm so close to the focus object. All I need to do is get him over the line. "I respect your integrity, but this item is special. I hope that my final offer of 2 million dollars is enough to get this deal done."

He swallows, the color draining from his face. "Two million . . . Are you mad?"

No, just desperate. "So do we have a deal?"

3

"He said no?" Gabrielle cries. "To 2 million dollars? Is he insane?"

"Maybe. Or maybe he has integrity."

"Dammit!" she says. "Did you try? I mean really try?"

"Yes, Gabrielle, I tried." I scowl at her. "Your threats didn't help, by the way. It would have been good to know just how far you'd taken things."

She looks sheepish. We've retreated to a row of green recycling bins but still have a view of the warehouse entrance. Gabrielle is seated on a stack of wooden crates, kicking her legs. I feel like we're skipping school. She pulls a pack of cigarettes and a lighter out of her bag and lights up. "You're positive the horse was in there?"

"Absolutely. He told me it was sold, but he's got it with him."

"Any clue on the buyer?"

"No, but if I had to guess, a Chinese businessman."

"Or woman," she counters.

"Or woman," I concede. "The rich soak up all the good stuff. The only reason any of us have anything is because a billionaire didn't want it."

She shrugs. "He'll have to leave eventually. When he does, we follow him and steal it."

"And if he doesn't have the case with him?"

"We break in and steal it," she says angrily, as though this is a reasonable course of action. She pulls ferociously at the cigarette and exhales a plume of smoke. "All we can do now is wait."

We watch the warehouse for a while, not talking. After ten minutes or so, I decide to make an effort. Gabrielle's mood regularly tosses its own coin, so this is probably a mistake.

"Tell me about this mission you're on."

Surprisingly, we land on heads, her good side. "I'm working with a load of homeless guys in Chicago, and weirdly, it's only seven years ago."

"You're only jumping back seven years?"

"Yeah, harder than it sounds, though. When you jump far, you don't forget you're traveling, but when you're close to your own time, it's easy to get confused. Most of the same stores on the street, familiar stuff in the news, people wearing normal clothes. They're an iPhone model or two behind us, but otherwise, it's the same."

"I can imagine. What do you have to do?"

She squints at me. "Help this homeless guy get his life together. He's going to end up running a center for alcoholics, but I need to get him to stop drinking first." Gabrielle helping someone get off alcohol? An unexpected casting choice. "Yeah, yeah, I know what you're thinking," she says dismissively. "On the plus side, at least it wasn't a mono. I had a hunch it was gonna be, but for once I was mistaken. I've got at least one more jump, maybe more. Plenty of time to watch a few more episodes of *Highway to Heaven* and learn how to be nice."

"What do you mean, a mono?"

"A one-jump mission. They're the worst. You have to figure

out what you're supposed to be doing on the fly, and fix it all in one jump."

"Is that even possible?"

"Of course, but they're tricky sons of bitches. And you don't always know immediately either. Sometimes it takes an hour or two for the watches to calibrate before you see the red light."

On my last jump to London, the final-jump warning came up on my watch before I even traveled. I don't mention this, because I unwittingly stole the London mission from Gabrielle.

"Must be nice that language isn't an issue," I say.

"When is it ever?" Gabrielle says. "Now that you have your microchip, you'll never need to worry about that again."

I stick my finger in my ear and wiggle it around but don't feel anything unusual: no bumps or scars. Gabrielle gave me the implant when we were on the Paris mission. It burrowed under my skin like a parasite, but it didn't hurt; it gave me the immediate ability to understand and speak French. Now that I think about it properly, it's bloody creepy. It must be able to read my brain if it's changing the language I'm speaking, so that means it can probably hear my thoughts too. I start to feel panicky. I don't remember signing anything about privacy. I guess I could get it surgically removed if I really wanted to. At least it didn't set off the security alerts at Heathrow. "Is it still in my ear?"

"It's permanent," Gabrielle says, lighting another cigarette. "It'll kick in whenever you travel, enabling you to speak the most common language of the place and time you've landed in. I totally take mine for granted, but it's a smart little device."

"What happens if, say, I'm in France, but someone speaks to me in Russian?"

"It would switch to Russian, like you'd do, if you were smarter."

"Can I make it work in the present as well?" I think about

how useful it would be to understand Dutch here in the Netherlands.

"You can, but you have to turn on the setting."

"How? Is it an intention thing?"

"Bang your head three times against a wall. Why don't you give it a go?"

We both freeze as a car approaches. It pulls up outside the warehouse, a high-spec BMW, its brake lights illuminating the nearby street and canal. A striking woman in business attire exits from the rear. She's tall, with platinum-blond hair. We duck down as she briefly scans the docks and then enters Decker's warehouse. The car waits, engine running.

I drop my voice to a low murmur. "Our buyer?"

"Maybe," she says. "If I had to guess, I would say she works for a man with a ton of cash."

"Or woman," I happily correct her.

Gabrielle growls at me.

"What makes you think she works for someone rich?"

"They have a *look*," she says, scrunching up her nose, "like they are trying too hard but have absorbed some of the entitled superiority."

We wait, and the minutes pass slowly. Gabrielle checks her watch. "She's taking a long time. You don't think there's another exit out back, do you?"

"I don't think so," I reply, seeing just water beyond the warehouse.

Gabrielle closes her eyes and, after a few seconds of concentration, she says, "It's weak, but I can feel its energy. It's still in there." She grunts. "There's something off about this one, though."

"What do you mean?"

She shifts her weight, her expression uncharacteristically concerned. I get the feeling I'm finally going to discover what she should have told me when she woke me up at 5 a.m. "We have a department at The Continuum that tracks focus objects. Its official name is Location Services, but that's boring, so we call them the Librarians. Anyway, they regularly cross-reference the archives with the actual location of all the focus objects we know about, to confirm they're where they should be. This horse got flagged as an anomaly, showing up as off course. That's when I called you. But when the Librarians ran it again, it came up on the system as having been destroyed."

"Destroyed? But that's not right." I point to the warehouse. "It's in there."

"I know."

"So what's going on?"

"Initially, we thought it might be natural. Objects with amazing potential get lost all the time. Tons get destroyed in wars and accidents, and time just rebalances and identifies new pathways and focus objects. But now we know the horse is still here." Gabrielle grinds her teeth, thinking. "I don't believe Felix is wrong, because he's a goddamn genius. I'm thinking either someone is messing with the data, or they're deliberately shielding the object in some way, so we can't see it."

"Why didn't you tell me this before?"

"Because you overthink everything."

Anger threatens to boil over, but she might have a point. "Scarlett has to be involved, right?"

Gabrielle bobs her head. "It's the most logical conclusion. There's been no trace of her since we saw her in Paris, though."

Scarlett is a time traveler. She had been part of The Continuum, but she left over a disagreement. She had sent Nils, another traveler, into the void, apparently on purpose, and then turned up on our final jump to help him land safely in Paris. Like Gabrielle, she's often confusing, and her motives aren't clear.

"Wasn't Felix building a tracker?" I ask. "A way to keep tabs on Scarlett?"

"Along with Kyoko, yeah. They're using data from Paris, but I guess it's harder than they thought, because—"

She's interrupted by voices and movement. Decker and the woman outside. They shake hands, and he passes her the case. They talk briefly, and then she's back in the car and it's pulling away quickly.

"What do we do now?" I ask, but I know the answer.

"We need to follow her." Gabrielle turns to me, panic in her eyes. "We are not leaving Amsterdam without that horse." Her gaze follows the car, which is heading toward the gated exit of the docklands. She turns to me. "We need a car."

We run along the port, past what feels like endless warehouses, until we get to the main road, just in time to see the BMW turn toward the airport in the distance.

"Where are all the damn cabs?" Gabrielle says. "Wait, I see one over there. Looks like he's dropping someone off." She heads toward the other side of the road and hurls herself over the central barrier, weaving between traffic, reminding me of when I followed her in a death-defying jaunt across a road packed with horses and carriages in 1873. I follow, but by the time I get to the other side, the taxi has gone.

Gabrielle curses, but I spot another one and flag it down. We pile into the back, and Gabrielle barks at the driver. "That way, toward the airport. We need to catch up with the blue BMW!"

The driver is a middle-aged woman with a peaceful demeanor. A crucifix hangs from her rearview mirror. To my surprise, she drives like a bat out of hell, and we spot Blondie and her driver up ahead, taking the exit into Schiphol.

Gabrielle instructs our driver to follow, but by the time we reach the exit we slow to a halt, blocked by a queue of traffic.

Ahead of us, Blondie's car disappears into the mass of vehicles entering the Departures lane. "Is there another way to the airport?" Gabrielle asks our driver.

"No, this is the only way," the woman replies calmly.

Gabrielle grunts in exasperation, undoes her seat belt, and opens the passenger door. And we're running, like a couple who are about to miss their flight. Behind us, the taxi driver shouts. Gabrielle is fast. I can only just keep up, but I'm gasping for breath by the time we reach the entrance to Departures. There's no sign of the BMW or Blondie.

"They're gone!" Gabrielle kicks a nearby trolley. A family heading our way deviates toward another trolley bay, and I notice one of the security guards checking us out and speaking into his lapel.

"Gabrielle, you're drawing attention," I say. "You need to calm down."

She turns on me. "Calm down! We were asked to come here to do one job, and we've totally screwed up. Another mission lost. What the hell do we do now?"

"I don't know."

"You never do," she snaps.

"Wait a minute, it's not my fault that we—"

"I told you, missions like this don't come around that often. We lose the object now, and it's gone for good. The Continuum won't be able to track it.

"We'll get it back."

"The Future Change Index is at a critical point. If it gets much lower, we don't know what could happen. There will be a point when we can't claw it back, do you understand?" She winces, shaking her head. "Missions this deep in the past . . . they start small, but the repercussions of a successful union are huge. We need this one."

"Gabrielle."

Suddenly, she's in my face. "We're always one step behind, and it's your fault!"

"Seriously?" I fire back, fed up with her bleating. "You're blaming me? You only told me half the story. What do you expect?"

"If we'd caught that first cab, we'd have got here in time."

"And then what? Assault the woman in broad daylight at a massive international airport, in front of armed policemen?"

Gabrielle folds her arms, her cheeks bright. Her mood has flipped to tails, and it's staying there for the foreseeable future. "If you hadn't been here hamstringing my every move, I would have been on my way back home with the goddamn horse already! I only invited you here so you could have one of your electric dreams!"

"Electric dreams?"

Gabrielle grits her teeth and stifles a frustrated scream.

She's talking about my viewings, my ability to see the past. Through my dealings with The Continuum, I learned that all travelers can see the past via a connection to specific objects. It's called psychometry, but recently, I received an upgrade. Why? No idea, but now my viewings aren't just limited to objects. In certain high-stress situations, if I connect with someone eye to eye, I might—big stress on *might*—get a glimpse of their past. As far as I know, it's unique to me. Gabrielle knows that I can't do it to order, though, and certainly there are no guarantees, even with eye contact. As with the missions, time itself decides what I see. Is she hoping that I get a viewing of Johan Decker? Could I? Honestly, I have no idea.

Gabrielle's watch buzzes, and she peers at the face, shielding it from the sunlight. "You have got to be kidding."

"What's up?" I ask.

"My second jump. I'm leaving tomorrow. This is just *perfect*."

"So, what do we do now?"

"If you ask me that again, I will scream."

"Sorry, but you're the experienced one, remember?"

"I'm getting drunk. You can do what you like."

"So that's it? Go and drown your sorrows?" If Gabrielle's not careful, she's going to be emanating alcohol from every pore when she turns up to her mission tomorrow with the homeless guys. I can't see that going too well.

She narrows her eyes. I swear if we weren't in a public place, she'd take a swing at me. "We all cope in our own way. Don't wait up." She turns on her heel and stalks off toward the city.

For the next few minutes, I stand outside Schiphol Airport, unsure what to do next. Gabrielle is right: we did kind of mess that up. Then again, she's not exactly playing on the same team. I'm just about to get a cab when I spot the BMW. My eyes dart around until I see Blondie, through a glass wall, inside the airport. I break into a fast jog, not wanting to draw attention to myself but not taking my eyes off her. By the time I get inside, she's cleared a short queue and is through a set of scanners. She grabs the case and heads toward the departure lounge.

What do I do? If I go crashing through security, it's a guaranteed fast track to an Amsterdam police station. But another few seconds, and Blondie will be gone.

Instinctively, I shout, "Hey, wait!"

Maybe it's all the running, the adrenaline, my anger at Gabrielle for being so unreasonable, but my voice comes out in a great, thunderous boom. People stare at me. I suspect a few of them are undercover staff and might be about to reach for their guns, but I remain focused on Blondie. She stops, turns, and looks straight at me. There must be thirty feet between us, but even at this distance, it's strikingly clear how attractive she is: strong jaw, flawless skin, high cheekbones. Her pale-green eyes narrow. She appears confused, probably wondering if I'm going to call out again, if it was even her I was calling for.

Suddenly the airport saturates with color, and a cool energy passes between us. It's as though a tiny invisible thread, like filament in a bulb, has just ignited. That's when I grasp that my subconscious had a plan, and I just needed to catch up.

Eye contact.

It creates a connection.

I'm buzzing with it.

We are two people, who up until this moment had been unconnected. And yet this horse brought us together, joining and weaving our disparate threads into the same tapestry. The same story. Does she feel it too? Maybe. She blinks, but her focus remains on me.

What now? My options are limited. Offer her 3 million dollars, right here at the airport? No. I think seeing her was enough. I hope it was enough. I raise my hands. "I'm sorry," I say, as sincerely as I can. "I thought you were someone else."

She studies me with cautious suspicion, then regains her cool, self-contained composure. Seeming to accept my apology, she walks away and doesn't look back.

Outside the airport, I see the taxi that Gabrielle and I ditched. I pay the driver using my phone, and she seems surprised but appreciative. She offers me a ride back into town, but I decide to walk in the cool, refreshing air after all that unexpected cardio.

Hunger pains gnaw at my stomach, and the mouthwatering odor of fried fatty food teases my nostrils. I follow my nose and end up in a food hall, packed with the stalls of different vendors. I go for the kiosk with the longest queue and end up holding a paper cone full of *poffertjes*, little hot puffy pancakes sprinkled with powdered sugar. They are delicious, and a full belly gives me renewed energy.

When I get back to the hotel, the concierge asks if I'd like to join the Friday happy hour in the bar. I'm tempted, but with a nagging sense that my connection to the woman at the airport could trigger a viewing, I head back to my room.

I run myself a deep, hot bath, hoping that some deep relaxation might trigger my abilities. I squeeze in the entirety of a small bottle of free bubble bath, creating a massive lather on top of the water, like the ridiculous head on a beer from a nearly empty barrel.

I sink into the water and close my eyes, thinking about the little Chinese horse, traded like a commodity for millions of dollars by people who don't understand its true value. *I'm not giving up on you yet, Mister Ed.*

I think back to Blondie, the connection I felt when I looked into her pale-green eyes. I think Gabrielle's right, that she's working for someone. There's more to this—it's layered. Do I know this for certain? How could I? And yet, the thoughts arrive, intuitive, laced with suspicion. It feels like an aching tooth just as painkillers are wearing off. A dull ache, manageable but impossible to ignore. Blondie's hiding useful information just below the surface.

Sliding deeper into the bath, I ask time to show me more.

4

I'm high above a city, hovering like a drone over tall pastel-colored buildings with curved gray roofs. I don't know where I am—it doesn't look like Amsterdam, there's no water, and the scale of the place is much larger. Directly below me a wide square is sliced through by an asphalt highway, cars creeping slowly along in the morning rush hour.

Viewings often begin like this. I have a sense of awareness. A dual consciousness that soon fades as the viewing consumes me fully, but for now, I'm a knowing observer. I glide smoothly downward, entering through a small open window on the fifth floor of one of the buildings, into a long, well-lit corridor with highly polished parquet flooring.

A woman appears at the end of the corridor, walking directly toward me. Tall, platinum blond, the woman I saw at Decker's warehouse. Her pale-green eyes face my direction. My instinct is to hide, even though I know she can't see me.

As I float steadily toward her, she strides along the hallway with the assured gait of someone used to getting her way, and when we meet, there's a rush of cool, florally scented air as I meld with her and finally lose all sense of myself.

She enters a bathroom and leans heavily against the solid, waist-height shelf. She regards herself in the mirror: checks her teeth for traces of food, licks her finger and dampens down an errant eyebrow hair, gently pulls at the skin on either side of her face and watches the lines around her mouth disappear. Her eyes are clear and intelligent but troubled, and her gut is a ball of tension. She's alone now and needs to look out for herself. If she plays it right, this could be her ticket to financial security. She stands tall and smooths her hair.

She leaves the bathroom and crosses the corridor into a spacious, brightly lit room. The décor is tasteful: high ceiling, pale-gray walls with a single piece of monochrome artwork, a Georgia O'Keeffe floral, hanging behind the elegant, minimalistic desk. She takes a seat on a cream-colored leather office chair, turns on the desk lamp, and lifts the lid of the white laptop beside it. The screen flickers to life, pure black with a single word in gold capitals in the center: EXTEMPERO.

As she moves the mouse, the log-in screen pops up. She types *Maria Hofer*, followed by a long password, concealed. A spreadsheet appears on the screen. A list of names: the first two *Kristin Meyer* and *Simon Conte*—

A call interrupts her.

"Ja?"

"It's me," a male voice says, young, professional, energetic. "I think I've found our fifth candidate. History professor at the University of Tübingen."

"Excellent. Net worth?"

"Just over 12 billion dollars, up nine percent last year. She donated 2 million in the last twelve months to a number of international development charities."

"Who put her name forward?"

"Miss Murata."

"Good. How about leverage?"

The other end of the line goes silent.

Maria grips the phone. "If we can't control them, they don't get invited. I was very clear."

There's a pause. "I understand."

"Do you? If we don't secure five qualified clients for this auction, we don't get paid. *I* don't get paid."

"I know. I'm sorry." His voice deflates. "I'll find someone."

"Don't let me down. If you can't deliver—"

He clears his throat. "I've got this."

"Don't tell me. Show me." Maria hangs up. She takes a folder from a drawer and places it on the desk in front of her. The cover is matte black, with the word *Extempero* embossed in gold. Beneath that: *Auction, April 20.*

She opens the folder and runs her finger over a photograph of a pottery horse. A nibble of anxiety gnaws at her chest. *We need to find someone soon. We're running out of time.*

Suddenly, a cold slimy creature attacks her.

Wrapping itself around her throat.

No.

Wait. It's attacking me!

What?

With a start, I wake up in icy water with a damp washcloth wrapped around my neck. I pull it away with a shudder, and although I'm aching with cold, I bound out of the bath, fling on the plush hotel dressing gown, and hurry into the bedroom in search of paper. I'm fired up by my viewing. I need to write down as much as possible while I still remember it. After discovering a small pad and pencil in the bedside table, I write the name of the woman I merged with.

Maria Hofer.

I've had viewings of the past since I was a teenager, but the whole eye to eye connection is still somewhat new. When I called out to her at the airport, I was hoping an intense connection would trigger a viewing. It happened with Scarlett, when I caught her in my shop, and now with Maria, providing information that I have no right to know. I shake off the sense of intrusion and recall Maria studying herself—and thus me—in the mirror. I could sense her anxiety. She was under pressure to deliver to someone, her boss maybe. It made her snappy on the phone. I write down:

> *Someone researching candidates.*
> *Fifth person needed.*
> *Wanted leverage—like an affair?*
> *Billionaires?*
> *Auction, April 20.*

I stop and chew the end of the pencil. What were those names from the list? I think one was a woman's name . . . Katherine? I close my eyes and will the scene to replay itself in my head, the list to reappear. I relax and breathe, and the two names slip effortlessly into the spotlight in my mind.

Kristin Meyer.

Simon Conte.

I'm convinced I've heard of Conte before. I grab my phone, google his name, and flick impatiently through the biography that pops up: billionaire, made all his money in gambling and casinos—and he's a collector of ancient Oriental artifacts. I check Meyer out too. She's another billionaire. She made her money in fragrances and cosmetics, and I'm going to guess she's into antiques too.

I drop my phone and sit back on the bed. Bingo. Extempero is a private sale for the superrich. Maria and her team are searching for potential buyers, and the Chinese horse is going to auction on April 20—that's only ten days away!

I call Gabrielle but get no reply. She's probably facedown in some seedy bar already. I dry off, fling on some clothes, grab my silver hunter, and head out into the city.

5

On the way out of the hotel, I swing by reception and ask a young man behind the counter where people go to party in Amsterdam. He checks the clock, which shows ten past 11, and then looks me up and down, probably wondering if I should be tucked up in bed with a mug of cocoa.

"Are we talking a quiet drink or a full-on session?"

"Extremely full-on," I reply.

"Cool." He offers me an approving grin, seeming to reassess me. "Head to Leidseplein. Do you need a cab?"

Twenty minutes later I'm navigating through streets crowded with people of every age, every color, and pretty much every nationality, checking out the bars and nightclubs and trying to imagine what might draw Gabrielle in. After working my way through a fifth heaving bar, I stop and try calling Gabrielle again. As it rings, I watch a man dressed as a turkey eat fire to the music of Mozart—an odd combination, but strangely gripping.

This time, Gabrielle answers. Dance music blasts out of my phone, followed by a wild, raucous screech that grates against every nerve in my body.

"Hello?" Gabrielle shouts, sounding shocked.

"It's me, Joe."

"Good timing," she says, her voice slurred. "I'm so drunk I might just forgive you."

"I had a viewing," I tell her. "I know what's going on."

"What did you say?" she screams.

"Where are you?"

A short pause. "Where are we?" Muffled chatter. "The White Flamingo," she shouts. "Rooftop bar." I hear laughter and Gabrielle giggling, so I hang up and ask someone for directions.

After paying an extortionate entry fee to a silent man in a full-body zebra-striped leotard, I go inside. The club has real palm trees and a white plastic flamingo the size of a T. rex in the center of the dance floor. The music is deafening. Young women dance on tables. Men laugh and drink and high-five. It's packed. I hate it. Awkwardly I push through the crowd of sweaty faces and climb the greasy staircase to the top floor, resisting the urge to plug my ears with my index fingers.

The rooftop bar is lit with white plastic flamingo lamps in a variety of poses and dotted with a few brown faux-leather sofas and dented plastic cacti in pots. It's hardly the classiest club in town, but Gabrielle seems to have found her spiritual home. She's sitting on someone's lap, and they're snogging like teenagers. She's holding a lit cigarette in one hand and a fluorescent cocktail in the other.

A bunch of blokes down pints of beer and chat loudly nearby, and from the lack of females in their midst, they seem to be on a lads' weekend away. As I approach, I'm surprised to discover that I recognize one of them. It takes me a while to place him, but then I recall I've seen him in a viewing. It was a while ago, in a viewing of Other Joe and Alexia at a wedding. I'm wondering if perhaps I've got it wrong, but he notices me with a slow, dawning recognition. OK, it's definitely him, whatever his name is. It feels like a huge coincidence, but when I think it through, it's not that unlikely to see someone I know in Amsterdam. What are the options for a cheap and dirty stag weekend if you live in the UK? It's basically here or Dublin. Most people have done one or the other at some point. However, I have no desire to enter a conversation with someone from Other Joe's life, so I keep my attention steadfastly on Gabrielle and walk over to where she is still eating this poor guy's face.

"Hi," I say loudly. No response. "Gabrielle!"

She pulls away from her conquest and scowls, lipstick smeared across her cheek, trying to focus. "That you, Bridgeman?"

Her eyes appear to be moving independently of each other. She's absolutely plastered.

"We need to talk," I say. "Here, give me that." I take her glass as she climbs off the sofa, leaving the man with a bereft expression. I tip the drink into the nearest cactus pot and guide Gabrielle to a bench well away from the edge of the roof. We sit down.

"Ahh, you came to rescue me," she slurs. "Come here, you." She strokes my face, and before I know what's happening, she leans in as if she's about to kiss me. There's a sudden flash, and I look up to see that the guy she was with has just taken a photo of us.

I'm half expecting him to attack me for stealing his *girlfriend*, but he's grinning. "Hope you don't mind, just wanted a memento of the best snog in Amsterdam before she gets stuck into her next victim." He waggles his tongue at her. Gabrielle flicks him the finger, and he walks away laughing. Lovely.

Gabrielle can hardly keep her eyes open. She's singing quietly to herself now, some kind of sea shanty.

"Come on, let's get you some coffee," I tell her.

It's a miracle, but we make it back down the stairs in one piece, battle our way through the bar, and emerge into the street.

I steer Gabrielle to a nearby coffee shop and order her a couple of double espressos, which she drinks in quick succession. Eventually, the alcoholic fog clears, and she stops slurring her words. It strikes me that Gabrielle is similar to Vinny. She can consume a huge amount of alcohol and yet still function comparatively normally. I would suffer the mother of all hangovers and need two days under a duvet. Finally, her eyes seem to focus on me properly.

"I need a hash cake," she says.

"No, you don't," I tell her, passing her a napkin. "You need to wipe your face. You have lipstick all over it."

She scowls, and for about the fifth time this evening, I feel like her dad, like a real party pooper. She licks the napkin, wipes her face, and checks her watch. "Woah. This is way past your beddy time, isn't it?"

"I had a viewing of the woman we saw at Decker's warehouse."

That seems to sober her up a little more. She leans forward, closes her eyes, and rolls her hand a few times. I tell Gabrielle what I saw, and she listens intently. When I'm done, her eyes ease open. One is a little bloodshot. She fishes her phone out of her pocket. "We need to talk to Iris," she says.

Iris Mendell runs The Continuum, an organized group of time travelers based in the year 2131. I glance around the café nervously, imagining various members of The Continuum suddenly appearing in holographic form. "I know this is Amsterdam," I say, "and half the people here are already tripping, but isn't that a bit risky?"

Gabrielle sneers at me. "We can just call them, you know, make a *normal* phone call." She tilts her phone screen toward me and scrolls through her favorite contacts, settling on one titled *The Future*. She checks around the café. The baristas wear headphones, but other people are within listening range.

"Outside," she suggests.

We walk hand in hand, the cool air refreshing for me and essential for Gabrielle. We head away from the crowds, down toward the maze of pathways that flank the canals. Gabrielle presses the Call button. "We can stick them on speaker."

Sure, let's put the future on speakerphone. Why not?

Talking to the future is not something you get used to, but I do have a vague understanding of what's going on. According to Iris, the work that Vinny and I did in London has enabled this technology. They call it ICARUS, which stands for Instant Communication Across Relative Universal Space-time. Vinny says it so often, it's burned into my memory.

Iris picks up after a couple of rings. "Hi, Gabrielle," she says, her calm, measured voice a welcome change. "How are you getting on?"

"We found the focus object, boss. It was in a warehouse here in Amsterdam, but we lost it again because Bridgeman needs to work on his cardio." My hackles rise immediately, but Gabrielle punches my shoulder playfully.

Iris ignores the gibe. "So where is it now?"

"We don't know, but Chosen One here had a viewing he wants to fill you in on." Gabrielle angles the phone toward me. "You speak now."

Irritably, I take the phone. "Hi, Iris."

"Hello, Joe," she says. "Thank you for lending Gabrielle your antique expertise."

"No problem," I say. Gabrielle mimes sticking her finger down her throat and vomiting. Slowly and methodically, I take Iris through every detail of my viewing. The woman, the laptop, the names. "From what I saw in the viewing, I'd say it's a business running private auctions for the ultrarich."

"Extempero?" Iris says thoughtfully. "I haven't heard that name before. Does it mean anything to you, Gabrielle?"

"Diddly-squat."

"Do you think Scarlett could be involved?" I ask. "I mean, she stole the radio. Could she have stolen the horse too?"

"I've been thinking the same," Gabrielle says, "but it doesn't add up. If she wanted to steal it, why go to the trouble of setting up an auction?"

"It's been bothering me too," Iris says, "but the radio had been allocated; it was comparatively vulnerable. The Tang dynasty horse, that's not common knowledge. It's top secret information, and there's no way Scarlett could have known about it. At this stage, we have no evidence that she's involved. I think we focus on Extempero and see where that leads us. When is the auction, Joe?"

"April 20."

"Just over a week's time," Iris says. "Thanks to your viewing, our plan is simple. Someone should attend the auction and win it back."

Iris is professional. She doesn't assume I'm willing to go. And that's fair. I have a life. I don't work for The Continuum. However, she knows I understand the importance of the focus object. Plus, my experience in the antiques trade will be useful here.

"I will happily attend the auction," I tell her. "There's just one problem."

"What's that?"

"Someone within Extempero has to vouch for me."

Iris pauses for a beat. "Remind me of the names you saw?"

"Kristin Meyer and Simon Conte."

"Let us run those names through our historical search index," she says. "See if it flags anything."

I wait, trying to imagine what she's doing. Through the magic of some quantum subatomic process, we are talking to each other across time. My future is her past, meaning everything that's happened is searchable and trackable, historical data that can be interpreted and used.

"Yes, this is very interesting . . ." Iris says. "I think Conte is our man."

"What've you got, boss?" Gabrielle asks, all but licking her lips, clearly loving this.

"Four years from now, Conte will be exposed for fraud. He runs a charitable trust supporting microbusinesses in South America, and he's been embezzling funds for several years already, in your time."

"Yes! What a spectacular bastard!" Gabrielle punches the air. I think the alcohol is having another go around her bloodstream. "Let me get my hands on that slimeball, and I'll hustle you an invite to that auction, Golden Balls!"

It appears I was right. The historical search index, as Iris called it, has just given us information that we have no right knowing: the destiny of the man called Simon Conte.

"I'm sorry to ask, but is this ethical?" I'm feeling alarmed at our speed.

"About as ethical as stealing money from all those people," Gabrielle retorts. "You play with fire, you're gonna get burned."

"I understand your concerns, Joseph," Iris says. "Under normal circumstances, resistance wouldn't allow such interventions. However, because we're trying to complete a mission, it should allow Gabrielle's conversation with Mr. Conte. Consider this. There is a chance, albeit a small one, that Gabrielle will convince him to stop defrauding the charities altogether. Our intervention may end up doing some good."

She makes a good point, which further clarifies my understanding of resistance. The rules can be bent, just a little, if the intention is good and the focus is on successfully completing a mission. In many ways, it's good to know that The Continuum can't just go around ruining lives because it's fun.

"OK," I say, "presuming you can get me an invitation, we have another problem." I give an embarrassed laugh. "They were very focused on personal wealth. There is no way I'm going to qualify."

"Have you learned nothing, Grasshopper?" Gabrielle says disparagingly. "The Continuum can give you a temporary identity tweak in the blink of an eye. They can lay data trails so that you appear to be a billionaire, plus they can transfer the money you need to actually buy the thing." She cocks an eyebrow and grins. "If you can manipulate data, you can rule the world." She sighs. "Having you pull it off, though, is gonna be a lot tougher. You don't look like a billionaire. You look like a doofus."

Iris ignores her. "Presuming we can secure your entry, you're willing to do it, Joseph?"

"Yes. Absolutely."

She lets out a sigh of relief. "That's good news. I was so worried that we were going to lose the focus object, watch it disappear into some private collection, never to be seen again. Thank you, Joseph. I know you will do your best. We will create a persona for you that sets you up as a silent billionaire, and Gabrielle will secure you an invitation to Extempero from Mr. Conte. Then all you need to do is win the auction. Sound OK?"

It sounds simple enough. I go to auctions all the time, so I'm used to the process. But what if the other bidders have a ton more cash than I do? If I can help Iris and the team secure a crucial focus object for a mission that's probably going to take place after I've fallen off my perch, well . . . if nothing else, it's a chance to leave a legacy.

"I can do it," I say.

"Excellent," Iris says. "Thank you, Joe. Gabrielle, I'll forward you the data you need on Conte. Keep me posted."

"Will do. Catch ya later." Gabrielle hangs up and grins at me.

"What?" I ask her, warily.

"You."

"What about me?"

"Pulling it out of the bag, as always," she says, curling her lip. "Top of the class, a gold star from Iris. I bet you were a real teacher's pet."

I scowl. "The total opposite, *actually*."

She smirks. "I'm only pulling your leg. You did good, Bridgeman. It's the reason I wanted you to come, that brain spaz of yours can be helpful."

"You can't say that."

She yawns loudly, rubbing her eyes. "I feel like we should celebrate, but you've sobered me up now. I can feel a hangover coming on. Wanna walk back to the hotel with me? I could use some fresh air."

Like all dedicated smokers, who often claim to be gasping or in need of fresh air, she lights up, and we stroll the midnight streets. We pass through the Red Light District. It's been raining, and the colorful lights of the bars and coffee shops reflect off the wet road.

"Nice shirt," I say, noticing that she's wearing the Vinny's Vinyl T-shirt that he gave her.

"How is the big guy?" she asks. "He's got meat on those bones, a real man. Let's give him a call right now!"

I chuckle. "It's a bit late. He'll be tucked up in bed, fast asleep. He's fine, though. He recently found out he's a dad."

Gabrielle stops. "You're kidding! Wow, congrats! I didn't know he was in a . . . When's the baby due?"

"What? No, Charlotte is a teenager. Vinny split up with her mum, years ago. He didn't even realize Kassandra was pregnant at the time. Then she contacted him out of the blue a couple of months back and told him the happy news."

"Why wait so long?"

"I don't know."

Gabrielle whistles. "That's great for him, but boy, too bad for me. All the good ones get snapped up."

"I didn't know you liked Vinny!" I think about how he flushes red whenever I mention her.

"Doesn't matter," she says. "Sounds like he's found his lobster."

"His what?"

She glares at me. "Phoebe? From *Friends*? Lobsters mate for life, apparently. Anyway, it's cool."

"I'm hoping Vinny will come with me again on a jump sometime," I say. "Assuming The Continuum is OK with it."

"It's not the army!" Gabrielle shakes her head. "He can come. I brought a friend with me on a couple of jumps, but you grow out of it. They're like training wheels, and that's OK, but once you get into the swing of things, they kind of slow you down. Plus, you don't want to put them in danger. Missions can be treacherous. Like Paris." She sighs heavily. "You gotta take care of Vinny. It's not often I meet a guy I like. Most of them are idiots, and the ones that aren't think I'm just a good-time girl, so they give me a wide berth."

"You are, aren't you?"

"A good time? Sure, but I wanna settle down someday, get the house, the kids, the dog . . ." She punches my shoulder. "Don't look at me like that! Is it so strange that I want those things too?"

"No, not at all. I just can't imagine a domesticated Gabrielle. Doesn't mean it's not right for you, though."

A bunch of lads, all of them hammered, walk past us, catcalling and leering at scantily clad women in a nearby window.

"Like I said, most men are idiots," Gabrielle says without irony. "I sometimes wonder if the human race is screwed no matter what we change or fix. Maybe we should just give up already."

"Wow," I say. "That's depressing."

"No. It's realistic . . . freeing, actually. Means I can be good at my job. The minute you believe your own publicity, that's when it all goes tits."

Ten minutes later we arrive at the hotel.

"Nightcap?" Gabrielle suggests as we push through the main doors.

"You're a lunatic," I say, wondering who might win a drinking competition between her and Vinny.

"You're a lousy spoilsport," she says. "But you figured out Extempero, so I'm going to let you off." She half smiles, heads off toward the bar, and in typical Gabrielle style, without turning her head, shouts back, "But if you don't get us that horse, Bridgeman, I will never forgive you. *Never*."

PART 2

6

It's midafternoon on Saturday by the time I walk through the door of Bridgeman Antiques. The flight back from Amsterdam was smooth and uneventful, but the coffee was appalling, barely worthy of the name, so I'm gasping for a proper hit of caffeine. The little bell above the front door rings as I enter the shop, and I breathe in the scent of wood polish, old leather, and the faint mustiness of much-loved furniture.

Molly sticks her head out of the kitchenette. She comes out to welcome me, wiping her hands on a cloth. "I've just been giving the teapot a proper clean," she informs me. "Standards, Mr. Bridgeman, you know."

"Always, Molly," I agree. Molly is not only my brilliant shop manager, she's also the Alfred to my Batman, always there in the background, keeping Bridgeman Antiques running smoothly.

"Good trip?" she asks, peering at my small flight case. "Did you procure the antique you went hunting for?"

"I'm in negotiations," I say. "I may have to go back and pick it up next week."

"Very good," she says, apparently satisfied with my response.

"Why don't you go on upstairs and get yourself sorted out. I can handle the shop floor. It's clear you could use a cup of coffee." She all but shoos me out of the back of the shop with her tea cloth. Gratefully, I let her.

Dumping my case on the bed, I check my phone in case the guys from Extempero have tried to contact me about the auction. Nothing. With a homemade, three-shot flat white in hand, I head to the terrace. The fresh spring breeze is invigorating, and as I look out over Cheltenham, I wonder at the magic of air travel. Three hours ago I was in another country. It's probably the closest thing to time travel most people will ever experience.

I sip my amazing coffee, reflecting on the rush of the last twenty-four hours, and wonder if there'll ever be a time when I can get my feet properly under the table of my new life. I never seem to have enough time. It's been full-on since I got back from saving Amy, and I'm only slowly getting to know my parents and my grown-up sister.

Mum and Dad found it hard at first to deal with my "head injury"—Amy and I came up with the idea of retrograde amnesia to explain why I couldn't remember anyone or anything—but they've started to accept that my accident may have caused a permanent personality shift.

Who knows what they really think about the new me, but I can tell they've chilled a bit because they've just gone on holiday to a posh hotel near Ullapool in the Scottish Highlands, and they're planning to be away for three weeks. The one fly in the ointment is that Dad was supposed to retire this year and hand his commercial property business over to me, but my accident has put paid to that. Mum's worried that Dad's working too hard, but I think he's secretly relieved he doesn't have to give up his business just yet.

As the sun dips toward the horizon, I shiver and go back

inside the flat, pulling the French doors shut behind me. I wander over to the wall and peruse the beaming photos of Other Joe, the version of me I replaced when I got back from saving Amy. He lived life to the fullest and had both a ton of friends and a love of sport and high-octane pastimes. His friends didn't seem to know how to approach me after the *accident*, and most have drifted away with the tide. I can't say I mind, though. I still have a handful of good friends and one brilliant one, Vinny.

The other special person in my life is Alexia. Today she moved into her new office, and I'm going to visit her tomorrow. She and I have had a bumpy ride. Other Joe dated her for a while, but she dumped him after he messed her around, so emotionally I've had a lot of lost ground to cover. Like a fool, he also evicted her from her office building, forcing her to rent a place out of town for her hypnotherapy business. Gordon, her now ex-boyfriend, spotted his opportunity and moved her into the office next to his, and boy, did he enjoy rubbing my nose in it. Now that the boot is on the other foot and Alexia's going to be working just down the road from me, I'm not planning to shout it from the rooftops, but if Gordon happens along my path, I might just drop it into conversation.

I sleep like a baby in my own bed, and Sunday dawns cloudy but dry. After a late breakfast, I head out for a much-needed dose of joyful normality. Half an hour later, I'm knocking on the door of Vinny's Vinyl with two takeaway coffees and a couple of all-day breakfast sandwiches from my favorite local café, the Daily Grind. The shop sign says Closed, but I know he'll be in there somewhere, sorting through recent deliveries.

"Vin! It's me!" I call through the letter box. "I've brought breakfast."

The door to Vinny's office at the back of the shop opens, and my best friend lumbers into view. He grins and lets me in.

"Morning, Cash," he greets me. "I had a dream last night that you turned up here with a load of food. And here you are."

Vinny loves food, music, and time travel—he traveled back to 1960s London with me once—and apart from Amy, he's the only person in the present who knows the truth about my double life. I look him up and down as he steps back to let me in. He's lost some of his tummy, and his skin hangs a little looser on his face. That wouldn't worry me, but he's pale and seems diminished, with less energy than the last time I saw him.

"You've lost weight, Vin."

"Have I?" he says distractedly, lifting his shirt and flashing a bit of hairy belly. "Come on through." He takes one of the coffees, and I follow him back through the shop. There's a strange smell in here today—the usual odor of sweat and dust are still perceptible, but they're joined by a sickly floral scent that reminds me of my grandma's house. Is that a bowl of potpourri by the till?

"Take the weight off, Cash," Vinny says, indicating the leather armchair in the corner of his office where I always sit.

"Cheers." I balance my coffee on the windowsill, take a sandwich from the bag, and pass the other one to Vinny. "Tuck in, mate," I tell him. "You need it."

Vinny takes a huge bite of his sandwich, and his face relaxes, the lines on his forehead smoothing out, his eyes crinkling at the corners. "That. Is. Amazing!" he says between chews.

"They're the best," I agree, taking a bite of my own. It doesn't feel right to interrupt his focus, so I wait for him to finish eating before I speak again. I've known Vinny a long time—we were best mates in my other life, before I saved Amy, and since I've been living in this timeline, we've become close again. He still talks often about our trip to 1960s London. "You look like you haven't eaten in days, mate. What's up? Have you been ill?"

He leans back in his chair, wipes his mouth, and his shoulders drop a couple of inches. "I'm fine, Cash," he says. "Honest. I've just been busy, not had time to eat. I think that sandwich just saved my life." He picks up the coffee and drains it.

"Have you been working too hard?" I ask.

"Maybe. I'm off on holiday next week, though." He rubs his hands, spots of color appearing in his cheeks.

"Yeah? Where are you off to?"

"Portugal. All-inclusive, mate. Kassandra booked it. She's bringing Charlotte too, so I can get to know her better. I can't wait. And *all-inclusive*!" He beams with delight.

"Sounds brilliant," I say cautiously.

Vinny is eternally optimistic. It's one of the reasons I love him, but there's no denying it: since Kassandra came back on the scene, he's changed. He's more stressed and nervous than he used to be. He seems smitten, so I guess the oxytocin is doing its job, but from the outside, I can't see why. Kassandra seems to be critical of his weight, his clothes, and most of his choices. It's hard when you're not sure about the person your friend hooks up with. I've decided to keep my own counsel and allow this to take its course, but it's not easy.

"How are things with you?" he asks.

"Not bad, mate. Busy too. I just got back from Amsterdam, actually."

"Amsterdam? Holy cashmolee! You cheeky little jet-setter. For a holiday?"

"No, I went over there to help Gabrielle track down an antique, a Chinese pottery horse statue."

"How was Gabrielle?" he asks, immediately blushing.

Vinny met Gabrielle recently and seemed quite taken with her. Now I know that the interest is mutual, I wonder whether I should mention it, but I decide against the idea. He's about to head off on holiday with Kassandra. I don't want to complicate matters.

"She was fine. Short-tempered, demanding, unreasonable. You know, the usual."

"So cool," Vinny says nonchalantly. "Say hi for me next time you speak to her. Now tell me about this horse."

"It's really old, from the Tang dynasty."

Vinny's eyes narrow. "Isn't that that new Chinese restaurant in town?"

"No," I explain, "the Tang dynasty is a period in Chinese history. It started back in the 700s and went on for about three hundred years."

"Sheesh madeesh!" Vinny says. "That's so long ago, I can't even imagine it."

"I know, me neither. Anyway, this horse statue is a focus object for some super important mission in China, so The Continuum needs to get it back. Gabrielle and I tried to buy it off the dealer, but he'd already sold it to this organization called Extempero."

"Extempero!" he cries.

"Er, yeah. Have you heard of them?"

"No, but they sound like a Bond villain. Anyway, go on."

I laugh. "It does, but as far as I know, all they do is run private antiques auctions for megarich clients."

"But you didn't get it back."

"No, but the cool thing is, we bumped into this woman who works for Extempero while we were in Amsterdam, and I got a viewing off her and found out what it takes to get invited into the club."

"Let me guess," he says, wide-eyed, "you have to drink the blood of virgins."

"Er, no."

"Record a film of yourself admitting all the bad stuff you've ever done, so they have complete control over you?"

"No, mate," I reply. "You just need to be absolutely loaded

and best chums with a load of billionaires so one of the existing members will vouch for you."

"That's you off the list then, isn't it?"

"You would think, but The Continuum manipulated my data, and Gabrielle is on the case. If she can wield her powers of persuasion, I'll get invited."

Vinny sits back. "Well, that's a done deal then, Cinderella. You shall go to the ball. I reckon Gabrielle Green could persuade anyone to do anything. If you've read any of her interviews, you'll know what I mean. Some of the stuff she's got people to do . . ." His voice trails off, shaking his head in admiration. "And when you get this horse back, then what?"

"The Continuum sticks it in a special vault in London until they need it for the mission."

"It's so exciting," Vinny says wistfully. "You're like a spy!"

"Just call me the Psychometric Detective," I tell him.

"Hang on a minute—store it in a vault? You're not going on the mission, then?"

"No, mate. The mission isn't going to kick off for another fifty years or so. The Continuum just needs to secure the focus object and keep it safe till it's needed."

Vinny appears relieved. "Well, that's good. Now I've got a family, I reckon my time-traveling days might be over, but I'd hate to let you down if you were heading back in time again. I'm going to miss those days, though." His face takes on a dreamy expression. "I think sitting in a Rolls-Royce within spitting distance of Harry Hurst was one of the highlights of my life." He chuckles to himself.

Vinny's reverie is interrupted when my mobile phone unexpectedly bursts to life. We both jump. The ringtone is an air-raid siren.

Vinny's cheeks turn pink. "Is that Gabrielle?"

"Yes."

"Answer it then!" he urges me.

I pick up. "How's it going?"

She launches straight in. "I had a little chat with Simon Conte. He denied everything, then threatened to kill me, then apologized when I told him I was recording the call, then cried like the sniveling, thieving little worm that he is. Bottom line, he's gonna vouch for you—let's hope it's enough to get you into that auction."

"You're a star," I say.

"Yeah, I know."

"Can I talk to her?" Vinny whispers.

"Who's that with you?" Gabrielle asks.

"It's Vinny. He wants to talk to you."

"Well put him on!" she says. I hand him the phone, and his face goes even redder.

"This is Vincent Fry," he says gruffly.

"Legend!" Gabrielle cries. Vinny walks away, and thankfully I only hear his side of the ensuing conversation. He spends most of it laughing and saying, "No *way*!" When he eventually passes the phone back to me, he's a changed man. His eyes are bright, and his energy has totally shifted to the old Vinny, the one I'm missing already. "She is a cracker," he says. "Shame she lives so far away. I bet she'd be a right laugh on a night out."

"You have no idea," I say wryly.

"Who would be a laugh on a night out?" comes a high, wheedling voice from the shop.

Vinny jumps up and rushes to the office door. "Kass!" he says. "I didn't know you were coming over this morning."

"I did tell you. Perhaps you forgot."

"Yeah, probably did. Sorry, love. Hey, come and meet my mate, Joe." He steps aside, and Kassandra appears at the door of the office. She's short and blond, with long black eyelashes and drawn-on eyebrows, giving her a permanently surprised expression. She proffers a limp hand, as though she's expecting me to fall to one knee and kiss it. "Hi, Joe," she says. "I've heard a lot about you."

"All good, I hope!" I say cheerfully. Kassandra doesn't reply.

"Who was that you were talking to?" she says to Vinny. "Who would be a right laugh?"

Vinny flushes. "Oh, just someone Joe works with. I don't really know her. I only met her once."

"Vinny tells me you're into antiques," she says, clearly not interested.

"Yes, I've got a shop in Cheltenham, not far from here."

"And that was a colleague of yours on the phone, someone who is into antiques but would be a right laugh on a night out." She puckers her lips, tightly.

"We can be a surprisingly fun bunch."

"Right." Kassandra scans Vinny, appraising him from top to bottom. "Weren't you wearing that T-shirt yesterday?" She scratches a bit of crusty spillage off its hem.

Vinny flushes again. "I'll get changed in a bit," he says. "I was just wearing some old gear while I got the stock sorted."

This bothers me. I try not to let it, but she has Vinny in a constant state of apology. A dark shadow appears in the shop behind him, and a small pale face under a shock of navy-blue hair comes into view. Vinny sees me looking and turns around. "Charlie!" He breaks into a beaming grin and flings his arms around the girl, who stands stock-still and silently puts up with the big man's embrace.

"Her name is Charlotte," Kassandra says.

The girl folds her arms around her little pot belly and sinks into her double chin. "I don't mind if he wants to call me Charlie."

"How are you?" Vinny asks, excitedly.

"All right," she mutters, glancing at me for a microsecond, then staring at the floor.

"This is my best mate, Joe," Vinny explains, "otherwise known as Cash."

"All right," she mutters again.

"Good to meet you," I say.

Vinny taps her on the shoulder. "I've got some brill stuff to show you," he says, "some absolute classics. A stash of old *NME* magazines going back to the seventies, and some albums I think you're gonna love:—the Cure, the Cult, and Echo and the Bunnymen for starters."

"Who are they?" she asks with what seems like genuine interest.

"Oh, my life, we have so much to do! When Cash has gone, come out back with me and I'll show you."

"We talked about this, Vincent," Kassandra says. "We agreed you were going to declutter, get rid of those silly magazines. Nobody wants old stuff like that."

Vinny looks crestfallen. "Let me just show Charl . . . I mean, Charlotte, and then I'll sort out some stuff for charity." He glances briefly at me.

A lot can be said with a single look.

"It's all right, Vin," I tell him. "I'm heading off."

"OK, cool. Grand. See you later, Cash." Vinny heads through the shop toward the storeroom, trailed by Charlotte. She's like a mini version of him, and I swallow a lump in my throat.

As I get up to go, Kassandra blocks my way. "I've been hoping I would meet you. I've got some things to say."

"OK."

"You've been a good friend to Vincent," she says pointedly.

"He thinks a lot of you, but he needs caring for properly, and I'm here to do that now. Do you know what I mean?"

"I think so." She's telling me to back off.

The sounds of Vinny guffawing and a little chirrup of Charlotte's laughter punctuate the moment. Vinny's a dad now, and there's a chance that this family might get a crack at being something, like time's gone into reverse. This is super rare, and I don't want to stand in the way. Even if it hurts, I must try and keep the peace. However, there are ways and means. I'm not going anywhere, so I decide to pee on my friendship, metaphorically.

"I think a lot of Vinny too. He's my best friend, and nothing is going to change that. The way I see it, Vinny is lucky to have us both. And although he's been doing fine, he told me how thrilled he was that after all these years, you've come back into his life."

She seems surprised, but then I remember she always looks like that. She stands aside to let me out of the office. "Goodbye, Joe."

I dial up the passive-aggressive. "It was *really* nice to meet you, Kassandra. See you again sometime."

"Maybe," she says. "We'll see."

7

April is the best month of the year. You get the famous showers, but Cheltenham also luxuriates in warmer, longer days, and the flower beds in the park are bursting into life but not yet loaded with the dreaded ammunition of hay fever season. As I make my way from Vinny's Vinyl to Alexia's new office, I breathe in the fresh spring air, trying to wrest control of my emotions. Not so long ago, Alexia could hardly bear to look at me. We've come a long way already.

I turn down a short, brick-cobbled side street, and the old Cotswold stone building that houses Alexia's new office comes into view. I was thrilled when I found it. It's small—it used to be a primary school—and there are only four units. The other three are rented by a physiotherapist, a nutritionist, and a craniosacral therapist, where my parents sent me when they thought I had a head injury. I was floating for days afterward. There's a kitchen, a spotless bathroom, and a waiting area with a couple of sofas and a water fountain. It's very different from the place Alexia was in before—that was rather grand, a tall, narrow Georgian terrace painted cream with iron railings and a very formal feel. This place is friendlier, intimate, and I'm hoping Alexia is going to love it.

The front door is propped open when I arrive, so I walk through the waiting area, saying hello to an old chap who's sitting there with his elderly collie, and continue through the single corridor to the last room on the left. The door's slightly ajar, but not enough to see in.

"Hello?" I say, knocking hesitantly.

"Hang on a sec." I hear a thud, then footsteps. The door swings open, and Alexia is standing in front of me. Her hair is blonder than I remember, up in a loose bun. She's dressed casually in what I would call *comfy gear*. Absently she touches a hand to her chest, as if to hide her shabby white T-shirt. "Hey, Joe! Come in. Excuse the mess, I'm still getting the place straightened out." She turns and quickly crosses the room, balanced and graceful. I'm not ashamed to say that I notice how amazing she looks in a pair of old jeans. The truth is just the truth. Awkwardly I follow her, picking my way through countless boxes to the middle of the room, where Alexia's wooden desk butts up against her chaise longue, like a little furniture island in the middle of a cardboard sea.

"I brought you an office-warming present," I say, proffering the plant I picked up on the way over. "It's a peace lily. I thought it might help to keep your patients calm."

"Thanks, it's perfect." Alexia takes it and places it on the windowsill. I get a waft of her scent: warm and spicy, familiar, and lovely. "Does it need much caring for?"

"Not too much. I didn't want to give you another job to do. The man in the shop said to water it now and then. That's about it."

"Great. Do you want to sit down for a minute?" She hauls a couple of boxes out of the way so that I can get to the chaise longue, then fills the kettle at the little sink by one of the windows. "Tea?"

"I'm OK, thanks. I'm pretty full of coffee."

"No worries." She puts the kettle on to boil.

"How's moving in?" I ask as she joins me on the chaise longue. "I didn't realize how much stuff you had."

She smiles. "It's bizarre, isn't it? You'd think a hypnotherapy business would be just me and my couch, but I have a lot of paperwork, and I've got a ton of reference books too." Being so close to her in bright daylight is almost shocking. I notice the freckles around her mouth, the faint lines on her forehead, the curl of her eyelashes. "So, what's new with you, Mr. B?" she asks.

I am determined to be as honest as I can with Alexia. I'm not going to dive straight in and tell her I'm a time traveler—there are limits—but I'm going to tell her as much of the truth as I can. I caused serious problems with Amy by trying to hide the truth from her when I was traveling back and forth to the 1960s, and I'm not doing that again.

"I'm just back from Amsterdam, actually, on the hunt for an antique for one of my clients."

"Wow, you went a long way for one object!"

"You could say that," I agree. "It's a precious one, though, a pottery horse from eighth-century China. They used to bury statues with their dead, for the deceased to use in the afterlife."

"Like the Egyptians?"

"Yeah, just like the Egyptians. The Chinese called the statues *mingqi*, which means 'spirit object.' They believed that some of the dead person's spirit stayed on Earth, and so the *mingqi* was buried with the body, to comfort them."

"That's fascinating, if a bit creepy," Alexia says. "I bet an object that old would have a ton of stories to tell you. Are you going to try and read it?"

"Maybe, yes."

"Exciting."

Alexia knows about my psychometry. Initially, she was skeptical and quite rightly wanted proof. She persuaded me to do a psychometric reading from an old fountain pen, and I was able to tell her, in great detail, what had happened to her great grandfather in the First World War. She wasn't skeptical after that.

"Mum's still blown away by the stuff you told us about Stanley's pen. She told all her friends about it, asked me if she could bring a few of them down here with the family heirlooms, do a kind of *Antiques Roadshow* with you." She laughs at my expression. "Don't worry! I told her there was no way, that what you did for her was a one-off. I know it's not some kind of party trick."

"Thanks, I appreciate that," I tell her. "I don't mind doing it occasionally, but it can get complicated if I'm not careful."

"I can imagine," she says thoughtfully. Then her eyes glitter with excitement. "You know, I've been reading a bit more about it. I wanted to understand how it works." She jumps up, walks over to the bookshelves, and reaches for an old book with a plain dark cover. "You're not the only Joseph who's into psychometry. Do you know this book?" She brings it to me, and I turn it over in my hands. It's Joseph Buchanan's *Manual of Psychometry*. I haven't seen this book in—what, twenty years? After we lost Amy and I started to get viewings of her life by holding her toys, I got curious about my abilities, and one day I went to Cheltenham library to see if I could find out more. I must have been about sixteen, and I remember pulling up the hood on my jacket so none of my friends would see me going into the library. I asked the woman at the front desk if she could tell me where I'd find books on people who could do crazy stuff with objects. After a bit of digging, she pointed me in the direction of the paranormal section, and I spent a few hours hunkered down on the floor reading books written by a selection of—I'm sorry to say—New Age wackos. The only book that made any sense to me was Buchanan's. He wrote with the clarity and conviction of a scientist and discussed at length the experiments that he and his associates had carried out. His was the only book that didn't make me feel like a freak, the only one that reassured me that I wasn't alone.

"I do know it," I say, handing it back to Alexia. "I haven't seen it for a long time, though."

"It's absolutely riveting," she says, flicking through the pages. "Some of the experiments Buchanan did were mind-boggling. If we learned more about psychometry, it could really change what we believe about history and time. We've always assumed that stuff happens, and objects just sit there, but maybe they're not inanimate, not the way we thought. Maybe they're more like silent witnesses."

"Silent witnesses . . . I like that," I say.

Alexia lays the book down. "I know most people would think I'm crazy, but I totally buy what Buchanan's saying. It makes sense to me, emotionally. It's fascinating when he talks about building a bond with the object, to get it to trust you and share what it knows."

"That's what I did with your mum's pen. I'd stopped halfway through the first time, so I had to reassure the pen that I was going to listen to its tale all the way through." I recall coaxing the story from the camera I found at the antique shop in Ludlow, when I was trying to find out what had happened to seven-year-old Amy, and tuning in to Alexia's earring when it wanted to show me a conversation she'd had with Other Joe at a wedding. "To me, it feels like respect, just like with a person. You don't muscle in. You give them space to step into."

"Absolutely." Alexia turns toward me. "Joe, do you think we

could try it sometime, just you and me? I'd love to have a go . . . Maybe you could teach me? Only if you want to, of course." Her smoky blue-gray eyes hold my gaze. She looks nervous.

"Sure, that'd be fun. I'd enjoy that."

She smiles. "People used to think that hypnotherapy was a load of mumbo jumbo, but it's solid science. I think it's important to keep an open mind. Sometimes a concept that sounds totally implausible turns out to be true. I mean, take quantum physics? Nuts or what?"

"Totally," I say, and the balance in my mind shifts slightly away from *Alexia is going to freak out and refuse to ever see me again* toward *Alexia is going to be fine about time travel.*

Do it now, the voice inside my head urges me. *Before you lose your nerve.* I swallow, and my throat clicks. Alexia must have heard it, but she doesn't react. "Alexia, I was wondering . . . I don't suppose . . . Look, it's fine if you'd rather not, but I . . . Would you like to go out for a drink sometime?"

"How about dinner?" she says.

It takes me a second to register that Alexia Finch has just suggested we go out for a meal together. When I told my sister that Alexia had split up with Gordon, she advised me to tread lightly. "Other Joe acted like an idiot," Amy said. "He abused her trust. This time you need to let her come to you in her own time. Like a cat." I think that's what Alexia just did. I modulate my voice to hide my excitement. "Dinner would be great," I say. "There's a restaurant I'd like to try, belongs to one of my customers. It's called Dialogue. Do you know it?"

My shop bell jangles for the hundredth time, and I don't even look up from the sales ledger. I can't remember such a busy Monday.

Molly and I have been constantly attending to customers since we opened, and even though it's only 3 p.m., we've already beaten our previous one-day sales record by over seven hundred pounds. Seems like Cheltenham is full of day-trippers from the North, and they've all been making a beeline for Bridgeman Antiques. It makes no sense at all. We never advertise, and it's not a public holiday or a special weekend, but I'm not complaining.

"Excuse me," says a familiar voice. "Can you help me find a gift for my brother? He never replies to my texts, so I need to remind him that I exist."

It's Amy, my sister. Her golden-brown hair is a little wild today, and her pale freckled cheeks have a hint of pink. She's dressed in her usual: layers, ankle boots, corduroy trousers, and a long flowing coat, earthy, neutral tones. I stand up and hug her. "Have you been trying to get hold of me?"

"Since Friday. Busy weekend?" she asks, green eyes playful. "Anything I need to know?"

"Not that kind of weekend, but yeah, there is some stuff I need to catch you up on." I seek out Molly, who's showing a group of middle-aged women a tray of marcasite jewelry from the shop window. "I'm just popping upstairs with Amy for twenty minutes," I tell her.

She smiles at Amy and gives me a quick nod. "Take your time."

Amy and I go upstairs to my man cave. That whole "absence makes the heart grow fonder" thing is true. It's also permanent. Having lived without Amy for so many years, every time I see her—and I mean *every* time—it feels new, joyous, vital. Amy and I have had a few ups and downs since I got back, but she's now in a much better place, mentally. We've been hanging out quite a bit and discovered a shared love of cheesy American TV comedies. We have regular TV nights, and I love every minute.

I slump down on the sofa, and Amy sits at the piano and plays the first few bars of "Chopsticks." "I keep forgetting you have Grandma Bridgeman's piano," she says. "I still miss her." She laughs. "Remember that day you were so naughty that she didn't give you a chocolate biscuit for the journey home? She gave me two instead."

"I do remember, Miss Goody Two-shoes." Amy often shares stories of when we were young, from before she went missing in my original timeline. This shared history is a place where we can meet.

She shakes her head. "I didn't wear that crown for long, though," she muses. "Anyway, tell me about your weekend. Where've you been?"

I fill her in on my trip to Amsterdam, the hunt for the Chinese horse, and my viewing of Extempero. "Basically, I learned that the biggest hurdle to getting an invitation to the auction is that someone who's already a member of Extempero has to vouch for you."

"Those rich boys love their exclusive events, don't they?"

"They do. Anyway, Gabrielle's spoken to the guy who's going to vouch for me, and apparently, he's going to talk to Extempero, so now I'm waiting for the call."

"Sounds intriguing," Amy says. "Very cool, actually. What an experience that'll be if you get to go! You said it's an auction for the superrich? How are you going to get in? I mean, I know you're running a successful shop, but still, unless Bridgeman Antiques is secretly some kind of money laundering setup, aren't you going to fall a bit short?"

"The Continuum is going to manipulate my data so that when Extempero checks me out, they will believe I'm a multimillionaire. I haven't asked too much about how they do it—I don't want to know—but I checked, and my bank account doesn't have any extra cash in it."

"How are you going to pay for this horse then?"

"The Continuum is going to send me a credit card."

She grins. "If you fancy taking your poor artist sister out for a posh dinner when it arrives, I won't say no!"

"Let's do it!" I say. "How are things going with your art, by the way?"

"Really good," she says. "I've been feeling very inspired by nature, painting wild landscapes, abandoned barns on windswept moors, that kind of thing. I lose myself in it, but in a healthy way. I can spend hours on one canvas and not realize how much time has gone by. I think it's what I'm meant to be doing."

My trips to Paris gave Amy repeated and disturbing visions of my future. She painted them, dark and abstract but also quite mesmerizing. The paintings were incredibly useful, and one of them helped me escape from the burning opera house. I was worried for a while because the process seemed to take a big toll on her mental health, but I'm happy to hear she's found joy in her art again.

Amy draws in a deep breath and sighs. "I've made a decision, actually."

"What's that?"

She spins around on the piano stool. "You know I had this feeling I was going to be traveling imminently?"

"Yes." I recall Iris telling me that Amy would be traveling soon, and that Amy had felt the pull. "Well, I think I had it wrong," she continues. "I thought I was going to be traveling in time, but I'm feeling a powerful need to go traveling in the traditional sense, do some exploring. I need creative input from other places. I've found someone to take care of the business for a while so I can go on the road, focus on my art."

"How long are you going for?"

"Six weeks to begin with, then see how I go."

"Wow. That's big news! I'm so happy for you." Amy's never taken her talent seriously before, so this is a positive shift.

She peers at her hands.

"What's up?" I ask.

"Oh, I'm feeling a bit guilty already."

"Guilty?"

"Yes, taking time off just to paint."

I laugh.

"What?" she asks, scowling.

"You don't feel like it's work, do you?"

"It isn't!"

Knowing it's a delicate subject, I tread carefully. "Amy, you aren't the first, and you certainly won't be the last, to feel guilty about following your passion. But listen to me now, and believe what I'm saying because it's true. The world needs artists. Music, film, novels, dance, theater, poetry—all of it matters. You're incredibly talented, and I think it's brilliant that you're carving out this time. It's an opportunity. Go and explore what you can do."

"Thanks," she shrugs. "When you put it like that . . ."

"What does Miles think?" Miles is Amy's on-off boyfriend. He's a passionate rock climber, and he spends a lot of time out of the country. When he's in the UK, they hang out, but they don't seem all that into each other.

"He's fine with it. We're on a bit of a break. You got me thinking when you asked me if my relationship with him was enough . . . I'm not sure it is."

It's been a while since I asked Amy if she was happy with Miles, but I know from my own experience that sometimes these questions don't land the first time around, especially when we're not ready for them. They bounce back and forth like boomerangs, and we keep throwing them, until one day we catch them and keep hold and finally let them in. "I hope I didn't overstep the mark."

"No, you didn't. It's like Mum says: if it's meant to be, you don't question it. I guess I'll find out if I miss him."

"What did Maude say when you told her?" Maude runs a gallery, and Amy's business supplies her, and a small collection of other clients, with artwork prints. I met Maude once. She's a great person, larger than life, and she really loves my sister.

"She was very supportive. She gave me this." Amy pulls out a pendant from beneath her shirt. It's a blue-violet stone set in silver.

"That's nice of her," I say.

"It's a natural crystal, called the Viking's Compass, apparently." Amy turns the pendant in her hand, and the color of the stone changes from blue to gray to clear and back again as she rotates it. "The Vikings used to use them to find the sun in the sky on cloudy days, and to help them navigate at sea. They're said to give the wearer direction and clarity. Lovely, isn't it?" She stuffs it back inside her top. "I'm a proper old hippie, aren't I!" She laughs and spins around on the piano stool again, her laughter warm and full. I feel like I'm getting my sister back, the happy, confident, sorted version of her that picked me up when I returned from saving her. Perhaps she's right, though: perhaps this is the travel she thought was coming. I can see that she needs to expand her horizons and reconnect with her muse, and I know she needs to do what's right for herself. I'm going to miss her, though. We will never catch up on all the time we missed, but still, you can't blame me for trying.

Amy heads off, and I go back down to the shop to help Molly with the last of the stragglers from the tour buses. At 5 p.m., I let her go. "I'll shut up shop," I tell her. "It's been a long day. You head off. See you tomorrow."

She doesn't argue.

I'm just flipping the sign on the shop door to Closed when a courier turns up with a package. I sign his electronic delivery pad, lock the shop door, and take a seat at the desk. The package is small, about four inches square and an inch high, and other than a small shipping label, it's completely black. Opening it up, I find a black credit card inside, an American Express Centurion with J. T. BLAKE printed on the front. I've never heard of a Centurion card, so I look it up online, and it blows my mind. This little slice of metal—it seems it's invitation only, you can't apply for one—has a five-figure joining fee, but it'll give me access to airport lounges around the world, top-tier hotel rewards, and best of all, an around-the-clock personal concierge. You just call them up and ask them to sort stuff out for you—book tickets or travel or whatever—and they do it. I can't wait to tell Vinny! The thought crosses my mind that I don't know how The Continuum makes its money. I just hope they do it ethically.

After a day in the shop, I'm keen for some fresh air, so I change into my gym kit, dust off Other Joe's mountain bike, and head up Leckhampton Hill, taking a waist belt to hold my house keys and the credit card, with the plan to stop in at Vinny's on the way back to show it off.

As I wind my way up the path, it occurs to me that this is the bike I told everyone I'd fallen off of when I sustained my imaginary head injury. Unlike Other Joe, though, I'm not hurling myself down the hill on two wheels; I'm panting my way up at a snail's pace. After about three minutes, I stop to wipe the sweat from my eyes and reflect on Gabrielle's comment about my fitness in Amsterdam. She might have a point. Time travel is unpredictable, and it would probably be helpful if I could run a bit.

I climb slowly to the top of the hill, and when I get to the summit, I turn around and gaze out over Cheltenham and the landscape beyond, appreciating the view. I'm still struggling to catch my breath when my phone rings. I fish it out of my pocket and check the screen—it's an unknown number with a plus sign in front of it, a sure sign that it's coming from abroad.

"Hello?" I pant.

"Mr. Blake?" asks a woman's voice. Her tone is brisk and efficient, with a faint Slavic accent, and I know at once it's the woman I saw in my viewing.

"This is he," I say, channeling a rich British aristocrat from the 1960s film for some reason.

"Mr. Blake, this is Maria Hofer from Extempero. I believe you are expecting my call?"

Oh my God, yes! "Yes, Miss Hofer, hi. Er, hello," I say, trying to sound like a billionaire and failing.

"Is this a good time?" she asks.

I do my best to catch my breath, keeping my mouth closed to avoid puffing into the mouthpiece. "Yes, absolutely," I tell her, almost saying *over*, as though we are using walkie-talkies. What is wrong with me?

"Our next auction takes place on April 20, and we have one spot remaining. Would you like to take it?"

"Definitely, yes. Yes, please."

"Excellent. Mr. Conte was most complimentary about your fit with the organization. He was quite insistent, in fact, that we invite you."

"How kind," I say, feeling bad. Gabrielle said he cried when she blackmailed him. I try to remember that he's a greedy, embezzling, fraudulent man who siphons money from his own charities. It helps.

"Normally we would put you through our extended welcome program, but as we only have a few days until the sale, you will naturally appreciate that we need to expedite the process."

"Of course," I say, not really sure what I'm agreeing to. "What are the next steps?"

"Just the small matter of the joining fee. This will give you membership in Extempero for twelve months and entry to all our events during that time. How would you like to pay?"

I notice in passing that she doesn't mention a price, so I don't ask. I guess cost is immaterial for people who eat caviar for breakfast.

"Credit card, please," I say, cursing myself. I must stop with the *pleases* and be more assertive. I fish the black card out of my waist pack.

"The long number, when you're ready," Maria purrs. As I read out the string of figures, a gaggle of Mamils (middle-aged men in Lycra) appears over the brow of the hill and streams past me. I hope none of them is within earshot long enough to get the whole number—I doubt this card has a limit. I give Maria the expiration date and three-digit code, and then wait for it to go through. Even billionaires have to wait for computers.

Maria's reassuring voice breaks the tension. "That's all fine. You'll need to arrive at Tivat Airport in Montenegro by three p.m. local time on the twentieth. We will pick you up from there. I'll send you an email confirming all the details."

"Perfect," I say confidently.

"We look forward to welcoming you aboard, Mr. Blake. Good evening."

"Yes. Good evening," I reply, parroting her. The line goes dead.

"Bloody hell," I breathe. "I'm going to Montenegro on Friday to buy a Chinese horse worth 2 million dollars." I'm running back through our conversation when a clap of thunder interrupts my thoughts. A raindrop lands on my shoulder, then another. The sky has darkened, and as I mount my bike, the heavens fall, and I get absolutely soaked.

I wobble my way precariously down a narrow track through woodland, gripping the brakes, determined not to add an actual injury to my imaginary, amnesia-inducing one. As I descend, thoughts shoot around my head, and I recognize that I'm terrified—not about the flight, or the posh hotel I'll probably be staying in, or knowing in what order to use all the knives and forks. Other Joe has racks of smart clothes I can just about fit into, so I can look the part. I'm happy as Larry, with almost endless cash on my new black credit card, and I know I can win that horse back for The Continuum. But the thing that scares me most of all?

Small talk.

I mean, what the hell do billionaires talk about?

8

A heavyset man with dark, leathery skin stands near the exit of the Tivat Airport arrivals lounge. He's holding a placard with the name JAMES THEODORE BLAKE printed on it. He takes my luggage and explains that he's here to take me to the Hotel Regent. I follow him to a brand-new, air-conditioned Mercedes, so clean he must have driven it straight from a local dealership. He loads my luggage, pops on a pair of classic Ray-Bans, and heads toward the town of Porto Montenegro.

My driver is silent as we glide smoothly along a wide coastal road. The glassy ocean and clear cyan sky are a welcome change from dreary old England. Montenegro has never really been on my radar, certainly not somewhere I would have considered a holiday destination. Now that I'm here, though, I'm wondering where it's been all my life. After fifteen minutes we leave the Adriatic Highway and wind our way down through narrow, cobbled streets. Porto Montenegro is a village spread over a hillside dotted with trees. Clusters of traditional stone buildings with terra-cotta roofs overlook a tranquil bay, the water so still it perfectly mirrors not only the town itself, but also the magnificent, dramatic mountains that frame it.

We arrive outside an impressive four-story hotel that exudes luxury. Even the ivy that drapes its manicured windows and doorways looks expensive. My driver grabs my luggage, and I give him what I think is an extremely generous tip. He smiles politely, but I get the impression that the amount was low compared to his usual clientele.

After the kind of effortless check-in that only money can buy, I'm shown to my room. A large deluxe with a sea view. The décor is elegant but generic: a calming palette of nautical blues and earthy shades of beige, finished off with a large amount of wood paneling. The view over the bay, though . . . that's priceless. All paid for by Extempero, which appears to do nothing by halves. Then again, when the cost of entry is this high, I guess I should expect a few perks.

I place my Louis Vuitton luggage on the bed. Gabrielle had it delivered to me. She said if I was going to play the part, I had to look the part. She also sorted out a tuxedo. She claims it's been tailored, although I'm pretty sure I would remember being measured up for a suit. Then again, Gabrielle has access to future technology that I doubt I will ever understand.

I get dressed, dial her number, and place her on speakerphone.

"Bridgeman!" she cries. "How's the tux, man? Does it fit OK?"

"Like a glove," I tell her honestly, although I wish she'd opted for a clip-on bow tie. This thing is a bitch to tie. Perhaps that was intentional. I finally manage to tie it, attach the cummerbund around my waist, and assess myself in the mirror. I'm totally faking it, but you can't beat a classic tux. "You know what, Gabrielle, I don't look half bad. Thanks for sorting this for me."

"Oh, it's my absolute pleasure," she says with her signature mix of positivity and sarcasm. "It's my dream to be your personal shopper, to help you become the ultimate version of you. In fact, I bet with that dark hair and square jaw of yours, you look like George Clooney."

"Wow," I say, taken aback. "I think that might be the first compliment you've ever paid me."

"It wasn't a compliment, moron. George Clooney is so obvious! Skinny. I keep telling you, I prefer my men with plenty of meat on their bones! Anyway, Mr. Blake, what did that broad from Extempero say happens next?"

"I received an email that said the auction begins at eight p.m. No phones or digital recording equipment allowed. I'm being picked up from the marina at six thirty."

"You're going on a boat trip?"

"Er, I guess so, yeah." I walk to the window and get my bearings. I can see the marina in the distance. Rows of boats gently bob on a calm, glistening sea.

Gabrielle lowers her voice. "Maybe they already suspect that you aren't who you say you are, and they're planning to ship you out to some deserted island so they can interrogate you in peace."

"That is not helpful," I grumble.

"I'm sorry. You're right, but I miss winding you up." She sighs heavily, like a sister who knows her younger brother won't be her personal punching bag forever. "OK, let's focus on the job at hand. All you need to do is play your part and win the horse. Your credit limit has been increased to 3 million. Use it if you need to. We need the focus object back, Bridgeman. If you can't win it, then just steal it."

My jaw drops.

"Oh, Christ," Gabrielle groans. "I can totally imagine your

worried little expression right now. When I say 'steal it,' I just mean borrow it. OK?"

"Right."

"You grab it, we do the mission, the FCI goes sky high, and we have it back with these rich assholes before they can buy another mansion. I mean, what's the worst that could happen? They figure out you're poor and boring and dull and ask for their champagne and caviar back?"

I laugh. I haven't left the hotel yet but can already feel that the pressure of keeping up with the Extempero crowd is going to be exhausting.

"Well, Bridgeman," Gabrielle says, "it's been a chore as always, and whilst I would love to rib you for a bit longer, I gotta split. Some of us have missions to complete. Good luck with your little horsey." Before I can say anything else, she hangs up.

Bizarrely, I kind of miss her. Things are never dull with Gabrielle around.

It feels strange leaving my phone in the bedroom, but Maria was clear on this. They don't want anybody taking photographs or recording the auction. Exclusivity comes at a price, I guess.

I head down to the marina, which is just a short walk from the hotel. It's early evening. The air is warm. As I walk the narrow streets, passing locals heading out to bars and the odd couple strolling happily hand in hand, I think about Alexia. I'd love to bring her here, spend some quality time together. I feel like that's what we need. Time to really connect and build a foundation. Then again, what do I know? When it comes to relationships, I'm thoroughly inexperienced. Losing Amy meant that my twenties were kind of robbed by grief. I had no time for relationships, couldn't find my way to loving anyone. It's why falling in love with Alexia was so unexpected, and now that I have a second chance, I want to ensure she knows how much she means to me.

The marina is a well-manicured lattice of wooden jetties that lead to a playground of small to medium-sized boats. It's clean, well-lit, and dotted with various shrubs and flower beds. The glassy water reflects a pastel-blue sky, just giving way to the faintest streak of peach on the horizon. I check my silver hunter—it goes everywhere with me now—and it's nearly 6:30 p.m. I glance around, wondering what to do next, when I hear the gentle hum of a motorboat approaching. A small cruiser enters the harbor. Sleek, stylish, and Italian, like something out of an Audrey Hepburn movie, its woodwork is glossy, and its hull is painted a rich dark blue.

The driver pulls up, loosely wraps a rope around a metal post, and steps onto the jetty. She's a young woman of slight build, in her midtwenties, I would guess. She wears a white shirt, black shorts, and deck shoes. Her blond hair, cut into a bob, sways as she walks toward me.

"Mr. Blake?" she asks enthusiastically.

"Yes."

"I'm Karen," she says, in a strong Australian accent. "I'm here to pick you up and take you aboard *The Valiant*."

"*The Valiant*?"

She smiles, exposing faint creases in the corner of her eyes that cut white lines through her tanned skin. "Mr. Zanak's yacht. He's looking forward to meeting you."

I perch on the pristine seating area at the back of the boat. The engine purrs, and we leave the marina, the stone buildings of Porto Montenegro glowing in the evening sunlight behind us.

We cross the calm bay, the only sounds the gentle hum of the boat's engine, the wind in my ears, and the bow breaking lightly over the water. The evening sun ignites the water into a million orange flames as we pass the headland and set out to sea. I decide not to think about Gabrielle telling me that I'm being taken to a deserted island to be interrogated.

I've seen yachts before, either on TV or moored up in Monte Carlo, but I've never seen one as big as the one we're approaching now. It's colossal: a multilayered, gleaming white megayacht. Long dark windows shine like gold, and its radar spins rhythmically. There's even a helicopter pad!

Various crew members—all looking suspiciously like clones of Karen—move efficiently around the rear deck. Karen doesn't appear to be slowing down. She's heading straight toward the yacht. I swallow, about to say something, when a large panel opens in the side of the yacht, revealing its own little marina within. The big boat swallows us, and the panel closes with a *wumph* as we gently slow to a stop.

Inside, another woman awaits us. She's dressed in navy-blue trousers and a white shirt with black-and-gold striped lapels. Her dark hair is pulled back in a ponytail, and her olive skin is radiant beneath a hundred LEDs.

"Welcome, Mr. Blake," she says in a rich Spanish accent. "I'm Captain Sofia González, and it's my pleasure to welcome you aboard *The Valiant*."

"Thank you," I say, feeling like royalty as I step awkwardly from the boat onto the yacht, which is packed full of seriously expensive gear. There is one of those military-grade rubber speedboats, a selection of neon-colored Jet Skis—who knows, you might need one for every day of the week—as well as various kayaks, paddleboards, wet suits, and life jackets.

Captain González smiles. "I see you're admiring her tender garage, fully equipped with all the water toys you would expect."

I've never heard of a "tender garage," and a selection of water toys is the last thing that I would have *expected*. I just nod, attempting an expression that suggests this is all perfectly normal, no big deal.

"Follow me," she says. "The other guests are already on deck."

Oh good. I'm fashionably late.

We pass cabins, crew quarters, a dining area, and a fully equipped gym, which Captain González describes as a beach club with a sauna, Jacuzzi, pool, and bar. The yacht has *its own pool*. It's a marvel of engineering and an incredible way to spend the equivalent of a small country's economy in one go.

We ascend a circular wooden staircase and emerge into a spacious lounge at the rear of the boat. The aft, I think. This is the luxury bit: a teak sundeck with various seating areas, tables, and patterned beanbags. Twenty or so extremely wealthy people drink, chat, and laugh beneath a huge canopy. They ooze a sense that they are meant to be here, an explosion of wealth expressed not only in their elegant clothes and expensive jewelry, but also in the way they hold themselves. Confident, comfortable, seemingly at ease with the world. To the left is a stunning mother-of-pearl bar. Two bartenders, Hollywood look-alikes of Tom Cruise and Brad Pitt, mix impressive cocktails. Behind them, various colored bottles sparkle beneath a myriad of lights. The staff serves canapés and champagne—nibbles and fizz, where I come from.

"Let's get you a drink," Captain Gonzáles says, "and then I can introduce you to some people, if you like."

I was already feeling nervous, but now panic sets in fully. "No, that's OK, I can mingle."

This isn't an auction. It's a full-on soirée for the dripping rich. How the hell am I going to blend in? This whole scene plays into one of my biggest fears.

Small talk.

Sounds pathetic, I know, but I'm terrible at it. I spent most of my twenties and early thirties in self-administered solitude.

A grief-ridden hermit. So when it comes to mingling at social events, it's not that I'm out of practice, I just never had any in the first place.

"I hope you enjoy the evening," Captain Gonzáles says. "Mr. Zanak is on his way. Please, help yourself to a drink. The auction will begin soon."

"Thank you," I say, managing to keep my voice steady.

Time to blend in, if I can. In the corner of the bar is a white piano, raised on a plinth. A woman in a red dress plays generic jazz that clearly isn't straining her abilities. I head in that direction, lifting a glass of champagne from a tray. I take a sip, and it tastes good, but I remind myself that getting drunk would be a bad look. I just need to make it to the auction, win the focus object, and get the hell off this party boat.

A middle-aged man approaches me. He oozes wealth and, based on his double chin and ample waistline, enjoys the finer things in life. He's wearing a classic tuxedo with a white silk scarf. On his arm is a tall blond woman in a black trouser suit. Her makeup is immaculate, her eyes so green they're visible from twenty feet away. I can't help but notice the age difference. She's a lot younger. His salt-and-pepper hair is receding, showing even more of his pale, mottled skin. It's a horrible presumption that he's the one with the money, but I can't help but wonder if she'd be with him if he was bringing in an average salary.

"Darling," he says to her, "just give me a few minutes, will you? I need to have a chat with Mr. Blake." She glances at me, her lips curling into a faintly seductive smile, generating enough heat to melt all the ice cubes on this boat, and then slinks off to the bar. She walks with grace and poise, as though paparazzi are hiding in every corner.

The man focuses his attention fully on me. Interesting that he knows my pretend name, but I don't know him. I hold out my hand and introduce myself. He grips my hand and pulls me close. I notice his scarf features an embroidered illustration of a roaring lion.

Why do I get the sense that I'm the gazelle?

Then I recognize him. *Oh no.*

It's the man Gabrielle blackmailed to vouch for me, securing my place at this auction. This is Simon Conte. A couple of years from now, an investigation will reveal the truth about his shady business operations, but for now, he sneers at me like a man very much at the top of his game.

He speaks in a hushed, gravelly tone, ensuring that no one around us overhears. "You've just clocked who I am, haven't you, Mr. Blake? If that's even your name."

"Listen, I'm really sorry about all that," I tell him honestly, "but I had to make it to this auction."

His cheeks redden. His right eye, encased in layers of pudgy skin, begins to twitch. "Let's just get one thing clear. I don't know where you and that bitch get your information, but this is a one-off. You don't keep coming back for more."

"Absolutely, a one-off." I stifle a smile. Gabrielle really does have an amazing effect on people. I start feeling guilty—I know what it's like to be blackmailed—but remind myself that he's as corrupt as they come.

Conte leans in. "Just understand this. If it leaks, I will hunt you down, and I will personally chop you into tiny pieces. Is that clear?"

I say yes, knowing full well that his destiny lies behind very different bars than the one he will frequent tonight. Knowledge of the past *and* the future is an extremely powerful combination.

I spend the next fifteen minutes attempting to avoid small talk with big people. When I do get dragged into conversation, they talk about where they've been, what they've done, and what they're planning to do. Luckily, they seem happy to talk about themselves and don't ask me too many questions. Perhaps they can smell that I am somehow *other*. I nibble on a canapé, a plump seared scallop with soy sauce, ginger, and spring onions. Water drips from an ice sculpture, an incredible carving of some Greek god surrounded by dolphins. There is an atmosphere of anticipation, but no mention of the auction, like it's some big secret. I don't like it. It feels like the setup for a horror movie, like I've been lured onto the boat so the elite can perform an ancient, ritualistic ceremony. I blame Gabrielle for putting these dark thoughts into my mind.

I spot Karen, the woman who picked me up at the marina. She's standing in the corner, arms behind her back, poised. The minute someone sets down a glass or a plate, or touches anything, she quietly removes the items or takes a rag from her back pocket and buffs the surface back to a gleaming shine. She sees me watching, and we nod at each other. I don't think anyone else notices her. I'm not judging. Having spoken to a few people here, they don't seem like bad sorts. They are different, though, from an alternate world to the one I live in, accustomed to luxury and desensitized to the practicalities of day-to-day life. In short, they expect 24-7 assistance.

A woman's voice, rich with the playful tones of Texas, brings me out of my thoughts. "You look like a man who needs a drink." She hands me a glass of champagne.

I accept, starting to feel a little tipsy but deciding that the Bridgeman wheels do need a little greasing.

The woman is buxom and short in stature, although her gray hair—swept back and blow-dried into submission—adds another four inches to her height. She's wearing a white suit, accessorized with various pieces of silver jewelry, most of them studded with diamonds. Her makeup is magazine photo-shoot-ready, making the guess-her-age game even more difficult. There are a few tell-tale signs—liver spots on her hands, a bit of gravity-induced sag to the skin around her neck—but the lifts, tucks, and ironing work she's had done have achieved that elusive less-is-more success. I'm going to go with early to mid-sixties, but she could be seventy. Either way, she looks fantastic. Her red lips break into a friendly smile, and she holds out her hand.

"Kristin Meyer," she says. "And like you, I'm not really like them."

"James Theodore Blake," I tell her as we shake hands.

"Oh, I know who you are." Her blue eyes sparkle playfully. "Conte vouched for you. You're new meat, fresh blood."

I am, and you're the other name I remember from my viewing. "Extempero?" I venture, deciding that someone here needs to say the word.

Her eyes widen, and she laughs. "You said it like you were saying *Voldemort*." She leans in. "Emil does love a sense of intrigue."

"Emil. Is that Mr. Zanak?"

She bobs her head. "He runs Extempero. He'll arrive soon." She waves her arms dramatically. "He always has to have the biggest entrance. He's such a drama queen, but I kind of love it." Her voice has the singing, infectious quality of Dolly Parton's. I like her, and I'm relieved to connect with someone I can talk to. "It's strange, you seem to have come from nowhere. I'm trying to understand how our paths never crossed." It makes sense. Being this rich is a club, and everyone tends to know everyone.

I babble some excuses about flying under the radar and my love of antiques.

"So, I'm right," she says. "You're a fish out of water like me."

"Yes, I suppose you could say that. This isn't really my scene. I'm just here for the auction."

"Well, watch out, Mr. Blake, because I feel lucky tonight!" She spends a long time on the word *lucky*, sounding every bit the country singer. She gazes around the lounge. "You can't really blame them. I feel like I've been through it and come back out the other side, but it gets harder and harder to scratch the itch."

"How do you mean?"

"I've never done drugs, but I suspect it's similar. The private jets, the skiing holidays, the multiple properties. Initially, they hit the spot, but where do you go from there? How do you keep getting that rush?"

"I guess you can get used to anything," I say, thinking about how time travel was once alien to me. "It's all relative."

"Exactly." She squints thoughtfully. "And that's what this is all about. At this level, people want to feel special. They want the drama, the storytelling, the promise of something hard to find, those elusive, magical moments they can't find anywhere else. When you get to a certain level of wealth, it's hard to find unique, authentic experiences."

As I soak in this lavish display of luxury, I understand what Kristin is saying, though I'm not sure this is unique and authentic. To me, it feels generic and fake, but each to their own. "So, when does the auction start?" There is no sight of an auctioneer or any of the usual signs of an auction.

"We have some fun first. Emil likes us to put our hands in our pockets to support some of his philanthropic endeavors. I'm down with that. It's worth it just to get this chance."

It's sinking in that I might have my work cut out for me, bidding against Kristin and the other successful people in the room, when I feel a vibration in the floor. I'm wondering if they've fired up the engines, but then the air begins to shake. The pianist stops playing, and a hush descends. All eyes are out to sea. Two heavyset men with wires in their ears are out on the deck, looking up at the helipad. A helicopter approaches, its rotors thrumming the air. When Kristin said that Emil Zanak liked to make a dramatic entrance, she wasn't kidding. The chopper flies low and fast over the sea like a dragonfly, reaches the yacht, and touches down on the helipad, bouncing gently before settling and powering down.

A dark-haired man in a sharp gray suit exits the chopper. He salutes the pilot and waves in our direction. People clap as he makes his way toward us.

"What's his story?" I ask Kristin.

"He's Iranian but spent most of his life in South Africa. Rumors are his parents fled Iran. They say the early years toughened him up. He's extremely successful, a very passionate man. He's going to want to meet you."

Oh goodie, another superpowerful person I'm going to have to lie to.

Zanak waves away the applause as he joins his own party, fashionably late. Dark-skinned, with heavyset eyes, black hair, and a neatly trimmed beard, he works his way around the room, confident, all smiles, clearly charming everyone he meets. At times like this, I really wish I could channel Other Joe, the side of me that led a very different life, who learned how to be successful, how to play this kind of role. I've read stories about characters with multiple personalities, where one side forces its way through because it wants to take over. Right now, I wouldn't mind that one bit.

Zanak makes his way over to us. He takes Kristin's hand and gently kisses it. He is solid, as though he would be just as comfortable in combat gear as he is in a tuxedo. In a strong South African accent, he says, "You look fabulous. Timeless, as always."

Kristin accepts the compliment with grace. "Is that a Brunello Cucinelli?" she asks, appraising his attire.

"Yes," he says, turning to me. "Kristin is about to tell me this suit is an investment."

"It is!" she announces.

"Mr. Blake." Zanak smiles, and we shake hands, his grip firm. "Emil Zanak, but please, just call me Emil. It's not very often we welcome a new member into our fold. Tell me, have you ever been to an auction on a boat before?"

"No," I tell him, "This is a first for me."

"A first time for everything, eh? Keeps us young and alive." He glances at Kristin. "I have a feeling, and I probably shouldn't be saying this, but tonight could be your lucky night."

Kristin raises her eyebrows. "About time, this is my fifth auction!"

Emil turns to me. "I have a confession to make. I asked everyone here not to ruin the surprise."

"Surprise?"

"If you will excuse me, for just a moment." Grinning, he takes a glass from a tray and taps the side with a ringed finger. "Ladies and gentlemen." His voice is loud, commanding. "The charity auctions will soon be announced. Please enjoy the entertainment, and remember, be generous." He wags a finger, and a ripple of knowing humor passes over the crowd. "The main auction will begin soon. Good luck to the select few." After a round of applause, he turns to me. "Welcome to Extempero, Mr. Blake. I hope you find what you're looking for here and enjoy the show."

Zanak makes his way around the room. I turn to Kristin. "What surprise? What did he mean, the select few?"

She sighs heavily. "I've been to loads of these, but if I win the lottery tonight, it will all be worth it. It's such a gorgeous piece, don't you think?"

"It is, but what do you mean, win the lottery?" Surely, these people have enough money.

She laughs. "I keep forgetting you're an Extempero virgin. Oh gosh, I remember my first auction. I'm almost envious of you. Let me explain how it works. Once you've attended a few auctions—Zanak decides how many—you get put into a lottery. Five winners are picked, and only those five can bid on the chosen antique. Don't worry, though, you'll get your chance eventually."

I stare at her, my heart sinking. I already thought this billionaire club was peculiar, but this is just ridiculous. In some tragic series of events, Extempero has unwittingly snaffled The Continuum's focus object as its must-have trinket of the month. And after traveling to Montenegro, taking on this fake persona, and ending up on this megayacht, I find out that I'm not even going to be in the running to win the bloody horse back.

This whole dumb charade could be for nothing.

9

Along with the other guests, I'm ushered into a spacious room that spans the full width of the yacht. The walls are floor-to-ceiling panes of tinted glass, exposing the harbor lights of Porto Montenegro twinkling in the distance. The décor is tasteful but sparse, with just a few seating areas arranged around the edge of the room. An enormous crystal chandelier dominates the center, dropping through the ceiling, which is cut to reveal part of the deck above. I'm guessing the architects had fun coming up with that idea. It's impressive. Below the chandelier is a lectern, and behind that, a six-foot banner featuring a close-up photograph of the ceramic horse. It's the first clue that the Tang dynasty focus object might make an appearance this evening. The room buzzes with anticipation. People position themselves around the edges of the room but remain standing. Kristin takes my arm and guides me to the right of the lectern.

Most auctions I've attended have been in the UK, and the majority have been low-key affairs: musty halls, cheaply produced catalogs, the usual competitive bunch of dealers, and a smattering of the general public hoping to nab a bargain. This, on the other hand, feels closer to a private sale, similar to one I attended in London, early in my career. It was more focused, the stakes higher, the money eye-watering.

As the chattering excitement builds, my hearing unexpectedly fades for a few fleeting moments. My spine feels like a tuning fork ringing true as a silent whisper of energy passes through me, making the hairs on the back of my neck stand proud. Objects have power, and since my trip to Paris, I've been tuning in to the subtle energy they emit.

The focus object is close.

Of course, I could just be feeding off the crackling excitement in the room, but I trust my inner compass more and more these days. W. P. Brown's advice, coming back around. I'm wondering if I could sneak off and try to find the horse when the security guards I spotted earlier block the exits. They stand motionless and solid, arms behind their backs, watching the room.

A balding man in a traditional suit and tie takes his position behind the lectern. He is lean, with strong features and ruddy cheeks. If you search *auctioneer* on Wikipedia, you will probably find a picture of him. He peers over his glasses and checks through his paperwork. A hush descends as he lifts an envelope. "Ladies and gentlemen, may I please have your attention." His voice has the pleasant, polite ring of expensive British education. "Thank you. On behalf of Mr. Zanak, may I welcome all of you to this, the seventh Extempero auction. A night that, I'm sure, will be as memorable and exciting as ever. As is customary, I will now announce the winners of the lottery."

Kristin loops her hand around my arm, squeezing it. In a hushed tone, she says, "I got a feeling you might be my lucky charm."

The auctioneer opens the envelope with a flourish and reads the first name. "Brian Schmidt."

After a brief round of applause, a young man with mid-length hair raises his hand. He seems almost embarrassed.

Kristin leans in. "Twenty-seven years old, a Silicon Valley whiz kid. Invented some tiny part used in automatic cars. A real thrill seeker too. Likes diving with sharks."

I was impressed until the shark bit. Now it's clear he's an idiot.

The auctioneer reads the second name. "Adebe Kanumba."

A kind-looking man with a beaming smile is patted on the back by a group of friendly associates. Kristin—who seems to know everything about everyone here and appears to have adopted me as her protégé—informs me that Adebe is Africa's biggest cement and salt producer. She giggles to herself. "You don't wanna get those two mixed up."

"And the third of tonight's winners is Fumika Murata," the auctioneer announces with apparent relish.

Kristin points out an old but sprightly Japanese lady. "Murata takes parts in samurai reenactments. She loves racehorses, and apparently, she's an Olympic-standard archer."

Oh, how the other half play.

The auctioneer peers over the crowd. "Two names remain." He milks the moment for all it's worth. "Number four: Quentin Lockwood."

The rakishly thin and bored-looking gentleman is into real estate. Kristin tells me he owns half of New York, but won't be happy until he has all of it.

Like a good comedian, the auctioneer waits for the applause to die down. The room is still. When he focuses his attention in our direction, I think that I might be the fifth winner. An unexpected clerical error? Instead, he announces, "Kristin Meyer!"

Kristin lets out a whoop. She turns to me, her eyes welling with tears. "You see! You're my lucky charm!"

Not wishing to burst her bubble, I offer a reluctant smile.

In my opinion, all she's done is make a shortlist of superrich people willing to pay over the odds for an antique.

People move around the room, seeking out the winners. Kristin is surrounded by people shaking her hand and effusively congratulating her, telling her that she *so* deserves it. I don't know these people, so it's impossible to ascertain if they're being genuine. A lot of them look as though they sail through life being anything but. I take a few steps back and try to blend in. Eventually, the fervor settles down, and the auctioneer announces that the main event will begin in just a few minutes.

Man, these guys really know how to drag out a single-item auction.

Kristin finds me again and subtly gestures toward the whiz kid, her expression darkening. "Brian Schmidt. I'm gonna have my work cut out with him. Everybody wants to win one of these auctions at some point, but I know for a fact that Brian is very competitive." She frowns, but her positive demeanor returns quickly. "You've done your bit, James, you brought me luck. I believe in karma. What will be, will be."

The auctioneer rings a small bell, as though beckoning us all to dinner, and patiently waits for the room to quiet. "Tonight our five lucky winners will be bidding on this exquisite Tang dynasty figurine of a horse." He glances at the banner behind him and then returns his full attention to the room. "This handsome horse has a stunning athletic body and rich, shiny mane. It's been depicted proportionally and realistically. Notice the great attention paid to its anatomical accuracy, the texture and embellishments, the exquisite treatment of color. This particular piece would likely have belonged to someone of great wealth."

And so, the circle will complete.

I've seen a few auctioneers in my time, and this guy is a real pro. He's relaxed, completely at ease, and enjoying the attention.

He leans close to his microphone. "Imagine if this piece could tell its story, what tales it would tell."

A ripple of entertained laughter passes around the room. I arch an eyebrow. He doesn't know how right he is. It certainly has a story. I just need to grab it so The Continuum can decide when to listen.

"Shall we start the bidding," the auctioneer says, "at, say, 1 million dollars?"

If I had just sipped my drink, I would have sprayed it halfway across the room.

What the hell?

Ordinarily, you would start much lower than the target value to build momentum. The idea is to attract as many bidders as possible. I suppose, with a fixed number of bidders, that isn't as important, but still, it's odd to start so high.

The auctioneer acknowledges a bid to my left, scans the room, and asks, "Do we have 1.2 million?"

Kristin raises her hand, and the bidding continues, a swirling mass of money building up like a cyclone. The auctioneer is good: plenty of eye contact and a dash of humor. He knows this is a performance. He gracefully moves his attention between the five bidders, ensuring that everyone feels part of the action. Within minutes we are at 2 million dollars.

I'm no expert on the Tang dynasty, but I know enough. That horse is worth 1.2 million dollars on a good day, an exceptional day, when the sun is shining, the stock markets are soaring, and people with money are itching to pull the trigger.

By the time we reach 5 million, my collar feels tight, and my mouth is parched. I'm not in the running here, yet I still feel queasy. The auctioneer switches it up by increasing the bid increments to one million dollars. Six becomes seven becomes eight in a whirlwind. This is absolute madness!

Emil Zanak looks pleased. I'm not bloody surprised. With a newfound respect, I consider what he's built here, this secretive club of high-net-worth individuals. The idea is simple but brilliant. You take what's in vogue—there's always one antique superstar; in this case, Chinese antiquities—introduce a grandiose location, one that reminds you that you're in the top one percent, and then simply pour over the secret sauce.

Clue. It isn't champagne and caviar.

It's scarcity.

Supply and demand. The universal multiplier. It doesn't matter how much money you've got, if you want it and someone tells you that the supply is limited, it just makes it worth more.

Zanak has taken an item of worth and added a thousand percent to the price. No wonder he's smiling. He's the smartest man in the room, and that's saying something, considering that the present company are all extremely high achievers.

He looks at me, his demeanor confident, but his expression also suggests a certain level of wariness. It feels as though he's deconstructing me, peeling back my mask. I hold his gaze and find myself doing the same. Interesting. I think we're both wearing a disguise tonight. Our mutual appraisal passes. He turns and continues talking with one of his guests. Meanwhile, the auction rattles on at pace, generating the perfect level of buzz, and more importantly, competitive bidding. It's impossible to guess how high this thing could go.

There are audible gasps in the room with each bid. Someone nearby cries out "Yes!" as Kristin bids 10 million dollars.

She's riding this horse to the moon.

After a few more minutes of madness, three of the bidders bow out. It's now down to Kristin and the Silicon Valley whiz kid, Brian Schmidt. She flashes a confident smile. He grins back and scowls at her playfully. It's a duel, a battle of wills, but I've seen enough auctions to recognize the look in his eyes. He already knows he's lost. He's way past what he was willing to pay. Now the game just needs to play out.

The auctioneer flicks his eyes between the two of them and settles on Brian. "Highest bid is currently with Miss Meyer at 28 million dollars. Can we say twenty-eight and a half?"

Why not? What's half a million amongst friends?

Brian swallows, rubbing a hand across his mouth.

"Fair warning," the auctioneer says respectfully, and after a few seconds of tense silence, he begins the countdown. "Going once."

Every single person looks at Brian.

"Going twice."

Silence. No one breathes.

Brian shakes his head.

Bang!

The hammer falls, and the room explodes into cheering and applause. The auctioneer leans into his microphone and proudly announces, "Sold to Miss Kristin Meyer for 28 million dollars."

I'm an antique dealer. I appreciate the item in question, even more so because I know it's special, but Kristin has just laid down 28 million dollars. For a ceramic horse.

Based on the envious expressions on everyone's faces, I'm the only one who's shocked by this. Clearly, none of these rich fools understands that she just paid about 26 million dollars in ego-tax. Kristin is ecstatic. Tears roll down her cheeks. Perhaps, for people like her, this is small change, like finding a few hundred in a savings account you'd forgotten about and deciding to treat yourself to a night out. It's all relative, I suppose.

And it was very, very exciting.

Emil hugs her, an overly dramatic embrace that I suspect is for the crowd. They chat for a while. He leans in and whispers in her ear. She glances at the door. Zanak nods. I'm distracted again by a wave of intuition. It washes over me like the invisible swell of a powerful undercurrent. The focus object. They're going to see it, and I need to go with them. As they head for the door, I cut them off and congratulate Kristin on her win.

She beams at me, eyes glassy. "Thank you, James. My heart is still going like the clappers! I'm so happy."

Zanak's eyes remain fixed on me. Considering he just made a lifetime's salary in about five minutes, he really ought to be happier. What's troubling him? I suppose it could be me, the unexpected new guy who doesn't fit in and smells of fake money.

"Mr. Blake, I do hope you've enjoyed your evening," he says in a way that suggests my interactions with him are already over. "There are more auctions to come, albeit smaller. Many of the charities I am most passionate about need all the help they can get. Please, do enjoy the rest of your evening, and I hope you will join us again."

Channeling Gabrielle, I ignore him and focus on Kristin. "Where are you going?"

"Miss Meyer and I have some business to attend to," Zanak says. "If you will excuse us."

She offers me a playful wink. "We're going to see what I just spent all that money on."

Yes, I know you are.

"It would be amazing to see the horse," I say coolly. "Would you mind if I had a quick look?"

Emil places a hand on my shoulder. "I'm afraid that won't be possible. We like to maintain a sense of—"

"Wait a minute, Emil." Kristin scowls at him. "I just won the auction. Do I need to remind you what that means?"

Emil regards her, unblinking. "This is Mr. Blake's first auction."

"I appreciate that, but rules are rules, and I choose him."

"Choose me for what?" I ask, my mind racing through my horror-movie back catalog again.

"You'll see." She folds her arms and smiles confidently, fixing Zanak with the same expression she had in the final run of the auction.

Emil raises his hands. "Why do I bother?" He gestures toward the door. "Seems you've jumped the queue, Mr. Blake. Shall we?"

We leave the buzzing chatter of the crowd behind us and work our way down to the lower decks. My heart races. I'm unsure what my plan is, but the idea of stealing a horse that's now worth 28 million dollars is feeling crazier than ever. We descend a second flight of stairs and walk silently down a long corridor. I feel the gentle thrumming of the yacht's engines, the cool, conditioned air. Zanak presses a key card to a wall-mounted reader. A door clicks open, and we enter a small luxurious room that wouldn't be out of place in a country manor. Subtle lighting. Dark-blue walls. Paintings, armchairs, bookcases. Zanak walks ahead. Kristin follows, her heels clicking on the polished mahogany floor. It's cold in here, sterile and unmoving. Spotlights attached to a beamed ceiling illuminate rows of glass cabinets. Inside are various artifacts: vases, ornaments, coins, weapons, an eclectic mix of antiques.

"This is my private collection," Zanak says. "Do you approve, Mr. Blake?"

I tell him I do, momentarily forgetting all about the horse and wishing I could spend a few hours in here perusing what appears to be an impressive collection, a proper mini museum.

He flicks a light switch, revealing five mannequins adorned with traditional Chinese clothing, replicas but very authentic looking. "Especially for you, Kristin," he says with a winning smile.

She claps her hands, laughing. "Oh, they're wonderful!"

They no doubt cost a fortune, but hey, I'm getting used to that.

In the center of the room is a plinth with small seats around it. It's strongly lit from above, but empty, as though a piece of fine sculpture has been stolen. So far, no horse, and I can't feel it anymore. I tune in to the room. Nothing. In fact, the opposite. A new and quite unpleasant sensation consumes me. It begins in my gut, a breath of ice that creeps through my body. For some reason, I really don't like this room. It's not just the sterile air. It feels like the opposite of energy, as though a dark and benign force has drawn the goodness and life out of here, like a sponge soaks up water.

"Are you all right, Mr. Blake?" Kristin asks. "You look awfully pale."

I manage a smile. "Yes, I'm fine, perhaps something I ate."

But it's not that. The objects in here are silent. Zanak's museum feels more like a tomb.

A tall blond woman enters the room. I recognize her immediately. It's Maria Hofer, the woman I saw in my viewing after Gabrielle and I followed her to the airport. She's carrying a case that is alive with the promise of the past. I don't need Schrödinger to tell me the horse is inside.

"Maria," Zanak says, "this is James Theodore Blake, our latest addition."

"Ah. We've spoken on the phone. Pleased to meet you, Mr. Blake. Welcome to Extempero." As we shake hands, she regards me with a puzzled expression. "Have we met?"

"I don't think so," I tell her, maintaining an innocent expression. She blinks a few times, clearly sifting through her memory, but eventually she releases my hand with a polite smile. She places the case onto the plinth. The dull metal gleams under the bright lights.

Emil thanks her and she leaves, heels tapping on the floor. She glances back at me but thankfully doesn't make the connection. Zanak turns to Kristin with a wide grin. "Your prize, madame." He unfastens the two catches and lifts the lid of the case to reveal the horse, snugly held in position by perfectly molded foam.

"Oh my," Kristin sighs. "It really is quite something."

I couldn't agree more. I'm struck by its beauty, and for a moment, all thoughts of stealing it go out the porthole. It's bigger than I imagined, around seven inches tall and cleverly articulated with a faux-fur saddle, intricate harnesses, and bell motifs. Its mane is short and neat, its tail upturned. Knowing I was coming here, I did a little research. Cobalt blue was the rarest and most prized of colors, so I'm not surprised to see it used in abundance here, although it's faded, of course. Well over a thousand years will do that.

Kristin explains that the Chinese believed that every person had two souls, one called *hun* and the other *po*, and that the *hun* soul is the one that leaves the body . . . but I'm distracted.

Something is wrong here.

I was so relieved to see the horse, so consumed by the natural attraction of a focus object, that I didn't really study the case. It appears bespoke, as though the parts have been assembled specifically for this job. The metal has a pearlescent sheen. Alien, yet also familiar. The question of why it's familiar taps around the edge of my subconscious like a moth against a lamp.

Embedded into the lid of the case are two glass cylinders. They remind me of an old valve amplifier, simultaneously high-tech and lo-fi at the same time. The retro vibe is broken as an incongruous-looking screen flickers on, displaying an array of complicated information. Charts, numbers, frequencies.

When I read the center of the display, a rush of panic

tightens around my throat and then sinks like a ball of ice. A gnawing suspicion that's been lurking since I walked into the room clarifies into a terrible certainty.

They know precisely what the horse is, and exactly what it can do.

On the screen, digital letters read: *Object Stable. Expected Year of Arrival: 743.*

Questions fill my mind. Who is the time traveler here? Zanak? Does he know about The Continuum? Is Scarlett involved? I try to swallow, but my mouth is horribly dry.

With an amused lilt to his voice, Zanak says, "I think it's just dawned on Mr. Blake why you paid so much for this." He's talking to Kristin but doesn't take his eyes off me.

Kristin laughs, clapping her hands. "It's been so hard keeping this secret. I'm so glad you finally know."

I stare at her, my mouth hanging agape as the events of the last couple of hours play back through my mind like a reel of cruel naïveté. I recall Kristin talking about not being able to find unique, authentic experiences anymore. She said people want to feel special, want drama and storytelling, the promise of something hard to find. Suddenly, the lottery, the storytelling, all the secrecy and exclusivity make sense. Emil Zanak offers experiences you can't find anywhere else on Earth. He deals in the impossible. The unobtainable. Extempero offers time-travel tourism for the megarich. And for all I know, the private jet is about to leave without me.

10

Time-travel tourism. All the secrecy, the crazy money, this specific object being the one they sourced and went crazy over at the auction. Finally, it all makes sense. The familiarity of the flight case suddenly clicks into place too. I think the silver metal might be triterbium, a grounding material used by The Continuum. I have a hunch that Zanak is using it to mask the energy of the focus object.

Staring at the horse, I feel a swirling mixture of excitement and dread. Excitement, because I think the connection between traveler and object is a two-way street: my blood tingles, as though lightly carbonated, the skin on my neck and arms shivers with anticipation. Dread, because I have a horrible feeling that Zanak doesn't understand the importance of its story.

Distant echoes of the past leave the horse and enter me. A conversation of sorts. It tells me that it's been waiting, that it's ready to talk. Willingly, I fall under its spell, but snap out again when I recall Gabrielle telling me about priming objects. I don't want to set this thing off. I just want to steal it and get the hell off this boat.

Reluctantly, I draw my attention away from the focus object and become acutely aware of Zanak and Kristin watching me. Their attention is uncomfortable, the room suddenly claustrophobic. Kristin attempts to reassure me. "This isn't a game or a simulation or one of those extortionate real-life experiences you can buy. This is real, James, this is time travel." In a tentative voice, she says. "It's incredible, ain't it?"

I nod slowly, still in shock, deciding to keep my mouth shut. I know time travel is real. It exists for a reason, to change the past. The first of what I suspect will be many questions arrives, and it's a significant one.

What kind of time travel is this? Purposeful? Or wasteful?

Emil watches me intently. "It's not every day you're told that time travel is real, eh?"

"No, it isn't," I reply.

Luckily, I remember to act surprised, channeling my own first experience of time travel. "I don't know what to say or how to feel about this. It's a lot to take in." I draw in a slow breath, trying to steady my heart rate and buy some time. "I'm sure you understand that I might be a little . . . dubious?"

"Of course, and you're right to be," Zanak says, a fixed smile carved into his face. "Although—and I must be honest now—there were a few times this evening when I thought you had already figured it out, or at least had your suspicions." His South African accent seems stronger, suggesting he tempers it for the crowd. He drifts off for a second, deep in thought, as though amused but also bothered. "I noticed the way you soaked the evening in, took it all in stride. I've seen smart and confident people struggle as they navigate this stage, but I've never seen anyone deal with it like you. You're different, almost as though you were expecting this. I don't know, call it a hunch."

As hunches go, it's a good one.

A few seconds pass, the silence gaining its own unique volume. Eventually, Kristin breaks it. She places a hand on her hip and offers me a beaming smile, exposing perfect white teeth. "Don't you mind him." She scowls playfully at Zanak. "He can be a little paranoid, which is understandable considering what he's offering. Rules are rules, though. The lucky winner of each auction is allowed to initiate someone of their choosing. Tonight, that was you, James. Think of this as a kind of fast track into our little club."

Sure, a club where you spend 28 million dollars to . . . what? Waste a change event? She crosses the room and stands close to me, studying the horse with apparent affection, her expression serious. "I've been through two cheating scumbag husbands, plenty of challenging business partners, and a heap of staff. It's given me the knack of sorting the heroes from the zeros. I consider myself a good judge of character. I took a risk, telling you this, because I felt a connection, felt I could trust you. Was I right? Can I trust you, James?"

When you're a long way from telling the truth and someone asks if you're trustworthy, it's hard not to feel guilty. As confidently as I can, maintaining eye contact with them both, I do my best to convince them that I'm one of the good guys. I'm in the club, their secret is safe with me, etc. All the while, I'm wondering how they risk showing people this? Surely, the more people you add to the mix, the bigger the exposure. Eventually, one of these rich idiots is going to talk, right?

Zanak's calm expression suggests otherwise. He doesn't appear concerned that his secret has been spilled. In fact, his demeanor suggests that he knows I won't tell a soul. Memories of the viewing I had in Amsterdam surface. I saw Zanak's assistant, Maria Hofer, in the process of recruiting just the right person to join the auction. She was pushing one of her minions to confirm that the final candidate matched a very specific profile, and if I remember correctly, she insisted they had lever-age over them. For them to choose me, Gabrielle must have included a juicy—and knowing her, quite sordid—backstory to bolster my James Blake persona.

Extempero demands leverage. If someone steps out of line, eject them from the mother ship with a healthy dollop of defa-mation and scandal. I play the scenario through, imagining the *National Enquirer* headline: Billionaire Claims Secret Society of the World's Elite are Time Travelers!

Discredited, threatened, and ousted. Who's going to believe them? It makes me think about all the secretive organizations that appear to run quite efficiently, right under our noses, with only the occasional leak. I can't help but think about The Con-tinuum: an organization with hundreds of time travelers that, almost magically, no one knows about.

"This is the first time we've discussed time travel with a new member," Zanak says. "Normally, we would have had three or four auctions, more vetting, more gentle conversations, allow-ing you to adapt. You're coping very well, Mr. Blake."

The initial shock is thankfully wearing off, and I give myself a metaphorical slap. Come on, Joe, get it together. What would Gabrielle do? I smile when I think of her in Paris, saying to me, *Now, we investigate.*

"So Extempero is a time-travel club," I say.

"Yes."

"And when you travel, what do you do?"

Zanak holds my gaze confidently, like a proud father. "We immerse ourselves, experience as much as we can, soak in the culture. It's unlike anything you've ever experienced."

"Do you change the past?"

He appears disgusted by the idea. "Of course not. We are mere tourists. We are extremely careful and leave no trace."

Is he telling the truth? If I had to bet, I would say he might be. I suspect they are time traveling in blissful ignorance, completely unaware that they're squandering focus objects.

"When are you leaving?" I ask.

"I'm thinking a couple of weeks," Zanak says. "I have a team of researchers putting together a fantastic itinerary. I'm still learning the language, which isn't easy. Plus, we have our clothing. Magnificent garments that are just receiving the finishing touches."

"We're going to the lantern festival," Kristin says, her voice practically trembling with excitement. "I've dreamed of this for so long. I can't wait; it looks wonderful."

I fix my attention on the screen as I figure out my next move. One option: tell them who I really am. It takes me less than a second to realize that's a terrible idea. The minute Zanak discovers he has no leverage, I turn into a liability. He has security guards. They probably have guns. We're on a boat, and accidents happen. Bad idea. I will maintain my persona for now. I don't know if Zanak is a time traveler, but I have to presume Scarlett is involved in this operation. Maybe he's the front man and she's the traveler? I can imagine her choosing to remain in the shadows, arriving in a couple of weeks to drag them both into the past. From personal experience, I know that Scarlett doesn't care about change events. Has she even told Zanak about them?

OK, I'm going down the rabbit hole here, without proof. My mind whirls. Zanak is studying me again, those dark eyes of his calculating. It won't be long before he suggests that I've probably seen enough for one night. Once I leave the boat, I won't see the horse again. Extempero will trigger the mission, and that will be that. Game over.

A plan forms in my mind. It's rough, but it's all I've got.

"I know it's a lot to ask, but is there any way that I could come on this trip with you?" I turn to Kristin before Zanak can reply, trying to connect with her. "You said to me earlier that you crave unique and authentic experiences, that they're incredibly hard to find. It's the same for me. I've always dreamed of time travel. This is a once-in-a-lifetime opportunity, and I would love to share it with you, if you'll let me."

Kristin blinks, her eyelashes fluttering. Her pained expression suggests that she's considering my suggestion, but she looks resigned when Zanak lets out a short little laugh. "That was a sterling effort, Mr. Blake, but I'm afraid it doesn't work that way. Kristin may have won the auction, but I'm the one who decides who travels, and I only ever take one guest."

Scarcity. Exclusivity. Control. Emil Zanak has it all.

My chance to go on this mission is slipping through my fingers. Kristin looks disappointed in me. "Listen, I like you," she says, "but this isn't how we operate. I wanted you to know the true purpose of Extempero, but I won this auction fair and square. Don't be a sore loser."

I glance at the horse, powerful yet benign, and realize I have no choice. I need to prime the focus object, bond with it, and go on this mission myself—now. The bonding process will form a permanent connection, rendering it useless to Extempero. Once I've made the first jump and found out what the change event is, then I can work out the next move with The Continuum. It's not a bad plan. The only problem is, I've never primed an object before.

"You heard the lady, don't be a sore loser," Zanak says, his fixed smile returning. "You may get your turn, but it's not going to be tonight. Now, if you'll excuse us." He gestures to the door.

I need to do what these guys have been doing all along. I need to buy some time.

Raising my hands in a gesture of defeat, I concede. "OK,

I understand. But it really is the most striking piece. Could I please have one more minute? I just want to admire it. Then I will go, no more questions." I'm pushing my luck here, but I'm relieved to see Kristin bob her head at Zanak.

His dark eyes study me like a panther. "All right, but no touching."

Interesting. He's nervous about touch. It makes me wonder again what his role might be in all of this. Ringmaster, traveler, or both.

Knowing I don't have long, I focus my full attention on the horse. Apart from the silent whispers and sense of attraction, it feels comparatively quiet. I need to get it singing, like the radio in my shop and the metronome Gabrielle used when we traveled to Paris. She told me that priming was all about intention. OK, I *intend* to get this horse fired up. Big time. Without moving a muscle, I reach out to the focus object and ask it to tell me its story before it's too late. The reaction is instant. The cobalt glaze saturates, as though someone skilled in restoration just wiped its surface. The wood, dark and cracked, lightens, revealing the original carved details. I hear distant sounds, chimes, voices on the wind.

I'm beginning to think I might be able to do this when it fades back to its original dull sheen. Dammit. What happened?

Zanak is standing next to me, tapping my arm. "Time to go, Mr. Blake."

Alexia's words come flooding into my mind, the advice she gleaned from the psychometry book. She talked about trust, how the objects need to feel that you have their best interests at heart. In a final effort of will, I imagine the horse as a child and project my heart and integrity into a bunch of sweet nothings that I whisper silently across time.

I'm listening.
I'm here for you.

But your story is in danger.

I'm a traveler, your best hope. I'm decent and honest. Whatever it is you want to show me, whatever it is that needs to be changed, I promise I will do my best.

Believe me. Trust me.

Let me bond with you.

This commitment pours out, as though already written: a poem, a love letter.

Without realizing it, I had closed my eyes. When I open them, I'm taken aback by the wonderfully familiar display of a focus object in stunning full bloom.

Primed, eager, agitated.

A cool mist cascades from the horse, spilling over the edges of the case and down the sides of the plinth like dry ice. Its cobalt-blue paint glows like a mysterious flame. Circles of crimson red, sparkling gold, and sulfurous green pulse, building in power until they become swirling spirals of brilliant light.

The promise of the past hits me like a warm gust of ionized air, sending a ripple of tingling energy over my skin. The room fills with a giddy static. Feeling like I've taken a mild hallucinogen, I begin to laugh helplessly. It's amazing. My own personal fireworks show.

It's calling me. The past is waiting.

The spell is broken by shouting. It's Zanak. He's cursing and shaking me. "What the hell have you done!"

Like a drunk man watching a tennis game, I move my attention between him and the horse. "You can see that?"

"Of course I can!" He growls, baring his teeth. "Why did you do that?"

Kristin approaches. "See what? What are you talking about?"

"This idiot just opened the portal!"

Clearly confused, she says, "But it looks exactly the same as when we walked in."

"For you," he says, jaw clenched, "but not for us."

Us. OK, several details have just been confirmed. The visual energy of a primed focus object can't be seen by "normal" people. I'm not the only time traveler here, and Zanak clearly wants to kill me.

The display on the case updates. Zanak leans over it, and when he speaks, his voice is thin and distant. "Jesus H. Christ, it gets worse."

The panel reads: *Object Activated. Departure: 3 minutes.*

A countdown commences.

"Three minutes!" Kristin covers her mouth with her hand. "But we can't leave now, we haven't prepared."

On that, we agree.

Zanak shoves my shoulder. He doesn't appear to put much weight into it, but it still knocks me back a step. "Whoever you are, I will deal with you later." His accent is harsh, totally unfiltered. He turns to Kristin. "You paid 28 million dollars for this expedition, and thanks to this idiot, we're leaving earlier than planned."

"We're still going?" she looks horrified.

Zanak points at the horse. "We only get one chance, and I'm not going to miss it. If you still want to come, that's your choice, but we're leaving now." Ignoring me, he walks to a cabinet, opens it, and stuffs various items into a rucksack: a flask, a couple of smaller bags, and a pouch. I'm guessing they were prepared for the trip he planned to take two weeks from now. The one I've just totally messed up. He straps a watch to his wrist and checks the dial. I can't tell if it's like mine.

My mind plays through what's about to transpire. When travelers touch primed focus objects, they become bonded to the missions. It's permanent, and the objects are no longer required. If Kristin decides she wants to go, Zanak will hold her hand and touch the focus object, and the two of them will be dragged into the past. Now we might be able to create a chain, join hands so the three of us travel. In theory, this should work, but it's dubious speculation at best. Either way, I think the chances of him agreeing to that idea are . . . zero. Which means there is only one reliable option left. I must be the one who bonds with the object, and I need to travel alone.

Stepping forward, I move my left hand toward the horse.

"What are you doing?" Kristin asks.

"No!" Zanak shouts, so loudly that it stops me in my tracks.

Keeping my hand over the horse, I turn to them. "I'm going on this trip alone."

"Wait, just wait a second." Zanak's voice has regained its original charm. He raises his hands in a passive, defensive gesture. "You *could* do that. It's your choice, but I must warn you, James. It's dangerous."

"This isn't the first time I've traveled." I manage to keep my voice steady, despite the focus object demanding my attention.

He nods patiently. "I guessed as much, but honestly, this is a shock for me as well. It's amazing to meet another traveler. I thought I was the only one." I consider this. He's probably bluffing, but I know the feeling, and it rings true. "You're in control here," he adds, "but when you land, you're going to be alone. You're not going to know where to go. I'm prepared. I know the landscape, understand the people." He takes a tentative step toward me.

"Back off!" I warn him, moving my hand closer to the horse. I can feel its cool energy dancing over my fingertips. They both stare at me like I'm a terrorist holding a bomb.

"Think it through," Zanak says. "There is safety in numbers. We can all go, that's the best move here."

Annoyingly, he might be right. As long as I'm the one who bonds with the object, there's nothing to stop me from dragging him along on this jump. Any subsequent jumps will be bonded to me and me alone. I can't deny it, though: his knowledge of where we're heading will be useful on this initial jump. I might need his help. Another idea crosses my mind. He hasn't talked about this being a mission and certainly doesn't seem to know that the object exists for a reason. If we travel together, I might be able to show him—maybe teach them both—the true meaning of time travel.

Sensing my uncertainty, Kristin says, "I trusted you. Seeing China is my dream. Please don't take that away from me."

"We don't have long," Zanak warns, gesturing at the display. Twenty seconds.

I'm talking before I realize the decision has been made. "We go together, but I'm the one who touches the object."

They both nod. Kristin looks relieved and terrified. I keep my focus on Zanak. If he rushes me, I wouldn't fancy my chances.

"We make a chain," I tell them. "Hold each other's hand first."

They do as they're told, and I split my focus between them and the horse. It seems to know that a connection is about to be made. Somewhere in the distance, I hear the deep, throaty rumble of a waterfall, the sweet song of a forest glade. A cool breeze washes over my face, carrying with it the scent of moist earth and wild grass. The pleasant jostling of wooden chimes travels on a whisper of wind, working its way through tall sighing trees. It's mesmerizing, hypnotic, magical.

I reach out and take Kristin's hand, forming a circuit of three souls ready to embark on an impossible journey. When I turn back to the horse, its paintwork burns like blue neon. The sounds of nature are joined by traditional Chinese instruments: metallic chords driven by pounding drums, flutes and violins, chanting and laughter. These discordant sounds resolve into a thrilling audio tapestry.

The object draws me. There is no choice now. The room swells, willing the connection. I feel the heartbeat of time itself joining our worlds. The present, so reassuring and constant, gives way, and for a breath I feel weightless. Then in a blinding whipcrack of light, the three of us are transported.

The year, 743.

The age of the Tang dynasty.

PART 3

11

We land awkwardly on rough, icy ground, and Kristin immediately loses her footing. I lend her my arm briefly while she catches her balance, then the three of us gaze around in awe. We're near the top of a hill, standing at the head of a gentle slope that leads down to a valley. Behind us the hill rises away, covered in fir trees. To the left and right stretches a vast plain, patched with snow and studded with the black skeletons of winter trees, and in the distance, undulating moors nestle at the foot of a giant snow-capped mountain range. The sun has just disappeared behind the highest peak, streaking it with pale ribbons of golden light.

Kristin shivers and pulls her silk jacket close around her. "Oh my, it's glorious," she says, surveying the impressive landscape. Her cheeks are pink with cold, and her eyes sparkle with wonder. A tear rolls down her cheek. In a voice thick with emotion, she says, "China. I can't believe I'm here, finally here. The Tang dynasty."

Clenching against the cold, I fold the lapels of my jacket up around my neck and soak in the view. Kristin isn't the only one feeling it. I've traveled a few times now, but never this far, and the sudden shift from a luxury yacht into the raw natural beauty of ancient China is extreme. Fear, excitement, and trepidation fizz around in me, possibilities stretching in all directions like roots.

Before I can focus on a plan, Zanak pushes me roughly backward into a tree. He jams his forearm against my chest. "We weren't due to travel for weeks!" he hisses. "Why the hell did you do that? Who are you?"

I try to free myself, but he has me pinned. "Would you please get your arm out of my face?"

Zanak stares me down, then releases me and takes a step back. He scowls. "Conte pretty much begs me to invite you to the auction, you wrap *her* around your little finger"—he jerks his head over his shoulder in Kristin's direction—"and then as soon as you get close to the travel object, you fire it up in a matter of seconds! You're obviously an experienced time traveler." He jabs a finger in my face. "You'd better start talking."

My plan, if you could call it that, didn't really extend to after we landed. I buy some time, smooth down my hair, and straighten my jacket. I have a chance to complete the mission, and that's all that matters. However, this whole stolen object setup has Scarlett written all over it, and if Zanak's in cahoots with her, he could turn nasty. I decide it's best for now to maintain my cover. I'm not going to mention The Continuum until he does, if at all.

"My name is James Theodore Blake," I say with conviction. "I'm a time traveler, like you." As is often the way when you're lying, a good dose of truth goes a long way.

Zanak folds his arms. "How did you find out about me? About Extempero?"

Thinking on my feet and sticking to the facts as closely as I can, I say, "Objects call to me. I was drawn to the horse, and then it was sold. It led me to you. I had to connect with the object. You understand that, don't you? The way they call you?"

I'm fishing here, but if I'm going to navigate this jump, I need to know as much as possible about Emil Zanak.

He regards me suspiciously. "How did you get Conte to tell you about Extempero? You're the first person he's ever introduced. He always said he wanted to keep it for himself."

"He didn't want to tell me anything, but I pressured him, and he cracked in the end." I'm aware that I might be dumping Conte right in it all over again. The poor guy is hardly a saint, but he doesn't deserve to have Extempero busting his balls too. "My fault entirely, by the way, not his. He has no idea I'm a time traveler."

Emil shakes his head. "You've got all the answers, haven't you? But I don't really care what you say. I didn't want you on this trip. You forced us to travel. Now give me one good reason why I shouldn't just knock you out and leave you here to fend for yourself."

"Listen here, you two," Kristin chips in. Her voice is resonant, but her teeth are chattering, and her lips are blue. "I paid a ton of money for this trip, and I did not pay it to listen to the two of you squabbling up here on this freezing mountain! Traveling back to this era is a dream come true, one I never thought I'd live to see. One time traveler or two, I don't care. We are here now, and all I want to do is soak in every tiny detail, but you idiots are distracting me." She shivers violently.

Zanak glares at me and then focuses on Kristin. "You're right, I apologize. We need to get you somewhere warmer." He stares pointedly at her strappy diamond shoes. "If it weren't for this fool, you would be wearing the clothing I had made especially for you." He gestures toward a well-worn dirt track at the foot of the hill. "Let's head down. I'm confident that road will lead us to a village, or people at least." He turns to me. "I don't care what you think you know, Blake. This is my trip, and you do as I say. Got it?"

"Yes," I tell him, without any angles.

"We stick together for now, until I decide what to do with you."

We work our way awkwardly down the hill. I'm struggling in my flat-soled shoes. I offer Kristin a piggyback but am kind of relieved when she suggests that might be more dangerous than walking.

When I get a chance, I surreptitiously check my watch. The date is Tuesday, February 12, 743. This is the farthest I've ever traveled. What is that, like twelve hundred years? My watch updates and displays our expected jump duration.

"My God," I murmur.

Zanak looks back. "What's wrong with you now?" he asks.

"How long do you think we're going to be here?"

He pulls a device from his rucksack, a simple black box, smaller than a phone with a basic display, and smiles. "You certainly picked a good one, Kristin," he says, as he helps her over a tricky bit of terrain. "This trip is going to be one of our longest ever. Nearly two days in total."

"Wonderful," she says. "At my age, every second counts. And I'll be even happier about it once I can feel my darn feet."

Two days. This will be my longest trip as well. The rules dictate you always land at the end of a story that needs changing and this is the first jump, a chance to prepare for what comes later. I keep my eyes peeled and my senses tuned in.

"We'll be at the road soon," Zanak reassures us. "Meanwhile—and listen up, Blake—I need to remind you of the rules. I am responsible for Kristin's well-being, not yours. Remain close; no wandering off. And remember, we're here as tourists only."

"Yeah yeah, leave only footprints," Kristin says, pushing something deeper into her handbag. "I've heard it all before."

Zanak stops and folds his arms, his brow furrowed. "Come on now. Empty your bag."

"They're plants!" she cries indignantly. "Just a small botanical collection. What harm could that do?"

He glares at her until she pulls them out and drops them on the ground.

He peers into her bag. "Is that all of it?"

She nods.

"Good." He mollifies his tone. "If you try to do anything that may have a long-term impact, time will push back, and you'll feel it. For your own safety, you must respect that. I've never lost a traveler, and I don't intend to start today."

"Do you ever try and change anything while you're here?" I venture.

"Christ, I just told you," he growls. "We're here as tourists only."

And so, it's confirmed. He's using focus objects as tickets for a time-travel safari and squandering missions in the process. A complex wave of sadness and anger consumes me, but I push it down. Now is not the time.

Zanak walks ahead, unintentionally allowing Kristin and me a chance to talk. Voice lowered, I say, "I'm really sorry for messing up your trip."

She frowns, playfully. "Don't be silly. Apart from freezing, I'm glad you came."

"Thanks, me too," I tell her honestly. "So, how many of these trips has Extempero completed?"

"Since I became a member, there've been three others, I think," she says. "I don't know how many before that. I couldn't believe it when this came up. I so wanted to visit ancient China. I am one lucky girl."

My heart sinks again. If Zanak is telling the truth, and they don't care or even know about change events, that means there have been at least three other squandered missions. All those opportunities . . . missed. No wonder the Future Change Index has been in the red. More determined than ever to complete the mission here in China, I grasp my silver hunter and make a silent deal with time. I will wait for a waypoint, connect with what time wants to show me, and then when I travel home, I will talk to The Continuum and get support and guidance on how best to complete the mission. I sneak a look at my watch and see that it's calibrating again.

Slowly, painstakingly, we wind our way down toward the track along the side of a steep valley. After about an hour, we emerge from a thicket of pine trees and pause in a clearing, cut into the hillside. "I have to stop," Kristin says wincing.

She rests on a nearby tree stump, takes off her stilettos, and rubs her feet in her hands. "I hope my toes don't give up on me after all this abuse," she says forlornly. "I've grown quite fond of the little guys over the years."

A cracking sound in the nearby trees catches my attention. "Did you hear that?"

Zanak makes a sign for us to be quiet. A moment later a sizable man emerges from the undergrowth. He is swarthy and strong-looking, with a neat mustache and an oily black beard. He's wearing a long-sleeved tunic in a bright red-and-yellow pattern, with ornate ribbon trim at the cuffs and around the collar. He pauses and studies us, his eyes shaded beneath a thick fur hat. He is followed by another man, this one shorter and stockier. His beard is peppered with gray, and he's wearing a similar outfit, along with a gilet and knee-length leather boots over a startling pair of leopard-skin leggings. He reminds me of the Jack on an old-fashioned playing card.

Kristin moves to my side, alarm flashing across her face. "Should we run?" she murmurs.

"No point," I reply. "We're hardly geared up for it. He might be friendly."

Zanak pushes a small device into his ear. "Leave the conversations to me."

Interesting. Clearly some kind of translation device. Where does he get his tech, I wonder? The screen on the focus object's case, a timepiece, and now this. And yet still no mention of The Continuum.

The tall man asks where we have traveled from. Zanak seems to understand what they're saying, as well as I do, which means the device he put in his ear is clearly working. However, it doesn't seem to stretch his brain in the same way as my implant, which means he's struggling to be understood.

The man appears puzzled and shrugs at his companion. "I believe he's trying to speak the local language, but I cannot grasp the meaning."

The other man studies Zanak. "At least he's trying. Most of them don't bother."

"True," the first man replies.

They consider us with fascination, appearing to fight off smiles. "He has not the appearance of a China man," says the short one. "I have never seen such apparel, not in a hundred moons. Are they from the circus? And look at the woman." He approaches Kristin with bald curiosity. "Why has she bare legs? And what torturous devices on her feet."

"Perchance she is a slave, and they are taking her to market," the tall one suggests. "Although she is past child-bearing age, she is of good health. Bright eyes, strong back."

"But I cannot understand why they wear so few coverings when it is the snow season," his friend continues. "And where are their camels?"

The men look bewildered. I decide it's time to step in.

Gabrielle gave me her usual sink-or-swim version of training. I recall her explaining that the implant works via intention. Silently, I instruct the device in my brain to speak the same language as these men, cross my fingers behind my back, and take a step forward.

"Hello," I say to the tall man, slowly annunciating my words. "Can you understand me?"

My words sound English to me, but judging by the astounded expression on his face, the implant is working just fine.

"You speak Sogdian!" he exclaims, laughing and smacking his sides.

Sogdian? Never heard of it. It briefly crosses my mind that if I could dig this device out of my ear and clone it, I'd be a billionaire like Zanak.

"Where are you from?" the tall man asks, now smiling at the three of us.

"Er, we are from a Western land," I say.

"How do you come to speak our language?"

"I am a traveler," I respond. "I speak many languages."

"Then you are like us, my friend," he says. *Not really, I have a futuristic microchip embedded in my brain.* "It is a pleasure to make your acquaintance. My name is Takut, and this is my friend Artivan."

Artivan beams, an excited and friendly smile.

Kristin turns to Zanak. "You wanted a reason to keep him around. Is the fact that he speaks fluent Sogdian enough for you?"

Zanak glowers at me.

"It's good to meet you," I say to our new acquaintances. "My name is James, and this is Emil and Kristin."

The Sogdian men chew on our names for a while, eventually achieving some semblance of English. Kristin laughs but then shudders.

Takut bellows, "The night is drawing in, and there is ice on the wind. Our caravan is just down there, in the valley. Your party will join us."

"Caravan?"

Zanak taps my arm and says, "Tell them we want to reach Chang'an."

I do, and Artivan nods. "Yes, yes, but you need suitable attire. We will trade and eat. You will stay the night with us, and in the morning, we go to Chang'an."

My watch hasn't yet given me any waypoints, but until it does, I think it makes sense for us to stick with these guys. They seem friendly enough, and although they could be luring us into a trap, it doesn't feel that way. Plus, we need food, clothing, and somewhere warm to sleep.

"Thank you," I say. I turn to Zanak and Kristin, remembering that they won't have understood a single word, and explain it all to them.

Zanak grits his teeth in irritation. "We need to discuss any plans before you make unilateral decisions," he snaps. "And I thought I told you not to interact with anyone."

Kristin steps in. "You couldn't make yourself understood, whereas James here speaks their language fluently. How fortunate that you've studied Sogdian," she says to me. "I bet you never thought you'd have the chance to try it out! And aren't their outfits fabulous? I'd just love a pair of those leopard-skin leggings."

"The sun is setting," Takut says. "We should make haste."

"We'll follow you," I say.

"But what about the woman?" Artivan points at Kristin. "How will she walk with those devices on her feet? The way ahead is rough and strewn with rocks."

"I will carry her," Takut announces and walks purposefully toward Kristin.

"What'd he say?" she asks me.

"The big guy's offering to carry you," I tell her.

"Well, hello there," she beams as he reaches down to collect her in his arms. I expect him to carry her against his chest, like a baby, but instead he throws her up over his shoulder in a kind of fireman's lift.

Kristin shrieks and laughs. "This reminds me of a time I went ranching and a cowboy flipped me upside down on the dance floor!"

Zanak and I follow the Sogdians and a grinning Kristin down the hill through rocky woodland. After about ten minutes, we reach the track and a long line of carts and horses that snakes away across the landscape, eventually disappearing behind the hills.

"Artivan!" a woman calls out. "Did you get rabbits?"

"No rabbits, but we found these strange creatures!" he calls back jovially. He bows to us and mounts a nearby cart. People stare at us, laughing and pointing. We must look like aliens in our modern evening wear.

Takut puts Kristin down gently. She smooths her suit and straightens her hair. "Well, I never," she says. "I can't remember the last time someone carried me. Thank you, sir."

"We will travel to the caravanserai," Takut says. "There we will camp for the night, and tomorrow we'll head onward to the Western Market in the great city of Chang'an." He smiles at me and gestures toward Zanak, who is quiet and seems a little nervous. "Tell your friend."

I explain what's happening. Zanak finds a thin smile but doesn't look at me. Not being the center of attention is clearly his kryptonite.

Takut talks to his people, loads us up onto one of the carts, and hands out thick fur blankets. They feel wonderful, and once wrapped up, the chill finally leaves my bones.

I don't know if we're heading in the right direction, but I do know that time tries to help. If these guys turning up doesn't whisper *subtle serendipity*, then what does? Eventually, my watch will catch up, and then I'll know whether we're going in the right direction. For now, this is my only option.

Takut suggests I sit in the front of the cart with him. We sit side by side on a bench. He snaps the reigns on two heavy horses, and we slowly lurch into motion.

From this height I get a good view of the caravan, a ragtag assortment of twenty or so carts and wagons. We are in the middle. The caravan moves with steady purpose, as though every person and animal knows where we're heading and nothing will keep them from their destination. Kristin and Zanak sit in the back. They talk but I can't hear them. There's constant jangling, braying, padding of hooves across rough ground, and the odd call from the animal drivers. A distinctly pungent tang permeates the air, which I presume is coming from the camels. I once read that they pee on their own legs to cool themselves in the heat and warm themselves in the cold. No wonder they smelled a bit fruity.

"Where did you say you're from?" Takut asks.

"From the West," I say again, vaguely waving my hand in what I hope is a westerly direction. "We have come an extremely long way. More than a thousand . . . miles."

He narrows his brow in confusion. "Why did you attempt such a trip on foot? And in such unsuitable attire? Where are your beasts of burden?"

"Er, we ran out of food and had to eat them on the journey," I improvise, looking at him hopefully.

He bobs his head sagely. "It is a great misfortune, but it occurs all too often."

We sit in companionable silence for a while, and I soak in

the caravan atmosphere. Am I afraid? Worried I might never get home? Of course, but that does me no good. I'm hardly experienced, but my previous trips form a base that I can build on, use to maintain a positive outlook. I draw a steadying breath and focus on the moment.

A camel in front of us is piled so high and wide with packages that I can't see around it, but farther ahead I see the trail of carts and pack animals leading us, and ascertain that the caravan is turning left into a gap between two high cliffs.

Takut taps me on the shoulder. "Jemz!" he says. "Tell your friends to hold on tight. We have to navigate a narrow path with a steep drop." I pass on the warning. Zanak languidly rests a hand on the side of the cart, but Kristin does as she's told.

The cart slows as we enter a narrow pass between the cliffs, the light fading rapidly as we cross into deep shade. After a couple of hundred yards, the cliff on the left separates from the path, and a precipitously deep chasm appears, its bottom too deep to see clearly. Takut slows the cart to a crawl, and we creep our way along the path, a foot or two from the edge, trying to keep our distance from the camel in front, which kicks when we get too close.

A hundred feet ahead, the cliff rejoins the path.

"Not too far now," Zanak reassures Kristin.

"Uh-huh," she says, her eyes glued to the front wheel.

The cart inches along the path, and we're within maybe fifty feet of safety when the horses suddenly bray wildly, buck in the traces, and bolt, dragging us with them. Kristin grips my arm so hard it hurts.

"Woah, woah!" Takut cries, trying to pull the animals up. The cart sways violently as we go over a huge rut in the track. It lurches to the left, and I watch various bags and small items fly into the air and disappear into the depths of the crevasse.

It feels like a lifetime, but it's only a few seconds before Takut stops the horses.

"Are you all present and well?" he bellows loudly, without looking back.

I turn to check on Kristin and Zanak. He brushes off my inquiry with a wave of his hand. "We're good," he says gruffly.

"All fine," I tell Takut. Once we are over to the other side, he gets out of the cart to check the wheels and ensure his animals aren't hurt, then walks to the edge of the crevasse and peers into the darkness, shaking his head.

Kristin leans forward. "My stilettos fell off the cart and down that gap." She shrugs. "They were killing my feet anyway. I'm going to stick to flat boots from now on."

As we resume our journey, I wonder if it was a mere accident that knocked her shoes off the cart, or whether it was resistance at work. Resistance can certainly be a powerful force. I remember it nearly choked me when I considered ways to stop the opera fire in Paris, so why wouldn't it get rid of a fashion item that the world isn't ready to see yet? It might sound dramatic and even silly to think that time would want to keep anyone from finding those shoes, but who knows how these things work? How many lives would be affected if the stiletto had been invented in 743?

The rest of the journey goes without a hitch, and at just before 5 p.m. local time, we round the edge of a small coppice and enter a wide, sweeping valley. About half a mile ahead, a sandy-colored stone building comes into view, a small fortress with towers at each corner like the fingers of an upturned hand buried in the landscape. I check my watch, but it's still calibrating. If I'm going to see what time wants changed, I'm going to need a waypoint and a change event. So far, I haven't had any sense that I'm witnessing a mission-related event, but if we're here for nearly two days, there's plenty of time. I'm just used to much shorter jumps. Maybe I need to relax a bit while remaining open to the clues and guidance that time might offer?

"Is that building over there a castle?" I ask Takut.

"No, that is the caravanserai," he says, "a place to stop and rest and trade. We will stay here overnight. You three shall be our guests. We will eat, drink, and be merry!" He pats his belly. "They make the best goat stew I have ever eaten. Just you wait and see."

12

The sky deepens to rich indigo as we pass through the torch-lit outer gates of the caravanserai. As Takut navigates the inner courtyard, I'm hit by the stench of manure, smoke, and sweat. Shadowy groups of people in a variety of attire surround campfires, their smoke winding up into the early evening air. Donkeys and camels graze nearby, tethered to stakes in the ground, tents and heaps of cloth bundles strewn about. It reminds me of a modern New Age festival. The sound of music carries on the wind, and I see dancing girls in the distance.

"What are you all gawking at?" Takut says, slapping me on the back. "You're like a nosy goose! Come on, let's find a spot to settle for the night."

He stops the cart, and we all climb down, stretching after being stuck in the same position for the last two hours. The occupants of the caravan decamp, drawn toward the welcoming glow of firepits. Only now do I see how many people made up our convoy. There must be a couple hundred, all bundled in thick winter clothes, and as they remove their fur coats and hats, it becomes clear that we've been traveling with men and women of many different races. There must be as many animals too, noisy camels, horses, and mules slurping from buckets of water and munching hay.

Zanak helps Kristin down from the cart. "They have these all along the silk road," he says. "I guess you could think of them like the precursors to our modern roadside service stations."

"It's wonderful." Kristin gazes around in awe. "Priceless."

A ginger-haired man approaches, looks the three of us up and down in astonishment, and much to Zanak's consternation, bursts out laughing. "What in the name of Adhvagh's beard are you wearing?" he guffaws, prodding my dinner jacket. He circles Kristin, "And what is she wearing? I have never seen clothes like this, not even in Chang'an. Can we trade?"

Takut steps between us. "Hands off, Varzak, they're with me."

The man bows respectfully, but his eyes flash with mischief. "Watch Takut. He has a silver tongue. He will trade your clothes and give you fresh air in return."

"What are they saying?" Kristin asks me.

I don't reply. I know that Zanak enjoys being the guide, that he needs to be the main man. If I can, I should let him. He says, "I think they're fighting over you."

"How flattering!" she says. "I quite like the look of the red-haired guy."

Takut beckons Artivan and a small group of Sogdians. "Now we trade," he announces.

Using basic words, body language, and gestures, Zanak manages to explain that we need warm clothing and sturdy footwear.

Takut grins at me. "And what do you need, Jemz?"

"Warm clothes and strong boots, please, and some leopard-skin leggings for my friend here," I tell him, indicating Kristin.

"She has legs like hairpins," he says. "I have no skin leggings, but I have good clothes." He rummages in the back of the wagon and pulls out a sack filled with a variety of garments and blankets, which he lays out on the ground for us to peruse. We pick out tunics and fur gilets and hats, and Zanak and I hold up a blanket for Kristin to change behind. Takut picks out three pairs of long leather boots. "These should fit you," he says, handing them over. I give the smallest pair to Kristin, who wraps strips of woolen cloth around her legs and feet to create makeshift socks, then pulls them on.

"How do I look?" she says, twirling around so we can admire her. "Cute, huh?"

"You absolutely look the part," Zanak says. "Are you warm now?"

"I'm toasty," she says. "Good to go. James, your outfit is incredible! It really suits you."

"Thanks," I say. I'm wearing a green tunic embroidered with blue roundels at the collar, cuffs, and hem, along with blue leggings that I've tucked into the boots. I also have a thick sheepskin gilet, and a brown woolen cloth around my neck. Zanak is in a similar getup, although he's chosen a brown tunic, leggings, and a black gilet.

"One thing missing!" Takut hands me a blue skullcap, which I perch on top of my head. "There you go. Now you're a true Sogdian!" He pats me on the back and belly-laughs with glee, then gathers up our discarded twenty-first-century outfits and runs his fingers over the cloth. "Incredible craftsmanship," he says. "I have never seen such even cloth. And what are these made of? Horn? Or shell?"

He's plucking at the buttons on my dinner jacket, which I suspect are made of plastic. "They are a special kind of resin," I say.

"Excellent," he breathes, his nostrils flaring with excitement.

"These will fetch a pretty price at market." He stuffs the clothes into an empty sack, secures it with a plaited leather strap, and throws it onto the back of the cart. I'm worried that we've messed something up by traveling back in modern dress, but unlike with the stilettos, time seems happy enough with this trade, and I'm glad to be warm.

Takut claps his hands. "Now we eat!" He leads us to a huge cauldron hanging above a roaring fire, where a group of hungry travelers waits patiently for the cook to dole out rations. "Make my day and tell me it's your legendary goat stew!" Takut says loudly to the plump, sweaty Chinese man stirring the pot.

"You're in luck," the cook says drily. "This is the end of last year's meat. After tonight there'll be no more goat till summer."

Trying not to think about how you keep goat meat fresh for months without electricity, I accept the bowlful of steaming stew and a hunk of tough bread with as much enthusiasm as I can muster. Once we all have steaming bowls, Takut pays using coins from a purse and leads us back to the Sogdian encampment. Rugs and cushions have been arranged beneath a makeshift burlap shelter near one of the arches. We sit cross-legged on huge blankets, surrounded by the chatter of many Sogdians. Artivan fills everyone's cups from a voluminous pottery jar.

"The finest Sogdian wine," Takut tells us. "The Chinese say if you drink this, it takes a month to recover! Want to find out if it's true?" He proffers a horn beaker full of the ruby liquid, and I pass it to Kristin.

"Sogdian wine," I tell her. "Apparently it's strong stuff."

"Bottoms up!" She takes a tentative sip. "It's excellent," she says, with the assured opinion of a seasoned drinker. Artivan hands me and Zanak a beaker each, and I try the wine. It's good, strong and full of tannins, a bit like a modern Australian Shiraz. The stew, on the other hand, smells like the school dinners of my youth, but with a bitter, gamey undertone. I take a small bite and chew. The meat's surprisingly tender, and I realize just how hungry I am.

Zanak offers Takut a gold coin in exchange for the food, but he refuses to take it. "Tonight you are my guests," he says. "Tomorrow, when we get to Chang'an, you will invite me!" Zanak glares at me. I translate for him, and he reaches out to shake Takut's hand. Bemused, Takut allows his arm to be pumped up and down.

"It's just a way to say thank you," I tell him.

"Aha!" Takut beams. "I love to learn new customs!"

A small group of colorfully dressed people clears a generous space in the center of the courtyard, about thirty feet across. They hustle people out of the way, seat them in a circle, and lay down six small circular rugs, spaced evenly, each around three feet in diameter and woven in intricate patterns. Then they sit, and one takes up a harp, one a flute, and one a double drum in the shape of an hourglass. The harp player is in charge, and on his signal, they play a slow, quiet tune, one I heard on the yacht before we traveled here. A lament to nature.

We listen to the music as we eat and drink. The wine does its work, and it's a relief to feel some of the stress dissipate like smoke swirling away into the night. Aware that I need to stay focused and ready, I pour out my second beaker of wine. Kristin talks in a quick, excited stream of consciousness to Takut, who watches her with sparkling eyes. He doesn't understand English, but he's transfixed anyway. Even Zanak seems to be relaxing, listening to one of the Sogdians play a lute and sing a soulful melody.

A buzz against my chest breaks the spell. Ensuring that no one sees, I check the screen. Finally, a waypoint. Close by. Time always helps you along if it can. I'm in the right place. I close the watch, shove it back beneath my shirt, and slip away.

As I'm leaving the camp, someone grabs me from behind.

"Where are you going?" Zanak snarls, holding my jacket.

"I'm just taking a look around." I gesture toward the huge gates, which are closed and guarded. "I can't go anywhere."

He studies me for a few seconds and then releases his grip. "Just don't mess this up for us, any more than you already have." He walks away.

The waypoint leads me to a shady corner of the court-yard, away from the crowds, where a lone figure, a woman, is unwinding narrow rolls of silk. Hesitating, leaning against the caravanserai wall, I watch for a while. The woman wears a dark-green felt jacket with tight sleeves and loose red silk pants. As the silks unfurl, they fall from her hands, and she teases them around her head and body, turning them through the air, weaving ephemeral patterns across the blue velvet sky. It's bewitching, and I move a little closer.

She lifts her head to the stars and flicks the ribbons in time with an imaginary drum beat, then taps her feet. Once she has found the rhythm, she spins on the spot, lifting her arms above her head and crossing them back and forth, behind, and then in front of her chest, weaving intricate patterns in the air, the silk strips trailing from her hands as she whirls faster and faster. As she rotates at dizzying speed, the color of her outfit suddenly grows even richer, supersaturated, fading the back-ground to a dull gray.

It's a form of attraction. Magnetic. Undeniable.

This happened in London when I was trying to choose which road to take to follow Frankie Shaw, and again in Paris when I was searching for Nils. The waypoint guided me here, and now time is reassuring me that this woman is connected to my mission, the attraction so strong that she may even be my primary focus. I'm relieved that my role is becoming clear at last. The woman pauses her dance to adjust her ribbons. Tentatively,

I approach. She spots me, and her face flashes with embarrassment. "Oh, I didn't know anyone was watching."

"I'm sorry, I didn't want to disturb you. It was wonderful."

"Thank you," she says shyly. Her hair is tied up in long braids, and a streak of freckles adorns her nose. Now that I'm closer to her, I can see how young she is, no more than sixteen. "I was just practicing."

"What is that dance?" I ask.

She frowns. "You speak my language better than any foreigner I've ever heard."

"I had a good teacher," I tell her.

Her dubious expression suggests she doesn't believe me, but she lets it go. "Foreigners call the dance the Sogdian whirl. It's a custom I learned back home in Panjikent. I'm going to dance before the emperor tomorrow night, with the rest of the troupe, to celebrate the lantern festival."

"Amazing. My name is James, by the way."

"Pleased to meet you, Jemz," she says. "I am Sayana."

"You dance wonderfully, Sayana," I say. "I've never seen anything like it where I come from."

She bows her head. "If Adhvagh blesses you with a gift, it is your duty and honor to share it." She clutches a wooden talisman that hangs from her neck on a leather thong, and it draws me in, wants to tell me its story.

I tune in to its energy. Love literally pours from it. If I could touch it and hear what it has to say, I'm convinced it could be a clue as to why I'm here, so I need to gain her trust. "Your necklace, it's from someone special, isn't it?"

Her eyes narrow. "How do you know that?"

"Objects talk to me sometimes."

"Really?" she says, dubious but interested.

"Yes, and like you, I feel that if I have a gift, I should use it . . . to help others, perhaps even offer a blessing." I'm reaching here, but I'm hoping this kind of language might appeal to her. "It's beautifully carved. May I see it?"

"It's precious," she says, enclosing it in her fist.

"I will give it straight back. I would just like to see it . . . and to listen."

"Promise me you will give it back."

I smile. "I promise."

She appears briefly unsure, but then lifts the talisman over her head and passes it to me. As soon as the smooth wood touches my hands, I feel the object's desperation to tell me its story, so I close my eyes and invite it to share. I'm able to use psychometry in the present, but the intensity of my abilities increases tenfold when I'm in the past. Images flood effortlessly into my mind. I see a grand palace, the emperor of China himself seated on his throne, and Chinese courtiers, one of whom is young, energetic, and ambitious—not for his career, but for his heart. I see the young Chinese man with an older man, an uncle perhaps, who guides him, teaching him about navigation using the stars. Then I see the young Chinese man and Sayana in moonlight. He has carved this necklace for her, his promise to her that they will be together . . . They are going to elope.

I open my eyes and return the necklace. It's a nice change to be involved in a mission based on a love story. Sayana lifts the talisman over her head and pushes it beneath her jacket. "Did you see anything?"

I nod. "A young man carved it for you as a gesture of his love."

Her mouth drops open. "You do have a gift."

"I hope you will both be very happy together," I tell her.

"We will be," she says, with the certainty of youth. "His name is Li Bai. He will be there tomorrow night, watching me dance, and then . . . we are to be married." Her expression darkens. There is more to this story, as there always is. "It's complicated, though." She looks at me hopefully. "Will you give us your blessing? Like you said?"

"Of course," I tell her, thinking of Alexia. "It's clear to me that you and Li Bai are meant for each other. Whatever challenges you face, love will find a way."

"You believe that?"

"Trust me, it always does."

She peers at the stars, her cheeks flashing red. "Thank you. I must go now. It was good to meet you, stranger who speaks and loosens my tongue. May Adhvagh bless your horses."

She leaves, and I consider what I've just seen. A love story with unseen complications. All I can do is hope that time will show me the end of the story on this jump, so I can understand what needs to be altered. Then, when I get home, I can do some research and figure out how to complete this mission. I check my watch. It's blank. I guess I've observed what time wanted me to see, so I head back to the others and the warmth of the camp.

"Ah, there you are!" Takut says, clapping me on the back. "We wondered where you'd got to. We must be up before dawn tomorrow if we are to reach the city in time for the lantern festival." He wags a finger at me, like a doting father. "It's time for sleep."

Fifteen minutes later Zanak, Kristin, and I are lying in a row under thick furs, our heads resting on bundles of cloth, surrounded by Sogdians. As we gaze up at a sky streaked with nebulae and studded with brilliant dots of light, Kristin says, "Look at all the stars. You can see the Milky Way. It's so clear."

"No light pollution," Zanak points out. "And have you noticed how sweet the air tastes? Preindustrial purity. You can't get that anywhere on Earth these days."

"You get what you pay for," I say, unable to help myself. Zanak doesn't reply.

"I still can't believe I'm here," Kristin yawns, "experiencing all of this firsthand. I fell in love with the Sogdians years ago, read all I could about them, and now, here we are. It's like a dream come true, all my Christmases at once!"

"I'm pleased you're enjoying it," Zanak says.

"I wish we could stay for a year," Kristin sighs. "A couple of nights just isn't long enough. I'm trying to store it all in my brain, but I'm worried I'm not present enough, that I will forget the details when I get back home. How do you cope with it, Emil?"

"I try and live in the moment, and focus on keeping my guests safe," he says. "Anything else is a bonus."

"Wise man," she says.

"Are you warm and comfortable?" he asks her.

"Snug as a bug," she practically sings.

"Let me know if you need anything, all right?"

"I will, Emil, don't you worry."

I glance at him and wonder again if he knows about change events. Maybe he was just playing innocent earlier to avoid a discussion with me. I decide to do a little more fishing. "Hey, Emil." He stares at me from under his dark brow. "I know you're angry with me, but it's amazing to meet another traveler. How did you discover you could do this?"

"I've always wondered that too," Kristin says.

Zanak appears visibly torn between blanking me and playing the role of the charming host for Kristin. He pulls his hat lower over his forehead and leans back against a bundle of sheep fleece. "Get some sleep," he says abruptly. "We're up with the sun, and tomorrow is going to be a long day."

Kristin yawns. "You're right," she says, putting her hands in a prayer position. "Dear Lord, we thank you for this incredible opportunity, for the chance to visit the past and see how our ancestors lived. Please help us to do the right thing while we're here, and give us the grace to appreciate all we have back home. Amen." She turns over. "G'night, boys."

I envy Kristin a little. I can see the attraction of time travel when all you're doing is soaking up the experience, and it's no wonder that Extempero is such a successful organization. Still, I hope that when we see the change event, and I can explain to Kristin and Zanak what we're here to do, they'll understand how important it is. They'll see why objects store so much energy and give us these one-in-a-million chances to travel back in time, and they'll understand that these trips are not for entertainment.

We're going to be here for a while yet, and I can't believe I'm ever going to get to sleep, so I stare up at the stars and think about Alexia. Eventually, my eyelids grow heavy. The present feels so far away, but I remember that she and I are going on a date soon. Instead of counting sheep, I count years. My date with Alexia will take place in 1,278 years. She's worth the wait. Slowly, the sound of the crackling fire and the peaceful quiet of a less populated Earth lull me to sleep.

Sometime later I snap awake, my heart racing. The campfire has burned down to ash and glowing embers, and there's a full moon overhead. The courtyard is a mass of people-shaped humps, gently breathing as they sleep. Aside from the occasional snore and the odd snicker from one of the horses, it's quiet. Why am I awake? I listen, on high alert, but the camp is peaceful.

As I reach for my silver hunter, it vibrates silently against my chest. Rubbing at my tired eyes, I see that a new waypoint has appeared to the east, toward the city.

That's good, but it's not all.

"Oh no," I murmur as a shiver of cold realization washes over me.

I tap the watch, but I know it's not malfunctioning.

The final jump indicator is lit, glowing red like a warning light. This is a single-jump mission, a mono. Gabrielle warned me about these. There will be no returning here from the present, no advice from The Continuum, no more jumps. The change event will happen here and now, and I'm going to have to figure it out alone.

13

My London and Paris missions both began at the end. I was shown what to do, was given more jumps. Why did this have to be a mono?

As I peer at the waypoint on my watch, I know I have some big decisions to make.

Distance: 10.7 kilometers
Expected Arrival Time: 4 hours, 52 minutes

The average walking speed of a normal human isn't the kind of knowledge I have at hand, but I think it's about 5 kilometers an hour, so I should make it easily, even if some of the terrain is a little rough. On our way into the caravanserai, I noted the city in the distance, almost due east. The waypoint matches up to that, and along with Zanak's knowledge that this jump would lead us to the lantern festival, this means my destination is Chang'an. The only problem is that I can't wait to travel with everyone else. I need to go now.

Cautiously, I sit up and extricate myself from the bedroll

as quietly as I can, grabbing my leather boots, sheepskin gilet, and fur hat. Neither Kristin nor Zanak stirs, so I stand and pick my way past sleeping people, twitchy mules, and snoring camels, across the courtyard to the wall. Once there, I pull on my boots but pause next to a pile of belongings. I'm not proud of myself as I rummage through them. Eventually, I find what I'm searching for, a shoulder bag with some basic supplies, various bits of food, and an animal-skin water bottle shaped like a kidney. I squeeze it to check it's full and whisper apologies to the owner as I steal it away.

I walk gently toward the main gates. The moon is bright and full, casting deep shadows and rendering my surroundings in sharp slabs of grays and blues. The night watchman is perched on a stool, snoozing, but as I approach, he snaps awake and stands upright. "The sun won't be up for another three hours," he says in a clear voice. "It isn't safe to be out there alone."

"I have to reach Chang'an early," I tell him, and in a flash of inspiration add, "secret business, for the emperor."

He considers this for a few seconds, then lifts a latch and pushes open a small door cut from one of the tall wooden gates. "Farewell and good luck." The door is only about four feet high so I half step, half crawl my way through, and the watchman pulls it closed behind me.

I jog away from the caravanserai for a hundred yards or so to a small clump of trees, spookily angular in the moonlight. Leaning against one of them, I pull out my watch to get my bearings. As I thought, the waypoint is directing me almost precisely due east. Far in the distance, I see tiny dots of light on the city walls and feel the pull of time toward the metropolis. OK, so I have plenty of time to get to the city.

It isn't safe to be out there alone.

I decide the safest option is to follow the road but stick to the tree line, so I'm out of sight to any undesirables I might meet along the way. "Right," I murmur, "the longest walk starts with a single step." Who said that, was it Confucius? Or Buddha? Blimey, for all I know, it could be someone local, and they might not have said it yet.

Hugging my pack around my body, I walk toward the edge of the coppice.

A voice calls out. "James! Stop!"

It's Zanak, with Kristin not far behind him. I consider running, but then decide it's best to talk to them. In fact, it might be time to tell them the truth. I wait while the two of them catch up to me. Zanak stands defiantly in front of me, blocking my path. "Where in the hell do you think you're going?" he growls. "Why are you going walkabout in the middle of the night?"

"What's going on?" Kristin says, panting a little. "Why would you sneak out here and try to . . . Well, what *are* you trying to do?"

"It's difficult to explain," I begin.

"You better try, Mr. Blake," Zanak says.

"But why do you care?" I ask, genuinely confused. "Why don't you just let me go?"

He studies me. "You know, I can't figure you out. You clearly have your own agenda, and you're obviously an experienced time traveler, yet you don't seem to know the most basic of rules."

"And what rules are those? Yours?"

"No, you idiot. If you go messing about with time and it doesn't like it, you'll get us all kicked."

That gets my attention. "Kicked? What's that?"

"You're even more stupid than I thought," he scoffs.

Kristin cuts across me, glaring. "I've waited my whole life for this. I won't get a chance like this again, James. Don't you *dare* spoil it for me."

"I'm not trying to spoil it," I say. "I'm actually trying to do the opposite."

"I've had enough of your glib repartee, Blake," Zanak snaps. "I want some proper answers. I want to know who you really are and what you're doing here. Start talking or I swear to God, I will beat it out of you."

Under normal circumstances, despite the threats, I would probably try to maintain the façade and stick with the James Blake cover, but now that I know the mission is a mono, I'm not sure I have much to lose in telling them what's really going on. I think it through. As soon as we get back to the present and he talks to Scarlett, he'll find out who I am anyway—that's assuming they know each other.

"OK," I say. "I'm going to tell you the truth. My real name is Joseph Bridgeman. I work with an organized group of travelers who identify events in the past that need healing and send people like me back to fix them."

"Events that need healing?" Zanak asks, his voice high, almost laughing. "What are you talking about?"

Knowing this might be my only chance, I do my best to sum up what The Continuum does. "Objects like the Tang horse connect us to the past for a *reason*. We call them 'change events,' and they give travelers like you and me the chance to go back in time and put things right. You are using objects to travel back as a tourist when you could be using them to fix time."

"*Fix time?*" he says scornfully, a deep furrow between his eyebrows, his arms folded tightly across his chest. "Seriously? And who decides what to change? You, I suppose?"

"No, there is a plan to all this," I say, deliberately keeping my voice calm. "Time knows what we can and can't do."

Zanak laughs. "Come on, we're going back."

"Let him talk," Kristin says, scowling at Zanak. "Tell me more about these change events. What do you have to change?"

"It's different every time," I tell her. "Once I had to save a woman from being murdered. Another time we had to encourage someone to set up a music school."

"And this time?" she asks.

"I don't know yet, but I do know it's going to happen in the city, and soon. It's linked to the festival, I think." And with Sayana and her lover—but I'm not about to tell Zanak specific details.

"But how do you know all that?" Kristin presses me.

I resist the urge to talk about my watch. They mustn't find out about it. "I get these feelings; I'm drawn to people and places. It's a kind of attraction, a force that time travelers experience naturally."

"If all of this is so 'natural,' how come I don't feel it?" Zanak asks.

"You have to lean into time, connect with the mission, tune in to why you're here," I say, "then you'll feel it."

"New Age bullshit," Zanak says. "I made the rules clear to you when we landed: we are visitors and we do not mess with anything. We spend time with the natives, enjoy the view, and then get the hell out again. Trying to change the past is dangerous. I've seen people get kicked back to the present, and it's vicious. It messes up the trip for everyone else."

I appeal to Zanak's better nature. "You're right," I tell him. "Trying to change the wrong thing is dangerous. It happened to me once. But altering what *needs* to be changed . . . that's the only reason we're here at all."

"That's enough," Zanak barks. "This is my gig, so it's my rules. Kristin paid a hell of a lot of money for this trip. She invited you along as her guest, but you're acting like a spoiled brat."

"I'm sorry, Kristin," I say.

She shakes her head. "No need."

"I have to go," I tell Zanak. I can feel the draw of the city, and every cell in my body is screaming at me to travel eastward. "Sometimes we get a couple of chances to make a change, but I'm only going to get one chance at this one. I won't do anything that gets you . . . kicked, and I understand if you don't want to be a part of it, but I need to do my job." I turn and walk slowly but deliberately toward the pinpricks of city light in the distance.

Kristin shrieks. "Emil, what are you doing?"

I turn around.

Zanak is pointing a gun at me. He fires, and I feel a sharp stab in my left shoulder. I look down and see the fluffy tip of a stubby dart sticking out of my tunic. I tug it out easily, leaving a tiny bloodstain on the fabric.

"You shot him!" Kristin cries out.

Darkness creeps rapidly across my vision, and I feel myself floating backward into a warm bath of *who cares*.

I hear Zanak's voice, distant and in slow motion. "It's all right," he says. "It's only . . . aaa . . . tranquilizerrr . . ."

I collapse to the ground and pass out.

The velvety darkness is silent . . . timeless.

At some point I wake, vaguely aware that I'm slipping into a viewing. A wheel within a wheel within a wheel. I'm not me, I'm not in China, and I'm not in 743. I don't know who I am or where I am, not yet.

I glide high above a city, swooping and wheeling between skyscrapers like an eagle. I settle lightly on the top of a tower clad in iridescent panels, but rather than landing, I sink through the floors in a rush of concrete, glass, and carpet until I come to rest just above a dark-haired man. He's seated uncomfortably at an impressive mahogany desk, shifting in his chair, and as I connect with his aura, my last thought of my own is that I recognize him. It's Emil Zanak.

"The markets aren't responding in the way we expected," says the man seated opposite Zanak. He leans his elbows on the desk and clasps his hands, fixing Zanak with his pale-blue eyes.

"What does that mean?" Zanak replies.

"Look, we both know your divorce has had an impact on your work here. Your numbers have been down for five months in a row, and this month they're disappointing again." Zanak's jaw tightens. He knows where this is headed, but he can't deny the facts. "I've had HR draw up a severance package," the man continues, pushing an envelope across the desk.

"Come on, Mike, this is just a blip. I was top of the sales league for nearly three years until things went south with Rebecca!"

"It's true. You were. But that was then. Things have changed."

Zanak tugs at his tie, which feels way too tight. "I just need time. The fund's about to turn the corner. The investors know this. They believe in me."

The man leans back in his chair. "No, Emil, that's where you have it wrong. They believe in Harrison Worthy."

"But who *makes* them believe?" Zanak says, hot anger rising in his throat. "With all due respect, Mike, I think *you* have it wrong."

"I'm the CEO, I don't do *wrong*," the man says. He pulls a telephone toward him. "Come on, Emil, let's not make this any harder than it needs to be."

"You're firing me?"

"Letting you go."

"What about my clients?

"We've spoken to them."

"You told *them* before you told me?"

"They aren't *your* clients Emil, they're Harrison Worthy's. They're mine."

Zanak stands up and strides to the door. Just before he walks out, he turns back to the man in shame and vulnerability. "This isn't over," he says.

The man remains calm, twisting an expensive pen in his fingers. "Good luck, Emil."

Twenty minutes later Zanak is sitting in the plaza, an empty espresso cup on a café table beside him, his box of personal items on another chair. There wasn't much to collect from his office; he got rid of the photos of Rebecca months ago. His eyes aren't used to the morning sunlight, and he squints as he draws heavily on a cigarette and wallows in self-pity. Why does this keep happening? Why doesn't anyone understand what he has to offer?

"Hey," a woman's voice says.

"I'll have another espresso," Zanak says.

"I'm not the server. I want to talk to you."

Zanak peers up at the smiling blond woman in front of him. She's wearing bright-red lipstick, a navy raincoat, and black patent leather stilettos.

"Who are you?"

"My name's Scarlett. I have a proposition for you."

"Unless you're offering me a job, the answer's no."

"It's not a job offer, Emil. It's better than that."

Zanak's curiosity gets the better of him. He's already lost everything he cares about, and the woman is attractive. He catches a waft of her scent on the breeze, subtle and expensive. He moves his box of belongings to the ground and pushes the other chair toward her. "Take a seat."

Scarlett sits neatly and crosses her legs. "I know what you're capable of."

He gazes at the shiny, spotless building opposite. "Shame they don't." He's overcome with a wave of exhaustion. "Look, I'm having a pretty bad day. Do you mind?"

Scarlett's still smiling. "I know about you, Emil. You're a time traveler."

He shivers, whether from excitement or fear, he can't decide. "Are you crazy? You don't know what you're talking about."

She laughs. "I know that you traveled once. I know that a few days later you were contacted by a man calling himself William Peter Brown, and that it went nowhere. He never contacted you again. I'm here to pick up where he left off, if you like."

How in the hell can this woman possibly know this? "OK, you have my attention. I was clear with Brown, though. I wasn't prepared to work for free. I've got bills to pay, like everyone else."

"Of course, I totally understand. I'm offering you a way to use your gift and get paid properly for the unique abilities you have. You're special, Emil, one in a million."

The scene fades.

Darkness again.

Nothing for a while.

Then, a bar. Neon signs, pool tables, and a TV showing American basketball. Zanak and Scarlett, hunkered down together in a maroon leather booth, two tumblers of whiskey on the table between them.

"Are you for real?" Zanak says. He laughs. "I can't believe this."

"I'm deadly serious," Scarlett says. "You front a time-travel tourism company, I supply the objects, and we split the proceeds."

"What are you thinking in terms of the split?" Zanak asks, wanting Scarlett to lay her cards on the table first.

"Seventy–thirty. I'm the one providing the objects, after all."

"But without me, you don't have a business. Seventy–thirty in *my* favor, and you have yourself a deal."

"Come on, Emil, without the objects, you don't have a business either!" She twirls a lock of hair around a finger, then lets it fall against her cheek. "Sixty–forty."

He picks up his tumbler and takes a thoughtful sip. "We need each other. Fifty–fifty."

She looks pained for a moment, then her face clears. "What the hell," she says. "Fifty–fifty." She holds out her glass to clink, but Zanak holds back.

"One condition. We call the business *Extempero*."

Scarlett tilts her head to one side. "Extempero," she muses, trying it on for size. "I like it. But why are you so set on the name?"

He indicates the Harrison Worthy building across the street. "It's the name of the fund that idiot up there just closed down on me."

"Screw him, you don't need them anymore," Scarlett says. "You have a gift they could never comprehend. This is yours, Emil, and no one can take it away." She raises her glass. "To Extempero."

"To Extempero," Zanak says, feeling a once extinguished fire in his belly flicker back into life.

14

A nasty crawling sensation moves up my left leg and snaps me awake. It takes me a while to remember where I am and what happened. My body is stiff, like I've slept awkwardly in a cold draft. My head aches too, which I guess is the comedown from whatever Zanak shot me full of. I try to rub my forehead, but my arms are tight against my sides. Looking down, I see a rope around me. It seems he sat me against a tree, then tied my hands behind my back and my body to the trunk. My legs are straight in front of me, but my ankles are tied too. I am well and truly stuck, and there's no way I can check my watch. I listen for a while but can't hear anything. I assume the caravan is long gone.

A fierce jab of pain in my calf forces me to cry out. "What the hell?"

That's when I spot the anthill, ten feet away. A few of the little buggers have taken an interest in me. I wriggle in vain, but all I can do is try and squash the ones that are biting me using my other foot. I'm not getting out of this on my own, so I decide to ignore the risk that the woods might be full of bandits.

"Help!" I shout. "I need help here!"

Nothing.

I wriggle a bit to get more comfortable and force myself to breathe slowly, attempting to calm my nerves. Someone is bound to turn up sooner or later. Kristin and I were getting on well enough. She'll eventually force Zanak to send someone back to check on me. I replay the viewing in my mind like a film reel. Scarlett supplies Zanak with objects, and he raises a ton of cash via Extempero, taking people on tourist trips into the past. Although I know he's wasting change events and damaging the future, I have to admit that it's ingenious. And I understand why Zanak took this opportunity, given the state he was in before Scarlett turned up. I hope that if I can show him what's happening here, he might understand and change his mind. But what I still don't get is why Scarlett's doing this. Why does she hate The Continuum so much? Doesn't she care about the future?

The last thing I want to do is fall asleep, but I can't help it. I guess I'm still processing the last of the tranquilizer. I drift in and out of consciousness. I wake up sometime later, shivering and confused. Time has passed—I'm not sure how much—but I'm covered in sweat, the sun is beating down, and the floor is alive. A stream of little coppery ants trots merrily toward my legs. The message has been relayed back to base: *Fresh meat, let's go.* I wonder if it's possible to die from multiple ant bites. I suppose it is if there are enough, but I imagine it takes a long time. What a stupid way to go. I stifle a sob, then call out again.

"Help! Somebody, please!"

Movement in a nearby bush sends my heart racing. Someone or something is watching me, and I realize that my cries for help could have attracted a hungry wild animal. Idiot. I have no idea what lives out here! Ants could be the least of my worries.

Eyes peer from the shadows. "Hello?" I ask nervously. "Is someone there?"

A small boy carrying a bundle of sticks pushes his way tentatively through the leaves. He's maybe six years old, wearing sandals, shorts, and a shirt buttoned up to his neck. He's impossibly cute, with dark hair and huge black eyes.

"Ah, thank God."

He frowns at me. "Why are you sitting under that tree?"

His Chinese accent is strong, but I can understand him, which is a huge relief. My clever little implant is a lifesaver . . . I hope. I focus on what a six-year-old, eighth-century Chinese child might identify with. "My friend tied me here for a joke, but then he forgot about me and went home."

The boy smiles, as though that's an excellent thing to do to someone. Oh dear, I think, he might be one of *those* kids, the kind that takes a magnifying glass to an anthill just for fun.

"The ants are biting me," I say.

The boy looks across at the anthill, then giggles. "Ouchy."

"Yes, ouchy," I agree. "Can you untie me?"

The boy points at my chest. My tunic has fallen open with all the wriggling, and my silver hunter is visible. "You want my watch?"

"Your necklace," he replies warily.

"Yes, OK," I tell him. It's a good trade. If my watch is taken, it always finds its way back not long afterward. "Untie me and you can have it."

The boy considers this, then shakes his head. "Necklace first."

"Can I trust you?"

He offers me an evil little grin.

Knowing I have zero bargaining power, I say, "All right, necklace first. Take it."

The boy dumps the bundle of sticks on the ground, pulls a small knife from his belt, and approaches me cautiously. When he gets near enough to reach, he lifts my watch over my head with one hand and stands there admiring it.

Firmly, trying not to scare him but sounding like I mean it, I say, "OK, it's yours. Untie me now."

He considers me, and for a horrible moment, I think he's going to laugh and run away. But then, I see a glimmer of almost reluctant kindness. He crouches down and slashes through the rope binding my wrists and waist. Then, perhaps expecting me to grab the watch back, he runs off, brandishing his prize in his little fist. Relieved, I pull myself free, unwind the rope from my wrists and ankles, and shake the ants out of my clothes. I examine the fiery red lumps where I've been bitten. They're sore and already itchy, but I'll live.

Without my watch, I'm going to have to double down on my intuition. There is still a chance I can complete the change event. I have to try, at least. I follow the magnetic pull in the opposite direction from where the boy ran. I walk for a few hours, the sun slowly sinking in the sky, until eventually I leave the woods and find myself back on the plain. Far ahead, the walls of the city glow pink in the evening sun, calling me. I wrap my gilet closer, pull my hat down, and set off.

By the time I get to the outskirts of Chang'an, the sun is low in the sky and the crows are circling the treetops, ready to roost for the night. I stop walking and take in the view. The thick earthen walls are at least twenty feet high, with tall lookout towers at intervals. Huge evergreen trees grow in clumps along the outer perimeter, partially blocking the walls from view, but between them I catch glimpses of curved rooftops peeping here and there over the ramparts, some red, some gray. The place gives off an aura of massive wealth and power, and I feel both excited and awestruck.

As I get closer—I must still be ten minutes' walk away from

the city—I can now see three city gates, a grand one in the center of the wall facing me, and two smaller ones, one to either side. Unsure which to choose, I decide to go for the middle one and veer slightly to my left as I adjust my trajectory.

"Oy!" comes a voice from behind me. "Watch your step!" I turn to see that I've just cut in front of an elderly man dragging a heavily loaded mule behind him.

The man is short, fat, and very old. His eyes are dark dots wrapped in layers of pale flesh. His bald head is mottled from years of sun damage. His donkey, the one doing all the work, is scrawny and clearly exhausted.

"Sorry," I say.

"Where are you heading?" he asks, long mustache twitching as he speaks. "You want to be aiming for the right-hand gate. The middle one's just for the emperor. They'll chop your head off if you go in through there."

"Thank you very much," I say, rubbing at my neck. I fall into step beside the old man and match his pace. He considers the reddening sky, huffing and wheezing. "Gotta hurry up, won't be long before they start the drums."

"Drums?"

"They close the city gates at dusk, play the drums just before they close them. My right ear don't work no more but I can't hear 'em yet."

I strain my ears, but I can't hear drums either. "I think we still have time," I say.

By the time we get to the city gates, the old man has told me about every one of his twenty-two grandchildren, and I've long run out of platitudes. The guards at the gate don't throw us more than a cursory glance, and we walk into the city unheeded. Inside the city walls, we're sheltered from the evening breeze, and I feel warmer immediately.

"Farewell," the old man says. "I'm off to prepare. Tonight I shall wear my finest clothes and give thanks. Enjoy the lantern festival, foreigner. May your face be round."

"Er . . . thank you. Yours too," I tell him. He turns right down a narrow street and limps away, his poor mule tripping over its own feet, the packages heaped on its back slipping precariously to one side.

I turn back and walk down the main street, following the stream of people making their way toward the city's inner sanctum. It's a bit like traveling with the caravan in here, and I weave along the street between Sogdians on swaying camels, Chinese pushing carts with enormous wheels, people of indeterminate gender riding horses dressed head-to-toe in black, others carrying bamboo cages of live birds and monkeys, and groups of children playing with hoops and dogs. The sound of human chatter is deafening, like being in the middle of London on a Saturday afternoon the weekend before Christmas, except that the hooting of buses and squeal of brakes has been replaced with the creaking of wooden wheels and the whinnies and calls of beasts of burden. It's loud, smelly, and exciting.

I'm so distracted by the activity going on around me that I narrowly avoid stepping in a huge pile of horse manure. "Mine!" yells a muscly, fierce-looking Chinese woman with a very red face. I pinch my nose to block out the stench as she nips in front of me with a bucket already three-quarters full of unspeakable contents, scoops up the manure with a little shovel, then hops out of the road again, scouting the ground for her next prize. A nearby group of little kids points at me and laughs at the expression on my face.

Ahead, the road rises a little, and as I get closer, I can see it's actually a bridge over a wide, busy canal. Boats and barges pass one another loaded up with crates, boxes, and live animals, and people call from the banks of the canal, doing deals with the boatmen as they float by. White square lanterns are strung along the sides of the bridge, and their reflections break and re-form as the boats cut through the water. On the other side of the canal is a tall pagoda, standing maybe a hundred feet high, tiered like a collection of ever-decreasing fancy hats. On each level, yellow lanterns glow at equidistant intervals like huge static fireflies, il-luminating a thrumming cluster of people pushing to get inside. I can feel the energy building, drawing me in, so I cross the bridge behind a man pulling a cart full of flour sacks and turn right to find myself in a wide street that is packed with people.

This must normally be the main thoroughfare. To the left, about three blocks up, an impressive pair of carved gates guard the entrance to what I assume must be the emperor's palace. Behind the gates I can see gilded roofs and strings of bright tangerine-colored lanterns. Between me and the gates are thou-sands of people. The edges of the street are lined with tables and trolleys of food and drink decorated with white lanterns. People sit and eat beneath trees hung with shining silver flowers. Ev-eryone is dressed in their finest clothes, and the air is buzzing with excitement and anticipation.

"The dragon is coming!" The call reverberates down the street, and the crowd parts as the sound of drums draws nearer. I find an abandoned wooden box beneath a small tree, so I upend it and climb on top to get a better view. A few hundred yards away, a marching band plays as it makes its way along the street toward me. Behind the musicians, a young man dressed all in red carries a white pearlescent ball on top of a pole, spinning it this way and that as he moves rhythmically. Behind him comes the dragon, its huge head ducking and weaving in time with the music, its body writhing sinuously behind as the dancers inside move expertly in time with one another.

I'm distracted by a silent vibration against my chest and, reaching my hand up, I discover with relief that my silver hunter is back. W. P. Brown told me I couldn't lose it because of its bond with me, and I've since discovered just how useful this is. "Hello, old friend," I murmur.

I climb down from the box, and I'm about to check my watch for updates when I notice a tall man stalking along the street toward me, ahead of the dragon procession. He wears a tall black cap, a long mustard tunic, and black boots. He looks smart and professional. His bearded face is set in a scowl, and he seems oblivious to the celebration going on around him. He looks familiar, but I can't place him.

My watch vibrates again as he passes me. It's given me another waypoint just a few hundred feet away, in the direction he's walking. I hide the watch inside my tunic and follow him.

15

If I were on my own here, trying to pick my way through the crowds, it would be like trying to get to the front of the bar at a music festival. But because I'm following Colonel Mustard, it's easy. People bow and move aside, allowing him easy passage, and in his wake, I'm able to follow like an obedient page boy. I keep my head down and avoid making eye contact with anyone so that nothing holds me up, ignoring the hands proffering pies, sweetmeats, and bunches of herbs.

A couple minutes later, my quarry stops suddenly. Directly ahead of us, the crowd thins out and I see a square lit with a thousand lanterns. On our right is a two-sided screen painted white with ornate patterns in black, red, and orange around its upper edge, each side around thirty feet long and ten feet high. Seated on the floor within its shelter is a troupe of a dozen musicians playing gentle, enchanting music. They are dressed in dark orange tunics and tall black caps with sparkling silver ruffles around their necks, seated in perfect alignment with one another, legs folded neatly beneath them. The men are clean-shaven, and the women have white painted faces with tiny blood-red rosebud lips. I watch them play for a while, spellbound by the ghostly music and marveling at the precision with which each player manipulates flute, zither, drum, or harp.

To their left is an enormous Persian rug, perhaps fifty feet square. I imagine what that might be worth in the present. The pace of the music steps up, and I spot a troupe of dancers emerging from behind the screen. One of them is Sayana, the Sogdian dancer I met at the caravanserai. She places a black-and-white carpetbag on the ground at the back of the group of musicians, near the drummer, pulls out a long piece of colored silk, and follows her fellow dancers onto the carpet, where each takes a spot, nine of them in all. Colonel Mustard seems to be transfixed. His shoulders have gone rigid, so I take the opportunity to slip away and move around the crowd to a spot where I can still see him but have a better view of the dancers.

Sayana is standing right in the center of the dance troupe, wearing a short white blouse that wraps around her torso and stops just above her belly button, with baggy green trousers loose around her upper legs but wrapped tight to her calves with white lace. Her ankles and wrists are adorned with silver bracelets and anklets hung with tiny silver bells, and her shoulders and arms are draped with the long strip of colored silk—vividly striped in green, blue, and red—which falls to the earth and pools at her feet. She looks amazing.

One by one, the instruments fade away, leaving the beat of a single drum. The dancers stand motionless, waiting. I watch Sayana, swaying almost imperceptibly, her big toe tapping out the rhythm. Then the plaintive sound of the flute floats through the air, and without any obvious signal, the nine dancers take up statuesque positions, heads tilted, legs bent, their arms held up above their heads at sharp angles, fingers extended in supplication to the moon. As the harp and the zither join the flute, the dancers slowly move, some balancing on each other like acrobats, some standing alone, creating intricately choreographed patterns reminiscent of the décor on the palace gates.

The drum picks up the pace, and the dancers move around the carpet, passing one another in rapid succession and teasing the silks that fall from their shoulders around their bodies, turning them through the air, weaving ephemeral patterns across the blue velvet sky. It's bewitching, and I move a little closer to the front of the crowd. The dancers lift their heads to the stars and playfully flick their ribbons in time with the beat. They spin on the spot, lifting their arms above their heads and crossing them back and forth, behind their backs, and then in front of their chests, weaving intricate patterns in the air with the strips of silk. The girls lift their legs and angle their feet outward, spin around on one leg, then move across the carpet and spin again, until the spectacle evokes a planetary system, girls rotating but also revolving in larger circles. The music shifts again, and eight of the dancers curl themselves gently to the ground, leaving Sayana on her own in the center of the group. Slowly, she turns on the spot, one leg pointed outward, her arms holding her ribbons high above her, flicking her head like a modern ballet dancer. As the musicians pick up the tempo and volume, Sayana whips around faster and faster, until she is spinning at such dizzying speed that the colors of her outfit blur into wild streaks. I hold my breath as this human whirlwind displays perfect balance and control, her skill and the beauty of her movements unifying the crowd, drawing us in. Then, suddenly, the music stops, and Sayana stands stock still in the center of the stage, her head bowed, hands limp by her sides. I burst into rapturous applause with the rest of the crowd. "More!" I cry, clapping and whistling. "More!"

The dancers get to their feet and line up to take a bow. When they straighten, a huge smile breaks out on Sayana's face, and she waves one of her silks at someone to my left. I follow her attention, and my eyes alight on a handsome Chinese man in the front row, his arms folded on his chest, his eyes blazing with pride. He's wearing a rust-colored wrap-over coat fastened at the waist with a thick leather belt. One edge of the fabric is embroidered with a bright-orange-and-lime-green floral pattern, and the pure gold thread that outlines each element of the design sparkles in the lantern light and gives away his royal connections. His shiny dark hair is held in a topknot by a pair of short sticks, and his cheekbones are high and prominent. It's the man I saw her with when I held her necklace, her lover. He bows, very slightly, to Sayana, and she gracefully reciprocates, nodding her head and holding out her arms, silks billowing like the wings of a butterfly.

Glancing across to see what Colonel Mustard thinks of all this, I can't locate him in the crowd. Annoyed with myself for getting so carried away with the dancing, I scan methodically and spot him chatting with the drum player. The conversation appears friendly, but flicking open my watch I see the waypoint needle pointing directly at him, so I push my way through the crowd until I'm just about twenty feet away. Colonel Mustard reaches inside his voluminous tunic and pulls out the statue of a horse with an ornate saddle and its front foot raised midstamp.

It's the focus object.

Throwing a nervous glance to either side, Colonel Mustard reaches down and slips it into Sayana's carpetbag. I resist the urge to jump to my first conclusion, the obvious one: he's planted it in her bag, framing her. It could be a gift. I don't know the customs here, and he could be her father for all I know, planting a surprise for after her performance. I work through various options, but none of them rings true.

Bill told me once that my natural instincts are heightened when I travel. It brings a whole new meaning to the phrase "gut feeling." Mine is screaming at me that my first idea was the right one. He's framing her, he's going to accuse her of stealing the horse, and I am here to stop him, to put right whatever tragedy is about to unfold. The only question now is what to do. I could walk over and remove it myself, which would scupper his plans, but recalling how Gabrielle and I approached the mission in Paris, I decide to let resistance guide me. If what I'm planning is the wrong idea, time will resist me.

"Help! Somebody, help her!" a man's desperate voice screams.

I turn to see what's going on. At the edge of the square, a small group of people stands horrified as a woman sinks to her knees, clawing at her throat. It's Kristin! I glance back and see Colonel Mustard walking rapidly away from the square. Sayana is talking to members of the public along with the other dancers, showing off their silks and costumes, so I make a split-second decision to help Kristin.

Running over to the stall, I put my arms around her shoulders. "I'm here," I tell her. She stares back at me, eyes bulging. Her skin is turning a worrying shade. "What happened?" I ask the stallholder, whose terrified face is as green as the herbs he's selling. "What did she eat?"

"Nothing," he says defensively. "She was asking me how she might grow one of my plants at home. I gave her a cutting to take with her, and she started choking! What's wrong with her?"

Luckily, I know, because when I was in Paris, resistance almost choked me too. What's wrong is that she wants to take a species of plant home with her that doesn't belong in the future. It might seem inconsequential, but if time doesn't want it to happen, it bites, hard. Who knows what this plant could do, how it might affect the future? It could run rampant, like Japanese knotweed, or it might cross-pollinate with something in the present and kill us all.

"Kristin!" I shout. She grabs me, eyes desperate, clearly struggling for breath. "Listen to me, you're suffering from resistance, because you're doing something that time doesn't want you to do. You need to think about something else. Think about . . ." I gaze around and catch a glimpse of the moon high above us. "Think about the moon, how it's been the same for thousands of years, how it's exactly the same back home in the USA." Gradually, Kristin's breathing slows until she slumps down on the ground and leans her back against my legs. "Put your head between your knees," I tell her. "You're going to be fine."

"What do you think you're doing?" Zanak's loud voice, spiky and accusatory, sends shivers down my back. I look up and see him approaching, his face creased in anger, his hand reaching inside his bag.

"Don't dart me again," I shout. "I was only trying to help."

"Are you all right, Kristin?" Zanak says, kneeling and taking her hand.

"I'm fine," she says weakly. "James was helping me. I couldn't breathe, I nearly died. It was the most distressing experience. Just awful."

"It was resistance," I add. "She's OK now."

Zanak glares at her, anger roiling over his face. "I warned you about that, why didn't you listen to me?"

"Just give her a minute," I say, holding up a hand.

He swats it away. "How did you get here?"

"Oh, you mean after you left me unconscious and tied to a tree? What does it matter? I'm here, and I just saved your guest. You're welcome, by the way."

He shrugs. "She would've been fine anyway."

"Maybe." I check on Kristin. She rubs at her neck, thanks me again, and tells me she's OK. I tell her I have to go, and as

I'm walking away, Zanak shouts. "Where do you think you're going?"

"To complete my mission," I say.

He laughs. "What are you babbling on about? *Mission*? Are you still stuck on this stupid idea that you're here to change something?" His face is contorted with anger. "What an incredibly arrogant point of view!"

"I'll tell you what's arrogant," I snap back. "Wasting precious focus objects for your own selfish gain. This is all part of a natural healing mechanism, but you don't care, do you? I know you're working with Scarlett. I know you cooked up the idea of Extempero together when you lost your job in the city."

"How in God's name . . . ? Has she been talking to you?"

I ignore his question. Viewings are my secret power, and I'm not about to tell someone who knows Scarlett how I get my information. "Focus objects exist so travelers like me and you can get to change events and fix time. It's that simple. You're a time traveler, Emil. So somewhere inside you, you'll know that's true. You'll be able to feel it! That's if you haven't killed that part of your soul." The anger is building in me now. The tranquilizer is well and truly out of my body, and I'm feeling the full fury at this greedy, self-centered man. "You're going to let me go and complete this mission just like time needs me to do, and you're going to keep yourself and Kristin out of trouble until we all travel home. And then you're going to tell Scarlett that you're not doing this anymore. Because if you don't, you're no better than a common thief, and sooner or later it'll catch up with you." I turn to go.

"You can't leave," Zanak says.

"Let him go, Emil," Kristin says. She stands and brushes herself off. "If he tries to do anything time doesn't want him to do, resistance will stop him anyway, right?" She looks at me. "I don't know quite what to think now," she says, "but thank you for helping me, and good luck, James."

"That's OK," I say. "By the way, my real name is Joseph Bridgeman, and I work for an organization called The Continuum. Hey Emil, you can tell Scarlett that Joe sends his best regards."

I leave them and jog back toward where I watched Sayana dance. I lost my temper, probably told him way too much, but I want him to know why I've come here. Is it naïve to hope that he might be capable of change? If he understands and accepts resistance, then maybe he can learn that attraction is part of the equation. I don't want to give up, but as I cool off, I can't help feeling I told him way too much.

When I get back to where Sayana was dancing, the crowd has moved on. The carpet is being swept by a couple of young boys with besoms. Cursing, I pull out my watch and wait for it to orient itself. It takes a few seconds, but then another waypoint appears, pointing east, to the right of the palace gates. It's the only lead I have, so I need to follow it, and I need to stay sharp. This is a one-jump mission, and I must complete it while I'm here. The pressure is enormous, and it crosses my mind how different the situation could have been if Zanak was interested in trying to heal time instead of letting it bleed out. I push the thought from my mind and walk along a network of quiet streets, away from the festival crowds, then turn right again and follow my watch toward the south of the city. The roads are compressed mud, planted intermittently with small trees and lined on either side with four-foot ditches. I'm grateful for the thin blue light of the moon.

Chang'an is laid out in blocks, much like a modern North American city, and at each intersection, wooden gates stand propped open. My watch buzzes again and, following its directions, I turn left and pass in front of a huge tower built of red brick and stacked in rectangular layers that get smaller the higher they go, like a wedding cake.

Two blocks farther, I'm standing outside a low wooden fence that marks the boundary of a graveyard, not a soul to be seen anywhere. If I weren't so focused on the mission, I would be seriously freaked out by the quiet all around me. My watch points at the gates, but I'm reluctant to go through in the middle of the night with no one about. Inside the graveyard are mounds of earth here and there, some marked with wooden placards, most heaped with fading flowers and baskets of fruit. The scent of incense lingers in the air.

While I'm trying to decide what to do, I catch a flash of movement behind one of the grave markers, a shadowy figure creeping around in the gloom. I don't believe in ghosts, but my nervous system doesn't seem to care. My teeth chatter, and I get goosebumps all over my back. I crouch and peer through the picket fence, and as the form takes shape, I realize it's Sayana.

"Sayana!" I call out, banishing the fear and walking into the graveyard. "What are you doing here?"

Her face falls when she sees me. "Oh," she says. "It's you."

"Were you expecting someone?"

"I had a message from Li Bai, to meet him here," she says.

"He's the one who gave you your necklace?"

"Yes." She brightens. "We are running away together tonight."

I attempt a smile, but this doesn't feel right. Not far from where Sayana stands is a freshly dug grave, gaping in the moonlight, and I have an unwelcome flashback to the night in the London churchyard when, in another timeline, Frankie Shaw took my life.

I remember the *mingqi* horse, presumably still in Sayana's bag. Urgently, I say, "I saw a man put something into your bag."

"What man?" She clutches her bag suspiciously.

"He was quite old, wearing a dark-yellow coat."

The color drains from her face. "Li Bai's uncle. He does not wish us to marry. He thinks I am not good enough for his nephew."

I nod, joining the dots from the visions I saw when Sayana gave me her necklace to hold. I knew the man looked familiar, but only now do I realize he was the one teaching his nephew about using the stars to navigate. "It's a horse statue, from one of the graves," I tell her. "I could be wrong, but I think he's going to accuse you of stealing. Get rid of it, quickly. I'm worried—"

We're interrupted by the sound of voices and the flicker of approaching torches. A loud, caustic voice scratches out impatient orders. "This way!"

Sayana grips my arm, her eyes wide. "It's him, Li Bai's uncle."

"I'll distract them," I tell her. "You need to go! Get rid of the horse."

"There's a gate over there, behind the cherry trees," Sayana tells me. "I'll go that way. And please, give Li Bai a message for me. Will you tell him I was here? And let him know I'll be waiting with two horses at the Wild Goose Pagoda at dawn."

She picks up her bag and runs into the darkness, only to be dragged back toward me by two burly guards, followed closely by Colonel Mustard himself, Li Bai's uncle. "Where are you running off to?" he bellows.

"Let me go!" she shouts. "You can't do this to me! I've done nothing wrong!"

By torchlight, I see that her accuser has brought a small group of people with him, a few locals from the city and five armed guards. The old man eyes me, a mean smile crossing his lips in a flash. He puffs out his chest. "In order to avoid any accusations of wrongdoing on my part, I have asked these good citizens of Chang'an to accompany me here, to bear witness to the events that are about to unfold." He points at Sayana. "Search her bag."

One of the guards tips the contents onto the earth. Out comes a tumble of clothes and silks, and the horse statue, followed by an audible gasp from the gathered crowd.

"What is this?" Colonel Mustard says dramatically, picking up the statue and turning it over in his hands. It sickens me to watch, but this was an age when drama and performance played the biggest role in the system of law, justice, and recrimination.

Her accuser presents the horse to the crowd. "Just as I thought—stolen from the grave of the emperor's grandmother!"

"That's not true!" Sayana cries, infuriated by the baseless accusation. She looks at me beseechingly. "You put it in there! Jemz tell them what you saw!"

I consider telling the truth, but what good would it do? He's hardly going to admit to it. I'm a foreigner on his turf, surrounded by his henchmen. "I stole it," I say.

"What?" Sayana says.

"I beg your pardon?" says Colonel Mustard.

"I stole it from the grave and then I put it in the dancing girl's bag. It was me. Let her go."

The guards holding Sayana look questioningly at Colonel Mustard, but keep hold of her arms.

He stares at me for a long moment. "I shall deal with you shortly. Guards, seize him." Two of the henchmen take hold of me, and one kicks the back of my knees, pushing me to the ground.

Colonel Mustard turns back to Sayana. "Your ridiculous, childish dream of a life with my nephew is over. He never loved you. How could he feel anything but contempt for a cheap, foreign dancing girl?"

"You're wrong," she sneers, baring her teeth. "Li Bai and I

are in love, and we always will be. Nothing can change that, not walls, not distance . . ." She raises her chin and glares defiantly at the uncle of the man she loves. "Not even death."

"Oh, you poor ignorant girl. I'm not going to kill you." He laughs heartily. "You will live a long and full life of servitude a thousand miles from here." Tears well in her eyes. He smiles. "From this day forth, you are banished from this empire. Li Bai will never know your fate."

Sayana writhes and sobs as she's dragged away. "Please tell Li Bai what happened. Tell him that I love him!"

"I will," I call back, determined to put this right. If Li Bai knows what his uncle did, I'm sure he'll do everything he can to be with Sayana, and I can still complete the mission. As I watch her disappear, though, the color seems to fade from the scene, and all the power and certainty melts away with it. Li Bai's uncle smirks, and I instinctively know that I've failed the mission. I bow my head in despair, my heart breaking for Sayana and Li Bai and the love they will never get to live.

16

I'm in a dark cramped cell, the cold air heavy with moisture and the odor of old stone, damp soil, and decay. A single shaft of moonlight spills through a barred window, enough to pick out a figure sitting on the floor in the far corner. His breathing has the unpleasant rattle of someone who's been in here too long. He watches me, eyes gleaming in the faint bluish light.

What is it with me and incarceration? First London and now this. Is it normal for a time traveler to get banged up constantly? The sound of distant music, celebration, and happiness drifts in on the wind. It makes me think of the mission, how those kids were guilty only of being in love. Call me old-fashioned, but love is love, and it's supposed to conquer all, right?

Man, I was so close. What am I going to do now?

Time passes. I remain standing, but the cold sinks into my bones, along with the realization that I'm on the clock. Li Bai's uncle told the guards that I should be detained without food or water, said I wouldn't be needing it. With gleeful enthusiasm, he told me, "Your trial begins at sunrise. It will be swift. The sentence for grave robbing is death by strangulation."

I shudder, rubbing at my neck.

A tingling sensation snaps me out of my thoughts. My silver hunter gently vibrates against my chest. Turning away from the shadowy figure, I pop it open and check the display. The screen is blank, just the otherworldly glow of its blue background, etched with a faint honeycomb pattern. The many hexagons flicker excitedly as two words appear on the screen: *Mission Failed*.

My heart sinks a little lower. My failure was obvious, but it still hurts to see it confirmed here. As quickly as the words appeared, they are gone again. The screen cycles through a busy animation and then: *Calibrating*. Interesting. This happened in Paris, after Gabrielle and I thought we had failed our mission. It was as though time reshuffled the deck, attempting to offer us a second chance. Why now, though? It's not like I can do much from here, even if time has figured out some clever opportunity for me to intervene.

Eventually, *Waypoint* appears. Above that, the top half of the watch becomes a simple needle, a compass guiding me toward a change event. I let out a frustrated moan. "What use is a waypoint, if I'm stuck in here?"

The screen flashes. Jagged lines and strange symbols appear. Broken words dance over the screen, like interference or corrupted data. The watch glitches and then goes dark. If it was interference, then whatever caused it seems to have gone. It leaves me with a glimmer of hope, though. A waypoint alert suggests that if I can escape, there might be a way to get these two star-crossed lovers together.

I'm distracted by movement to my left. The scratching of feet on the stone floor.

A stocky, dark-skinned man steps into the silvery moonlight, too close to me. He's clothed in multiple layers of stained linen, a thick piece wrapped around his waist like a belt. His arms are exposed, revealing sinewy muscles. His thick beard is unkempt, and his dark eyes shine with suspicion. He begins to talk, growling and hacking at his words, an unfamiliar language that sounds vaguely Arabic.

"I'm sorry," I tell him, "I don't understand."

He tries again, shouting this time. He shoves my shoulder, pushing me back. I feel a sudden sharp pain shooting into the center of my brain like a spear. For a second, I'm convinced he just stabbed me in the head, that my death sentence came earlier than expected, but then the pain subsides, evaporating quickly.

The man is up in my face, his breath sour. "They put you in here with me deliberately. You're a Persian spy, aren't you?"

Persian spy?

"No," I tell him, "I'm a . . . er, I'm a Westerner."

The shift in his expression is so fast, it's comical: focused aggression to shocked bewilderment in a flash. If I weren't so sure he was about to kill me, I would laugh out loud.

He regards me with deep suspicion. "How do you know my language? How do you speak it so well?"

Suddenly, the pain in the center of my head makes sense. In retrospect, it wasn't exactly painful, more of an unpleasant kind of swelling that made me panic and interpret the shock as pain. I think it was my language chip filling my brain with an entirely new language. Initially, I couldn't understand a word, but I seem to remember Gabrielle telling me that it adapts on the fly.

The man grabs me and pulls me close. "You had better start talking, before I cut out your tongue!"

"I'm a traveler. I'm just visiting. I don't know anything about you or this place." I'm babbling, but I figure I just need to keep him talking. I continue making excuses, but then both of us are distracted.

The cell door has a barred window at head height, a couple of feet square. Through it, oily shafts of pale kaleidoscopic light punch through the gloom like an old cinema projector. The air fizzes with excited energy.

"What is this sorcery?" my cellmate asks, his voice trembling with fear.

I'm wondering that too. He backs away, terrified. I'm more confused than anything. Unusual weirdness is becoming my new norm. The light show has faded by the time I press my face to the hatch and peer out. Big blue eyes stare at me. I yelp, stumbling back, heart racing.

A cautious voice asks, "Joseph, is that you?"

It's a voice I recognize, the clipped British authority of a newsreader, utterly incongruous in these surroundings. I rush back to the door and gaze out on the welcome sight of W. P. Brown. He smiles, blue eyes sparkling. "Seems you've got yourself into a bit of a pickle."

"Bill," I manage to say, my throat tightening.

W. P. Brown is one of the founding members of The Continuum. There's a lot I don't know about him, but I understand his role was to recruit new travelers to their cause. Case in point: he was recruiting me when my orientation was derailed, and he ended up blackmailing me and then, rather confusingly, saving me. He's about the same age as he was the last time I saw him, in a church in London in 1963. And that's when the logical stuff kind of runs out because the man standing before me is dead. He threw himself in front of a shotgun blast, sacrificed his own life to save mine.

And yet here he is, very much alive.

Seeing him again causes the fabric of my understanding to weaken at the seams. When it comes to time travel, death appears to be extremely relative.

"Are you OK, my boy?" he asks.

A thousand questions and emotions rush around, an explosive relay between my mind and my heart. I try to assemble words. "You're . . . you're alive!"

His expression transitions through various emotions. Shock. Understanding. Determination. He composes himself quickly. "Now listen, Joseph. The top priority is to get you out of there, but you must, I repeat *must*, refrain from telling me details that may impact our shared history. Do you understand?"

"Yes," I tell him, and I do, but it's not the end of the conversation, not by a long stretch. I'm simply parking what I know will be an in-depth discussion because we have more pressing concerns.

"Good. Let's break you out, shall we?"

He assesses the situation with his usual air of optimism. He moves out of view for a second, and I hear the clattering of metal. When he returns, he's holding a long spear. He wrestles it into what I presume is the lock and begins prying away at the wood. Bill is strong for someone in his midsixties. The wood cracks and splinters, and something eventually gives way. He jams the spear into the side of the door and pushes it, leaning forward and grunting until the door cracks and yawns open.

I step out, blinking against the warm glow of nearby torchlight. I'm followed by the other man in the cell. I'd forgotten all about him with Bill's unexpected arrival. I was right: he does look strong, but also emaciated and scared, his eyes wide like a wounded animal's. He creeps away cautiously, gaze flicking between me and Bill.

"Not so fast," Bill says.

The man sneers, exposing the remnants of his teeth. "Are you going to try and stop me?"

"Not at all," Bill says. "I just released you, my good man, but

I must ask, do you believe in serendipity?" Now the man isn't sure whether to be worried or confused, or both. He doesn't speak. "I don't know why you were in there," Bill continues, "but you have been given a second chance, and in my experience, they don't come around that often. Don't squander this opportunity."

The man frowns, clearly trying to decide what he makes of Bill. I can sympathize. Bill is hard to figure out. To me, he sounds old-fashioned—in fact, everything about him belongs in the past—and yet his native timeline is thousands of years in the future. God only knows what this Tang dynasty local makes of him. The faintest hint of a smirk passes over the prisoner's lips. People often see caring as a form of weakness, and I half expect him to rush at us, but he doesn't. Instead, his expression shifts subtly, a swimming emotion lurking way back in his dark glassy eyes. Is it respect? Understanding? Perhaps both. It appears he knows this moment has weight. The connection passes in a flash, and he's gone, disappeared into shadow.

When I turn back to Bill, standing in the reflected glow of crackling torchlight, I get my first proper look at him. Now I understand my fellow inmate's smirk. Bill is dressed in checked tweed trousers tucked into half-length Wellington boots, a matching padded jacket with shirt and tie, and a deerstalker hat. No one in his right mind would choose to travel to eighth-century China in this outfit. He sees me assessing him and chuckles. "Caught me a little unawares. One minute I'm fishing—I felt the twitch of the rod, convinced I had a bite—and the next I'm here!" He breaks into a mischievous grin. "It's good to see you, my boy. Very good indeed." He glances around, soaking in our surroundings, a narrow tunnel somewhere in the bowels of the city. "Now, to business," he says. "When are we? Where are we? And what are we doing here?"

"Tang dynasty, 743."

He claps his hands together. "Wonderful, just wonderful." He narrows his gaze, focusing on me intently. "And the mission?"

"It's a mono." I tell him.

His eyebrows shoot up. "You know about those?" And then he adds, "Actually, don't answer that, just tell me what we have to do."

I bring him up to speed on the basics, but for brevity I leave Extempero out of it. I tell him about Sayana, and how she was banished.

Bill nods and says, "So her boyfriend is some kind of dignitary or prince?"

"Yes, and I believe the mission was to get them together."

"A union, how marvelous." He pulls a pocket watch from inside his jacket and taps it against mine, synchronizing them. Gabrielle did the same when she dragged me to Paris. Bill holds up his watch. *Calibrating* changes to *Waypoint*. He smiles, blue eyes sparkling. "Shall we?"

We work our way through a cavernous network of tunnels, occasionally creeping and hiding, but thankfully not meeting any guards. Part of me suspects that most of them will be involved in tonight's celebrations. Along the way, Bill ditches his jacket, hat, and tie. A Westerner wearing a shirt and trousers will still stand out, but he won't be the beacon of oddity that he was. We emerge into a quiet, dark courtyard and follow the waypoint, which aligns with the vibrant sounds of people and celebration. It's full dark now, but the sky is illuminated by a bright, full moon: a perfect silver coin dominating the sky above the city. We pass a few people, dark silhouettes holding lanterns, all heading in the same direction. The humming buzz of conversation is accompanied by beautiful music. We join a flowing sea of people, a street alive with the glow of a thousand lanterns. Tall posts with huge paper lanterns line the street, each emblazoned with a red symbol. There must be tens of thousands of people here. In the far distance, a gleaming palace of golden light, comprised of flamboyant red pagodas stacked five levels high, towers over the crowd. I check my watch. It updates, and *Waypoint* is replaced by two words that I've come to love: *Change Event.*

Bill once described this process as akin to barometric pressure. Our interactions create a kind of force, which the watch can then interpret.

Below the alert is more information.

Distance: 0.7 kilometers
Time to Change Event: 17 Minutes

We join the crowd, but our progress is too slow. I tap Bill's shoulder. "This is taking too long. We need to find a quicker way through."

"Agreed." He points to a dark, deserted side street.

Not wishing to draw unnecessary attention, we resist the urge to run and instead walk quickly. It feels counterintuitive to be working against the change event, but as we snake our way along the blocks of the city, keeping the temple in sight, I feel like we're making progress. That feeling doesn't last, though. Turns out Chang'an is a maze, with various dead ends. It's arranged into blocks, each one walled and separated by checkpoints where numerous guards keep watch. I have no idea how they might communicate, whether they know that I've escaped and are therefore searching for me. But there's no way we can risk trying to pass through one of these checkpoints. It could easily end up being a ticket straight back to the dungeon. Instead, we pass through quiet neighborhoods, gardens, and small temples, burning precious minutes, constantly hitting roadblocks until we eventually find ourselves facing the perimeter wall. The wall must be fifteen feet high, blotting out the night sky and casting a deep shadow over the road behind us.

"Five minutes left, Bill," I say, panting with frustration. "We're not going to make it."

He nods. "The fact that time has given you a change event means it wants you to succeed. We need to tune in, allow it to reveal a route."

"Psychometry," I murmur, as Bill places his hand against one of the huge blocks of stone and closes his eyes. I do the same, the stone cool against my touch, the darkness absolute.

Gabrielle showed me that it's possible to tune in to buildings too. I used psychometry in the opera house to find a secret passageway that ultimately helped Nils and I escape. Since getting back from Paris, I've tried this at home, a few times now. Most of my attempts have failed. Once, I received a flicker of information, but nothing like the depth and clarity I experienced in the opera house. Gabrielle told me that all the laws of time travel are accentuated during a jump. Attraction, resistance, psychometry—all of them heightened.

And so it is now.

The past floods into my mind, the evolution of a city, once much smaller and split into suburbs. Chang'an was planned and created. A grid system of districts, split by avenues like New York, takes shape in my mind's eye. I see the plans, how each stone was placed according to a detailed blueprint. Roads fan out over a parchment, snaking and revealing their secrets like invisible ink, a treasure map of the past. I don't see myself, but I feel my place within this construct, can visualize where I am and where I want to be. The palace. A staircase. Ramparts. A walkway that circumnavigates the city.

My eyes snap open. Bill is staring back at me with a knowing grin.

"The city walls," I say, excitedly.

"You've come on a long way, Joseph. I'm proud of you." He gestures toward a dimly lit alleyway, and after working our way through it, we emerge into a courtyard and see the steps I envisioned. They rise from a central point, up and out in a V shape to the full height of the city walls.

We race up the steps. My vertigo threatens to buckle my knees, so I put my head down and push on. There are no handrails, no warning signs or HR department to worry about us tumbling over the edge. Breathing heavily, hearts pounding, we reach the summit and stumble out onto a walkway the width of a single-track road with parapet walls on either side. Orange lanterns sway in a gentle breeze.

For a few seconds, time holds its breath. I'm taken aback by the unbroken view. The moon is shockingly white, its timeless power illuminating clouds that seem to stretch forever in an unpolluted sky. A canopy of trees stretches for miles, eventually kissing distant mountains that have the appearance of layered parchment paper, matte silver and charcoal gray.

Back down behind us, the full scale of the city becomes apparent, an immense slab of sharp angles carved into the landscape. Glowing rivers of people pulse like shimmering blood through the dark, symmetrical body of the city. Thousands of them, lanterns at the ready. The intoxicating sounds of an ancient civilization swell on the wind. Thundering drums pound the air, increasing in speed until they match my thudding heartbeat. Rhythmical chants follow, a countdown to the release of the lanterns. My skin ripples with a growing appreciation of what I'm witnessing, but my mind takes over, focusing on the job at hand.

We head to the far corner of the city. With the palace near, I start planning how to handle Sayana's story, but as we pass a huge pagoda, its dark shape cutting an imposing silhouette against the brilliant moonlight, Bill and I come to a halting stop. Ahead of us, a group of men in suits of armor, holding spears and swords and bows, appear from a building. Their gold armor gleams, their purposeful movements almost robotic.

"What do we do?" I ask Bill.

"Keep walking, act like we belong here."

It's good advice, and under normal circumstances, it might have worked, but when another man appears wearing a mustard-yellow tunic, I know that our luck has run out. More soldiers appear behind us, blocking any hope of escape. The light from their torches sends our silhouettes dancing nervously over the cobbles.

Bill edges to his left, stands on his tiptoes, and leans over the edge of the wall.

"You!" Colonel mustard shouts. "Stay exactly where you are."

Like a ventriloquist, I hiss at Bill. "Why are you looking over the wall? It's bloody miles; we can't jump!"

He glances back at me with a desperate look in his eyes. "I'm terribly sorry, Joseph, but it seems I'm leaving."

"What!"

He winces, a hand touching his temple.

"No," I cry, my voice cracking with nervous energy. "You can't!"

The guards move in formation behind him, but all I can think about is the icy pain that Bill's feeling in his head, the brain freeze that indicates his imminent return. I don't feel a thing because I'm not going anywhere, not yet anyway. I'm attached to this mission and will only return to the present when time decides.

Colonel Mustard strokes his white beard. "I had planned to show leniency, decided that you would receive two hundred blows, a warning to anyone who interferes in my business, but now this." He turns to Bill, cocking an eyebrow. "You, whoever *you* are, have helped this wanted criminal to escape." He draws in a long, steadying breath. "By the power vested in me as local magistrate of this great city, you leave me no choice."

In a strong voice, Bill announces that we would simply like to go on our way. Then to me, he says, "I have less than a minute. You're coming with me."

"With you?"

My watch buzzes, but I don't want to see the alert. Not just because I'm worried that the slightest movement might set these guys off, but because I think I know what it's going to show. Even with a second chance, I think I've just failed this mission.

"We don't have a choice," Bill says, glancing briefly at the tall pagoda. "I'm not leaving you here!"

The soldiers reach for arrows from the quivers on their backs. With bows down, they position the arrows and stretch their loaded weapons until they creak loudly. They pause, their keen expressions suggesting they are up for a little target practice. This was a time when people were blindly obedient to their emperor, didn't ask questions or doubt authority. As far as I know, it was *shoot your arrows and ask no questions later*, not even quietly to yourself. These men are strong and efficient. They wouldn't think twice about decorating me and Bill like porcupines. I hear movement behind me, the same taut groans of power waiting to be unleashed.

There's a weight to the air.

It all happens at once.

The soldiers step back and raise their bows.

The city explodes in a brilliant cacophony. Drums, cymbals, screams, and cheers. The residents of Chang'an release their lanterns, and yellow and red squares of light float into the sky like a million pixels of fire. I catch myself thinking that if this was the last sight I ever saw, it could be a lot worse. It's also the perfect distraction. Bill grabs my arm and pulls me up the nearby steps.

We only just make it inside the pagoda as numerous arrows sink loudly into the wood around the entrance. A couple embed deep into the floor just a few feet behind us. In the movies, arrows appear light, as though the tip wouldn't penetrate that far. These are long, thick spears that hit the wood at incredible speed, as though shot from a cannon.

Now it's my turn to pull Bill along. We clear two steps at a time, passing golden statues bathed in warm candlelight. He's struggling; a man of his age isn't designed to run like this. He stumbles, and I grab him and pull him up, willing him onward. The third floor is a sparse room surrounded by windows on all sides, a watchtower designed for defense, not for jumping out of. Bill immediately heads to one of the windows and eases himself onto the ledge. Below us, I hear the cries of soldiers, organizing themselves, running up the stairs. Too close.

Bill turns back. "Come along, what are you waiting for?"

Oh, I don't know . . . the cavalry? Reason? Sanity? I stare at the old man in disbelief as he squeezes himself onto the roof. No time. I follow Bill into the cool air, the view even more spectacular from this perilous outlook. We creep out onto the curved tiles. I lean over the edge, estimating the drop. I would guess the wall of the city is twenty feet high, but the drop here is more like fifty or even sixty feet. Below us is a slope of jagged rocks and trees that look like sharpened teeth. Even if it is sixty feet, it will still only take seconds for us to hit the ground.

An arrow whips through the air and sinks a full inch into the window frame behind us. Way, way too close. I turn to Bill, his skin translucent, shimmering like a ghost in a shaft of moonlight. My brain clenches when I try and figure out what would happen if we both died here. Where do the paradoxes end?

Seeing my hesitation, he holds out his hand. "We need to jump, now!"

"Wait, if we jump, and travel while we're falling, surely we'll take the momentum with us." I have visions of us shaped like cartoon accordions.

"We're going to travel into water, very deep water," he says. "Trust me, my boy, our landing will be fine."

Willing away my vertigo, I inch toward him and take his hand. It feels horribly cold, suddenly frail. He leans back, pulls me along, and we run and leap awkwardly into the empty darkness.

For a long second, we are weightless.

Time condenses.

I've heard that a near-death experience can feel like this, the seconds more like minutes. A natural form of time dilation. The scenery intensifies, lines sharpen, colors appear almost edible.

The sky is a blanket of stars. Villages vibrate with excited light. Smoke trails sneak up into the night in smudges of silver-blue, thick like icing. The air rushes past, loaded with promise. The sound of arrows whipping overhead is so loud, I'm convinced I could pluck their trails like guitar strings.

It's quite beautiful. The only problem with falling, though, is that you eventually hit the ground—or hit something, at least. I'm reminded of Vinny revving his motorcycle and assuring me that he was "good at soft landings."

He wasn't. It hurt. A lot.

Bill said we're going to land in water, but that requires some very specific timing. We need to leave the past and travel now, and I mean *right now*. With the whistle of air rushing in my ears, I pinch my eyes closed and brace myself for what I hope will be a wonderful and reassuringly wet collision between the past and the future, rather than some horrible, bone-crunching end to my final, failed mission.

PART 4

17

We land in water, just as Bill said we would. We don't break the surface, just arrive surrounded by it, freezing, shocking, and all-consuming. It knocks the wind out of me. We continue our acceleration downward, the pressure building in my ears. This isn't the first time I've time traveled into water—in fact, I think it might be the third—so I don't go into full panic mode, but I still have to push away the flashbacks of my sister kicking and screaming in the lake that took her life. As I push my way to the surface, I consider how this might have gone: death by multiple arrows or smashed to pieces on a slope of jagged rocks. In comparison, this cold, wet landing is almost pleasant.

Breaking the surface, I quickly take in my surroundings. Above me, thick clouds are broken by pastel-blue explosions of morning light. Mountains all around. I'm treading water in a massive lake. I'm not far from the shore, where I can see a huge stately home bathed in warm yellow light. I recognize it immediately: Greystone House. This isn't a lake, it's a loch. We're in Scotland and, I presume, the future.

Bill pops up next to me, sucking breath and laughing.

Unexpectedly, I find myself grinning back at him, and then I'm laughing too. Near-death experiences will do that to you.

"Joseph!" he cries between gasps. "That was one hell of a jump!"

"From the roof or in general?"

He laughs again. "If my calculations are correct, we just traveled nearly fourteen hundred years!"

No wonder I'm feeling so discombobulated. Losing your sense of *now* is one of the hardest things about time travel. It turns out the present isn't constant. It's within you and outside of you. Lining them up is the real trick. We swim toward the shore, and I try embedding myself in this new present. The moon helps, timeless, constant. Unlike in China, it's giving way to the sun but also waning, the faintest magical hint of a sphere behind a fading white crescent. I remember marveling with Kristin at the fact that we were seeing the same moon. My mind does a little wobble as I think about the thousands of years that now separate us.

We heave ourselves out of the water and crunch loudly over tiny pebbles. Bill appears to be around the same age he was when I last saw him. He told me then that we had many adventures *ahead* of us, and he asked me to remember them for him.

That was just before he died.

Seeing him again is a shock, but deep down, not a huge surprise. I've thought a lot about what he said in London, so I've been expecting his return at some point in my life. However, it doesn't change the fact that it's like seeing a ghost. He looks back out over the loch. "I'm not entirely sure what happened to *Ladybird*."

"*Ladybird*?"

"My little boat," he says. "I was sitting in her, doing a spot of night fishing when I traveled. I even brought the bloody lamp and fishing rod with me!"

He lets out an easy chuckle that builds into an infectious belly laugh, and we're off again, both of us laughing. But then my body convulses in a sharp, involuntary shudder. The air is freezing, and we're soaking wet.

"Come on," Bill says. "It's only a few minutes to my house from here. Let's get dry."

"That sounds good," I tell him, my teeth beginning to chatter, "but how long do you think I am going to stay here?"

Bill ponders this and suggests I check my watch.

My silver hunter informs me that the local time is 5:15 a.m. October 21, 2131.

Below that, the word *Displacement*.

Interesting, I've not seen that before. It's joined by the ever-familiar *Calibrating*. I show it to Bill. He nods. "You jumped to China, then I dragged you here. With all this bouncing around, your poor watch has lost track of where you're supposed to be, but don't worry, it will update at some point. Time will put you back where you belong."

It isn't just the watch losing track of where I'm supposed to be. I feel stretched, like an elastic band around a swelling pack of time-travel playing cards. Where do I belong?

Bill guides us up a narrow path, trees on either side, tall enough to form a canopy. He illuminates the way using a lapel-pin light like the one I used in Paris. It creates an incredibly strong beam that doesn't dazzle, just outlines the scenery clearly. Very clever. It's slow going, though. Our clothes are sodden and heavy. Through a gap in the trees, I see Greystone House, serene and even more impressive than I remember. I've visited the future before, but only using an advanced, hyperrealistic form of VR. I remember Iris explaining that they were holding back some of the details, taking it easy on me. This time Bill dragged me, meaning it's the first time I've traveled to

The Continuum headquarters in the flesh. The training wheels are off.

Above us a speeding silver lozenge cuts an impressive line across the blue sky. Light glints from its surface. Dark orange blasts from its rear, leaving an acid-blue trail of light behind it. It's moving impossibly fast.

"What . . . is that?" My voice trembles with the cold.

Bill looks up. "Ah, yes, of course, no virtual suppression this time."

The craft disappears over the horizon. It only takes a few seconds.

Flying cars. Just wait until I tell Vinny.

We continue walking, trying to beat the cold. The path widens and comes to a fork. Greystone House is off to our right, close now. I ask Bill if it's OK for me just to turn up like this, unannounced. He glances back over his shoulder and winks. "Unexpected arrivals are my specialty, but you don't need to worry. It's usually quiet around here during weekends. My house isn't far now."

The thought of people in the future having time off at the weekend seems funny. Normal. Mundane. I mean, why wouldn't they? It makes this feel even more real, somehow.

My watch vibrates. *Origin Confirmed*. I ask Bill what it means.

"It's just figured out where you came from," he tells me.

Casting my mind back makes my brain ache. My origin was Emil Zanak's yacht, a couple days ago. That feels like another world. All these timelines, interchangeable yet all playing simultaneously. I imagine the yacht, its anchor at the bottom of the ocean. I'm forgetting what that kind of certainty feels like.

"Time remaining, forty-seven minutes," I tell Bill.

He turns back to me, grinning. "Ideal. I'll put the kettle on."

It's reassuring to know they have kettles in the future, that some things never change.

We round a tall hedge and arrive in front of a modest stone house surrounded by a well-maintained garden. It reminds me of a cottage my family stayed in once, somewhere on the coast, before Amy went missing, back when we were happy, normal. Behind the house, at the edge of a forest, trees whisper in the breeze, shafts of moonlight flickering between a dense canopy of leaves.

A dog crashes through a hedge and tumbles around our feet, panting and wagging its tail. "Basil!" Bill cries, with warm affection. The brown-and-white springer moves between the two of us, craving affection. Bill strokes and pats his companion. "He's used to me disappearing on him, aren't you, boy? He waits patiently for me to come back. It's nice to have a warm welcome."

Shivering, I agree, and we head inside.

Lights glow into life as we enter. Bill's home feels welcoming and comfortable, if a little old-fashioned for a house in the future: a faded carpet on a flagstone floor, simple glass wall lights the length of the hallway. Bill shows me to a guest room, hands me a towel, and says he will find me some clothes. It's a relief to be out of my wet Sogdian clothing and wrapped up in a huge fluffy towel. Bill pops his head around the door and hands me a gray sweatshirt, jogging bottoms, socks, and a pair of plain white running shoes. He leaves, and I get dressed. The fabric feels unusually smooth against my skin. It could be my imagination, but I swear as I put the clothes on that they adjust slightly to form a snug fit.

Seems the future has autoadjusting loungewear.

It's doubtful these clothes belong to Bill. They just aren't his style. To have them at the ready like this, though, suggests that Bill was expecting me, or maybe he often has random visitors in sudden need of clothing.

I study the room, hoping to pick up some details of the future, but Bill's house is more like going *back* in time. Perhaps, if something isn't broken, the future doesn't feel the need to fix it. Apart from the fact that we stare at screens most of the day, how much have our lives and our needs really changed over the years?

Bill calls me into his study, a spacious, very untidy room. A window seat is crammed with rambling plants in shabby pots. Various papers are taped to the walls and books lie in piles all over the floor. Shelves are packed full of maps and files, shells and pebbles, cups and saucers. In the corner of the room sits a glass cabinet with a strange collection of items—an old pair of leather boots, a glass jug, a feather, some coins, a rolling pin—and I wonder if they're used-up focus objects. The desk is covered with an assortment of retro notepads, some futuristic-looking technology made of glass and chrome that I would love to get my hands on, as well as a set of meerschaum pipes on stands.

Bill's study smells of open fires and something rich, sweet, and earthy: cherry tobacco, an evocative scent that reminds me of the first day I met him. Smell is one sensory input that VR doesn't get right. It's critical to immersion, to life. Smell transports us, a potent form of mental time travel in and of itself.

Two leather chairs are positioned in front of a wide, redbrick fireplace with the ashes of an old fire still in the grate. Logs are piled up on either side of the chimney in a neat stack.

Bill throws a few logs on top of the ash and says, "Roaring fire."

The fireplace glows, and within seconds, the wonderful heat draws me close.

Voice-activated fire. Noted.

Bill hands me a steaming cup of strong, sweet tea. "My finest china," he says with a grin.

We sit quietly for a few minutes, sipping tea and warming up. Basil joins us by the fire, shaking and spraying a fine mist, then flops down on a nearby rug with a long sigh.

My teeth stop chattering. Now warm and dry, my mind kicks into overdrive, and all the questions and feelings that I parked when Bill arrived outside the dungeon in Chang'an come rushing forth.

"You're thinking about the mission," Bill says. "We must be careful. Probably best we don't talk about it now." He frowns, sipping his tea. "Just know this. Monos are the hardest missions, my boy. They often fail, and you mustn't be too hard on yourself. I doubt there's anything you could have done."

"I feel terrible about what happened," I say, "but that's not what I was thinking about. I know we're in Scotland, that this is the future, but when is this for you and me, in terms of our chronology?"

He purses his lips, blinking a few times. "It's somewhat complicated, but I will do my best." He focuses on the fire, prodding it with a poker. The logs release glowing embers. "Let's see, a few days ago you and I had a conversation in Cheltenham at a bandstand."

"Wait . . . what?" I say, my mind racing.

"It was raining, and we sheltered beneath the bandstand. It was a difficult conversation, for both of us. You remember?"

"Bill, for me that was months ago."

His demeanor shifts, his expression darkening and his voice somber. "Then we must be extremely careful. Our chronology must be protected at all costs. The fact that you are OK, that you are here now, could be affected if you tell me something that changes the outcome. Do you understand?"

"Yes, but I'm not sure you do." I work it through. If Bill recently came to see me at the bandstand, he will be drawn to me once more in Cheltenham before heading back to 1963, where he will sacrifice his life to save mine. That event may be in *my* past, but for him, it lies ahead. "Bill, I can tell you what's going to happen in London. We could change it."

He regards me with compassion, his blue eyes unblinking. Then he gets up and walks to a nearby wall, staring at an engraved gold shield mounted there.

> *Respect the Past*
> *Protect the Future*
> *Trust in the Great Unfolding*

He turns and offers me a warm, compassionate smile. "People often ask, if you could know the day, the exact time of your death, would you want to know?" He holds my gaze. "Most people wouldn't, but I'm glad I know."

"Are you saying you know what's going to happen to you in London?"

"Not the details, but I guessed the outcome when I arrived in China. You weren't just surprised to see me, you looked at me like I was a ghost, like you couldn't believe I was alive."

"Bill, I'm so sorry." The words get stuck at the back of my throat.

"It's OK, Joseph. It's not your fault that I guessed. Logic is at play here. The fact that you exist in a timeline beyond the Romano mission, that alone tells me that what I'm about to attempt will work." He swallows, blinking a few times, and then looks directly at me. "It's evident that I die saving you."

A strong hand squeezes at my insides. "This can't be right, Bill. I can't let you do this. We can change it."

He returns to his chair, his attention fully on me. "Let me ask you this. When you were trying to discover what happened to Amy, what if someone had told you that she was a time traveler, that she drowned in that lake. What if they also told you that in order to save her, you would die. Would you still do it?"

"Of course."

He offers me a gentle smile.

"That's not fair," I growl.

He stokes the fire. "You know now that I'm not blackmailing you, that I had to tell you Amy was in danger to ensure you completed the mission?"

"Yes."

"I'm glad. It's been hard for me."

"There must be something we can do. I can't let you go through with this!"

He nods slowly. "I understand. You believe we can alter the outcome to our preference?"

He's good at navigating these conversations. I suspect he's had similar debates many times. "We focus on simply avoiding your death, Bill, that's all."

"Joseph, the simple fact that we are having this conversation is already putting your life at risk. Any details you tell me now could alter the outcome. Your advice could literally endanger your very existence. It's an impossible, paradoxical dilemma. It's written, safe. I am not going to risk changing my plan now. Do you understand?"

Reluctantly, I tell him that I understand. Time travel is a gift, but it can also be a weapon, powered by information.

"This is bigger than me or you," he says. "I trust in the plan. Saving you is part of a much bigger picture. If we risk changing the events of that night, then we risk the chance that I fail. Originally, you died in that church—it was over—but the fact that you are here means it works. I beat resistance, and you're alive."

I stare back at him, a man I hardly know, yet who is willing to lay down his life for me. He told me once that time travelers can sometimes live a friendship in reverse, and I think I'm beginning to understand what he meant. Then a phrase that he just used circles back to me. "When you say you beat resistance, what do you mean?"

"Sorry?" He focuses on the fire again, his eyes glazing over a little.

"You just said that my being here, alive, means you beat resistance." My thoughts spin and reinsert themselves in my mind until my emotions are like a complex ball of wool. I think of Felix telling me there was something strange about the data on Bill's watch. And then it becomes clear.

As travelers, we often get to see the end of the story first. We see opportunity, what *can* be changed. For me it was witnessing Lucy Romano gunned down in an alleyway and the opera house fire destroying the life of Philippe Chevalier. I had presumed that Bill arrived at the end of my story, saw my death, jumped back, and changed it, but now I'm not so sure. "You tried but failed to save me. The change event closed. The mission was done."

He nods, a small, almost imperceptible gesture.

"And yet, you're planning to go back and save me. How?"

He looks up at me, seeming to age before my eyes. "You deserve to know, but what I'm about to tell you, you mustn't tell a soul. I have worked on this alone. Iris, Felix, they would never sign off on this. If they found out, this could undo the fabric of The Continuum."

I lean in. "Just tell me what you're planning to do."

He sets his jaw, eyes moist with emotion. "I'm going to reenter the change event, beat resistance, and change the unchangeable."

Visions of numerous versions of Bill, moving at impossible

speed around the church, come back to me. "I'm no expert, but I thought that was impossible."

"It should be, but I found a way, and your being here is proof that it works." He brightens a little, but then shakes his head, seemingly angry at himself. "I'm not proud of it, such double standards. It's one of the traits I despise most in human nature, and it's me doing it. I have broken all the established rules that The Continuum created, but I must save you."

Ideas swirl. "So I'm clear, your mission was to save me, but you failed, and the change event closed. It was over?"

"Yes. But I never gave up." His voice catches. "I'm coming back to save you, my boy."

"I'm here to give you a second chance," I murmur.

"What was that?"

"Scarlett." I frown, trying to cast my mind back to a time when I didn't trust Bill, thought he might even be working with Scarlett. My brain hurts.

"You know that Scarlett planted the radio in your shop. You believe me now?"

"A lot has happened since then, I need to tell you about—"

"Be careful," he warns me. "You mustn't tell me information that could alter The Continuum's approach to future problems."

"OK, I won't tell you the details, but her activity is linked to what you did when you saved me. I'm convinced of it." I think back to Nils, trapped in the void in Paris, of the viewings I had of Scarlett. "Scarlett put another traveler in danger. I had a viewing, saw her messing with his watch. She told the traveler she was giving him a second chance. I heard her thoughts too. The words were clear, as though she had spoken them to me. 'I have to know how he did it.' I think Scarlett was talking about you, Bill. I think she's trying to replicate what you've done."

Angered by the constant need to think about this from multiple chronological perspectives, I add, "What you're *about* to do!"

Bill's expression is thick with worry. "But I've been so diligent, worked alone, hidden my plans from everyone. I know this knowledge is dangerous, that it mustn't fall into the wrong hands."

"Felix is suspicious," I tell him. "He analyzed the data on your watch, said that something wasn't right."

Bill smiles. "He's a clever one, he won't give up easily, but I assure you, before I jump back to save you in London, I will erase the data on my watch and destroy all my research. Scarlett will not use what I've discovered."

"But what if you miss something. What if Scarlett has figured out how you saved me. What's the worst she could do, Bill?"

Before he can answer, the warm, cozy tones of his study flatten to an aquamarine hue. Brain freeze nips at the base of my neck, its icy fingers creeping up and over the top of my skull. "I'm leaving soon," I tell him, "but why has the room gone blue? I haven't seen that for a while."

"You bonded with the focus object."

"Oh, I get it." Being dragged along is different from being bonded. I check my watch: three minutes.

Bill wouldn't have allowed me to tell him about Extempero, would have freaked out about me breaking even more rules, but I can't fight the feeling that it would have been so helpful for The Continuum to know, ahead of time, who took the horse.

Extempero.

A wave of panic washes over me as I remember where I'm going to land. My place of origin. Emil Zanak's yacht! "I dragged two people with me to China, Bill. I'm going to be in trouble when I land."

He taps a finger against his chin, thoughtfully. "You dragged them from your present?"

"Yes."

"Hmmm." His eyes dart around in deep thought. "And then I dragged you here . . . Interesting." He focuses back on me. "When you arrived here, your watch had to calculate the displacement. The same will be true when you return to your place of origin. Your watch will advise you, but you've traveled deep into the past and then been dragged far into the future. The displacement could be considerable."

"Considerable?" I nervously picture myself landing off the coast of Montenegro, hundreds of years from when I originally left.

"I had a similar situation once," Bill says. "It caused at least ten minutes of displacement, gave me a chance to get ready—interesting one that. Have you ever been to Egypt?"

I tell him I haven't, but my mind is already drifting. We walk to the center of the room. I stare at Bill, feeling mixed emotions as I always do when leaving his company. I think back over his impending sacrifice. "How do you expect me to look everyone at The Continuum in the eye, knowing what you're planning to do? Knowing I might have been able to stop you."

He clenches his jaw, eyes glassy with determination. "You must. You have no choice."

"They miss you, Bill, especially Iris."

His chest rises and falls. "Try and help her to stay focused on the goal, she's good at that. She always said she would take care of Basil for me. That will keep her busy."

"Gabrielle misses you too."

He raises his eyebrows. "You've met her?"

"We worked together on a mission," I say, aware that I shouldn't share details.

He smiles proudly. "I'm so pleased. I knew you would make an amazing team."

I scoff. "I wouldn't go that far."

He lets out a hearty laugh. "She's a tough cookie, eh?"

"She is."

I'm aware of the blood pulsing in my veins, the ions crackling in the air. I feel the presence of time like some omnipresent god. It's the observer effect. It's found me and wants to put me back where I belong.

As time travelers we resist the urge to shake hands. "Thanks for coming to my rescue, Bill. In China, I mean."

"It was a most unexpected pleasure."

I peer down at my hands. They have an iridescent sheen. Time compresses around me. I wondered so many times, since that night in London, what I would say to Bill if I ever saw him again. I've spent time with him now, and yet I don't feel I've said half of what I planned to. Words tumble out in a rush. "You saved me," I tell him. "I've done a lot since then. I want you to be proud of me, Bill. I want you to know that I'm using my gift, that I'm really trying."

"I know," he says kindly. "I am proud of you, very proud. You're becoming the traveler that I know you can be. You will be a great leader one day, Joseph."

I clear my throat and swallow. "Thank you for what you're about to do."

"It's a sacrifice I'm proud to make," Bill says, "but please remember. Don't mourn me. Not yet. I will see you again soon, and many times after that."

I manage a smile. "Because we have great adventures together."

He smiles back.

And then I'm gone.

18

My arrival back onto the yacht is instantaneous. After all my pinging around and Bill's recent revelations, it's a relief that returning to your place of origin is still one of the golden rules. Emil Zanak's museum is cold, quiet, and deserted. The sterile, filtered air is a stark contrast to Bill's warm and very much lived-in home.

My watch updates, informing me that the local time is 4:52 p.m.

Displacement: +17 minutes

I'm going to presume the plus sign indicates that I've arrived ahead of Zanak and Kristin, meaning they are due back from the year 743 in seventeen minutes. I'm under some time pressure here, but I can't help staring at the pottery horse, exactly where we left it, entombed in its triterbium case. I consider stealing it, but there's no point now.

A crushing sense of guilt consumes me. That horse carried its story for all those years, all the emotion, desire, optimism fossilized within its fibers. I made a promise, told it to trust me, assured it that I would listen and not let it down, and I messed up.

I see Sayana, the Sogdian dancing girl, and her lover frozen in time as though trapped in amber, and my heart aches. I doubt I will ever know their fate, the opportunity lost forever. At least, that's the way I thought it worked. My unexpected meeting with Bill has cast a dubious shadow of doubt over everything I've been led to believe. No time to think it through now, though. I need to get off this boat, ASAFP.

As I turn to go, something catches my eye. Hanging on the wall near the back of the room is a photograph enlarged onto a canvas. As I approach, the cold sinking feeling I felt when I first entered this room returns. The photograph features various grinning members of Extempero holding objects. I count twelve people in total, including Zanak, who stands in the center of the group, smiling proudly. With growing horror, I realize these are the assembled winners of the previous time-travel auctions, displaying their grim trophies like tourists on a big-game hunt.

"Fools," I murmur, trying to remember—perhaps finding it harder now to believe—that they don't know the damage they're doing. I already thought this room felt like a tomb, and now I know why. The surrounding glass cabinets contain the spent, benign objects from the photograph. I don't want to look, but I force myself, knowing that it might be useful to mentally cata-log them. I walk the room quickly, hoping to feel a glimmer of the past, but all of them are deathly silent. I pass a set of scales, a wooden medicine box, and medals—tarnished silver, one from the Crimean War. On the other side of the room a small leathery brown globe, a set of engraved buckles, and an ancient dagger. This is so wrong. These focus objects were special; their stories waited for years, hundreds, maybe some of them even thousands, to be triggered and unleashed, and then, ultimately ignored. They are the equivalent of grotesque stuffed animals, devoid of their previous energy and vitality. All that remains is the eerie silence of wasted opportunity. I've seen enough. I sneak out of the room and work my way along the corridors of the yacht, heading toward the upper deck. I pass a member of staff and do my best to act like I belong. She says hello and asks if I need anything.

Unless you can fly a helicopter, I'm good.

When I reach the upper deck, I sneak around the edge of the boat and find myself near the bar, where I first met Kristin. That feels like a lifetime ago. A woman's voice behind me makes me jump, her Australian accent immediately jogging my memory. "Mr. Blake?"

I turn, trying to appear relaxed but failing. "Karen, right?"

She raises her eyebrows. "I'm impressed you remembered my name. I thought all the guests were off the boat. How come you're still here?"

I'm going to assume that the megayacht staff aren't in the know. "I've been spending some time with Mr. Zanak. He's on his way, actually."

"Oh, OK." She looks a little confused, but clearly isn't in the business of pushing guests to explain themselves. "Can I get you a drink, something to eat perhaps?"

"No, I'm good, thanks . . . I really just need to . . ." For reasons unknown, I mime an embarrassed, cross-legged clench.

Her concern is immediate. "Ah, the toilet is just down there on your left."

"Thank you," I tell her, walking away, unsure what to do next. The coast of Montenegro appears deceptively close, but there is *no way* I'm swimming ashore.

The sun is low in the sky.

The sea calm.

Sharks.

Or *tarkies*, as my dad would shout, grabbing my leg in the swimming pool when I was a boy. Immense damage done there. Whatever you call them, sharks love nothing more than a nice sunset meat feast.

Surprisingly, even with the grotesque vision of screaming and churning in a foaming red sea, I find myself smiling. I've just come up with a plan that would make even Gabrielle grin with reluctant appreciation. With seven minutes to go before Emil Zanak reappears, I make my way down to . . . What did the captain call it? A water barn? A toy shop of floaty playthings? Whatever it's called, I'm relieved to see it's still packed full of boats, paddleboards, and Jet Skis.

Four minutes remain. I'm gone in two with a bit of luck.

First step is to get the garage door open. I find one of those red emergency-style buttons on the wall. There's a load of warnings about not operating it when the boat is moving. I press it and the massive door lifts, bathing the garage in the warm glow of evening sun. OK, part one of the plan executed. I grab a life jacket from the rack and clip it on, for the obvious reason of not wanting to drown, but also, I'm still wearing the clothes that were given to me by Bill in the future. They don't belong here, and at some point, time's going to notice and send them home, leaving me in my birthday suit. If that happens, at least I can wrap the life jacket around my waist.

There are three Jet Skis to choose from, individually branded and splashed with fluorescent colors. I go with the biggest, hopefully the most stable. I climb on, wobbling a bit as the Jet Ski rebalances in the water. My next challenge is figuring out how to turn it on. As far as I can tell, there is no key. I spot a green button with the word *Start* above it. Sounds straightforward. I press it, but nothing happens. Crap.

On the wall is a box labeled *Keys*. Metaphorically smacking my forehead, I leap from the Ski, find a plastic key on a lanyard that matches the garish livery, and hop back on. The key is an unusual U shape. I can't find anywhere to put it.

I hear voices close by and check my watch: one minute to go. Panicking, I rapidly press the green button. Then I figure it out. The key has one of those stretchy cables. On the Ski is a button labeled *Auto Stop*: a cut-off device! I pull the button out a little way, slide the key underneath, and press the green button. The Jet Ski roars, kicking up a swell of bubbles from its rear. "Yes," I cry and twist the right-hand grip. Nothing.

"Come on!" I gasp. "How do I make you go?" I squeeze what looks like a brake lever and lurch backward, smashing the Jet Ski into the side of a dinghy. Right, throttle confirmed. Apparently, Jet Skis don't bother with brakes. Now I just need to figure out how to go forward. There's an *R* switch, so I click it to *F*, and this time when I gingerly squeeze the throttle, the Jet Ski eases forward.

As I leave the garage, my watch buzzes. If it's correct, then Zanak and Kristin have just got back from the Tang dynasty. How long until they figure out that I was a few minutes ahead of them, that I've stolen one of the Jet Skis? "OK," I say quietly to myself, "let's do this." I put my head down, pinch my legs against the thrumming chassis, and squeeze the throttle all the way.

The power is instant. I streak like a rocket over the glassy waters and find myself laughing and whooping. It's exhilarating, so fast I can hardly keep my eyes open. I'm constantly on the lookout for dorsal fins, but even the logical fear of being eaten alive by a perfect predator gets pushed to the back of my mind. Jet Skis are fun. Why haven't I done this before?

As I approach the harbor, I ease off the speed, not wanting to draw attention. It wouldn't take much for Zanak to phone ahead and arrange for one of his goons to greet me. All I can do now is hope that he doesn't bump into Karen or check his water-toy inventory for a while.

After ditching the Jet Ski and life jacket in the harbor, I steal a towel from the top of a nearby boat, in case of wardrobe malfunctions, and head toward my super posh hotel. It was booked by Maria Hofer from Extempero, but I need my luggage, phone, passport, and money. Luckily the woman at reception recognizes me and lets me into my room. I can't stay here—it's the first place Zanak will look—so I get changed double-quick, throw all my stuff into my suitcase, and disappear into the cobbled maze of Tivat. Eventually, down one of the narrow side streets, I find what I'm searching for. A small boutique hotel. I pay the deposit in cash, and only when I close the door behind me and let out a huge sigh of relief do I feel remotely safe. I've done some crazy stuff since I discovered time travel, but the last forty-eight hours take the top spot.

The transition from the past—or in this case the future—to the present is beginning to get a little easier. I learned a lot when I traveled with Gabrielle, and her attitude when we returned from Paris really stayed with me.

It doesn't do you any good to dwell on the impossibility of it all. It's best to just get on with it. I take a long shower, and if any of my thoughts threaten to spin me out, I let them run off the surface of my mind, like the water over my skin. As I'm drying off and getting changed, I'm not surprised to discover that the clothes and shoes Bill gave me have disappeared. I wonder about the process. The dinner jacket I took to China, has that been returned too? Did it suddenly appear in the present in a Chinese forest, or perhaps in a city somewhere? Did anyone see it? And what about the Sogdian clothes I was wearing when Bill dragged me into the future? Did they end up back in whatever Scotland is called in 743?

I order room service. Gabrielle would be proud. I actually can't remember the last time I ate. Was it in Chang'an? If so, that was many, many hours ago. My stomach isn't just growling, it's howling. I guess the adrenaline kept my hunger at bay, but it's become a painful, pinching sensation that runs the full length of my torso.

Half an hour later, I stare at the remnants of plates and dishes on the table. Spaghetti carbonara, bread rolls, chocolate pudding and cream. Enough for an entire rugby team, but as Grandma Bridgeman used to say, "It hardly touched the sides."

My stomach cramps. I break into a cold sweat of nausea, and for the next few minutes, I can't move. My digestion makes some very worrying noises. I ate goat stew in China. I really hope I don't spend the next few days laughing at the toilet. Gradually, the calories seem to remember their job, and my nausea subsides.

Finally, I can think straight.

I should call Iris and update The Continuum, but something Gabrielle said to me once circles back. She talked about how she couldn't maintain a relationship, that time travel made it impossible. I grab my phone, planning to call Alexia, but then see I've missed several calls from my mum. Mostly, my previous timeline—the one in which we lost Amy—has faded in my memory and feels more like a dream. In that life, Dad had committed suicide and Mum developed dementia, but in this one, they're both relatively healthy for their age. Moments like this bring the old timeline back to life. My heart sinks, instant flashbacks of the day my dad took his life rush forth. I banish them and make the call.

"Hello, darling," Mum says.

"Hi, Mum. I missed a lot of calls from you. Are you OK?"

"Yes . . . Well, no. My phone keeps telling me it's full. What's the cloud?"

Discussing the cloud with my mum is a unique form of torture. She never understands, but today I don't mind. Just hearing her voice is a comforting pleasure.

Every connection matters. If I hadn't known that before, I *feel* it now.

"Your father wants to know if you're coming back to work," she says, clearly under duress.

By *work*, she means the property business that I have no idea about. Dad and I have discussed this, at length, but he keeps chipping away. I think he's trying to be helpful, trying to cajole me back to the life they expect me to lead. "I'm still not sure," I tell her. "I feel like I want to do some traveling, maybe help people in some way."

I hear movement, a door closing. In a quieter voice, she says, "He thinks you're having a midlife crisis. Is that true? I think you might be. It's quite fashionable, apparently, but you shouldn't call it a crisis. It's an opportunity. Is that what's going on with you dear, a midlife opportunity?"

I tell her it's something like that, but not to worry. She says worrying is her job. We chat for a while longer. She asks what I think about Amy going off to paint, and I suggest that Amy might be having an "early life opportunity." Mum laughs. It's the best sound. As I hang up, I'm relieved she didn't ask me where I was or what I'd been doing.

I decide to call Alexia. Just seeing her name on my screen sends my heartbeat up a notch. It's a universal metric, perhaps the only one you need. If someone makes you feel this way, don't ever let them go.

"That's so funny," she says. "I was just thinking about you."

"Really?"

"I was just watering the plant you bought me and thinking how much I like my new place. I mean, I liked my old office, but this is even better." Her calming voice soothes me, and I'm suddenly overwhelmed by the need to be close, to hold her. I fall in love with her more every day. "Joe? Are you OK?"

"Yes," I tell her, my throat tightening. "I . . . I just wanted to hear your voice."

"Where are you?" she asks softly.

"A hotel in Montenegro."

"Wow, that's impressive. What are you doing there?"

I remember the cloud of orange lanterns filling the Chang'an sky like fireflies. "Chasing antiques," I say lamely, knowing that the next time I see Alexia, I'm going to tell her about my time traveling. Not just because it's the right thing to do, but because I want to. I want to share the pain of failing my mission in China with her—the good, the bad, all of it.

With a hint of playfulness, she says, "I never knew that the life of an antique dealer was so exotic. I'm definitely coming next time."

"I would like that." I find myself talking without thinking. It seems my mind has some catching up to do with my heart. "Listen, Alexia, I just wanted to say that there's a lot going on at the moment, some work stuff that I would like to talk to you about when I see you next, but I just wanted you to know that you're really important to me."

The line is silent.

"Hello?" I say, tentatively.

"I'm here," she says quietly.

"I know words are cheap, I just wanted you to know that I think about you all the time." I pause, blinking. "I miss you."

After a brief pause, she says, "OK."

She's still wary of me, or perhaps I should say, wary of *him*. The version of me that she dated lived a life shaped by completely different events. Alexia knows the worst of me, and it's going to take a while to show her the best, and even longer to prove that the real me is here to stay.

"Do you mean that?" she asks. "That I'm important to you?"

"Yes." I think of the star-crossed lovers all those years ago in the Tang dynasty. "I feel really lucky that we've been given this second chance, and I really appreciate you trusting me, giving us another go."

She sighs.

"I've gone too far again, haven't I?"

"Maybe, but . . . No, I like it." She lets out a little laugh. "I just wish you hadn't needed to fall off your bike to realize this."

We chat for a while longer, but eventually I let her go, reluctantly. She wishes me luck and hopes that I find what I'm looking for. I don't tell her that I already have.

Right, time to do my duty and tell Iris the bad news.

Smartphones are present-day miracles, but I have ICARUS. After placing a Do Not Disturb sign on the outside of my door, I lock it, draw the blinds, and place my silver hunter facedown on the center of the bed, where it can scan the entire room. A few twists and turns later, and my pocket watch turns into an expensive sci-fi movie's special effect. A cloud of tiny green glow bugs flutters out silently, working its way into the uppermost corners of the room, where the bugs attach themselves. Multiple arcs of sparkling green light scan the room, mapping it in three dimensions.

Joe, calling the future. Come in, future. Over.

"Connect to Iris Mendell," I say aloud. I'm pretty sure I could use my mind, but that's just a little too weird.

Words hover above the bed, so real and solid I swear I could reach out and grab them.

"Request acknowledged, please wait . . ."

After a couple of minutes, a glassy humanoid shape takes

form. The faint honeycomb mesh over its surface resolves into a rich and detailed simulation of Iris Mendell. She's tall, dressed smartly in a blue trouser suit. Her gray hair is styled in a wave, and her high cheekbones and pale skin glow with an otherworldly luminescence. Although the technology is incredible, it's not good enough to completely fool my brain. Her burgundy lips raise into a smile, and her eyes focus and fully connect with mine. That feeling of human connection is the part that really matters.

Sometimes her German accent hovers around the edges of her voice, but today it seems more pronounced. "Hello, Joseph," she says. "The auction has been on my mind. I'm keen to hear how it went." She looks tired, a little weary.

"We have a lot to talk about," I tell her, and as the events of the last couple of days begin spilling out, she holds up a hand, deep concern etched on her face.

"Felix and the others need to hear this," she says. She takes a step toward me, her right leg cutting through the edge of the bed. She glances around, then focuses back on me. "The technology we're using here is quick, useful, but there is another level."

My eyebrows lift. "Another level?"

She nods. "An avatar can be created here, enabling a more immersive form of communication. You will be able to move around, fully interact. The experience will be practically indistinguishable from reality. Now that you've used ICARUS a few times, I wonder if you might be ready?"

I can't remember if Neo accepts the blue pill or the red pill. I decide I might as well chug down the whole bottle. "Sure, let's do it."

"Are you able to lock your room?"

"Yes."

"Good. Time will pass slowly in your present. It's a form of hypnosis, and you won't be moving, so sit down, make yourself comfortable." I do as I'm told, choosing a low chair in the corner. "Now focus your attention on your watch. Don't focus on the lights, just breathe and relax."

This reminds me of my first hypnosis session with Alexia, which originally unlocked my time-travel abilities.

A series of dots appear and flash. I close my eyes, open them again, and allow my vision to blur slightly. A myriad of lights spirals faster and faster, pulsing and growing in a hypnotic, trippy display. I glance around the room, noticing dust particles that seem to hover in the air in impossible stasis. The LED lights strobe and flicker. Each breath seems to take an age.

"Are you ready?" Iris asks.

I tell her I am, my voice sounding like it's traveling down a long tube.

When using the previous version of this futuristic virtual reality, the location was comparatively fixed and would build around me like scenery. This time, the transition is instant. The hotel room disappears, and I find myself in a glass-and-steel atrium, with plants, trees, and a sparkling waterfall trickling through an odd crystal formation. It's bright, fresh, expansive. This no longer feels like a simulation. I am fully and completely present. The sound of moving water is spatial, dimensional, along with the distant murmur of conversation and echoes of footfall. The temperature of the air, the faint smell of polish, the light filtering through the glass that forces me to narrow my eyes—all of it real.

Iris stands still, quietly and patiently waiting as I just adjust. There are glass work pods scattered through the space. People are chatting, and someone is throwing images onto a screen with just a hand. People walk nearby, going about their business. They pay us little attention, as if it's normal for someone from the past to materialize suddenly in an armchair. That's odd. The chair from the hotel seems to have come with me, or at least a version of it.

Like anyone entering a new virtual reality for the first time, I peer down at my hands, rotating them. "They look real," I say, getting up from the chair to take my first virtual steps. "This is incredible. How does it work?"

"ICARUS technology, working alongside your implant, fools your brain into believing you are here. Back in the present, time is passing slowly. You are in a highly cognitive but relaxed state. If for any reason you are interrupted in the present, you will simply return there."

I study my body, feeling the texture of my clothing. "But I'm physically . . . here! You look real! Do I seem real to you?"

"Your physical presence here is a network of billions of nanoparticles working together to create a perfect, moving replica. You are making them move as your brain interprets your intentions and experiences."

If I'm made of magic ball bearings, I can't see how they join. I clench my hands into fists. I squeeze, feeling my fingertips pressing into my palms, the skin growing pale as I apply more pressure. Vinny told me he was investing in the metaverse, said it would be like *The Matrix* crossed with *Ready Player One*. When I get home, I'm telling him to double down on that investment.

I look at Iris. The uncanny valley has evaporated now. Her hair is no longer a luminous gray, but a pure white sheen. Her pale-blue eyes contain the depth that only comes with reality, or at least one we believe is real. "It feels like I'm meeting you for the first time," I tell her.

She smiles knowingly. "I've used the technology many times, but even I still marvel at its ingenuity." Her expression darkens a little, and frown lines that I haven't seen before crease her forehead. "Now, if you're ready," she gestures for me to follow, "I'm keen to share what you just told me with the team."

Iris leads the way, her back straight as a ballerina. She moves with poise and grace, acknowledging people as we walk. I notice a slight limp, but she covers it well. We enter a tubular glass corridor that cuts through a forest glade, reminding me of a submerged tunnel in an aquarium. We're alone now, surrounded on both sides by a lush green tree canopy, with clear blue skies high above us. I see an enormous dome at the end of the tunnel, glinting in the sunlight.

I've seen this dome before, but I've never been inside.

"Where are we going?" I ask.

Iris turns to me. "After what you've been through, I felt it was time for you to see how The Continuum began. What Felix created drives and shapes everything we do. It's part of the reason I wanted you to take the next step, to be present here so you could experience it fully." Her cool blue eyes sparkle, and for a fleeting moment, her glowing anticipation and pride remind me of Bill. "It's time you saw Downstream."

19

We pass through a narrow, dimly lit entrance tunnel. Iris places her right hand against a panel in the wall. Green light passes over her face. As she says her name, a circular door opens like a retina adjusting, and we walk into the dome.

"I don't get to spend much time in here," Iris says. "It always takes my breath away."

The colossal dome initially appears to be transparent, but as sunlight cuts through a thin layer of cloud, it highlights a honeycomb mesh cut into the glassy surface. The air is cool, pure, and still. I gaze up in wonderment at the cyan-blue sky. The lush green forest I saw earlier is visible all around us, even the mountains in the distance. I force myself to remember that my physical body is seated, motionless in a hotel in Montenegro, and yet here I am, magic marble-man walking around in the world's largest snow globe.

A man approaches wearing a white shirt, cream-colored chinos, and shiny black shoes. If it weren't for an extravagant red bow tie, he would be your classic scientist.

"Hello, Devon," Iris says.

"Iris . . . Always nice to see you here." The man's voice is deep, with a hint of the Caribbean somewhere around the edges. His black skin is smooth and unblemished, but specks of gray in his hair and beard betray his forty or so years. "Joseph Bridgeman, it's good to meet you." He holds out a hand, and we shake. "Professor Devon Campbell, but please, call me Devon." He has a cheerful, youthful disposition. He gazes around the dome. "Welcome to the Observatorium."

"Thanks," I say, "it's impressive."

To Iris, Devon says, "We just fired a pulse, should have the data in a few minutes."

"Excellent. Where's Felix?" Iris asks.

"You know Felix, he's downstairs with his baby." Devon offers a sideways grin, but when Iris doesn't reciprocate, he asks if she's all right.

Her brow narrows. "We've received some rather disturbing information. Would you mind letting Felix know that I'm here with Joseph? We need to talk."

"Will do." Devon heads to a nearby console, where a young man and woman are talking and interacting with projected visuals and objects.

Iris turns to me. "Downstream is how we study the past, a unique way of visualizing history. This is how we find focus objects and change events. Without it, there would be no Continuum."

I follow her toward a circular railing in the middle of the dome. A cylindrical chamber, twenty feet in diameter, descends into the earth, a gleaming chrome sphere in its center. The upper third of the ball is gloss black, with the dome's honeycomb pattern reflected on its surface: a metal eye, surveying the sky. Cables spill out from its base, connecting to an unseen power source that throbs faintly beneath us. Circling the ball is a spiral staircase, lit neon blue. A man ascends the stairs, illuminated head to toe. The last time I saw Felix Greystone, I was surprised by his laid-back demeanor and attire. It's less of a shock this time, but Felix certainly stands out among his peers. He's lean, with dark unkempt hair down to his shoulders. He's wearing a tightly fitted jumper unbuttoned at the front and pulled up to his elbows. His linen trousers are baggy, almost covering his sandals.

He spots us, waves, and meets us by a console of light that displays data I will never understand. He says hello to Iris and then focuses on me. "It's good to see you, Joseph. You've taken your first steps into a more immersive version of ICARUS, I see." His accent has the relaxed, honeyed warmth of an American surfer. "How are you finding it?"

"It's incredible," I tell him, honestly.

"I'm glad you like it, but just wait until you see this." He glances around the dome like a proud father. "I've been looking forward to finally showing you Downstream." Now that he's closer, I see his dark, freckled skin is peppered with stubble, and there are shadowy bags beneath his eyes. It appears he's been burning some futuristic version of midnight oil.

"Devon told me you've just fired a pulse," Iris says.

Felix rubs his hands together and then turns to me. "In order to analyze the past, we send a pulse back through time. It takes a huge amount of energy, not to mention the processing power involved in analyzing that data. We don't fire it every day, so your arrival is good timing. You get to see the fireworks."

Iris draws in a breath. "Felix, I'm afraid that Joseph has some rather disturbing information to share."

"Oh," Felix looks concerned and suddenly weary. "What's happened?"

I take a moment to think before I open my mouth. Being here, in this new form of presence, is one thing, but chronology is another. When Bill dragged me from China into the future, we arrived on the grounds of Greystone House, not far from here. For me, that was just a couple of hours ago, but for Felix and Iris and everyone here, that was months ago. Not that they know I was here, of course. They are still mourning Bill, and the reason he died was me. We have secrets, Bill and I, secrets I don't think I can share with the colleagues he trusted. Bill was adamant that I shouldn't tell him anything that might change future events. What does that mean now? At this precise moment in the timeline? Surely, it's OK to tell Iris and Felix what happened to me in China. Right?

"I need to ask you something first," I say. "I know I'm in the future, but is there anything beyond now? Is this as far forward as I could go?"

Felix grins, deep dimples appearing in his cheeks. "It's an excellent question, and the answer is simple. To maintain chronology, our travelers always arrive at time's arrow. You are at the very head of time, Joseph. There is nothing beyond. Everything unfolds from here. Why do you ask?"

"I just want to be sure that what I'm about to tell you doesn't damage anything that's already occurred."

"Spoken like a true traveler," Felix says.

Iris agrees. "Bill taught you well."

She doesn't know the half of it, and I'm realizing it may have to stay that way. I need to explain the events that led to my unexpected trip to China, but I decide that it's safer to leave Bill out of it.

"Joseph, would you mind telling Felix what you began to tell me?" Iris asks.

Carefully, I explain the events that led to priming and bonding with the focus object. They listen without interruption as I tell them about the Extempero auction, being invited onto the yacht. When I describe Emil Zanak's arrival by helicopter, Felix stops me. The color drains from his face. "Why do I recognize that name?"

Iris draws in a long breath. "We tried to recruit him. It must be twenty years ago now. He had completed his first tethered jump. As is the way, Bill was drawn to him, but it was clear from the start that it wasn't going to work."

"Why not?" I ask. "What happened?"

Iris considers this for a moment, blinking as though scanning a slideshow of memories. "Usually when a person discovers they can time travel and successfully alter the past, they feel a debt. You felt that, didn't you?" I nod. "Once they're introduced to The Continuum, most people join us in some form, willing to make a positive difference to the world, to play their part in the Great Unfolding. However, occasionally they feel the debt works the other way. Zanak wanted payment for his services. That's not how we work. Of course, we ensure that travelers are compensated for their time, but Zanak saw this primarily as an opportunity to make money. I remember Bill being quite upset about the numbers that Zanak suggested. The recruitment stopped, really before it began. Bill tried to persuade him, but Zanak became angry, resentful. Sometimes it goes that way."

"How did Zanak get access to the focus object?" Felix asks. "How did he know where it was?"

"Scarlett," I tell him.

Felix takes a few seconds to absorb this. "It makes sense, I suppose," he says, almost to himself. "Scarlett is young, impressionable. She's seeking purpose, a dangerous mix." He looks at Iris. "It must have been easy for Zanak to recruit her."

"No," I say, "it was the other way around."

"How do you know?" Felix asks.

"I had a viewing, while I was in China. I saw Scarlett. She approached Zanak. Extempero was her idea, all of it."

"And how did you end up going on the mission?" Iris asks.

"By the time I figured out that Zanak was a time traveler, it was too late," I reply. "I could feel the chance slipping through my fingers, so I took a risk. I primed the object and dragged all three of us into the past."

Felix cocks an eyebrow. "That was brave, Joe. Really brave."

"Maybe," I sigh, shaking my head. "But the mission was a mono, and I wasn't prepared. I failed."

The silence lasts only a few seconds, but it feels like an age.

"You did your best," Iris says, "under very difficult circumstances. When I asked you to join Gabrielle to try and get the focus object back, I didn't know about Emil Zanak's involvement."

"I know," I tell her. "I'm just sorry I didn't complete the mission."

"None of this is your fault, Joseph," Iris says.

An alert flashes on the screen in front of Felix. "We've received the data from the pulse." He looks at Iris. "What would you like to do?"

Iris raises her chin, her expression stony. "It will be tough to see, but I would rather know the damage."

"Of course," Felix says. He's joined at the console by Devon, the scientist we met on the way in. Devon moves his hands silently over a keyboard made of light. Charts and graphs and dials appear. He interacts with them using a form of sign language, as though coding with light.

Felix focuses on me, compassion and excitement in his eyes. "As I said, I've been excited about showing you Downstream. I wish it was under happier circumstances."

The dome darkens, leaving only the faintest hint of security lighting at floor level. The ring of blue light encircling the chrome ball beams outward in powerful strobes, as the huge eye lifts from its cradle with a whirring hiss, rising toward the center of the Observatorium like a majestic moon. The top of the sphere twists open, bathing us in warm light. A pulse of energy passes through me like a shock wave as we're plunged into total darkness. Lacking sensory information, I reach blindly for the handrail in front of me.

The empty space fills with an explosion of kaleidoscopic colors, vivid twinkling stars, a projected blast of pure light. There must be millions of them, each connected to others by a thin neon web of interwoven lines, creating a dazzling, radiant tapestry. Excited flashes of energy travel along synapses like living dreams. The projection of time swirls around us, immersing us fully. My breath comes in juddering bursts, and my heart beats loudly in my ears.

Felix's voice is proud and clear. "What do you think?"

"It's . . . beautiful," I say, deeply moved.

"This is the space-time continuum, rendered and displayed in all four dimensions," he says. "You are seeing human history, our story, mapped in as much detail as we choose to show. Now, I need to find your recent mission. The process of priming and discharging an object gives off a huge spike of energy, which means it shouldn't be too difficult to find."

A small square block made of textured yellow light appears in front of him. He places his hands around it as though it was perfectly solid and interacts with it using a combination of complex gestures and rotations. Felix and his creation, acting as one. Dozens of glowing orbs light up, a cluster of orange suns, each with a fluorescent tail tapering away like comets and connecting back to the green stars. I'm busy making my own connections. I believed Iris when she told me it wasn't my fault, but it doesn't change the fact that I feel guilty as hell. And now I'm about to see the details of my failure, woven into this vibrant tapestry.

"These are focus objects," Felix says. A stream of light plumes from one of the comets, snaking across the void and attaching hungrily to a nearby green star. They pulse in time with each other. "See how they link back to a change event?"

"Yes, I see them." My voice is the only thing grounding me here.

"OK, Devon, let's work back from the eighth century." Felix spreads his hands and performs a complex gesture, seemingly without thought, and Downstream switches focus to a new constellation. A fresh web of incandescent color fills the dome. Felix glances over his shoulder. "We can track the horse through time and see the exact moment you primed it." He and Devon manipulate the light show, rotating and spinning and zooming, as though we're a satellite shooting at impossible speed over a vast ocean of fiery beacons fringed with soft flickering edges.

"I don't understand." Felix turns, his features partially lit. "I can't find it. There's absolutely no evidence that an object was triggered at all." He tries again, sighing in frustration.

"Let me try," Devon says. After a few minutes, he finds something. When he speaks, his voice is flat, resigned. "I've found it." He zooms in on a dark circle haloed by a pale white light. In comparison to the other vibrant stars, this one feels like a black hole.

"Another one?" Iris says, sounding disappointed.

"I'm afraid so," Devon says.

"What is it?" I ask.

"The Tang dynasty horse," Felix says. "It was never primed. The mission wasn't triggered. It was destroyed shortly after you arrived in Montenegro, and the change event was lost."

"No," I say, "that's not right."

Silently, Felix stares at the black hole where the horse should be.

"I don't know what you experienced, Joseph," Devon says, "but Downstream doesn't show us what we *want* to see, it shows us what *happened*. It's a lens into the past, and it's never wrong."

"Well, I'm sorry, but it's wrong this time," I tell him, aware that I'm no expert but confident of the trials I've just been through.

In the silence, I hear Felix breathing and imagine his mind as the explosion I see before me. He pulls back from the constellation. "I want to show you something," he says, rotating the landscape and zooming in on a different cross section of time. "This is the Romano mission. All your jumps to London in the 1960s are visible." It's chilling to see my experiences reduced to characters, dots, and lines. New shimmering trails of light pierce the darkness, the spokes of a ghostly wheel flaring out from the change event. "Each time you travel back and observe more of the past, we receive new information. You can see the energy here, clearly."

"I can," I say, confused, "but I'm telling you, the focus object wasn't destroyed. I went on the mission. You're just not seeing it."

Iris suggests we've seen enough. Felix agrees, and the light show recedes, the darkness gradually replaced with the dome. I've heard astronauts talk about what it's like to see Earth from space, and as my eyes adjust to the light, I wonder how long it will take for my mind to assimilate what I've seen, this new and expansive perspective on time itself and my place within it.

Felix turns to me, forcibly suppressing a frown. "We're not doubting you, it's just hard to believe that we wouldn't be able to see the immense energy given off when the focus object was activated."

Thinking back over the events, I have an idea. "They transported the horse in a case. I thought the metal was familiar, it might have been triterbium. Could Scarlett have been hiding the horse?"

Felix rubs his chin and says. "Using triterbium to shield the object. It's possible, I suppose."

"Also, there was a panel with data about the jump," I add. "I don't know if it's useful to know this."

"It is," Devon says. "It shows that Extempero knew we might be watching. Downstream shows us data, but what if that has been tampered with, hidden from us. What if Scarlett has discovered a way to change the status of focus objects?"

"Is that even possible?" Iris asks.

Felix's eyes glaze over as he processes this idea. "Even if Scarlett can change the status of the objects, I'm still trying to figure out how she got the information in the first place." He turns to Iris. "Have we been compromised? Is someone leaking information from the archive?"

"I don't know. We must explore all avenues," Iris says.

"What about the other objects?" I ask. "Have their data been altered too?"

After a pause, Iris asks, "What do you mean, other objects?"

"Scarlett has been supplying Zanak with objects for months, maybe years," I reply. "The focus objects were in display cabinets. They were silent; it was horrible."

Felix has a deep frown etched on his brow. "How many objects did you see? Exactly?"

"I can't be certain. At least ten, maybe more."

"And you're certain they were focus objects?" he asks.

"I believe so, yes. I saw a photograph of previous auction winners, all holding their focus objects like trophies."

"No," Iris murmurs.

Devon's expression suggests a dark realization building within him. "What if all the focus objects we thought had been destroyed had actually been used, wasted?"

"Exactly," Iris says. "If Scarlett has been manipulating

the data, then we've been under attack, and we didn't even know it."

"I don't understand. What's going on?" I ask.

Iris visibly shakes herself into focus. "I apologize, Joseph, this is a lot to process." Her German accent is sharpened. I think it happens when she's afraid. "We've known for a while that something wasn't adding up. The Future Change Index wasn't balancing, and we couldn't understand why. Now this . . . the possibility that numerous missions have failed, and we didn't even know . . ."

Devon swallows with a loud click in his throat. "It gets worse."

Iris tilts her head. "How can it possibly be worse?"

"Downstream is an incredible machine," he says, "but it's only as clever as the data it receives. It never crossed our minds that the information we are interpreting could have been manipulated."

"What are you saying?" Iris asks.

Devon stares at the floor.

"We thought our calculations were wrong," Felix says, "so we've been . . . compensating."

"And what happens to the Future Change Index if we remove the compensation?" Iris asks.

Felix slowly turns to her, his expression grave. "You don't want to know."

20

We leave Devon sifting through an unimaginable amount of data. I follow Iris and Felix into one of many meeting rooms positioned around the upper rim of the dome. I've been in one like this before, using what I'm now thinking of as VR Version One. The room is ultraminimalist, with gently curved walls made of a smooth white resin. One wall is a floor-to-ceiling pane of glass, offering an impressive view of the interior of the dome. In the center is a table, surrounded by chairs, all made of the same material. Light panels, flush with the ceiling, give the room a sharp, even brightness.

Iris taps a panel on the wall, and a curved door slides from the wall and seals us inside with a pressurized *whumph*. In a quiet voice, she says, "Set Security Level One."

A robotic voice replies, "Security Level One activated."

Apart from the robotic voice and the sterile cleanliness of it all, this room could just about pass for a meeting space in the present. There is even a healthy-looking plant with glossy green leaves. On the opposite side of the room is a console table, replete with a jug of water and glasses. Felix walks to it and asks

Iris if she wants anything. She tells him she's fine, and he pours himself a coffee. He turns to me and offers an apologetic shrug. "I'm afraid you can't drink, Joe. The nanopresence tech is clever, but it draws the line at sensory input like taste."

"No problem," I say, my mind doing a little wobble. I'd kind of forgotten that I'm not actually *here*.

Felix sits down at the table and drums his fingers on its surface. Then he's up again, pacing the room. Iris stands beside me, peering over the dome. She's quiet for a while, then gathers herself and speaks. "What Joe has discovered leads to only one conclusion. Scarlett has been receiving inside information. We have a leak." For the first time since I met her, she seems genuinely afraid.

Felix nods, staring at his coffee.

"Devon said you've been compensating, that things are much worse," I say. "What did he mean?"

Felix looks up. "Downstream showed these objects as lost, and if that happens naturally, then the damage is usually minimal. But that's not the case here. These objects were triggered and the events wasted, which means the damage is worse." He takes a sip of coffee. If I had to guess, I would say he's in pain, a form I recognize: guilt. His invention has been tricked into outputting the wrong information.

"Time offers change events," Iris explains, for my benefit. "It wants us to complete missions successfully. Occasionally, though, objects disappear from the timeline. This is usually a natural occurrence. For example, many focus objects were lost during World War II bombings. You would think that this would have a catastrophic effect on the future. But time is clever. It recalibrates, finds a new way to heal. But when a mission is squandered like this, the damage is worse than if we lost it or never even tried."

Felix lets out a long breath. "Losing an object is bad, but failing a mission causes irreparable damage to the Future Change Index."

I'm slowly getting my head around the problem. "Gabrielle mentioned the Index. It's how you measure the impact of the changes, right?"

"Exactly," Iris says. "Every time you complete a mission, it has a positive impact. Consequently, a failure is negative."

"But how do you decide what's positive or negative?"

"A good question," Felix says. "The FCI is our own metric, a way of tracking the health of time, along with our progress." He pauses, rubbing his hand thoughtfully over his stubbled chin. "Have you ever traded on the stock market?" I tell him I haven't. He waves it off. "There are various ways of analyzing and tracking them. Markets go up and down, sometimes in the green, sometimes in the red. Volatility is normal, but nobody ever wants them to crash completely."

"So, the fact that these missions were triggered and wasted adds a load of negative points to the Index?" I ask.

"Yes, unfortunately," Iris says. "That's what Devon is working on now, removing our compensation. The Index was already hanging in the balance, and we're about to find out how bad the situation really is. The biggest difference between the FCI and something like a stock market is that if the FCI crashes fully, it won't ever come back."

"And what happens then?" I ask.

Felix glances at Iris. An understanding passes between them, but I can't ascertain what it means. The silence builds, neither of them wanting to be the one to tell me. My mind cycles through various doomsday scenarios, fueled by all the movies and books I've consumed about the end of the world. Nuclear war, viruses, zombie outbreaks, global warming . . . Why do we love these stories? Is it a way of facing our fears? Do we watch them to learn how to avoid these awful scenarios? I don't know, but I've seen my fair share, so my imagination is rampant.

Iris stares out the window, her back to me. "Resistance, attraction, objects, and change events," she says quietly. "The immune system evolved for a reason." She turns to face me, her expression fearful. "It's protection."

"Protection against what?"

"A dark future," she says, her voice uncharacteristically cold. "There's a decade when the dominoes of humanity's story crash into themselves, one after another, and it all comes to an end."

That sends a chill through me because this isn't guesswork, a hyperbolic prediction, or scaremongering. The Continuum exists in the future, peering over the edge of an abyss that feels comfortably far from where I come from.

The words forming in my mind are dramatic and over-the-top, but I can't help myself. With a steady voice, I ask, "Are you telling me that the world comes to an end?"

Iris looks at me kindly and shakes her head. "Not the world, Joe. Our place within it. If we don't succeed in healing time, then humankind's story ends."

I can't deny that a very small part of me wonders how bad it would be for the planet if we weren't here anymore. Was Gabrielle right when she said there wasn't much hope for us?

As though she can read my mind, Iris offers me a pensive smile. "We believe that humankind is worth saving, that we have great potential to do good. I don't say this from an egotistical perspective, but because we give the universe meaning, Joseph. We observe, and our story has yet to blossom. Our potential is . . . untapped." Her voice is imbued with a rare passion. "We must alter our destiny. In its own way, time knows this, and that's why it created the immune system."

Humankind's place in the universe.

It rings a distant bell. Perhaps a documentary I saw about the impossibly slim chance of intelligent life existing anywhere in the universe, and it raises some big questions. Are we alone? Does scarcity make us important? After everything I've just been told, there's one word that comes back again: *potential.*

Iris glances at Felix, seeming to weigh things up. "We need to talk about Scarlett," she says.

"I know," Felix says. "Kyoko should be here too."

Iris moves her hand over the center of the table. An interface materializes, thin lines of light that appear solid. She taps the air, and Kyoko's head and shoulders fade into view, projected into the center of the room along with the fringed outline of trees and surrounding gardens.

"Hello, Miss Mendell," Kyoko says.

Iris bows her head. "Kyoko-san. We have a situation here and would appreciate your wisdom and input. I'm with Felix and Joseph Bridgeman. Would you be able to join us?"

"Of course," Kyoko says.

"We can establish full presence, if that's OK with you."

Kyoko nods, and the keyboard and projection disappear.

Iris turns to me. "Kyoko isn't on the grounds, but she can join us in physical form, the same way we brought you here. So please, don't be alarmed."

Felix watches me, a faint smile in his eyes. "You will like this."

A circular hole about three inches in diameter appears in the far wall, the opening of a tunnel. Part of me expects Kyoko to be delivered through it like a squashed torpedo. At this point, nothing would surprise me. A thin tray slides out a few feet. On it is a graphite sphere, seated in a cradle. I hear it first, a faint but deeply resonant buzzing. The sphere lifts and hovers for a second before flying to the corner of the room, its buzz growing in intensity. The hole in the wall closes as the ball bursts into a swarming mass of microscopic fragments. My mouth hangs open as the tiny dots begin to move together in tightly choreographed swirling shapes, like a great murmuration of starlings at dusk. It's hard to identify the exact point at which the dark cloud transforms into a recognizable shape because it occurs so quickly. One minute it's a techy mass of flying weirdness, the next it's Kyoko Kojima, standing before me.

Kyoko is an elderly Japanese lady, small in frame and stature. Iris described her as *the watchmaker*, whatever that entails. She was heavily involved in planning and building a triterbium lantern that enabled me to pull Nils from the Paris opera house back into the present. She's dressed in sandals and multiple layers of floral-patterned clothing. A cream-colored dress flows from her neckline down to her ankles. A thick chocolate-colored obi wraps around her waist and over a blue shawl comprised of multiple folds of silk that cut pleasant angles. She bows gracefully. "Joseph-san," she says, her Japanese accent pronounced and pleasant. "It's good to see you again."

I have no idea of the proper etiquette, but I bow in return. "You too, Kyoko-san."

She folds her gnarled hands loosely in front of her and listens as Iris explains what we've discovered. Emil Zanak. Extempero. The squandered focus objects. Kyoko rarely betrays feelings or emotions, but her jaw tightens when Scarlett is mentioned. "How does Scarlett know where the focus objects are located, and where they lead?" she asks. "She has no access to Downstream. This information is secure." She looks at Felix with concern. "How is she doing this?"

"I have no idea." A flash of frustration burns over his face. "We've been so careful."

Iris shakes her head. "We have to presume it's coming from inside The Continuum."

"Location services?" Felix asks.

"We must consider every possibility."

"What does Scarlett want?" I ask. "Why is she so against what you're trying to do?"

Kyoko and Felix both look at Iris. "Scarlett never bought into the concept of an immune system. She never liked the rules, always felt we should be doing more."

"If she wanted to do more," Kyoko says, "why is she wasting the change events now? It makes no sense."

"Whatever she's up to," Felix says, "this isn't just about time-travel tourism. We need to figure out how Extempero ties in with Nils and what happened in Paris."

I think of my recent conversation with Bill. He made me promise I wouldn't say anything, but that's getting harder by the minute.

With a frown, Iris says, "Shouldn't our priority be to stop her?"

"We need to find her first," Felix says.

Iris looks at Kyoko. "Do you have an update on Project Slipstream?"

Kyoko nods and turns to me. "Scarlett travels in the wake of other travelers. Project Slipstream is a scanner. Our hope is not only to track her movements but also to study her jump history."

"Is it working?" Iris asks.

"I'm afraid the answer to that question is complicated," Kyoko says. "The wake scanner is operational, but in order to locate and track Scarlett's movements, we need to capture her unique travel signature."

Felix slowly paces the room. "So Scarlett can attach herself to the wake of any traveler in any time zone. When she travels, we can't see her. She remains undetected. For the scanner to work, we need to capture her signature, but to do that we need to know which traveler she's going to attach herself to, and when."

"Precisely," Kyoko says.

"But guessing her movements is futile." Felix lets out a frustrated laugh. "And she isn't exactly going to tell us, is she?" He looks at Iris, frustrated, but then finds a faint smile. "I'm sorry, it's just driving me mad that we can't see what she's doing."

Iris's expression darkens. "I'm just glad Bill wasn't here to see the damage she's done. It would break his heart, and Scarlett already did a pretty good job of that."

Felix cocks his head slightly, as though listening. "Devon wants to join us, says it's important."

Iris looks unsure, The Continuum's leak clearly playing on her mind, but then reluctantly agrees. A shape materializes in front of the window. Dancing shards of luminescent blue form into the glassy outline of a man fringed with impossible dark light. The image resolves, solidifying in color and depth, into the lifelike figure of Devon Campbell.

With Kyoko in the room, the difference between true presence and a hologram is more apparent. Although still incredibly realistic, Devon has a faint glow about him. His dark skin shimmers as he moves, occasionally revealing a translucent quality. He takes in the room, his eyes burning with excitement.

"What is it?" Felix asks.

"I'm sorry to interrupt," he says, "but you need to see this. Can you bring up the on-chain analysis of Joseph's recent mission?"

Felix walks to the table and swipes his hand over the center. An interactive panel appears, and he gets to work. The lights dim, and a now familiar constellation of stars fills the center of the room. Felix drags and manipulates the past, zooming in and highlighting two dark-red orbs—the focus object and the change event—connected by an arc of glittering light. He turns to me. "This is your mission to China, a mono jump. The red indicates that the mission failed."

A fresh wave of guilt washes over me.

Devon moves to Felix's side. "I captured this a few minutes ago." He rotates a circular dial, and the past begins to animate. A second trail of luminescent energy shoots out from the glowing red orb of my failed mission. It streaks across the dark sea of time and then explodes in a brilliant flash of white. What's left—connected to my failure by a burning rope of light—is a perfect green orb. Gentle waves of light ripple from its edges as it slowly rotates.

Iris's voice trembles. "Please tell me that's what I think it is."

"I checked and double-checked before I came to you," Devon says. His face, reflected in the glow, breaks into a smile so wide it sends a shiver of gooseflesh over the back of my neck. "It's a quantum chain."

The tension in the room breaks. Felix and Devon grin at each other, then begin to laugh. I half expect them to dance around like prospectors who just struck gold. Iris looks relieved, wiping a single tear from her cheek. Even Kyoko seems happy. Poor old me has no idea what's going on.

When the fervor dies down, Kyoko takes pity on me. "A quantum chain is extremely rare, an example of time recalibrating and trying to help us."

"It's a specific immune response," Felix adds, still grinning. "There's no way of predicting one, but occasionally when a mission fails, a quantum mission is born." He turns to Iris. "This gives us a chance to pull it back, a potential silver lining."

Iris wipes at her eyes and composes herself. "There is no doubt this is an amazing opportunity, but it's crucial to remember that a quantum chain is also a multiplier."

"A multiplier?" I ask.

Iris nods. "As Kyoko said, this opportunity is twinned with the failure of the Tang dynasty mission. It's a chance, but the stakes are higher. Success means that the Future Change Index will be strengthened, perhaps even more so than the Tang dynasty mission alone could have accomplished. However, failure can damage with the same intensity."

"Double or quits," I murmur.

"A good analogy." Felix taps the green orb, and a panel appears, filled with data. He and Devon pore over the information. "A quantum chain is unique. The observer effect and resistance haven't hardened yet. We have a very small window of opportunity."

Kyoko studies the projection. "Do we have a focus object?"

Devon shakes his head. "Not yet, but the flare point is narrow, so the window of opportunity will be small."

"How small?" Iris asks.

"Hard to say, could be a week from the original bonding with the horse."

"Same epoch?"

"Yes," Devon confirms, explaining to me that this new quantum mission is directly connected to the Tang dynasty jump, which means that the focus object will need to be activated in the same local time period—or *epoch* as they called it—as the horse.

My present.

Iris folds her arms, concern etched over her face. Felix asks what's troubling her. "As soon as the focus object location is known to us," she says, "we have to presume that Scarlett will also have that information."

"Do we try and turn that into an opportunity, trap her maybe?" Devon asks.

"We catch her, and then what?" Kyoko asks. "Hold her

captive? Is that who we are now?" Her expression is grave but not judgmental.

Devon looks down, blinking. "You're right, Kyoko, of course."

My mind crackles, connecting unseen dots into the germ of an idea. "Wait a minute," I murmur. "Kyoko was just saying that to get the tracker working, she needed to know exactly when Scarlett was going to jump."

Kyoko's intrigued expression suggests that she knows where I'm going with this.

My voice and confidence build as the idea takes shape. "You find out where the focus object is, you allow that information to leak, and when the traveler activates the mission, Scarlett follows, allowing you to capture her jump signature. That could work, right?"

Kyoko's thin lips break into a rare, if somewhat faint, smile. "Ingenious, Joe-san. It could work, yes."

Iris considers this, unblinking. "We have no guarantees that Scarlett will follow."

"She will," Felix says, his voice resigned. "You said it yourself, the stakes are higher. She will want to see us fail. She won't be able to help herself. Information is already leaking. Presuming that we deliberately avoid tightening our security, then as soon as we know the location of the focus object, she will know too. And she'll bite."

I've often felt like a spare part, whether it was trailing Gabrielle across Paris or in conversations like this. I'm always out of my depth and far from my comfort zone. And yet I feel like I might have helped here. A spark that began with me has unlocked a quantum mission. An opportunity born of failure. A chance to put things right.

"I'll go," I say.

Iris, Felix, Kyoko, and Devon all look at me with expressions of surprise.

"Joseph, you don't have to do this," Iris says. "China wasn't your fault."

"You can say that, but I want to make up for what happened. I want to try and pull things back if I can."

"There are significant differences that you need to understand before you commit," Felix says. "Quantum missions are an anomaly. The same principles of bonding apply, but the levels of attraction and resistance are heightened. We have very little information before the jump. We won't know what the mission is, where it will take you, or how many jumps you might get."

I smile at him and shrug. "So what's new?"

For the first time since I met The Continuum, we laugh in the face of adversity together, as a team. It feels good.

Felix draws in a long breath. "Bill was right about you, Joe. You're brave."

In my mind, Bill stands beside me, bathed in the green light of the display. I recall his happiness when he found me in the jail cell in China, his bravery and determination when we jumped from the roof of that pagoda. Bill didn't hesitate to do what needed to be done, and neither will I. "I don't know about being brave," I reply, my voice calm and assured, "but the quantum mission only happened because of me. It's linked to my failure, and that means it's linked to me. This is mine."

PART 5

21

After returning to the present, I check out of my hotel in Montenegro and catch the next available flight home. Upon arrival, it takes me a while to settle. Reality feels a little thin and untrustworthy. I'm fully expecting an evening of insomnia, so I'm relieved when my body shuts down the Bridgeman CPU for the night.

After a good night's sleep, I'm feeling unusually refreshed, and I'm down in the shop by just after 7 a.m. For the first time in ages, Molly has taken a day off, and she left me a surprisingly long list of jobs that need doing, the first of which is polishing the brassware. What a strange dual life I lead. Mad to mundane, bonkers to boring.

I clean two coal scuttles, an umbrella stand, five sets of horse brasses, and a small brass candlestick. The work is a welcome break, fiddly and smelly, but on the plus side, the pieces look more expensive now, and I line them up at the front of the shop so customers can admire and appreciate the added shine. I wipe the last of the smears off the candlestick and place it proudly on the occasional table to the right of the front door. Molly will be pleased. When I first arrived here after saving Amy, I thought

Molly worked for me, but honestly, it feels like it's the other way around. I don't mind, though. I've hardly been here recently, and a bit of cleaning is literally the least I can do.

The day passes quietly, with just a few regulars and a smattering of tourists. By the time the evening comes around, my recent time traveling has that strange, distant quality, as though I watched it in a film rather than living through it myself. I prepare a meal, and with my concoction bubbling away, I head out to my balcony, cold beer in hand. It's near dark, the sky an angry bruise. I sip my beer and watch the clouds scudding across the sky, feeling grateful that I returned home safely.

My phone buzzes. A text from Gabrielle, her longest yet.

Call me.

When I do, her voice explodes in my ear. She sounds genuinely happy, which is disconcerting. "Good news, GB!"

"GB . . . er, as in Great Britain?"

"Golden Balls, you idiot." She sighs. "Anyway, good news. The focus object for the quantum mission has been located. It's stateside. Guess who got the job?"

"SB?"

She pauses. "It's *Something* Bitch, right?"

"Sarcastic," I say, as sarcastically as possible.

"That works!" She laughs, and that sets me off, playing one-upmanship with Gabrielle is fun. "It's a long drive, but I'm going to pick it up now. As soon as I have it, Iris will let you know and arrange delivery."

"That's awesome. Do you know much about the object?"

"Nada." She's quiet for a few seconds, and when she speaks again, her voice is unusually kind, like a kid's in a horror movie. It doesn't sound right. "Listen, Joe. Iris told me you stepped up and offered to do this mission, but you don't have to, you know."

"Yeah, I know."

"It wasn't your fault."

"Yeah, it was."

Her tone is gentle. "I'm just saying, if you change your mind, no one is going to blame you."

"Wait a minute," I say, "you're worried I'm going to mess it up!"

"Of course, and also . . . I want to do it."

"I knew it," I say, smiling.

"Right, I'm heading out . . . so . . ."

"OK, take it easy."

"I prefer taking it good and hard." She hangs up.

Gabrielle *has* to have the last word. I vow that the next time we speak on the phone, I'm going to hang up the minute she asks me a question.

Even Gabrielle's smutty humor can't ruin my appetite. As I stir a huge pan of goodness, I decide to call Vinny. We have so much to catch up on, and it feels wrong that the big man is so out of the loop. I opt for a video call.

"Vin! How are you, mate?"

"Hiya, Cash," he says, his voice oddly lackluster. He rubs his face, looks tired.

I switch to the rear-facing camera on my phone and show him the huge pan of bubbling chili con carne. "I made it just how you told me, four squares of dark chocolate and a teaspoon of Marmite."

I'm poised, waiting for my *lovely jubbly* like a dog waits for a treat.

It doesn't come. Instead Vinny groans. "Showing me that is bloody torture."

Vinny is always my pick-me-up. Whenever I'm feeling blue, he's there to help me see the world in a more positive light, so his response wobbles me. I'm hoping his mood might improve when I blow his mind with my latest adventure. "Vin, there is so much to tell you, good news and some bad."

"No bad news," Vinny says. "I can't take it." He rubs his mouth, and I hear the rasp of his stubble.

"Are you all right, mate?" I ask. "I'm a bit worried about you."

He stares at me. "It's not all about you, you know."

"Yeah, I know that."

"Did you even remember that I'm on holiday?"

Wincing, I admit that I didn't. Now I feel terrible. He presses his lips together and squeezes his eyes shut for a moment. Then he speaks in a hushed tone. "This place isn't what I thought it was, Cash. This holiday is a bit of a nightmare."

"I thought you were heading off on an all-inclusive luxury package to Portugal."

"Well yeah, but Muggins here didn't ask what the all-inclusive included. I assumed it would be beer, pizza, ice cream, your basic food groups, but no. It's an all-inclusive"—he swallows—"juice cleanse."

"Yikes," I say. "That does not sound good."

Vinny shakes his head, and for a second I think he might be about to cry. "I haven't eaten solid food in days, Cash. My body's gone into shock. I can't feel my fingers or toes, my head's splitting, and my guts . . . Well, they've gone on strike, if you know what I'm saying."

"How are Kassandra and Charlotte getting on?"

"Charlie isn't even here! Kassandra said it wasn't good for someone who's still growing to limit her calories, but then why did she bring me? I'm still growing, Cash. I even told her I get growing pains at night sometimes." He leans in close to the screen, so close that I can see the broken veins on the end of his nose, and lowers his voice. "Can you get me a food package sent over? DPD or UPS or one of those guys? I'll pay you back."

"How long are you going to be there?"

"Three more days," he says forlornly. "Seventy-two hours. Thousands of miserable minutes."

Kassandra must've known that this would be his idea of hell. Credit where it's due, I think Vinny is a little overweight, and I worry about his health, so if I were being kind, I'd say she's trying to help, but this is not the way to do it, and certainly not without his consent. It's deceitful and controlling, and I don't like it. Vinny needs to be happy, with space to be himself, and his girlfriend should not be tricking him into experiences he doesn't want.

It's hard when someone you care about hooks up with someone you don't like, but I need to be careful. After a friend of mine split with his girlfriend, I told him I thought she was a screaming banshee, and then the idiot ended up marrying her anyway. I didn't see him much after that.

"Why didn't Kassandra tell you that it was a juice cleanse?" I ask.

"She said she wanted it to be a surprise."

"Really, though?"

"Yes, really." Vinny frowns. "Why?"

"It's just . . . She knows you love food, right? I mean, have you ever actually asked her to help you lose weight?"

"What are you getting at, Cash?"

"I just think that she should have been honest about this 'holiday,' then you could have made up your own mind."

Vinny's face darkens. "If my girlfriend is generous enough to take me on a surprise holiday to a luxury resort, then that's no one's business but ours."

"Yeah, of course. I'm sorry, it's just—"

"I didn't want to believe her," he says. "I defended you, told her you wouldn't say things like that."

"What are you talking about?" I say, thoroughly confused. "Things like what?"

"She told me what happened in the shop."

I pause, blinking. "I'm sorry, mate, I don't know what you mean."

"She told me how you were rude to her, warned her not to come between us. She means a lot to me, Cash—best thing that's ever happened. I've got a family now. I can't believe you'd say that."

"I didn't, Vinny."

Did I? I mean, I remember marking my territory a little, but she's a bully. I was only standing my ground. I knew Kassandra was bad news, but I thought I could handle her. She's clearly smarter than she looks. She didn't even declare war, she just invaded without warning, and now I need to be very careful. Kassandra's behavior is unhealthy, and Vinny is going to figure that out sooner or later. But he's tired and hangry now, so I probably need to cut him some slack.

"Listen, mate," I say, "maybe Kassandra and I got off on the wrong foot, but I'm sure we can sort it out."

Vinny looks behind him, then back at the screen, a worried expression etched on his face. "I've gotta go, Cash."

"Vinny, wait."

A willowy shadow falls over him, and a sharp voice says, "Vincent, seeing as you missed the lecture, I brought you some wheatgrass. Drink it up now."

Vinny's face freezes as the call disconnects. He disappears from the screen.

First Gabrielle, and now Vinny hangs up on me too.

22

The next couple of days drag along in a malaise. I'm lucky and have nothing to complain about, but this feeling isn't about me. My mind isn't even in the present. It's busy trawling through the past and imagining a terribly sad future, the one Iris described as a dark decade when several key moments in humankind's story all crash into each other. Not the end of the world, just our place within it.

The Continuum talks of healing time, making small changes that can have a huge impact further down the line. The idea appealed to me, immediately. But failure means the end of our story. No more chances to go back and fix anything.

This growing sense of helplessness makes me miss Vinny even more. I've texted him a few times, and he's replied, but his words are terse and distant. Our falling-out doesn't feel like a big deal, but I need to be mindful. Hairline cracks can grow into canyons if you let them. Vinny has a daughter now, and that means Kassandra might be a permanent fixture in his life. I need to make it work, somehow.

Amy calls late, bubbling with stories of her travels. Ironically, she was in Scotland. Little does she know that in the future, that's where The Continuum's base will be. Maybe she's drawn there? Who knows, but she's having a good time, the paintbrush is moving freely, and she sounds expansive and happy. I didn't allow my feelings for Extempero to tarnish my chat with Amy. She tells me she loves me. It's good to know that whatever happens, some things can't be changed.

My old friend insomnia comes knocking, so I head to my den, set my superclever lights to warm yellow, and settle in with some vinyl goodness. I work my way through the Fab Four's early work but then decide it's time for a little *Magical Mystery Tour*. I'm not surprised when, halfway through the opening song, I'm interrupted by my silver hunter buzzing against my chest. It's a call, an impossible connection: the future, now. I lift the needle from the spinning vinyl and check my watch's display. Text moves across the screen—*The Continuum*—along with buttons asking whether I accept or reject the call.

Right now, the idea of rejecting the future appeals, but I click Accept, of course.

"Joseph, it's Felix."

"Hi, Felix."

"I apologize," he says. "Finding a suitable window for the connection can be tricky. I don't get to decide the hour. I know it's late for you."

"It's fine," I tell him with a shrug. "I wasn't sleeping anyway."

"Oh, why is that?"

I decide to be honest. "The whole Extempero thing. It's playing on my mind, I guess."

"Me too." He's quiet for a moment. "I was wondering if we could talk . . . It's about Bill."

"Of course," I say, sharpening up.

"Good. I can bring you here, use full presence, if that would be all right?"

"Yes, just give me a second."

I lift my silver hunter over my neck, press and rotate the winder, and then place it facedown on my coffee table. As I click open the rear plate, it thrums with silent energy.

"OK, I have you," Felix says. "Just relax, you'll be here in no time."

Instead of the little glowing cameras, I'm treated to another mesmerizing fireworks display, each pulse of spinning, multicolored light disconnecting my mind from my current surroundings and lulling me into a hypnotic state. Dust particles pause in the air, the vinyl on my deck grinds to an almost imperceptible spin. My breathing slows, and the present fades away.

Unlike holographic VR, which sort of paints a new environment over the original, this full-presence VR is more like waking inside a dream. I can't quite remember how I arrived, the precise moment I slipped into the illusion. Did I close my eyes? I can't say. And yet, here I am. It's the closest thing to time travel that I've experienced. I suppose, in a way, it is time travel.

My present is now the future.

Blinking, I adjust to my new environment, a bright glass-paneled room. It's spacious, about the size of a tennis court, and filled with a variety of trees, plants, and shrubs. Above me, an indistinguishable white canvas bathes me in crisp white light. In the center of the room is a large metallic tube. Water cascades down its edges. The air feels purified and pleasantly cool.

Felix stands in front of me, dressed in loose-fitting linen and a thin over jacket that almost reaches his knees. Unlike the last time I saw him, he seems rested and calm. His mid-length hair is swept back over his head, and he's clean-shaven. Around his neck are several pendants and necklaces. Dressed like this, he gives off a New Age kind of vibe.

To my right, a small shelf retreats into a circular hole in the wall. On it is a cradle holding millions of tiny nanoballs— my name for them—compressed into a sphere and delivered through a system of hidden tunnels. The hole twists, like water down a drain, and then disappears. The wall is white and shiny again, with no edges to suggest the tunnel that was just there.

"You're managing the presence transition well," Felix says.

"It's amazing what you get used to," I tell him, glancing around. "Where are we?"

"This is my home," he replies. "Thank you for agreeing to come here. Let me show you around."

We leave the peaceful, if a little sterile, garden and walk into a long tunnel. The floor is stone, polished to a perfect sheen. The tunnel is lit by warm, unseen bulbs. Felix walks beside me.

"Where are we exactly?" I ask him.

He tilts his head in thought. "Currently, we're beneath Greystone House."

"We're underground?"

"Yes. In the early stages of construction, Downstream needed to be kept cool. I expanded the area so I could live down here during that phase and . . . well, I just stayed. I like it down here. It's peaceful. I can concentrate on my work."

We pass through a circular door into a spacious, open-plan living area. I'm slowly getting used to the differences in the architecture, the clever use of hidden lighting and curves rather than straight edges. Leather seating areas are dotted around, and there appear to be a couple of dedicated workspaces. It's hard to tell, as there aren't any screens or computers or the usual signs of a present-day working environment. In the corner is a small kitchen that looks reassuringly familiar, apart from a few superfuturistic appliances. The floor is a polished mosaic of warm wood, and paintings adorn the walls, mainly landscapes of the Scottish Highlands. Through glass doors is another atrium, filled with plants. It's familiar in terms of style, chic and understated. The space feels lived in, calm and peaceful. Having been a hermit myself, I can see the attraction. Greystone House is a bustling, intense place, and I get the impression that Felix might be on or off, with very little in between. Or perhaps always on, but on his terms. In the center of the room sits a circular glass table. Above it a projected hologram of the space-time continuum rotates slowly.

Felix turns to me. "We have much to discuss, but I wanted to show you something first."

We walk across the room and stand in front of the holographic display. He waves a hand over the center of the table, and the image is replaced by a detailed photograph of Felix, Bill, and Iris, much younger than I've seen them. They stand proudly around a machine that wouldn't look out of place in a factory in my present. It's roughly the size of a car and is built of metal plating, tubes, and glass. At its center is a familiar dome, inside a projection of the space-time continuum. Felix leans on the table, a pained smile on his face. "This was my first prototype of Downstream. It was a good day. We had been fighting for so long, almost lost hope. But then, a breakthrough."

I study the holographic display, imagining a time when The Continuum was smaller, uncertain of its purpose. They look proud, optimistic. Felix has a hand on Bill's shoulder. It hits me that a considerable amount of their lives has been spent together, within this organization.

Felix studies me. "I told you that Downstream was an accident, didn't I?"

"You said you were trying to build a time machine."

"My brilliant failure, so much more than I could ever have

imagined." His eyes glow as he considers his invention. "It enabled us not only to study and change time but also to find other travelers. That is Downstream's unexpected gift." He spins the photograph, zooming in. "Bill was the first traveler I found, here in the future. Iris arrived shortly after." He frowns, shakes his head, and for a while doesn't speak. Eventually, in a quiet voice, he says, "He is sorely missed, by all of us. He was here from the beginning, but it's not just the role he played. Bill was a good person. The Continuum made sense with him here." He turns to me, his eyes glassy. "It's not until people go that you realize all the good they were doing. How crucial they were to your purpose, your life, your well-being. I took him for granted."

I'm not sure what to say. I offer a brief smile, because I think I understand how he feels. I don't know what they went through, but I understand loss and regret.

Felix brings his hands together, and the image disappears. With quiet efficiency he gesticulates a complex sequence, and a section of time appears, a dark cloud pricked with multicolored stars. He pushes his hands into it, traveling deeper, until more details become apparent. "What we're seeing here are different eras in history." A few clusters light up in a sequence as Felix talks. "Here are World War I and World War II. Over here, the Black Death, and the Renaissance." He zooms in further. "Major events, all with unique signatures, unique data. The French Revolution, American independence, the discovery of antibiotics." His voice grows stronger and more excited as he moves through time. A section of the map clouds over in dark red, swarming with activity, like a thousand angry flies around a lamp.

"What's that?" I ask.

"The observer effect," says Felix quietly. "Resistance." Orbs of green appear within the red swarm, like irradiated diamonds. "And those are change events. This is where we work, in the shadows, the small unseen opportunities for change." He turns to me, his voice laced with pride. "It's quite magnificent, isn't it?"

"Yes," I say, mesmerized. As I gaze at these rare jewels—each one an object with a secret, each with the potential to change a life—I feel their power.

Felix pauses, pensive. "Tell me, have you heard of the Fermi paradox?"

Relieved to have at least a clue about this, I tell him that I have. "It's the idea that intelligent life could exist elsewhere in the universe, but the chances of finding it are minuscule."

"Exactly."

"Wait, you're not about to tell me that aliens exist, are you?"

He leans his head back and laughs. "No, but do you know why the chance of meeting intelligent life is so unlikely?"

I think for a second, wanting to get it right. "Because the chance of another civilization existing at the same time as us is just . . . so unlikely."

He bobs his head. "Consider Earth's beaches. For every grain of sand, there are ten thousand stars. If only one percent of those stars could support life, it means there have been millions of intelligent civilizations." His eyes narrow as he peers at the projection of time, pushing through cobwebs of light, zooming out to reveal numerous constellations. With a swipe of his hand, he highlights a section. Multiple blue dots light up. "These are travelers, like you, hundreds of them, dotted across time. Each exists within an epoch. Think of it as a zone or pocket of time. They are rare, Joe. Special. The Fermi paradox sums up The Continuum's greatest challenge. Reach and distance. Connecting with travelers." He rotates the display, and with another swipe of his hand, the dark nebula fills with a scattering of colored orbs.

"What are they?" I ask.

"Potential," he murmurs. "New travelers who have completed their first tethered jump."

"Tethered? What does that mean?"

"Travelers who are strong enough to break the bonds of their own timelines; they are unleashed, they become part of the immune system. It's survival of the fittest, I suppose you could say. This is how they appear in Downstream, their destinies yet to be decided."

As I stare at the kaleidoscope of potential recruits, I think about my first jump and saving Amy. I was tethered to my own timeline, but now I've been set free. Each of those sparkling orbs is a person, their latent ability revealed and unlocked.

Felix watches me processing all this. "Bill started out as a traveler, just like you, but then one day, he was drawn spontaneously to another traveler, and that was just the beginning. Bill was able to join these dots in a way we thought impossible, and once the connection was made, we could communicate, organize. He was the one who found and recruited every traveler who is part of The Continuum today." A deep frown etches his forehead. "Bill was the glue, our connection through time. No one else is or has ever been drawn to new recruits like he was. We all miss him, terribly . . . but from a purely practical perspective, how do we reach them now?" He eyes the holographic display, runs his fingers through his hair. "We hoped that Bill might have reached enough of them, but new ones appear all the time. New change events too. The immune system constantly adapts. Bill was our only recruiter, and without him, all these travelers will be adrift, alone and without purpose."

I turn to him. "You just said the immune system adapts, that Bill started traveling spontaneously. Maybe someone else will fill the void?"

Felix manages a thin smile. "Maybe, we can but hope."

He sinks his hands slowly into the center of the display and draws them out until the swirling mass is a complex universe of twinkling lights. "I can spend hours analyzing a single pulse," he says, gesturing at the display. "Devon thinks I'm losing it, but I'm convinced I can see symmetry in the shapes, secrets in the code. I hope you're right, Joe, that time will find a way to adapt." He looks out through the glass doors over his garden, his slice of organized nature. "Downstream and The Continuum are my family. I've given my *life* to this." He glances at me, looking suddenly embarrassed. "Sorry, I'm not complaining. I did it willingly, but I can't see it fail, not now."

"I understand," I tell him.

"I know you do. Thank you." He smiles, but it's brief, and his expression shifts quickly to one of deep concern. "And now we have a new threat: Scarlett."

I think back over our conversations. "You told me that Scarlett didn't like the rules, hated the fact that most of the past can't be changed." He nods but doesn't speak. "You told me Scarlett wanted to fix everything: famine, disasters, wars. So why waste these missions? Why set up Extempero and just squander the objects? That doesn't sound like someone who wants to do more."

Felix shows his palms, and his frustration is obvious. "I don't know, but this is why I wanted to talk to you." His lips form into a thin line. "I have a theory." He presses his forefingers to his temples and breathes quietly for a few seconds. "I believe that whatever Scarlett is doing, it's connected to what happened in Paris, but also the Romano mission. It's why I asked you here. I think this all links back to you."

"Me? Why?"

"I told you there were anomalies in the data from Bill's jump to London. The speed of Bill's movement, the number of jumps. The more I study it, the more connections I see. Romano, Bill saving you, wiping the data from his watch." He studies me as though I'm now the puzzle to be figured out. "Why would he do that?" There's another pause, this one longer.

I remember Felix wanting to know the details of Bill's death. It seemed harsh at the time, but I know what it's like to have someone disappear, the need for details about what happened to them, so you can process, grieve if necessary. Is all this uncertainty driving Felix to the wrong conclusions? Is he seeing connections that aren't there?

With a frustrated swipe, he kills the display, walks to the window, and looks out over his garden. "Paris," he says. "Scarlett altering Nils's watch, wiping the data, just like Bill did." He grits his teeth, almost snarling in frustration. "It's all connected, and now someone is sneaking around The Continuum, accessing Downstream, stealing our data, sharing it with Scarlett. Bill and Scarlett *both* covering their tracks." He shakes his head in tiny motions. "It's driving me mad." His pain is evident, and it's frustrating for me too, not knowing how to help. When Felix speaks again, his voice is flat, resigned. "I know Bill. He was up to something. What was he messing with?" He turns to me, eyes pleading. "Joe, if you know anything, please tell me. What was he doing? What was he planning, did he tell you? I have to know, because what he achieved is impossible."

Frowning, I murmur, "I have to know how he did it."

"Sorry?"

I said it before I could think, but it's too late now. "One of Scarlett's thoughts bled through in a viewing I had when she was tampering with Nils's watch in Macau. 'I have to know how he did it.'"

Felix blinks, deep in thought. "She wants to know how who did it? Is she trying to emulate what Bill did?" He sighs heavily.

"Please, Joe, if Bill told you any details of what he did that night in London, you must tell me."

My mind shoots back to Bill, sitting by the fire, telling me that he was messing with forces he knew he shouldn't, sneaking around, not telling his colleagues what he was up to. He made me promise not to tell anyone, but how can I keep this to myself? The people Bill has left behind are in pain.

Felix observes me silently. I draw a deep breath, knowing that what I'm about to say matters, that it could send possibilities crashing through numerous timelines, like heavy hail through a thin glass roof. "If I tell you, you must promise me that you won't pursue this."

"How can I promise?" Felix says, without judgment. "I will do whatever it takes to keep The Continuum safe, you understand that?"

"I do, but what I'm going to tell you is supposed to reassure you. If it does that, if we can focus on stopping Scarlett, you must promise not to change the past, to undo what Bill achieved. It's important, Felix. Bill believed that The Continuum's timeline and my existence depends on it."

He considers this and then bobs his head in reluctant agreement.

I draw in a slow breath. "I can only tell you what I know, but I think the person sneaking around behind your back was Bill."

"What was he doing?"

"Saving me," I say.

Felix frowns. "Yes, we know that. You became Bill's mission. Downstream showed us your fate, but Bill had a second jump, and he saved you. He successfully completed his mission."

"I think that's what Bill wanted you to believe, but he failed, and the change event closed."

"No," Felix says quickly. "That's not right."

"I don't know how, but he figured out a way to reenter the change event, beat resistance, and save me."

"It's impossible." His gaze darts around and eventually find me again. "He told you this?"

"Yes."

"When?"

I explain how Bill arrived during my Tang dynasty mission and saved me by dragging me into the future. The real complication was the fact that Bill had been drawn to China during the late planning stages of saving me in London.

"Poor Bill," Felix says with a heavy sigh. "Why didn't he tell me?"

"He was worried you would try and stop him."

"Stop him from saving you?"

"No, from breaking the rules."

"The rules," Felix repeats, clearly disheartened. I can see his mind actively processing this new information. "It makes sense, I suppose. The only person who would know how to hide this from me is Bill." He sharpens his gaze back onto me, his expression blooming with fresh concern. "And you think Scarlett's trying to emulate what Bill achieved, to somehow beat resistance?"

"Maybe, but Bill said he was going to double his efforts, be extra careful, and cover his tracks."

"But that doesn't work, does it?" Felix snaps, voice suddenly jagged with anger. "We're still in this mess. His secret isn't safe. We may have to go back in time and find that data, destroy it."

I'm already doubting whether I've played this right, but I couldn't leave Felix not knowing. "Obviously, I'm no expert," I tell him, "but I don't think changing the past is the answer. I told you because I wanted to give you closure. Bill broke the rules to save me. He knew it was dangerous, that he was messing with a power he shouldn't have. Right now, I think we should focus on Scarlett, on stopping her."

Felix bows his head. "You're right, of course. I just wish the silly old fool had talked to me." After a pause, he adds, "Thank you for telling me. I can assure you I understand how critical it is to maintain the timeline, but it helps me to understand his sacrifice. I will keep this information to myself, but it's incredibly useful."

"I'm sorry I didn't tell you before."

He shakes his head. "You're in a difficult position here, and for what it's worth, I would have done the same."

"Really?"

"Yes."

I think about the auction, the boat, the lavish lifestyles of the rich and privileged, all the focus objects they've wasted. How do you deal with people who care more about their own immediate gratification than they do about the future?

Felix's chest rises and falls. "I'm afraid, whilst there are genuinely good people in this world, some things never change, and there will always be people who are selfish and think only of themselves and their needs."

The thought saddens me because Felix gets it. He knows you can't negotiate with people like Emil Zanak or Scarlett. They take, they consume, and they don't care about the cost. The only way to deal with people like that is to stop them.

I just wish I knew how.

A small bell chimes, a pleasant sound. Felix holds up a hand. He blinks, then his eyes move up and to the left. I've seen this before, his attention focusing on an unseen communication. "Are you positive?" he asks. He listens, nods, and then turns his attention back to me.

"What is it?" I ask.

He smiles faintly. "There's someone who wants to see you." He glances over my shoulder. I turn, and a sizeable sheet of glass, previously opaque, reveals an enclosed garden beyond. Standing there, among lush green trees, is an elderly woman with long gray hair. She bears a striking resemblance to my mother, but it takes me a while to join the various strands of my life together before I realize, in a flush of excited panic, that it's Amy.

23

A doorway reveals itself in the wall next to the window. Felix waits, doesn't speak. Part of me wants to ask him what I should do, how I should handle this, but why am I afraid of the years that exist between me and Amy? She's my sister, and I'm finally going to meet the version of her that spends her time here in the future.

As I approach the door, it rolls silently open. With my heart beating and my mouth dry, I pass into a small domed area with a bench and various plants and trees. Glowing shafts of warm yellow light filter through the leaves. A gentle, seemingly natural breeze carries the babbling sound of running water.

Amy stands by a fountain. Her style is familiar, flowing layers of linen, but the tones are more muted. Blacks and grays beneath a warm cashmere jacket that almost reaches her knees. I wonder how I'm going to do this. Ever since Amy sent me her letter from the future, I knew that I would meet her one day. I also knew I was never going to be ready.

She smiles, and all the years and concerns melt away. I soak in her serene beauty, all that she has become. I would guess she's in her late sixties, perhaps early seventies. Up until a few months ago, Amy was forever seven years old in my memories. In my present, she is in her thirties, and now she alternates between those ages in my fragile mind: a young girl becoming a woman in the dawn of her middle-age, and now this, decades gone in a flash. It threatens to send me into a spin, but I hold on to one simple fact, a reassurance. I saved her when she was seven, and Amy lived this long. It's a guarantee that most of us never receive about our loved ones.

Her long wavy hair is pure white at the roots. It cascades down over her shoulders, deepening to a slate gray. Her face is timeworn, her skin pale, etched with lines and freckles. She wears no makeup but glows with a healthy radiance. Time has done its work, but Amy has gracefully allowed it. She looks amazing. Her distinctive green eyes observe me patiently. The familiar wisdom is there, cannot be defined by age.

She smiles again. "It's good to see you, Joe." Her voice is different, softened by age.

"It's good to see you too," I tell her. "You look beautiful."

Her expression is one she often pulled when she was younger and thought I might be lying. A playful grin laced with suspicion. It sits comfortably on her face at any age.

"You're probably wondering why we haven't done this sooner," she says. "I've been wanting to talk to you, but I knew I had to wait."

"For what?"

She considers me thoughtfully. "For you to be ready. It's quite an adjustment," she says quietly, "for us both. Bill prepared you for this, in a way, taught you that lives and relationships can be relative."

Bill talked of friendships in reverse, about how we build on our experiences. Amy and I share a comfortable silence for a few seconds, listening to the gentle and calming sound of water running down sheets of steel at the edges of the room. With each passing second, I relearn the contours and differences in my sister's appearance. A half smile crosses her lips. "I'm sure you have a lot of questions."

I grin back. "You know me too well."

She's right, of course. I have hundreds. What happens to me? To our parents? When and how did they die? Is Amy married? Does she have someone special? Did she ever have kids? Did I, for that matter? As I attempt to sort them, I'm surprised to discover that I don't want to know the answers. I want to find out naturally because that's part of the magic of life. We crave certainty, yet the not knowing is part of the fun. Life should be a journey of discovery, so I decide to keep it simple.

"How often do you come here?"

"Initially it was only once or twice a year, but as time moved on, I was drawn here more frequently. Now I choose to come. I can control my traveling, just like you said I would, all those years ago."

The image of my seven-year-old sister, shivering beside a lake, flashes through my mind. That was back when I hoped Amy might learn to stop time traveling. How things have changed.

"How long do you stay?"

She ponders this. "Again, that's changed over the years. I used to spend just a few hours here, but gradually the duration of my visits increased. Now I can sometimes stay for weeks."

"Weeks? Is that . . . OK?"

Her forehead furrows. She seems almost surprised by my question. "Do you ever feel like you were born into the wrong era?"

I think of my adventures with Vinny in the 1960s. "Sometimes, I suppose I do, yeah."

"I feel as though I belong here, at time's arrow. I have friends, colleagues. I spend more time in the future now than I do in our present."

Her lengthening stays remind me of my elastic-band theory. When I first began traveling, the farther back in time I went, the *less* time I would get to spend there. I wonder if it's similar for Amy, but in reverse? The more she travels to the future, the longer she stays?

"Why are you drawn here?" I ask her.

"Because I'm needed. I can be useful." Amy explains that her role in the future is to teach and guide other travelers to use their gifts. She did this with me during my Paris and London missions, so I have some experience of what it's like when Amy has your back. I'm proud of her. She's continued to develop her gifts. She tells me that she still paints, still sees the future. "I have a team of students," she says. "They are good people."

I think back to the young girl, always trying to help others. The light of the Bridgeman family made people feel better, and I bet she's doing that now. Life tries to change us, but seeing Amy like this makes me realize that all we need to do is be ourselves.

"When did you first travel here?" I ask.

"I have vague memories of traveling here when I was very young, seven or eight years old. I visited Greystone House at various points in The Continuum's history, but then there was no traveling for many years. I was dormant, I suppose you could say. My traveling here began in earnest when I was in my early thirties." She looks at me thoughtfully.

"Early thirties," I murmur.

"Yes. For you, that's soon, isn't it? Relatively speaking."

I nod. "A few months maybe. What caused you to start traveling again?"

Her eyes grow distant. "There is one specific moment in time, a key event." Her eyes gleam with secrets. "That's why I wanted to see you today. I want to show you something."

We walk through a smooth archway of light into a vast circular room. Amy moves differently, slower, a little labored, but also gracefully. The walls are darker here and give the impression of being formed from a single piece of wood, as though the room itself was drilled through the center of an ancient oak. The floor is tiled. Our footfalls echo.

Above us, an impossible sky, bright and pale blue. I lift my head, feeling a pleasant and familiar warmth on my skin.

"It's a virtual sun," Amy says with a smile. "Felix spends a lot of time down here, needs to get his vitamin D somehow. The air is also infused with vitamins and minerals. He told me once that it's about the healthiest place you can be."

In the center of the room, suspended at eye level by an unseen force, is an impressive artwork encased in a thick slab of resin. It must be twenty feet wide and lit to accentuate a kaleidoscope of colored glass ground so fine it sparkles and shimmers with the slightest movement of my head. We stand in silence as I pore over the details. The colors form a central shape, an unusual sweeping arc, that tapers like a soundwave. Flashes of color dance, cones of red, green, and blue reaching like hands across an ocean of possibility. It's mesmerizing, magnificent in its beauty and creativity, and evokes strong feelings, like all good art should.

Amy watches me, calm, peaceful.

I turn to her. "You made this, didn't you?"

She nods and considers her work thoughtfully, without pride. "When I began this piece, I didn't know what I was doing. I didn't realize it would end up so big and complex, and I certainly never intended for it to become revered like this."

"I can see why it's displayed, though. It's incredible."

"Thank you," she says easily, without ego, but also with no hint of the self-deprecating Amy from my present. "I've always used my art to process and express my experiences. I created this because I wanted to celebrate not only an important turning point in The Continuum's history but also a very formative event in my life."

She points out a plaque at the base of the work.

The Extrapolation Event—2112

"What's the Extrapolation Event?" I ask.

She places a hand against the glass, touching it tenderly. "It was nineteen years ago. Iris, Felix, and Bill had formed The Continuum. They had a prototype of Downstream. They could see focus objects and travelers, but they couldn't reach them. They didn't know why this had been shown to them or what to do with the information. They were losing hope. After years of struggle, they were about to give up." She turns to me, her eyes shimmering with emotion, her mind deep in the past. "Imagine, The Continuum, so close to disbanding . . . but then our stories came together. I was drawn here. I was thirty-two when I arrived . . . and something magical took place. My arrival created a breakthrough, which gave much-needed direction to The Continuum. The future and the past finally joining as one. The Extrapolation Event marks the day The Continuum found its purpose. My presence here, on that day, solidified our values, brought us together, gave us a unified goal."

I frown, processing this information. Each time I've visited The Continuum, it's been the year 2131, just like today. Iris described it as time's arrow, said there was nothing beyond. I hadn't really considered the history between my present and now.

Amy takes my hand, her skin cool, her expression pensive. When she speaks her voice is warm but wavering with emotion. "You and I are responsible for all of this, from a certain perspective . . . It all started with you."

"Me?"

"You saved me . . . My destiny was forged on the side of that lake, interwoven with The Continuum's story. Without you, I would never have arrived here at such a crucial juncture." She smiles warmly and waits for me to hold her gaze, her eyes shimmering with emotion. "I'm the fourth founding member of The Continuum, Joe. The Continuum we know now was really born on that day."

She watches me as though grading my reaction. I get the impression she's trying to guess whether I knew some of this. I didn't, but it makes sense. The chain of events that led to this moment solidifies in my mind. Simple ideas join and complexity arises. If I hadn't saved Amy all those years ago, W. P. Brown would never have arrived in my shop. The Continuum would have given up . . . It wouldn't even exist. Everything is connected, paradoxical loops forming a chain.

"You see how important it is that I arrived here in 2112," Amy says.

"Yes, although I don't fully understand what happened when you did."

"I can't tell you the details, because we mustn't risk the timeline being altered."

"I understand," I assure her.

Her expression darkens.

"What is it?"

"I wanted to tell you because I fear this event may be in jeopardy."

"What do you mean?"

"I have been working with my team, studying timelines, a different approach to what Felix can see with Downstream. It's less accurate—speculative—but what we've seen is deeply troubling. It's possible that key moments in our history are being strategically altered in the past. Joe, we must be vigilant. The past shapes our future, but it's shrouded in secrets and lies, becoming less clear by the day."

"Scarlett?"

"Maybe, but it's more than that. If it is her, she isn't working alone. There are multiple attacks. Specific changes. I fear that we may lose all of this. That's why I risked telling you about the Extrapolation Event."

"What can I do?"

"In your present, it's nearly time for me to travel to 2112. I traveled here alone, completed the Extrapolation Event, and set The Continuum on its course, but if that gets changed . . . if I don't make the trip for some reason, then you need to find me."

"And do what?"

"What you always do. Take care of me."

"I need more, Amy."

"If my journey is threatened, help me make the leap . . . I can't say more than that. We must trust that time has a plan, that this may all be part of the Great Unfolding."

"Bill talked about this. Iris too. What is the Great Unfolding?"

"It's time's plan for us, a way through the darkness, to become what we can be and reach our full potential. It's how things *should* be and *will* be, *if* The Continuum plays its part. That's why we cannot lose the Extrapolation Event. It's all connected."

My own connection with Amy, here and now, suddenly feels closer than my connection to her younger self. It's a strange feeling, a form of unusual betrayal. It weighs heavy on me.

"It's hard, isn't it?" she says. "To navigate."

"Yes."

"Eventually, we both learn to cope. I think of it like a river. The direction of flow is important, but it's all water."

I smile. I know what she means. "So what happens now?"

"We carry on."

"Will I see you again?"

"Yes, our connection is strong. Our timelines cross over many decades and ages." She pauses, breathing, considering. "I can't tell you much more, but I will tell you this: You set wheels in motion when you saved me. I then played my role in unlocking The Continuum's purpose. But this is as much about you as it is about me."

"What do you mean?"

Her voice takes on a distant, breathy quality. "I protect the future, and you heal the past. Your destiny is to lead, Joe, to be an inspiration to others."

I sigh. "You seem so sure."

"I've seen it," she says, "You are a great time traveler, and you lead by example. People trust you, respond to you."

I feel the years that Amy's spent here, watching me. I'm overcome with a claustrophobic sense of my life being already written. It chills and excites me in equal measure. A leader? Me? Christ, I can hardly get my own life in order.

Amy shivers.

"Are you cold?" I ask.

"No, I'm traveling soon," she explains. "You should get back to Felix."

"You aren't coming with me?"

She shakes her head. "I've been here for nearly a week now. I was heading back to the present but felt drawn to you, today specifically. I trust those feelings."

"Do I tell the younger you about this?"

She smiles, but only briefly.

"I don't, do I?"

"Not yet. Soon. And Joe, keep this conversation between us. You are the only one I trust."

"What about Iris and Felix? Are you saying they could be involved?"

"It's doubtful, but until we know how Scarlett is getting her information, we should be cautious. For now, the fewer people who know, the better."

"OK," I say, a little reluctantly.

We hug. She feels warm but frail. When we part, she begins to shimmer, her skin sparkling as though made of starlight. "Goodbye, Joe. I'll see you again soon."

I watch Amy fade, a ghost from my future, and I'm overcome with loss. I remind myself that she's alive, that all is well, but her words haunt me. Someone is tampering with the history of The Continuum. Amy talked of the Great Unfolding, but it sounds more like the Great Undoing to me.

In a kind of daze, I walk back through the garden and into the room where I left Felix. A hologram of Iris's upper torso floats in the center of the table beside him. They both acknowledge me.

Felix offers me an almost fatherly smile. "How did it go?"

"Good. I think."

"It must be quite an adjustment, seeing Amy," Iris says.

"Yes, but it's a relief, too, to finally connect with her here." I don't elaborate, and the air grows thick. I think of Amy, the fourth founding member of The Continuum, telling me to keep her concerns and our conversation private, of Bill and Felix, secrets and lies. In an organization like this, if you lose trust, tiny cracks can grow into canyons that are eventually impossible to traverse.

Iris breaks the silence. "I have an update from Gabrielle. It's not good news, I'm afraid. She was on her way to pick up the quantum focus object. We had a rough location. It had been there for years, but then it disappeared."

Felix visibly sinks in his frame, his expression tired. "Scarlett," he murmurs.

"We should assume so."

Felix straightens, focusing. "Devon ran another pulse through Downstream earlier."

"I know," Iris says, "I just spoke to him."

"Don't tell me," Felix replies, "the focus object is registering as destroyed."

Iris shakes her head. "It's showing as missing."

"Probably only a matter of time," Felix says.

"I agree," Iris says. "We should assume that Extempero now has the object, that it will soon be squandered like the others."

I realize now how naïve I was to think I could stop Zanak, that I could teach him the true meaning of his traveling. He's with Scarlett, he knows about The Continuum, knows exactly what he's doing, and just doesn't care. You can't negotiate or reason with people if they don't share your values. Are they the ones trying to undo all of this? What is their endgame?

"I didn't see this coming," I say, needing to say something.

Iris waves off the notion. "This isn't your fault."

"Devon and I need to work on this," Felix says. "I'm heading to the Observatorium."

"What can I do?" I ask.

"We will keep in touch," Iris says. "If we hear anything, I'll let you know."

24

How do you go on living your life, knowing that the very future of mankind is in jeopardy? Knowing that your sister's destiny is to give The Continuum its purpose, but the very people whose job it is to keep the future safe might get erased in your sleep? Knowing that precious focus objects are being squandered? Not to mention that, apparently, I'm going to be an inspirational leader one day.

"Sheesh madeesh," as Vinny would say. It's too much. Luckily, I am a black belt in compartmentalization. The future weighs heavily on my mind, but there are people who matter to me here, in the present. I'm desperate not to mess things up with Alexia. Meeting Gabrielle and Felix has expanded my world, but their situation is also a warning. They are so dedicated to their work that they've ended up alone and seem to have accepted that as a reasonable cost of getting the job done.

I'm not willing to make that sacrifice. I want a life as well as a vocation. That's not too much to ask, is it? Alexia and I have made progress, and I want to continue that. So a few days after my meeting with Felix, I meet Alexia for dinner at Dialogue.

"That's your table, over there," says the waitress, a gratingly confident teenager with a nose piercing and no discernible sense of customer service. "I'll come over in a bit for your drinks order." She pulls out her phone and types with two thumbs, at impressive speed, tutting audibly.

Despite the lukewarm welcome, Dialogue is a very stylish restaurant that seats only a couple dozen people. Its walls are painted in a dusty gray-blue and dotted with gold-colored lamps. The tables are lime-washed oak, and the chairs are all different designs painted the same shade of cream. My table is right inside the little bay window, separated from the rest of the restaurant by a small aisle, so I feel like I'm in a fish tank. A movement from across the street catches my eye, and I look up to see Alexia waving. I wave back, butterflies fluttering beneath my ribs. She is radiant. Her hair is loose, and she's dressed in a cream-colored silky top, cropped navy trousers, and high heels, with a caramel leather jacket slung around her shoulders. I swallow with difficulty, realizing my mouth is dry, and call to the waitress for a jug of water. She arrives with it just as Alexia walks in, and the two of them do an awkward maneuver around each other as Alexia takes a seat opposite me.

"Sorry I'm late. I had a last-minute wardrobe malfunction," she says. "The zip broke on my black trousers, so I had to change."

"You're not late," I say, admiring the way her hair curves at the top of her shoulders. "And you look lovely."

"Thanks. You're looking pretty swish yourself."

The waitress brings over the menus, and once we've ordered a selection of tapas and a bottle of Malbec, I finally relax. I ask Alexia about her day, how she's getting on in her new office. She asks about the shop. After we've exchanged niceties, there's a pause, and we each take a mouthful of food to fill the space.

"This is weird," she says.

"What is?"

She pauses, chewing. "My head knows you and I have dated before, but my heart is telling me it's new, and that's odd. You've changed so much. I mean, don't get me wrong, I think the changes are actually good, but if I need to go slower than you're expecting, that's why."

"I'm fine with that," I say. "And I think your heart is right. This is new. The way I see it? You and me, in this timeline, we're starting from scratch."

She swallows. "'In this timeline'? Are you talking about parallel universes again?"

I flush. I didn't mean to use that phrase out loud, but this is our third version of events. Old Alexia and I got close before I saved Amy; then Other Joe and this Alexia dated, although he screwed that up; and now here we are, this Alexia and me, starting out fresh once again. It's funny, though. As we get to know each other better and create new memories together, the edges are blurring between the different versions of my life. Where Alexia and I are concerned, I think our hearts would connect in any situation, any era. The separation of Sayana and her Chinese lover flashes through my mind, and I feel a rush of gratitude that Alexia and I have another chance together. Do I deserve this, though? When I failed the mission, did I let Sayana down?

"What are you thinking about?" Alexia says. "You're miles away."

I want to tell her I'm a time traveler, that she helped me save Amy. I want to share with her how I'm feeling, the craziness of Amsterdam and Montenegro, my insane trip to China. But Alexia and I are rebuilding, mending the damage that Other Joe did, and I'm loving every second of it. If we ever get out of first gear, I'm going to tell her the truth, all of it, but right now I don't want to risk derailing our progress. I just want to live the dream a little longer.

"I was just thinking about my sister, Amy," I say, images of her in the future blending with the younger version who sat at my piano not so long ago and played "Chopsticks." "She's gone off on a road trip for a while, and we haven't spoken in a few days. It doesn't seem to matter how old she gets, she'll always be my little sister, and I worry about her sometimes. Silly, isn't it?"

"Not at all." Alexia puts down her fork and studies my face. "What?"

"This isn't like you, sharing your life, telling me how you feel."

"Sorry."

"It's not a criticism." She passes me the plate of *patatas bravas*, and I help myself. "I like it."

The rest of the meal passes in a merry blur, and I'm disappointed when we come to the end of our evening together. We stand outside the restaurant, both a little uncertain.

"Thank you for a lovely evening," Alexia says.

"It was my pleasure."

"I had a great time."

"So did I."

She takes a microstep toward me, her eyes locked onto mine. I lean toward her and, very slowly, with infinite tenderness, kiss her cheek, breathing in the sweet, musky fragrance of her, sensing the warmth and softness of her skin.

As I pull back, she says, "I was wondering . . . Do you need to rush off?"

"I'm in no hurry," I say, with studied nonchalance. "What are you thinking?"

"Would you like to come back to my place for coffee?"

"I would love to." I try not to jig like a leprechaun as we walk the street together, side by side.

When we get to Alexia's place, I'm relieved. It's the same house we worked in together to save Amy. It's impossible to know for sure how far the ripples extend when you alter your timeline, and I'm glad that the seismic shifts in my life didn't affect where Alexia lives. We head inside, and Alexia pauses in front of the kitchen door. I hear snuffling and scratching on the other side.

"Jack," I say, smiling.

Alexia tuts. "Oh, so you remember the dog!"

"Yeah," I say. "Amnesia can be random like that."

"Why don't you wait here? I'll put him in the conservatory."

"You don't need to. I'd like to see him."

Alexia looks at me dubiously. "You two don't get along." She means Other Joe, and I smile. Dogs tend to be good judges of character. "He bit you, left a scar, there on your hand." She points at my right hand, then takes it in hers, studying it. "Hmmm. That has healed remarkably well," she murmurs. "Anyway, probably not a good idea."

I place my hand on the doorknob. "Let's see what happens."

"I really don't want to go to the hospital tonight," Alexia sighs.

"We won't."

It's a relief when Jack scuffles his way across the floor to me, first sniffing my shoes and then jumping up and trying to lick my face. He's just as I remember, a gray scruffy lurcher with a black nose and eyes that peer right into your soul. He works his way around my legs, tail thrashing. After some fuss, he rolls onto his back, legs in the air. Total submission.

Alexia laughs. "Isn't that the turnaround of the century?"

I smile back at her, thinking how right she is.

Alexia makes coffee, then fills Jack's water bowl. He drinks noisily, then drips water all over the floor. We leave him in the kitchen and head to the sitting room.

"Have a seat," Alexia says, indicating the low velvet sofa.

She sits next to me, plunges the cafetière, and hands me a cup of black coffee. She takes a sip of hers. "When I invited you back, I had ulterior motives."

That sends my heart racing. It's unavoidable. My face flushes red.

"Oh God!" she says hastily. "Sorry! I meant I was thinking it could be fun to try a bit of psychometry together. Are you up for it? No pressure, though, only if you fancy it. We could always do it another time."

I laugh. "Sure, why not."

She goes to the cabinet in the corner of the room, pulls five or six books off the shelf, then sits in the armchair at one end of the coffee table and spreads the books out in front of me.

"Ta-dah!" she says. "Here are my psycho books. I've been studying these for weeks now. They're all interesting, but this is the one." She picks up Joseph Buchanan's *Manual of Psychometry*. "I've read it cover to cover probably three times now. I don't really understand how it all works, but I know that theory only takes you so far. I've always found the best way is to practice."

"It is." I think back to the early days, when I used to hold Amy's toys and envision her playing with them, to those anguished hours when I would clutch Amy's hair ribbon and beg it to tell me what had happened to her. As I've become more used to my gifts, I've become more confident using psychometry in my shop and on missions, but it was only recently, in Paris, that Gabrielle showed me that it was possible to read the psychometry of buildings.

That sends me back to China, hands pressed against the

Chang'an city wall. It's a reminder of the fact that the focus object for the quantum chain mission is missing, a crushing loss of potential. I will soon hear from The Continuum, and the object will probably register as destroyed, but we know what that really means now. It will have been squandered, its story and all the potential benefits wasted. I picture the members of Extempero, gathering for yet another celebratory photograph, clinking glasses of champagne, talking of their incredible and unique adventures.

"There," Alexia says, snapping me out of my daze. She studies me. "That's what I was talking about earlier. You sort of drift off, lost in your own world." She shrugs. "Perhaps it's the curse of the therapist: I see things when I wish I didn't."

That makes two of us.

She regards me with empathetic eyes. "Look, you can tell me that it's none of my business, but my gut tells me that whatever you're thinking about, it's troubling you. You can talk to me, you know. If you want to."

Our faces just a few inches apart. I feel the timelines tugging at the fabric of our relationship, threatening to pull us apart. I open my mouth to speak, convinced that the truth will come pouring out, but after a few seconds, I close it again and stare at the floor.

"I'm worried," she says.

"Worried?"

"I had a really nice evening," she says, her voice pensive. "I feel like I'm getting to know you, the real you. But you put on this . . . mask, and it's scary. I'm worried you're going to change back to how you were, or maybe into someone else."

Now *I'm* worried. Instinctively, I reach out to take her hand, but she pulls away.

She breathes deeply. "I need to know if I can trust you, Joe."

"You can," I tell her, knowing that I'm about to pull the pin on the time-travel grenade. I really don't have any choice. "We need to talk," I tell her. "Can I just use your bathroom first?"

"Of course," she says, looking somewhat relieved that I'm lowering my guard.

She directs me to the bathroom, one floor up, second door on the right. When I reach the top of the stairs, I glance down the hallway and notice her bedroom door ajar. I imagine spending time in this house together, building, growing. Sunlight pouring through the windows, filling us up, warm and expansive. I enter the bathroom, close the door, and eyeball myself in the mirror.

"Right, listen up, Bridgeman," I say to myself. "This is it. You did it once before, and she took it well. You go downstairs, and you tell her everything." I pause. Well, maybe not everything. I shouldn't tell Alexia that we've already fallen in love in a timeline that has since been erased. "No, that wouldn't really get us anywhere," I murmur. "But anyway, it's happening now. Go down there and spill the beans, all of them, and then live with the consequences."

I flush the toilet and run the tap, ensuring that Alexia hears and knows that I'm a good boy, clean and tidy. As I descend the stairs, my heart rate increases with each step. My lips are dry, my head is pounding. *Be brave*, I tell myself and walk into the room.

Alexia appears to be upset already. Her cheeks are flushed, her jaw set.

"What's wrong?" I ask.

She swallows, and when she speaks, her voice trembles slightly. "I think it's time you told me what's really going on."

"Absolutely," I say. "I was just telling myself the same thing."

She remains seated, her gaze fierce. "I've known for a while that there was something you weren't telling me."

"There is, and I—"

"Just hang on a minute," she says, pointing at me. "I want you to really think about what you're about to say. This is your last chance to tell me the truth."

"Right," I say, really confused now.

"Well?" Alexia says, her voice pricked with anger.

I take a steadying breath and begin. "I'm part of an organization known as The Continuum. We help people."

"What are you talking about?"

I blink a few times. "You asked me to explain, I was just telling you—"

"No." Her expression cools, grows stony. "I want you to explain *this*."

She holds up her phone, displaying a photograph of me and Gabrielle at the rooftop bar in Amsterdam. From this angle it appears we are locked in a passionate embrace. Text beneath it reads, *Isn't this your boyfriend?* It's followed by the emoji that evokes Edvard Munch's painting, *The Scream*.

Yeah, this is bad.

The room spins a little. "I can explain that."

"Oh really?" Alexia laughs bitterly. "Don't tell me, this is yet another relationship you can't remember."

"It's not like that."

"Please tell me that you aren't going to pretend it isn't you."

"No, it's me."

She places the phone on the coffee table and looks up, her eyes swimming. "Are you in love with her?"

I laugh, and instantly regret it. This is Gabrielle we're talking about, and I genuinely couldn't think of anyone worse to fall in love with. "Her name is Gabrielle. She's a colleague. I met her in Amsterdam. She got really drunk, I went to find her, and some guy she was with took that photo. It's not what it looks like. I missed you when I was there. I'm not in love with her!

How could I be when I'm . . ." My words jam in my throat. I decide not to say it, not now.

Alexia folds her arms and leans back, waiting for me to continue. Once I start, I can't stop. I tell her about my psychometry unlocking my ability to time travel, how I was contacted by The Continuum, my recent missions. Alexia stares forward, her eyes glazed. I end up telling her about the Tang dynasty, my failings there, and how we recently lost the focus object.

After a few seconds of silence, I ask, "Are you going to say anything?"

"What do you want from me?" she says, without looking up.

Everything.

All of you.

"I want you to talk to me," I say. "Tell me how you feel about what I just told you."

"I can't figure you out," she says, her head shaking gently. "Your psychometry is amazing, but this is completely different. Do you really expect me to believe this?"

"I know it's hard, but it's the truth."

"You're a time traveler."

"Yes."

She gets up from the sofa and paces back and forth. She finally turns to me, anger simmering in her eyes. "You know what hurts the most? The fact that you would make up a cover story so stupid, so pathetic, so over-the-top, just because you have a bloody girlfriend in Amsterdam! I can't believe I let you back into my life."

In the awkward silence that follows, I hold on to the fact that people only tend to get upset with someone they care about.

"I really think you need help," she says, perhaps trying to reassure herself. "You really believe that there are all these people that work for a futuristic organization, going back in time and completing missions, for . . . What did you call it?"

"The greater good," I say, embarrassed now.

She lets out a solid laugh. "This is the sort of story a ten-year-old would make up, but you're an adult, and you're clearly lying. Why can't you just admit you're having an affair?"

"I'm not having an affair," I say sharply. "I wouldn't do that. All I want is you."

My phone howls in my pocket.

"You should answer it," Alexia says chirpily.

"It's OK. It can wait."

"Is it *her*?"

"I don't know," I tell her honestly, but then I remember that Gabrielle has her own special ringtone.

My phone beeps.

"She left you a message," Alexia says. "Why don't you listen to it? Put it on speaker."

"Alexia, please."

"What are you afraid of?"

I check my phone. The number is unknown. I don't really have much choice. I place the phone on the coffee table, select Voicemail, tap Speaker, and wince when I recognize the voice.

"James?" Kristin says, clearing her throat. "Oh sorry, *Joseph*, I keep forgetting to use your real name." She sounds nervous, breathy. "It's Kristin. I have information. It's important. We need to talk." She hangs up.

Alexia looks hurt. "Who is Kristin?" she asks. "Why did she call you James?"

"Kristin is one of the rich people who came with me to China. She was the winner of the auction I was telling you about."

"How many women do you have on the go? How many lives?"

Now *that* is a question.

"I don't have any women on the go," I say. "And just so you know, Kristin is like seventy years old!"

Things are going badly, but there's a small part of me that's relieved, like I've opened Pandora's box and shaken it all over the place. In comparison to all the secrets, the chaos feels somehow welcome.

"Listen, I know I've been holding back. I know this all sounds impossible, unbelievable, but it's real."

"But, Joe, how do you expect me to believe you?"

"I don't," I tell her. "But if you're willing, then I would eventually like to show you."

"Call her back," Alexia says sharply.

"OK, I'll call her, on speaker. You can listen, but will you let me talk to her, and then you and I can talk afterward?"

Alexia smiles and draws a pretend line across her lips. We all have sides to our personalities, and this is one of Alexia's that I could really do without.

Kristin picks up on the first ring. "Joseph?"

I feel Alexia stiffen but she remains silent.

"Yes, it's me," I reply, "but call me Joe. I got your message. How are you, Kristin?"

"Traveling is amazing. I mean, it was wonderful, right?" Her voice sounds hoarse, as though she's been crying.

"It is, but not the way Extempero does it. You said you had information?"

"I do. I thought a lot about what you said in China. I've been feeling so guilty, Joe. I believe you. I listened to what you said about time travel having meaning, a reason, and it rings true." Her voice cracks a little. "And the more I thought about it, the more I realized that I've been going along with it. Alarm bells were going off, and I just ignored them. Emil is greedy, they all are. They don't care." She pauses, sniffs. "He called a flash auction. He handpicked a few of us, said a new object had arrived, said it was an unexpected opportunity. The price was a joke, eye-watering even for him, but people signed up."

This isn't a huge surprise. We knew that Zanak had hidden the quantum focus object. And now, he's going to waste it, just like all the others.

I hear Kristin sniff again. "I just thought you needed to know."

"Thank you," I say. "I really appreciate it. Do you know when and where the auction is?"

"It was supposed to be tonight," she says, and then really begins to sob.

Alexia leans forward, concerned now.

"Kristin, are you there?"

"Yeah. I hope I've done the right thing."

"What have you done?" I ask, as calmly as I can.

She sniffs again. "I stole it."

"What?"

"I went to see Emil. I took it and I ran."

"You have the focus object?"

"Yes." She speaks quickly, babbling now. "I'm in the UK. I didn't know where you were, so I flew into Heathrow. Am I in danger?"

"No," I tell her. *Maybe.* "Just don't tell anyone else, OK?"

"OK," she says, her voice wavering.

"Where are you?"

"The London Savoy. Room 612."

My mind is scrambling, but I don't hesitate. "Right. Don't call anyone, stay where you are, and I'll be with you in a few hours."

25

"Was that phone call real?" Alexia regards me with a mixture of skepticism and annoyed amusement. "This could all be an elaborate setup to cover your tracks. She sounded like an actress."

"Why would I do that?"

"You tell me."

She folds her arms, and in the frosty silence that follows, I feel the tendrils of all my timelines trying to wind themselves around my throat. Or maybe they're roots that could bring truth and life. I just don't know anymore.

"Alexia, when I saved my sister, it unlocked an ability in me." I don't tell her that in another timeline, she helped.

"What do you mean, you saved your sister?"

This is a can of worms for another day. I decide to change tack. "Think back to when I told you about my psychometry. You didn't believe me, but it was true, wasn't it?"

She scowls. "Your ability with objects is amazing, but it's completely different. You're talking about traveling through time!"

"It's connected," I say with a shrug. "Objects are the link."

Another pause. Long seconds tick by. "You're going to see this Kristin woman now?"

"Yes."

"And what happens then?"

It's a good question. "I will use psychometry to prime the object, and then travel back in time."

"Travel back in time," Alexia repeats sharply. "What, you'll just disappear, will you?"

"Yes."

She stares at me like I'm a madman, which is fair. Sometimes I wonder if I am, but then I see a subtle shift in her expression. Dubious becomes determined. Her eyes snap to mine. "I'm coming with you."

"Alexia, I don't know if that's a good idea."

"Why?" she shoots back. "Because then you'll have to prove it?"

"No, because I don't know if it's safe."

She purses her lips. "If you expect me to believe you, then I need to see it for myself."

The way she's looking at me hurts, but I understand how she feels. She needs to see it with her own eyes. It's the only way to break down this wall between us. Could she be in danger? Maybe, but it's doubtful. As far as I know, the three of us are the only people who know the focus object's location. Even if Kristin is followed, and Zanak is waiting when we arrive, I don't think people will get hurt, not in the present anyway. He wants the object, and I just need to ensure that Alexia stays out of harm's way.

"All right," I tell her, hoping that when this night is over, she'll still want to be with me. "You can come, but we need to go now."

A foreboding sky gives way to a dark rainy evening. At least the roads are clear. I drive in silence for a while. A couple of times, I ask Alexia if she's OK. She nods, staring ahead. I give her space.

Rain patters against the windshield, streetlights flash by.

Alexia asks why Kristin called me James.

"I had a fake persona to get into the auction," I tell her, knowing how lame it sounds.

"Right." She lets out an exasperated sigh. She's angry and upset, and although it's difficult, I think it's a good sign. Anger is often born from the disappointment of someone we trust letting us down. And the only people who can hurt us are the ones we care about.

As I drive, I think about Kristin, the bravery it must have taken for her to steal the focus object. If it weren't for her ingenuity and quick thinking, this would all be over by now. I wonder what the object might be, where it might take me, and that leads my thoughts to The Continuum.

Felix once showed me a huge globe in the atrium of Greystone House. It was a map, the location of all the time travelers. And guess what? I've got a microchip in my head. He could be tracking me right now . . . I could be a little flashing icon on its merry way to London, while The Continuum members scratch their proverbial beards, wondering what I'm doing, what I'm planning.

And I thought Facebook and Amazon were evil.

"What are you thinking about?" Alexia asks as we approach the outskirts of London. She seems to have cooled a little. Maybe she's worn-out with all this loopy time-travel nonsense.

"I'm thinking about the people I work with and the fact they need to know what I'm doing." I glance at her. "They have problems. Someone on the inside is leaking information."

I'm expecting a dry response, but Alexia asks, "What are you going to do?"

"I'm going to talk to them, but I need to be careful. I probably won't tell them everything."

"Yeah." She sighs and focuses back on the road. "You're good at that."

I grip the wheel, frustrated. "I'm sorry, Alexia. There were so many times I wanted to tell you, but we were getting on so well, I didn't want to mess things up between us."

"I think it's a bit late for that."

I let it go, knowing that once she sees me travel, we're going to have a lot to talk about. We ditch the car on the outskirts of London and take a tube to Temple station. It's 9 p.m., and London is busy but not packed. We sit facing each other on the tube. Nobody talks in London, so we fit right in.

The Savoy Hotel overlooks the River Thames, its glowing windows and clean white walls give it the appearance of the world's biggest and most expensive Advent calendar. Near the entrance, a steady stream of gleaming cars circles an impressive fountain. A suited concierge in a top hat whistles and directs traffic, welcoming his guests with a confident smile. Alexia and I head inside. We walk the checkered black floor of the cavernous marble entrance hall, gazing around at the impressive opulence.

In a hushed tone, Alexia says, "If I'd known we were coming somewhere this posh, I would have spent the entire day getting ready."

"You look amazing," I tell her.

She glowers at me, but I'm relieved to see a glint of playfulness.

We exit a mirrored lift on the sixth floor and head to room 612. I tap the door. A few seconds later, Kristin's voice calls out, "Who is it?"

"Joseph Bridgeman."

The door opens. Kristin is as striking as ever in an expensive suit with flared trousers. I can't help but notice her bright-yellow Converse. They shouldn't work with such a stylish outfit, but they really do. She appears relieved to see me, but beneath her immaculate makeup, I notice her puffy eyes. She's clearly been crying. She smiles at me and then looks at Alexia.

"Kristin Meyer," I say, "meet Alexia Finch."

"A pleasure," Kristin says.

Alexia smiles awkwardly.

Kristin ushers us inside and locks the door. As expected, her room is probably the most expensive suite in the hotel. We pass through a marble-floored foyer and emerge into a spacious lounge. It's grand with impressive, modern elegance. Gold-leaf wallpaper, comfortable seating, chandeliers—the works. The view over the River Thames is spectacular. Boats and barges wind their way slowly over the water. Numerous iconic landmarks are visible: the Houses of Parliament, Big Ben, the London Eye.

I'm hoping Alexia might be distracted by the impressive location, but she appears to be scanning the room for hidden cameras.

"I really appreciate you coming," Kristin says, gesturing to a seating area in the middle of the lounge. "Please, make yourselves comfortable."

"I was worried about you," I tell her.

"That's real kind of you," she says, forcing another smile.

It's good to see Kristin again. Under different circumstances, I think we might be friends. I enjoyed my time with her in China. She has a positive energy, but recent events have clearly diminished that. We sit, each of us awkward in our own way.

"It's silly," Kristin begins, "but I was suddenly afraid of Emil, especially after what he did to you in Chang'an." She covers her mouth. "Gosh! Have I gone and put my big foot in it? Does she know?" She glances at Alexia. "I'm sorry, I don't mean to be rude."

Alexia cocks an eyebrow. "Are you asking if I know about time travel?" Her tone is laced with sarcasm.

Kristin lets out a big relieved sigh. "Oh good, you know." She doesn't seem to have picked up on Alexia's sarcasm, or perhaps she's choosing to ignore it.

"I only told Alexia earlier this evening," I say. "She hasn't seen anything yet."

Kristin raises her eyebrows. "Well, before this night is out, you will become a believer." In her country way, she kind of sings the word "believer," like she's on TV, pleading with Alexia to reach out and touch the screen.

"I really want to believe," Alexia says, flashing me a hurtful look. She turns back to Kristin. "Who is the man you're afraid of?"

Kristin draws in a deep breath and gazes out over the Thames. "His name is Emil Zanak, a time traveler like Joe. He uses the special antiques for tourism, though. It's made him rich and powerful. I'm out of the club now, and there's no going back." She glances at me and lets out a sorrowful laugh. "No going back . . . That's kind of a joke."

I lean forward. "The Continuum is a much better club. They are good people, trustworthy. They know the true purpose of time travel and won't let anything bad happen to you. You did the right thing."

Kristin looks down at her hands. "I hope so."

I didn't want her to feel any pressure when we first arrived, but I decide it's time. "Where is the focus object?"

She doesn't look at me.

My heart sinks. "You do have it, right?"

She nods, looking up. "It's here, but I want something in return." Her eyes narrow, and she offers me a tentative smile. "I told you on the phone earlier, I believed what you told me in China. I want to know more about what you do. I need to know I can trust you."

Seems to be the theme of my week.

I explain to Kristin that I'm new to this, but that I will tell her what I know. She listens intently as I explain the basics of time travel, how focus objects link to human stories, small protected pockets of time that we call *change events*. I do my best to explain the immune system, how The Continuum sees the past, healing and fixing where it can.

I feel Alexia's eyes on me the whole time. Her expression is dubious and concerned, as though we're about to burst out laughing, pointing and shouting, *Hahaha! We got you! You believed us!* Mostly, though, she just looks exhausted, like she can no longer find the energy to piece together all this madness.

Kristin notices and takes pity. "I remember when I first learned about time travel," she says, her soothing voice kind and reassuring. "It was a reminder that there is much in this world we don't understand."

"Very true," Alexia agrees. She purses her lips, staring blankly ahead.

Kristin stands and asks Alexia if she would like some tea. "I have a selection. I'm guessing you don't need caffeine."

Alexia stifles a reluctant laugh. "You're right, there. Anything herbal, please."

Kristin turns to me. "Thank you for telling me about The Continuum." Her expression darkens. "I feel terrible. I genuinely didn't know we were doing harm."

"I understand," I tell her. "All that matters now is that you're doing something about it."

She raises her chin. "You're right. I'm glad I'm out of the club."

After serving Alexia's tea, Kristin leaves the room and returns with a familiar metal case.

It's a relief to see it. Since her phone call, the pessimistic side of my personality believed that Kristin might double-cross me. I'm glad I trusted her, though. She genuinely wants to put things right.

Kristin gingerly places the case onto a low wooden table. I wonder if it might have a tracker, but I don't think Extempero was expecting it to go missing.

"Do you want me to open it?" Kristin asks.

"Yes, please." My heart thumps. Being this close means I can feel the object now, like a warm breeze.

She thumbs the latches and lifts the lid.

"Seriously?" Alexia exhales loudly. "That's it?"

Inside, entombed in foam, is the quantum focus object: an original Nintendo Game Boy.

"The poor thing looks like it's had a tough life," Kristin says.

She's right. The D-pad and buttons show some wear, but the tiny screen has a deep, diagonal crack across it. The bulky outer casing is horribly split and dented.

"Do you want to touch it?" Kristin asks.

"Not yet," I say. "Let's leave it in the case for now."

I notice some frayed wires and bent metal attached to the inner edge of the case. "There was a screen," Kristin says. "I thought they might be able to track me, so I ripped it out. Is that OK?"

"Yes," I assure her. "Zanak isn't here, which means they probably don't know where it is. Not until I prime it, anyway."

Alexia looks between the two of us worriedly.

"Do you have any idea where it will take you?" Kristin asks.

"None," I tell her. "All I know is that it's a rare type of quantum mission, born out of my failure in China."

"Oh," she says, frowning.

"What's wrong?"

"You failed the mission."

"Yes."

"Because we wasted the focus object."

"No, because I messed up," I explain. "This new object is a second chance, but The Continuum has very little information. They don't even know where it's going to send me."

"It's connected to the age of the object, right? Like the horse?"

I nod.

"When were these released?" Kristin asks.

In a monotone voice, Alexia says, "Late eighties."

I look up at her.

"My brother had one," she says with a shrug. "Late eighties for sure." She studies the Game Boy. "So how does this work? You touch the object, and your psychometry helps you imagine you're in the past?"

She's fishing for a reasonable resolution to my madness, but I shake my head. "Focus objects charge up with emotional energy, once it's primed and I touch it, then I physically travel back in time."

Alexia has the look of someone who's just stumbled onto the set of *Two Flew Over the Cuckoo's Nest*.

I walk to the window and gaze out over the city, a gleaming sea of stars. "Emil is working with a woman called Scarlett. She was once part of The Continuum. She's the one who's been sourcing the objects, stealing them, but we can't locate her. I've been formulating a plan to help find her, but I can't do it on my own. I have to talk to The Continuum." To Alexia, I say, "This is about to get very real." I lift my silver hunter from around my neck and place it on the bed. "The Continuum is based in the future. I communicate with them using this device."

"It's a pocket watch, Joe."

"Inside is technology they call ICARUS." I spare her the details. "What you're about to see is a hologram of someone who exists in the future."

Alexia folds her arms and smiles. "Sounds great. Please, go ahead."

I ask Kristin to draw the blinds and double-check that the door is locked. When she comes back, the light show starts. A stream of glowing green projectors forms into a shimmering cloud of hypnotic light.

"Wow," Kristin sighs, "it's beautiful."

The shiny bugs head toward the corners of the room like synchronized swimmers, attaching themselves in formation around the ceiling. They flicker silently.

Alexia is pale already.

"Contact Kyoko Kojima," I say.

Text hovers above the bed: *Connection Made, Please Wait.*

After about thirty seconds, I risk looking at Alexia. She's frowning at the fully dimensional text, fascinated. Slowly, she works her gaze around the ceiling, her face reflected green in the glow.

Gradually, Kyoko's compact frame forms. Initially she's a translucent gold statue, but then the color blooms from her center until her solid form resolves and she joins us in the room. She's wearing a long jade kimono. Her hair is scraped back and pinned in place. Her dark eyes scan the three of us and then settle on me. "Hello, Joseph," she says, her voice relaying no emotion.

Alexia's breathing grows heavy. Her cheeks are red. She looks amazed, excited, petrified, like she's just completed her first skydive. "Holy shit," she murmurs. "This is real?"

"It's OK," I tell her, doing my best to sound reassuring. "Kyoko is a colleague of mine." I almost say *friend*, but we aren't there yet. I respect and trust her, though, as much as I can trust anyone right now.

"Where are you, Joseph-san?" Kyoko asks.

"I'm not sure I can tell you that."

"Are you safe?"

"Yes, but I can't take any risks."

As briefly as I can, I explain the situation, filling Kyoko in on Kristin and Alexia and how we all ended up here.

She listens without moving, and when I'm done, she looks at Kristin and says, "You took a risk. Thank you."

"It was the least I could do," Kristin replies quietly.

Kyoko fixes her attention back on me. "Why trust me?"

"Because I need the tracker."

Kyoko's lips set in a thin line. She narrows her eyes. "You have the focus object?"

I bob my head.

"And you're hoping Scarlett will follow?"

"Yes."

Kyoko considers this for a second and bobs her head, once. No fuss, no argument. Free of emotion, she sees my logic. "The tracker is untested," she says, "but if Scarlett follows, it will capture her unique signature. I can update your timepiece remotely."

"Thank you." I let out a long, shuddering breath, only then realizing that I had been holding it. "How long will it take?"

"No more than twenty minutes. You will be alerted when the update is complete."

"How does it work?"

"Her jump signature will automatically be captured. I will assign a map showing her location to a secondary function. A single press of the winding crown will switch from your usual display to the tracker. If her signal is acquired, her geographic location will be displayed. When are you planning to travel?"

It's a good question. I could have waited, moved the object away from Kristin. I could have spoken to The Continuum, planned all of this, taken my time. But that's how things go wrong. That's how we lost it in the first place, and the radio that sent me back to London too. I don't know if Zanak is about to burst through the door, but I know that once I prime the object and travel, then it becomes useless to him, leaving him no reason to track any of us down.

"I want to leave as soon as I can," I tell Kyoko. "I just need to prime the object."

She glances at the open case. "That's it?"

"Yes."

She nods, as though a Nintendo Game Boy is perfectly normal, expected even.

"Joseph-san," she says. "I must share this information with the rest of the team immediately. They must know that you have the object and plan to travel." She's right, of course. Here I am being overly cautious, but we need this information to leak so that Scarlett will follow me. "I will call a meeting and ensure your plans are known," Kyoko says. "All we can do then is hope that Scarlett takes the bait."

"Sounds good."

"You should know, your subsequent jumps may occur in quick succession."

"How do you mean?"

"We only have a small number of quantum missions with which to compare, but the time between each jump was short. Be ready."

"OK, anything else?" I ask, wincing slightly.

"Attraction and resistance will be intensified. Use the enhanced attraction to your advantage, and obey resistance." She slowly bows. "Joseph-san, you continue to impress me. Travel well and good luck." She bows to Kristin and Alexia and then fades away.

And just like that, we are three again. Alexia looks close to tears.

"How are you doing?" I ask.

"I'm OK, all things considered." She half smiles, looking confused and embarrassed. "I'm sorry I didn't believe you."

"How could I expect you to, really?"

She glances at the Game Boy, and then back at me. "You're really going to do this?"

"I am."

Kristin clears her throat. "I'm going to give you two some space. I'll be in the room next door for a while."

She leaves, and Alexia and I stand at the window. The external world is the same, but we both know our lives have just changed forever. I turn to her, hoping . . . praying that she isn't angry.

"I'm not quite sure what to do with this," she says. "How to process what I just saw."

"It takes time," I tell her. "But it's a relief that you finally know."

She frowns, deep in thought. "There's more to this, isn't there? The fact you've changed. Your amnesia, your bike accident. Is that even true?"

"It's all connected. When this is over, we can talk more."

Her face creases in deepening confusion. "Part of me feels like I don't know you at all, but then . . . another part feels like I've known you forever." Her eyes search mine. "Does that make any sense?"

"It does." Way more than she could know. I wonder if there is a silent but powerful force that connects all our experiences together. Spooky action at a distance across the multiverse. And then my mind stops working and my heart takes over. "I'm glad you came," I say. "I'm glad you know, because none of this makes any sense without you. This might sound crazy, it might seem way too fast, but I'm going to say it anyway." I take a step toward her and hold out my hands. She places hers in mine. Quietly, but with conviction, I say, "I love you, Alexia."

She stares at me, her eyes swimming.

"It's OK," I assure her. "I didn't say it because I want you to say it back. I just didn't want to leave without . . ."

She steps toward me, her face just a few inches from mine, and places her head on my shoulder. We hug, and I feel the warmth of her breath on my neck. We stay like this for a few seconds until she pulls away. I'm lost, and then we kiss, slow and sensual, full of tenderness and respect. All our complicated history falls away, and I feel our energy combine and soar up and outward, expansive, brilliant, dancing across the sky. I feel as though I'm finally, *finally* home.

Time travel makes you question reality. It brings a whole new meaning to "living in the now." And in this perfect moment, that's all there is. Love, pain, happiness, and loss.

Everything.

Now.

Slowly, the world comes back. Alexia's body is warm and welcome against mine. We smile, but I see a flash of confusion on her face.

"Are you all right?" I ask. "Was that . . . OK?"

"Yes," she says with a slight frown, "but you've never kissed me like that before."

"Like what?"

"Like it was the first time."

I've been through a lot since I left Alexia on Leckhampton Hill. The journey back to her felt impossible and yet, here we are. There are powers in this world that we don't understand.

Love is one of them.

She kisses me again, and we're holding hands like schoolkids when Kristin returns.

She beams, clasping her hands together. "Well, ain't you two just cute as a button."

We flush with embarrassment, but Alexia's hand remains in mine.

It's the little things.

Kristin's expression shifts. "I've been thinking," she says. "Do you want me to come with you? I don't mean as a tourist, I mean to help you do whatever it is you do."

"It's kind of you, Kristin, but no. It's best that I go alone. I don't know what I'm heading into."

As we wait for my watch to receive its update, the mood shifts, the air brimming with anticipation. Alexia has taken all this remarkably well, like I knew she could. But now the reality is sinking in, for all of us.

I'm leaving, and soon.

I turn to her. "When I bond with the object and travel, it becomes useless. They won't be looking for it anymore."

"How long will you be gone?" Kristin asks.

"I'm not sure. China was much longer than I've been used to. Normally, it's a few hours."

"We'll wait," Alexia says, "however long it takes."

"Thank you." I take Alexia's hand in mine. "Don't answer the door to anyone. Call reception, call security if you need to. Just be safe, OK?"

"Don't worry about me."

"It's a bit late for that," I say. My watch buzzes. I check the screen. "It's an update from Kyoko. The tracker has been installed. I guess I'm ready to go."

I stare at the Game Boy, its faint energy a whisper compared to the horse's. It hasn't been primed yet, but I use one of Kristin's silk scarfs to avoid skin contact and lift the Game Boy from its case. I place it on the coffee table. The three of us position ourselves like witches around a cauldron. I need to cast a spell, but on that front, I'm not exactly an expert. I think back to priming the horse, how I gained its trust. I close my eyes and whisper silent promises. I assure it that I'm here for it, that it can trust me. I feel a minute tremor, like the wings of a tiny moth beating against my palm.

"It's waking up," I murmur. I breathe lightly, all my focus on the Game Boy, but the tremor fades away. Kyoko described a quantum object as delicate. I think I know what she means. "It feels timid, almost scared, like it's locked away."

Alexia takes my hand, and the warmth and softness of her skin give me goosebumps. "Breathe with me. In for four, hold for four, then out for seven. Ready?" I close my eyes and listen to her voice. She speaks slowly, her husky purr reminding me of the very first time I met her. "In, two, three, four . . . Hold, two, three, four . . . Out, two, three, four, five, six, seven."

We breathe in unison like this for a while, I don't know exactly how long, and I feel myself sinking deeper into my sub-conscious mind. Gradually, I feel a connection building, like threads of rope winding and fusing together. Finally, a weak ripple of energy travels through me. Without sound or touch, I hear the drone of a car radio, feel the buttons of the Game Boy clicking.

In the darkness, Alexia's voice asks. "You feel anything?"

"Yes," I tell her, and when I open my eyes, my peripheral vision fades to black and white, though the focus object is deep and rich in color. Blooming digital fractals pulse from it. Steam seems to pour from its edges and tiny speaker vent. It begins to change shape, as though going back in time ahead of me. Its dull plastic brightens. The dings and dents in its casing ease outward, re-forming into sharp edges. The cracked screen re-solves into a pristine, glassy surface.

And then there's the smell: new plastic, the sweet smell of new toys.

"Is anything happening?" Kristin asks.

"Oh yeah," I say, my voice trembling. "It's happening all right."

The focus object crackles with energy. A sharp chime rings out, the digitized chirp of a retro audio chip, and the Game Boy boots up. There's no game cartridge in it, but that doesn't seem to matter. The dot matrix display flashes, dark-green pixels over the olive-green background. The word *Tetris* descends from the top of the screen, jerkily animated. The tiny Start button depresses, and a jarringly happy tune begins to play, a tinny snare drum driving a stylized rendition of *The Nutcracker Suite*.

And then those iconic blocks start to fall. Units of four: squares, bars, L-shaped pieces, and more. They fall and slide into place. Whoever is playing is good, and the bottom third of the screen soon fills into a solid mass of blocks with just a single column's gap.

The buttons glow, telling me it's time to take over. The battery light flashes, slowly at first, then faster and more urgent. It's now or never.

I stare down at my hands, my skin shimmering. I glance at Alexia. A tear rolls down her cheek. But I feel disconnected now. I don't belong here. I'm already on my way.

As I reach out, my fingers tingle with pent-up energy. The Game Boy crackles and fizzes with excitement. I pause, no more than an inch away, and it swells, growing bigger, trying to close the gap.

I look at Alexia again and know, instantly, that I will never forget this.

Her expression says, *You're crazy. You're perfectly sane. You were telling me the truth. I love you too. Please come back to me.*

She tells me all this without words, and my heart swells with happiness.

And then I'm drawn into the past, and I leave her, again.

Traveling to who knows where.

PART 6

26

Our brains are not equipped to cope with replacing reality. My stomach flips. My ears pop. I don't know if it would be better to keep my eyes open, but I doubt it. The backs of my eyelids glow orange. I feel the pleasant warmth of sun on my skin. Slowly, I open my eyes and take in my surroundings.

I've landed in a quiet clearing surrounded by trees. Above me a clear blue sky, leaves swaying gently in a warm breeze. It's peaceful and calm. Late summer, perhaps? As jumps go, it's a good result. Well-trodden tracks cut angles into the side of a hill. My pent-up fears and trepidation become curiosity and an appetite to discover why time has brought me here. I follow one of the trails. The trees whisper in a light breeze, which carries with it the hint of sea salt and the rich aroma of hot dogs and warm rolls. The smell of America, along with the distant sounds of music and the echo of a significant crowd.

I check my watch: *Calibrating.*

As I reach a fork in the path, I physically cross my fingers, hoping that this mission is not another mono, but rather a *normal* time-travel mission, if there is such a thing. I head up the hill and after a couple of minutes reach its peak, a vantage point with an incredible panoramic view. The air is clear and warm, a cyan-blue sky unbroken by clouds. A flash of adrenaline ripples over me as a soak in the iconic vista. A vast expanse of water meets a city, and in the far distance, the unmistakable silhouette of the Golden Gate Bridge.

San Francisco.

My watch vibrates against my chest. No change event, just a date: *October 17, 1989.* It feels familiar for some reason.

I click the dial, as Kyoko told me to do. The layout changes. In the corner of the screen, the words *Wake Scanner Active.* In the center, a pulse moves outward, like a ripple on a pond. I presume it's scanning the area and so far, has nothing to report.

Shielding my eyes, I stare out over San Francisco, allowing myself a brief moment to marvel at the wonder of time travel. The thrumming sound of an excited crowd draws me around the edge of the hill, a nagging memory of the date pecking at me as I walk. I pass through another clearing of trees and emerge on the other side of the hill. From this angle I can still see the Golden Gate Bridge and, below me, a baseball stadium, packed full of fans, a sea of colored T-shirts and caps. The air buzzes with a tangible sense of anticipation. I know absolutely nothing about baseball, but it might be fun to watch a game. A few stragglers run inside the stadium. I could have guessed this was the late 1980s, even from this distance. The cars, the fashion, the hairstyles. Unmistakable. Inside the stadium are massive advertisements for recognizable brands like Coca-Cola and Safeway, along with ads that jar against my present-day sensibilities, like the Marlboro Man with his cowboy hat and cigarette. A huge illuminated sign with big orange letters on a black background reads:

Welcome to Game Three
of the 1989 World Series

Players warm up on the field, which is bright green and mowed into neat stripes. Music plays. I hear the commentators through the PA system, their slick voices whipping the crowd into a frenzy. They obediently clap and cheer. I check my watch: 5:02 p.m.

Time has brought me here for a reason, to witness the end of a story, a chance for change. I wonder what it wants me to see. The wind dies down, deadening the sound from the stadium. An unsettling stillness descends over the world like a blanket, as though Earth itself needs a long, deep breath.

Something catches my eye, an unusually dense flock of birds flies over the stadium, agitated and shrieking. I'm overcome with a primal urge to run, but I have no idea why. The audible swell of the stadium returns, the wind acting as nature's volume dial. Impatient fans pound their feet in the stands, so hard I can feel the vibration all the way up here.

That's when things stop making sense.

Distant thunder fills the air, despite the clear summer day. Trees begin to sway in a sickening rhythm. Dust on the ground dances from side to side, as though God Himself is panning for gold. A throaty rumble builds into a deafening roar, like a jumbo jet taking off beside me. It's everywhere, an all-encompassing din so loud it vibrates the earth.

The sound I heard wasn't fans banging their feet.

It's an earthquake, and I'm right in the middle of it.

A violent vibration sends my teeth rattling in my head like loose screws and turns the hill into a bucking bronco. I steady myself against a nearby tree, but that doesn't help. In fact, it makes it worse. I'm thrown to the ground, watching its surface roll and shimmer in waves. I scream but can't hear myself, the quake loud as a freight train. I'm utterly disoriented. Trees moan and splinter. I lose track of time. All I want is for this terrible sensation to end. When it does finally stop, I'm on my hands and knees. I feel the earth spasm, sending seismic ripples through my body, one after another. And then, finally, an eerie, deafening silence. Tentatively, I get back up, terrified that the quake isn't over, but after a few minutes, the only thing shaking is me. I force myself to take long, deep breaths. Each exhalation comes out in a shuddering effort. An unusual smell permeates the air: dust and oil mixed with minerals, as if the ground had belched ancient peat moss.

Looking out over San Francisco, I'm convinced that I see a ripple of the quake traveling over the landscape, shaking trees and lifting houses like blocks on a graphic equalizer before reaching the shore and dissipating into the ocean. From the coastline I see clouds of dust pluming, and a few smoke trails. I knew the date was niggling at my brain: 1989, the World Series quake. I know very little about it, but I vaguely remember news reports.

"Is this why I'm here?" I murmur. "You expect me to stop this?"

As if answering my question, the sound of a cheering crowd hits me, totally incongruous after the earthquake. The world desaturates, and my attention is drawn to the baseball stadium. Its glowing green pitch and bright-red seating call to me. I remember Kyoko telling me that attraction and resistance will feel stronger on a quantum mission. Time wants me down there, now.

The first pinch of ice travels over the back of my skull. Brain freeze. I'm not going to be here for long. I check my watch, and a countdown begins. Eighteen minutes. Feeling humbled by the power of nature, I slowly work my way down the hill. The path is clear and the descent gradual, but my legs feel weak. The Earth may have returned to its solid self, but I'm not convinced I will ever trust it again.

Signage informs me that the baseball stadium is called Candlestick Park. Is this place about to collapse? I don't think time would bring me here if that were the case. This is my first jump. It wanted me to experience the quake, but now it wants me to see something else. I need to find out as much as I can. No one tries to stop me as I walk through the stadium entrance, via a long tunnel, and emerge into packed stands.

There has been no mass exodus, no stampede for the exits. Quite the opposite. The stadium is buzzing with excitement, people everywhere, some making their way back to their seats. A few appear shocked, but most seem to be in a state of mild euphoria, clapping, cheering, and whistling. A woman next to me holds up a handwritten sign: *That was nothing—wait till the Giants bat!*

I can't help but smile, but she didn't see what I saw. The city, the smoke. I glance around the stadium. There are substantial cracks in some of the walls. A few lights are out. I notice a slab of concrete, about the size of a coffee table, that has fallen from above and landed on a seat. A crowd has gathered around a tall man with a mustache, who is busy telling them that he went to get a hot dog and when he came back, the concrete had stolen his seat.

"You're lucky to be alive," someone calls to him.

We all are, I think.

A nearby man shouts, "We're San Francisco, man! Earthquakes are what we do!" People laugh, raising their fists to the sky in jubilant triumph.

Their defiance is infectious. Even I feel like chest-bumping someone.

The public address system crackles to life again, and the thumping drums and multilayered hand claps of Queen's "We Will Rock You" begin. People stomp and clap along, laughing and singing.

There are no smartphones, no news feeds, no Twitter

disseminating information within seconds. These people have experienced an earthquake, but so far I can't see anyone with a discernible injury. The sky is still blue, the stadium still stands. Today is a World Series game. Life goes on, right?

I hear people asking if the game is going to be canceled, but most are still cheerful, chatting about their incredible shared experience. Some players walk out onto the field in their green-striped uniforms. Some in caps, others rubbing their hands through their hair. The stadium erupts into a cacophony of mixed reactions, some cheering for the players, others waiting for the opposing team to make an appearance.

Instead of waving and accepting the applause, the players wave their hands downward, calming the crowd. Their expressions are shocked and somber. Gradually, a hush descends. I spot a couple of men listening to a boom box. People gather around them, anxious for news. Snippets of information begin to spread. The mood changes, people's hands cover their mouths, stunned eyes gaze out in disbelief.

"The Bay Area has been hit hard."

"The bridge has collapsed."

"People are injured."

"People are dead."

The whole stadium feels like a question. Both teams are on the pitch now, and fans join them. The mood is quiet and respectful, and the gradual building silence is eerie, the unmistakable sound of fear. It's written on every face too. A classic black-and-white police car, its lights strobing, drives slowly into the center of the stadium. If there was any doubt, it's gone now. Today's game isn't going to happen.

A police officer addresses the crowd. The PA system squeals, then he pulls back the microphone and says, "Folks, can I please have your attention?" He pauses for a few seconds but needn't have bothered. All eyes and ears are on him. "It's important now that we don't panic." He holds up a hand. "You do not need to leave in a hurry, but you may want to check on your loved ones. That was a major earthquake. I have reports of serious damage across the Bay Area. I'm afraid I'm also hearing unconfirmed reports of loss of life. Some buildings in the Marina District are on fire, and the upper deck of the Bay Bridge has collapsed onto the lower deck. Again, please do not panic. Leave the stadium in an orderly fashion." People cry out and gasp in shock. The expressions on their faces mirror my own. A few minutes ago, these fans were worried the game might be canceled, but now they realize they are the lucky ones.

We play games on this Earth, but sometimes it plays games with us.

My watch tells me I have four minutes remaining. The last thing anyone needs after such an event is to see a mystery man vanish from the scene. I head back down the stairs, and as I walk through a tunnel, I feel a crushing sense of sorrow. I witnessed a tragic event today, but I was removed from the worst of it. Just a few miles away, people lost their lives. Near the edge of the tunnel, I pause. People are running to the parking lots. There's a long queue for a pay phone. People's attention is everywhere except me—that's good.

I fade from the past and return to my present.

My reality cross-fades like a screen saver. The early evening air of San Francisco is replaced by the sterile air of Kristin's hotel room, with its hint of perfume and jasmine tea. Delayed shock takes a bite out of me, and the ground suddenly feels untrustworthy. It's still moving, sending waves of nausea through me. I feel like I've been on a boat for hours, and even though I'm on dry land, my legs haven't received the message. Alexia and Kristin are at my side, steadying me. Grounding me.

"Are you OK?" Alexia asks.

It's so good to see her. I fight back the stinging pain behind my eyes.

They guide me to a chair. I ask for water. Kristin grabs a bottle from her mini fridge and hands it to me. "That was quick," she says. "I was just telling Alexia we might not see you for days."

I look up at her, confused, but then remember the only experience Kristin has had of time travel was China. Slowly, the room stops spinning and my heart rate settles. Kristin and Alexia wait patiently. Alexia holds my hand.

Finally I'm able to think, and as I fill Kristin and Alexia in on my jump, I'm processing the events myself. Concern is etched on both their faces.

"Now what happens?" Alexia asks.

"We wait," I tell her. "The number of jumps is still unknown, but there will definitely be at least one more."

"How can you be certain?" Kristin asks.

I tap my silver hunter. "A final jump is indicated by a red light on my watch. There wasn't one. It means I will travel again."

"To the earthquake?" Alexia asks, frowning.

I consider this. "Not necessarily, it could be some time before. It depends on what time wants me to do. It showed me the earthquake for a reason."

In the silence that follows, I suspect all three of us are thinking the same. Some events you can alter or even avoid entirely, an earthquake isn't one of them.

Memories of the quake shudder through my brain like aftershocks. It was vicious, scary as hell, a brutal but incredible display of raw power. I drain the small bottle of water, and I'm just about to ask Kristin for another when my watch buzzes against my chest. My hand trembles as I pull it out, just in time to see the word *Updating* disappear from the screen.

A countdown appears.

"Fifteen minutes?" Alexia says, quizzically. "Until what?"

I swallow and look up at her. "My next jump."

27

Kyoko warned me that individual jumps in a quantum mission can occur in rapid succession. Fifteen minutes and I'll be gone again. The clock is ticking. The coppery tang of adrenaline dances over my tongue as I click into action mode.

"Kristin, we're going to need to do some speedy research. Do you have a laptop?" She shakes her head. "An iPad?"

"Yes, let me get it."

Alexia holds up her phone.

"Great." My words arriving in a flurry. "I landed near a baseball stadium, Candlestick Park, but that doesn't mean I will land there this time. In fact, I would say it's unlikely. I witnessed the end of the story, so hopefully I land well before the quake. Whatever happens, I need to know as much as possible about what I'm heading into." I think about the observer effect, how certain events are baked into time. "Focus on smaller stories."

"What sort of thing?" Alexia asks.

"Isolated incidents, human stories that didn't have many witnesses. I need to call Iris."

"Who is Iris?" Alexia asks.

"Iris is the boss."

My research team gets to work, tapping and scrolling in silence. Via the wonders of ICARUS, Iris joins us in the room. She's alone. I introduce her to Alexia and Kristin, who briefly acknowledge her but remain focused on the task. Alexia remains clearly shell-shocked, but the countdown of my impending travel has sharpened her mind, leaving no room to process the impossibility of Iris's arrival.

Iris listens intently as I explain the situation. I have thirteen minutes before I leave. She's as professional as ever, unfazed, calm under pressure. "You acted quickly and decisively," she says. "You primed the object, and you've seen the end of the story. Now you have a chance to complete a quantum mission. For what it's worth, I'm proud of you, Joseph. Felix and Devon are readying another pulse, so we will be able to track your progress."

"What am I supposed to do?" I ask her. "I can't stop an earthquake."

Her cool blue eyes connect with mine across the vast expanse of time. "The change event and increased attraction will guide you," she says. "Let time be your guide. It won't intentionally put you in danger, won't ask you to do anything you aren't capable of." The shadow of a supportive smile crosses her lips. "All you can do is your best."

My thoughts circle back to my jump. "Kyoko's wake scanner didn't alert me. I presume Scarlett didn't follow."

Iris shakes her head. "Your jump will have been a surprise to her. Hopefully now she knows you've activated the focus object and is preparing to follow you on this next jump. If she does turn up, your watch will show her location. But please remember, capturing her signature is a bonus. Your focus should be on the change event and completing the mission."

The events of Paris come flooding back. Scarlett is such a mixed bag of contradictions. "Is she going to try and stop me?"

Iris considers this. "Maybe, but I know Scarlett, and she isn't evil, Joe. If she does follow you, it's not because she wants to harm you. Whatever she's doing, it's because she's lost her way, that's all. I hope that if we can communicate with her, then we may be able to find a way forward."

My imagination kicks into overdrive: the locations, the possibilities. "People die in this earthquake, Iris . . . Can I help them?"

She draws in a slow breath. After a few long seconds, she says. "It's one of the hardest realities for a traveler, to obey the laws of time." Her voice is kind, compassionate. "Resistance, change events, focus objects. It's all natural. Time weaves a delicate path, only it knows what can be done safely. Obey resistance and attraction, and you will be all right." She pauses, seeming to acknowledge the fact that Kristin and Alexia are listening too. "There is so much bad in this world," she says, "a billion wrongs that we wish we could put right. But how can we possibly know the impact of seemingly obvious choices? How do we know whether our interventions might make matters worse? It's a moral dilemma, one that I'm relieved we don't have to face. Time decides. It knows. All we must do is listen and trust."

Although I haven't had much experience, I understand what she is saying. I've felt it myself. Thrown back in time, the weight of many possible futures hanging over me. So many wrongs that could be put right. But what is right? If time has a plan, then I'm glad it's the one in charge, not me.

"It's difficult, jumping into the unknown," Iris continues, "but I will remind you again, just as I did before you jumped to Paris: do what you can, but don't risk your life. Come back safely, and we'll cope with the outcome together."

"I'll do my best."

"I know you will. Safe travels, Joseph, and good luck."

She fades away.

Time is short, but I need a couple of minutes alone to gather my thoughts. I tell Kristin and Alexia that I'm going to the bathroom. They acknowledge me, but their attention remains fixed on their screens.

The bathroom is about the size of a small one-bed flat. Black-and-white marble tiles on every surface. A roll top bath, a huge walk-in shower, and a double sink unit, big as a breakfast bar. I lock the door behind me, splash water on my face, and let out a jagged breath. Fear sets my muscles twitching, my own little aftershocks as my mind plays through the quake, its sheer overwhelming power. The man in the mirror looks afraid, already beaten.

"Listen," I tell him, "you're going to be OK. You're going to jump back in time, complete the change event, and come home." I force myself to breathe, slow and steady. "And then, you're going to live a long and happy life, hopefully with Alexia. It's all going to be fine."

Three knocks on the door. Alexia's voice. "Just checking you're OK in there."

"I'm fine," I call back. "Be out in a minute."

I dry my face but can't look at myself. A part of me wants to stay in here, just crawl into a corner and hide, but there is no hiding from time. It's coming for me, my trip nonnegotiable, a metaphysical contract, because once I bond with an object, I travel, whether I like it or not.

I don't have a choice.

Where is it going to put me? In the city? I thought the quake was bad on the hill, but it must have been scary as hell on the streets of San Francisco. I think about the people on the bridge, inside buildings. I don't suffer from claustrophobia, not really, but like any sane person, I don't like being in tight spaces. I shake it off. There's no point thinking like this. I've only just told Alexia that I'm a time traveler, and I'm hoping that when this is over, she and I have a chance at a relationship. I don't want her to see how fearful I am. I focus on what Iris said: just follow the rules and do my best. The change event knows what I'm supposed to do.

There is a plan, order within the chaos.

My watch informs me that I have eight minutes. That's four hundred and eighty seconds to cram for my earthquake exam. I straighten my back, stand tall, and walk back into the lounge, playing the part of a confident time traveler.

Faking it helps.

Kristin and Alexia are huddled around the iPad. A YouTube clip plays live coverage of the 1989 World Series. The commentator delivers a slick, effortless monologue, recapping a previous game, ". . . allowing Jose Canseco to score, and he fails to get Dave Parker at second base, so the Oakland A's take . . ." He's interrupted by the sharp hiss of static, the screen rolls and flickers, the commentator repeats the word *take*, and then another wavering voice interjects. "I tell you what, we're having an earth—"

Static hisses over a snow-filled screen.

A green title card appears with the words *World Series*, along with an ABC logo in the bottom corner.

Dread fills my belly. The coverage was like a movie, chilling and perfectly edited for maximum impact. But this isn't a Hollywood disaster film. It *happened*.

Kristin and Alexia are so engrossed that they jump when they see me. Their faces are pale, like those of the people in the stadium. "Sorry," Alexia says, tapping the screen to pause the broadcast.

"It's fine," I assure them. "We have about eight minutes. Tell me as much as you can."

"I wasn't there, of course, but I remember it on the news," Kristin says. "The Loma Prieta earthquake. It struck at 5:04 p.m."

"Lasted fifteen seconds," Alexia adds.

"Wow." I frown. "It felt like fifteen minutes."

Alexis explains that it was the first major earthquake in the United States to be broadcast on live television. Game Three was just about to get underway.

In a low voice, I ask, "How many died?"

"Seventy-four people in the Bay Area."

"My goodness," I murmur.

"It would have been a lot higher," Kristin says, "if it weren't for the fact so many people attended the game."

Alexia flicks through photographs on her phone. Crumpled buildings, some of them on fire. After Paris, I don't want to be anywhere near a burning building ever again. I do my best to keep my fear below the surface. She pauses on an image. "This is the Oakland Bay Bridge. A section of the upper deck fell onto the one below."

My heart sinks. A huge section of concrete, like a massive trapdoor, collapsed. It's horrible. People died. I sigh, feeling the weight of the past.

"Again, because of the game, the traffic was a lot lighter than normal," Kristin adds. "That's a blessing, in a way."

I nod a few times, blinking away the pain. "I know this is hard, but keep going. The more I know, the better."

"You need to see this one," Kristin says. "The Cypress Freeway." She shows me another collapsed section of road. A snarled gray stretch of freeway has been ripped apart, leaving a mangled cross section of concrete and metal. Within its triangular gaps are crushed vehicles and pillars leaning at precarious angles. Fearless people crawl over the wreckage, and medical workers gather at the base, along with ladders and fire engines.

"Most of the casualties were here," Kristin says, her voice somber.

Leaning on Iris's advice, I try to remember that I can only change the small things. This part of the quake has been heavily observed, baked in. Surely, I can't change this.

"People were saved," Alexia says. "Police, doctors, and residents worked through the night. They risked their lives getting people out."

This makes me rethink a little. I can't stop the quake, can't change major events, but as I stare into the shadowy nooks and crannies, I wonder . . . Is this where time might play?

"Where is this?" I ask.

Alexia taps the screen. "The Cypress Viaduct is across the bay, in the Oakland area." She brings up a map, and I get rough bearings.

"All right, thank you. Anything else?"

"Probably not relevant," Kristin says quietly.

"Go on."

"You did say to focus on the smaller stories . . . They played the World Series eventually. The Oakland Athletics went on to sweep the San Francisco Giants."

"That could be useful to know." I tell her, "Thank you." My voice is distant, my sense of place fading. I feel the tug of time, like I'm made of sand and the tide just washed over me. Alexia stands and reaches out to take my hand. I pull away.

"What's wrong?" she asks.

"We mustn't touch. I could drag you with me."

Her eyes widen. "Oh, OK." She offers me a pained smile. "This is so strange, Joe. What you can do, I mean."

"I know, but you get used to it." And then I laugh. "That's a lie. You don't."

Concern remains etched on Alexia's face. "I heard what Iris said. She's right, you know. Don't risk your own life."

"I won't," I tell her, knowing it's probably a lie.

"Come back safe," she says, almost crossly. "I mean it."

I tell her I will, feeling stretched. My heart is on Leckhampton Hill, but my voice is coming from the other room. The world is quiet now. There's love, companionship, unity, but I'm disconnected from it all. I belong in the past. I have work to do. Alexia and Kristin study me with an almost repulsed form of fascination. The incredible vanishing man.

My reality shifts, and the confines of the hotel room are suddenly replaced by a vast expanse. I'm standing on a road. It's a relief to have arrived on solid ground. A pleasant sun warms my skin, the omnipresent hiss of crashing waves nearby. A light mist, heavy with sea salt, fills my nostrils. A jogger appears, then a cyclist behind me. They pay me no attention.

To my right, the bay, and in the distance, Alcatraz. Ahead of me, the iconic Golden Gate Bridge, its rust-red metalwork clear and bright against a pastel-blue sky. The road snakes up and around to meet the bridge.

It's 3:45 p.m. on the day of the quake, which doesn't hit until 5:04 p.m.

Knowledge of the future hurts. For some people, this will be the last day. I dismiss these dark thoughts, knowing they aren't going to help me. Resistance won't allow me to warn the masses, but I wouldn't be human if I didn't at least consider it. I focus on the rules and the restrictions of the observer effect help to stop my conscience from eating itself alive.

I'm relieved that time didn't drop me into the epicenter of the disaster, or perhaps even worse, the aftermath. I have roughly one hour and twenty minutes before the quake hits. Who knows, I might even miss it completely on this jump.

Waves crash on the rocks as I look at the Golden Gate Bridge. Kristin and Alexia didn't mention it, and I don't think it was affected. In fact, somewhere in my trivia data bank, I seem to remember that the bridge had been altered or repaired after an earlier earthquake.

So, why has time put me here?

My watch buzzes. *Calibrating* disappears from the screen, and *Change Event* appears, along with a waypoint.

My relief is huge. I can't undo the terrible events of this day, but I can play my part, and I will do that to the best of my ability.

My watch buzzes again. An alert appears on the screen: *Wake Scan, Signal Acquired.*

I stare at it in disbelief. It worked! Scarlett has followed me here! The Continuum has a chance to track her, maybe even stop her. It's good news, but this euphoria is immediately followed by panic, crashing over me like the waves of the Pacific. I wanted her to follow me, but suddenly feel nervous. She's here, in San Francisco.

Focus, Joe.

I click the winding ring on my silver hunter and access the wake-scanner mode. As I hoped, the pulsing signal has been replaced by a map. I can see myself on it, a green dot surrounded by basic dimensional topography of the landscape. The map slowly zooms out, and I see a flashing red circle: Scarlett. According to the map, she's 3.4 km away, moving in the opposite direction of my location.

This is unexpected. I thought she would immediately try and find me. Then again, unless she has a way to track me, San Francisco is a big place.

I remind myself that capturing Scarlett's signature was

secondary. That's done now, so I focus on the change event. I click my silver hunter back to its normal setting and align my waypoint: the Golden Gate Bridge. It feels good to be moving as I jog along the road and then scramble up the bank. When I reach the head of the bridge, I can't help but marvel at its construction. I've probably seen it a hundred times in photographs and movies but never actually visited. The magnificent rust-red peaks, the tension cables tapering into the sky, the wonderful, impossible physics of its suspension.

Traffic is light. There is a walkway ahead of me, a woman jogging in my direction. She passes and says hello. Resistance tightens like a knot in my stomach. I force a smile, resisting the urge to warn her, hoping she will be OK.

Magnetism draws me. I felt it in Paris, but it's stronger now. I could resist, but it would be hard, the tug of the change event undeniable.

I step onto the walkway, my footfall vibrating on the latticed steel. As I walk, cars pass in both directions. I'm alone on the walkway now. The sun is warm, but the air is cooler up here. The wind sings and whips over the huge cables, a pleasing, powerful sound. The view is both incredible and deeply troubling, like paradise holding its breath. Near the middle of the bridge, I notice a red Toyota pulled over to the side, its hazard lights blinking. Someone must have broken down. Luckily, there is just enough room for the traffic to continue to flow.

I double-check my watch, and my heart sinks.

Red light.

No more jumps.

This is it.

A small part of me is relieved. I don't relish the idea of experiencing multiple earthquakes, but the finality of seeing that red light is always a shock. My sense of magnetism increases, the tidal pull of time guiding me. The colors in my peripheral vision fade, but the bridge remains bright and saturated, and that's when I see him, a middle-aged man on the walkway ahead of me. He had been obscured by a concrete support, but I see him clearly now and don't need my watch to know that he's my quantum mission. He places his hands on the railing and peers out over the bay. It's a beautiful afternoon, but I know that he's not here to soak in the view.

He's planning for this to be his final jump too.

28

Not wishing to startle him, I inch forward. He doesn't turn, just stares out toward the city, motionless. My senses feel heightened, soaking in every detail. He's tall, middle-aged, midforties, wearing standard office attire. His dark hair is receding, flecked with gray at the edges. A young couple heads in our direction. He still hasn't acknowledged my presence, but I think he knows I'm here. He remains fixed to the spot. The couple sees us and hesitates. They know what this looks like. I tell them everything is fine. They nod, but there's a flash of concern.

"It's OK," I assure them, "I've got this." An understanding passes between us, and they continue crossing the bridge.

We are alone again, two men standing at a crossroads.

Below us the expanse of the bay is filled with the white triangular sails of tiny boats, Alcatraz, and the glowing buildings of the city in the distance. The late afternoon sun warms my skin, but it's losing the battle against a strong breeze whipping up off the Pacific.

The man turns and regards me with obvious suspicion. He has a kind face, long features, sloping eyebrows. His eyes are vacant, his jawline darkened with stubble. He turns away, places both hands on the railing, and draws in a long breath.

Panic bubbles up. How am I going to deal with this? I'm sure there are steps to follow, phrases you should and shouldn't say. I take my own deep breath, reminding myself that any opportunity is better than none. I'm no expert, but sadly, I have some experience with suicide. In the timeline I changed, my father had taken his own life. Years later I found myself immersed in research, trying to understand it more. I delved into what pushes someone to this, and although that hurt, sometimes pain is necessary to feel and explore and accept, but most of all, to understand.

From that research, I learned the importance of speaking calmly, maintaining a gentle manner, and showing kindness. One terribly sad story stayed with me. A man had left a note, saying that if just one person had smiled at him on his way to the bridge, he wouldn't have jumped. No one did, and I'll never forget that. All it would have taken to save him was a little kindness. A simple smile can alter history.

"Hi," I say, quietly, so as not to startle him.

He tilts his head slightly.

"Got any plans later?" I ask. "Going to watch the game?" Talk about the future, avoid the idea of *now* being the end.

"Baseball isn't my thing," he replies without looking at me. "It's just a game. It doesn't matter."

"What about tomorrow? Any plans?"

His knuckles whiten as he grips the railing. After a few seconds, he turns and engages with me properly for the first time. "Listen," he says, his voice steady, "I don't want to cause a scene. I just want to go quietly. Please, leave me alone."

My heart lurches, but I remain still. I don't know this man, but I know something about what he just said. Most of the time, when someone says they want to be alone, it isn't true. With gentle compassion, I hold my palms up. "Just give me five minutes, that's all I ask. Talk to me. After that, if you still want to jump, then you can." My only job is to buy time.

His eyebrows narrow. "You're hoping if you can get me talking, I'll change my mind."

"Maybe. What's your name?"

"Aaron," he says. "Aaron Pennington."

"I'm Joe," I tell him. "I'm an antique dealer."

"Oh yeah?" he says, his Californian accent clearer now.

"What about you, Aaron. What do you do?"

His eyes wander as he tells me he's a pediatric surgeon at a nearby hospital. He frowns. "Sometimes, it doesn't matter what you do, there's just no way you can save them."

This resonates, more than I can tell him.

His expression darkens, then his shoulders sag and a worrying calm descends over him, a kind of trancelike acceptance. "I've heard you experience a sense of relief and peace on the way down," he says. "I'm sorry, Joe, but this is as far as I go."

The image of him falling, unobserved, jolts me into action. I could try to grab him, but that could go quickly and horribly wrong. Instead, I must reach him with words, using the same steady precision I suspect he uses when he wields a scalpel.

"Listen, Aaron, this might be the wrong thing to say, and if it is, I'm sorry, but I think I know how you feel."

He glowers. "You think you know me? That you understand my problems?"

"Not at all, but I might understand a little of what you're going through," I tell him, channeling my past. "Pain, loss, regret. My sister went missing when she was just a kid, and I thought about ending it too, many times."

Only now do I realize I've been hiding this dark and regretful truth from myself. The thought of checking out of this world often whispered to me when it became clear that Amy was never coming back. If I had gone through with it, I would never have known that time travel was waiting for me. The pain was unbearable, but all I had to do was tread water, live with the pain, and eventually life found me again.

He tilts his head, blinking. "What happened to her?"

"Years later, she came back. We found her. I understand regret, believe me, but life can suddenly change in the most unexpected ways. You don't know what's around the corner. Don't jump, please."

"Why do you care?" he asks, without any edge. "What does it matter to you?"

"Because I need your help," I tell him without thinking.

"What do you mean?"

I think for a long second. "I believe you might still have work to do."

He lets out a surprised laugh. "This is not how I want to leave, with some crazy guy babbling on. Just go, please, just leave me alone."

What do I tell him? How can I talk about what's going to happen? Most people, when pressed, will admit they believe in something outside of their understanding. Ghosts? Most will say they believe it's possible. Aliens? Sure, probably. Premonitions? Again, maybe.

It's time to channel my inner Amy.

"I'm not crazy," I tell him, "but I do see things."

"What kind of . . . things?"

"The future," I say. "Premonitions of events that are about to occur."

"I suppose you're going to tell me that you saw this," he gestures around him, "that you saw me?"

"No, I didn't know about you until I got here." We stand in silence for a few long seconds. The air feels thin and untrustworthy. "There's going to be an earthquake."

"Welcome to San Francisco, buddy," he says. "We're always waiting for one."

"But I know that it happens tonight at 5:04 p.m."

He shrugs. "That would be a shame for the World Series."

"They reschedule."

He glances at me. "You're just telling me this so I won't jump."

"Honestly, I'm not sure what I'm doing. All I know is that you're not supposed to do this. In less than an hour, there are going to be a lot of people who need help."

The wind picks up, and the moment sharpens. I swear I can feel the powerful flow of the Pacific Ocean below us. Trying to hide my desperation, I ask, "What if I'm right? What's an hour?"

He stares down at his hands. I can see he's holding something, but I can also feel it. There's energy, and for a second, I wonder if it's the Game Boy, but of course, it isn't. It's so small I haven't noticed it until now, but it means a lot to him.

"What's that you're holding?" I ask carefully.

In a monotone voice, he says, "It's a symbol, I guess."

"May I see it?"

He blinks for a few seconds and unfolds his hand, revealing a *Star Wars* action figure.

"Boba Fett," I say, nodding. "You a *Star Wars* fan?"

His eyes glisten, and he swallows. "It's not mine."

The familiar action figure thrums with psychometric energy. It's part of his story, part of the reason he's here. "I told you I see things," I say. "Can I show you what I mean?"

"What are you asking?"

"Let me hold the figure for a second."

He shakes his head. "You're going to try and grab me."

"I won't do that," I tell him. "I promise you can have it straight back."

He nods faintly. Very slowly, I close the gap between us and take it from him. It's a risk, but I close my eyes and cup the action figure. After a few seconds, images appear in my mind. A snapshot of the life of Aaron Pennington, pediatric surgeon. A children's ward. The staff and the kids love him. He's a good man, but he's not coping anymore. I feel a breaking point, a loss of purpose. I pull back, trying to focus on the events that led to this moment. There were happier times. A boy, very cute, with a heartbreaking smile. My eyes remain closed, as I begin to talk through what I'm seeing.

"His name was Daniel. He was very ill. You lost him in surgery." His pain becomes my pain. Sadness consumes me, the loss, the guilt. "You've always been so careful not to become attached, but you did this time." I open my eyes, and my vision swims.

Aaron lets out a juddering breath, a tear runs down his cheek. He wipes it away absently. "How do you know about that?" His voice is thin.

"Objects show me people's stories." There's more to this one. I allow it in and relay what I'm seeing to Aaron. "I know about the funding too, that you blame yourself for not raising the money, but it's not your fault. You tried so hard."

His jaw drops. "Who are you? How could you possibly know all of this? Have you been following me?"

I ignore his question. "Life changes today, for a lot of people, you included. I want to help you, Aaron. You have a lot to do."

The snapshot of a special period in the lives of two people, shown to me by Daniel's favorite toy bounty hunter, was a complicated one. Aaron Pennington believes that if he had secured the funding for a new specialist wing of the hospital, then Daniel might still be alive. He believes he's responsible. I doubt that's true, but it doesn't make any difference. He believes it, and the guilt has been eating him alive. Daniel didn't live, so why should he? Aaron Pennington doesn't think he deserves to be here. He's wrong, but that won't stop him from jumping.

That's when an idea surfaces, a way to play the cards I've been dealt. Memories of Kristin choking in Chang'an come back to me. Will resistance allow this? All I can do is try.

"I appreciate that you're not a baseball fan, but what if I told you that I know who's going to win the World Series."

Aaron shrugs. "Most people around here can predict the future with absolute certainty when it comes to baseball."

I cross my fingers behind my back and try to find the words, but each time my mind forms a sentence, the words flip and get jumbled around. I feel the pressure of time all around me, tightening my chest and throat.

Could telling him really negatively alter the future?

"What's the matter," he asks, "having trouble guessing?" There's a hint of sarcasm there, which is good, I think. At least his mind is off the jump.

I need to navigate the delicate resistance, find a way to tell him in a manner that time will allow. Speaking silently to time, I ask it to trust me, but then I realize it's not about time trusting me, it needs to trust Aaron.

"You were trying to raise money for a specialist ward, right?"

He nods. "They couldn't find the budget, the fools."

"How much did you need, exactly?"

He regards me with a confused expression. "Three hundred thousand, at least."

"Could an anonymous donor fund it?"

"Sure," he says. "They aren't going to turn the money away, but who's going to do that?"

"You are."

"What? How?"

"I'll tell you the result of the World Series. You bet on each game and compound the winnings, but here's the most important part. You must promise me that you will calculate the bet precisely, so that you win only what you need."

A reassuring warmth emanates from my center. The idea is sound, and if I can get him over the line, time might just allow this.

He shakes his head. "This is crazy."

"I agree, but I can only tell you the winner if we have a deal."

"Kind of ironic." Aaron lets out a laugh. "You want me to swear on my life?"

"A simple promise will do just fine."

For the time being, his mind is on the crazy man who has joined him on the bridge. I can almost see his thoughts dancing around the possibility of funding his ward, saving lives. He's confused, dubious, concerned. "What you said just now, you're right about Daniel. I don't know how, but you were right. He was such a great kid." He pauses, his eyes welling up again. "I will never understand how, but you knew about the funding too, so yes, if you're right about the earthquake, I'll place the bet and ensure that it's just enough to fund the ward."

We're talking about later. He's making plans.

The tightness in my chest releases, and the throbbing in my temples that I hadn't even been aware of recedes. Words form freely now. In a clear voice, I tell him what Kristin almost didn't tell me. "The Oakland A's sweep the Giants in four games."

"A sweep?" He frowns. "Even I know that's unlikely."

"It's the way it plays out," I tell him, with absolute certainty.

"So, what do you think is going to happen? The quake, I mean."

His question is a welcome bridge back into the moment. I think back over the news reports, the information that Kristin and Alexia gathered for me. One story stood out from a human perspective. "It hits at 5:04 p.m. There's a freeway. I'm not sure of the name. Two levels. It collapses."

"Could it be the Cypress Street Viaduct?" he asks. "People call it the Cypress Freeway."

"That's it." I recall the image of the upper tier collapsed onto the lower one, the concrete crushing the cars like tin cans. "It's going to collapse. People will need your help."

"If you're so certain, we should ask them to close the bridge, stop people going onto it."

"I know exactly why you would think that," I say, "but I'm afraid it doesn't work that way. Just get somewhere safe, and then help the people you can."

He's looking at me like I've slipped into mad mode again. "Who are you?"

"Someone who, like you, is doing his best. We can't save everyone, that's not our job. All you can do is your best, help the survivors, and don't be on the bridge when it collapses. OK?"

He shrugs, a gesture of, *What else am I going to do?* His expression is that of a man who knows he just stepped back from the edge of life. Confused, but willing.

I hand the action figure back to him. "You have a lot to live for."

He stares down at it fondly, a thin smile crossing his lips.

My watch buzzes against my chest: *Mission Complete.*

Swells of emotion blur my vision. I wipe at my eyes. The time is 4:10 p.m. My watch begins to count down. I will return to the present in one hour and twenty minutes, which means two things: I'm going to be here for the earthquake, and I have some spare time on my hands.

"Good luck," I tell Aaron.

He stares back at me and manages what might be the best smile I've ever seen. "Where are you going now?"

I click the central dial of my pocket watch and see Scarlett's flashing signal on its display. "There's someone else I need to talk to."

29

Ideally, I would just find somewhere safe to ride out the earthquake, a wide expanse of flat land, or a park, maybe. Instead, I'm planning to head into the heart of the city. In terms of wise decisions, this feels low on the list, but I can't pass up the opportunity to find out what Scarlett is doing here.

I exit the bridge and walk a road that cuts through parkland. I check my watch. Scarlett is 6.9 km away. How long will it take me to run? Who am I kidding? I can't run for more than about five minutes. Oh, the practicalities of real-life time travel. Nearby, I hear kids screaming and playing. As I pass a rack of bicycles, I'm surprised to see very few of them locked. Nervously, I glance around, choose one that matches my height, and steal it. I'm not proud, but needs must.

The display of my silver hunter isn't like a modern satnav. It doesn't give me a route, just shows me a basic map with Scarlett's location. What is Scarlett doing here? Why would she follow me only to head to a different part of the city? It doesn't make sense. Questions, always questions.

I head roughly in the right direction, cycling the wide

sun-dappled streets. It's quiet, just a few cars and the odd cyclist, most of whom smile and say hello. I pedal hard, the wind in my face, still glowing with the satisfaction of a successfully completed mission. When I left Aaron, he seemed happier, but I know how easy it can be to wear a mask. I'm not naïve enough to think that my intervention today is a guarantee that he won't try suicide again, but I did my job. Aaron Pennington's life reboots today. What happens next is up to him.

As I join Lincoln Boulevard, I hit a steady climb. My legs howl, and by the time I reach its peak, with its spectacular view of the ocean, my heart is hammering and I'm pouring with sweat. I really do need to get fit at some point.

Finally, I sweep downhill and enter a residential area. This is the San Francisco I've seen in the movies, with rows of two-story buildings painted in sunshine colors. Considering the time of day, it's unusually quiet. I get a sense that the only people moving around are those who either don't care about baseball or are on their way to watch the game somewhere.

I see a family walking together down the street and the crushing knowledge of the future weighs heavy on my mind. Could I warn them in a way that time would allow? I consider telling them to get somewhere safe, but just the thought creates an unsettling sensation of pressure around me. This is how resistance works. Boundaries and rules. So much of this day can't be changed, compressed by years of observation until each unchangeable moment is strong as a diamond. If I stick to time's agenda, then my jump will be comparatively straightforward, but if I step out of line, try to meddle in events that could cause problems further down the line, time will remind me who's boss.

The family stops walking and glares at me, as though I just shouted at them. They appear suspicious of the lone cyclist who seems to have taken an interest in them. The mother, a woman with an amazing head of dreadlocks, ushers her children into a car. The father glares at me, and I feel a crackle of confrontation.

I think about warning him, but my throat tightens and my head throbs. Rules are rules. If I go too far, eventually, the pressure will crush me like a can, so I stop thinking and clear my mind, fully accepting that I am only here as an observer. In an instant, the tension dissipates. The man shakes his head and gets into his car. The moment passes, and they drive away.

Not being able to warn people is genuinely the hardest part of being a time traveler.

I reach a busy intersection and pause to check my watch. I've been cycling for nearly twenty minutes. Scarlett's signal is close. I join Divisadero Street. Signage tells me that I'm in the Marina District. The buildings are taller here, three or four floors, representing a variety of architectural styles: modern, Art Deco, old-fashioned. It's mostly residential, with a few cafés and office buildings. I pass a park with wide steps and welcoming grassy areas. People walk, kids play. I check the time: 4:42 p.m. Twenty-two minutes until the quake. It's so strange to think that everyone I see is about to go through the same awful, shared experience. Only three people in San Francisco know about the impending disaster: me, Aaron, and Scarlett.

As I join Grove Street, I see her.

She's standing on a curb, facing an apartment block on the opposite side of the road. The last time I saw her was in Paris, in an opera house consumed by fire, smoke, and uncertainty. In comparison, this meeting is subdued and peaceful. No dramatic entrance this time, just a woman alone on a street. She seems small, insignificant. Ordinary. I'm on the opposite side of the road, a couple of hundred feet away. She hasn't spotted me yet.

I lean my bike against a tree and slowly walk toward her. She's wearing baggy jeans and a black hoodie. Her hair is long and straight, down to her shoulders. It's tinted purple. She looks more like she did when I first saw her in my shop. She turns, and when she sees me, she raises her right hand, her expression calm. I instinctively raise my own hand.

Just two time travelers, saying hello.

Unexpectedly, she beckons me over. As I close the gap, I can finally get a decent look at her. She's younger than I thought, in her mid to late twenties. Her eyes are heavily made-up in dark tapered flashes that give her a catlike appearance. Her skin is pale, her cheekbones accentuated. Her lips are painted the same dark purple as her hair. She's goth, she's emo, she's grungy—all of them and none. She could probably disappear into pretty much any time from the 1970s onward.

Scarlett is a chameleon.

"You don't seem surprised to see me," I say.

"I figured you'd have a way of tracking me," she says with a nonchalant shrug. "How did your mission go?"

I scowl at her. "What are you doing here? Choosing locations for Zanak's next trip?"

She ignores me, holding out her hand. In it is a silver disc, domed like a paperweight.

"What's that?"

"A sensor." She glances back at the building, holds her hand open, and moves it across her body a few times. The disc glows like a bulb each time it lines up with the building. "I'm double-checking that I'm right."

"About what?"

"The location."

I study the building, a four-story apartment block rendered in cream paint with bay windows and numerous front doors, classic San Francisco.

Scarlett looks at me, her expression serious, and when she

speaks, her voice has the quiet determination of someone on a mission of her own. "In fifteen minutes, the whole Bay Area will be razed to the ground."

"I know. I've been here already."

"Here?"

"Close enough."

"This location is special. Can you feel it?"

I look at the building again. A subtle but potent resistance emanates from it. Scarlett points out a specific apartment. I focus on it, opening my senses a little more.

And then I get the strangest feeling: resistance fades slightly. The tension in my stomach eases, a noticeable shift.

"You can feel that, right?" Scarlett asks, her tone encouraging.

I nod.

"What do you think it is?"

I swallow. "There's less resistance here."

She smiles. "And soon, if I'm right, there won't be any at all."

A tingle of adrenaline buzzes across my arms and up over the back of my head. "I don't understand," I murmur. "What does this mean?"

Her jaw sets. She appears older, a woman now. "It means we can do more."

"Enough riddles," I tell her. "What are you planning to do?"

"There are people inside." She gestures toward the house. "They don't make it. They die in the quake."

"A lot of people die today. It's hard, but there's nothing we can do about that. My mission is done."

"I understand why you might think that, but we can save them." Her voice grows in confidence. "This is what I've been trying to do. It connects with Nils and Paris."

Anger builds at the reminder of what she put me through. "You messed with his watch and deliberately sent him into the void."

"That was a mistake. It wasn't supposed to go that way. I was experimenting, trying to weaken resistance to give him a second chance."

"You're the one who made him fail!"

Scarlett draws in a slow breath. "Failure is part of the equation. All I wanted was the data from his watch, and it almost worked."

My anger simmers just beneath the surface. "You nearly got us both killed."

She fixes me with a pained expression. "I'm sorry, but the work I'm doing is important, Joe. I believe I've discovered an opportunity bigger than anyone at The Continuum could imagine. You can feel it, resistance is weak. Think about that. There is so much more that we could do."

"Enough with the *we*!" I shoot back. "All you've done is cause trouble. You planted the radio in my shop and sent me back to London. Bill died saving me—*died*, because of you."

Her jaw tightens, and she looks down. "What happened to Bill is the biggest regret of my life, but what he discovered . . . is incredible. I knew it was possible to beat resistance. That's why I sent Nils into the void. I was trying to unlock the final secret."

"Yeah, well I hope it was worth it."

She holds my gaze, her eyes pleading. "What I've discovered means we could save thousands, perhaps even millions more. I need your help, Joe."

"What are you talking about?"

"I can travel, but I'm not like you. I can't change the past. You're the only one who can save the people in that house."

"That's why you're here? You knew I would track you down?"

She nods, and I can hear Gabrielle warning me that Scarlett's a parasite, manipulative and clever.

"If there are people in there," I say, "why don't I just go in there now and get them out?"

"We must wait for the right moment," she says, "when resistance is at its weakest."

"Don't tell me," I say, shaking my head, "when the quake hits?"

She shrugs and offers me a wry smile. "It was bound to be, wasn't it?"

"I'm not buying this," I tell her. "You're talking about saving people, yet you've been helping Emil Zanak waste change events. Why?"

"The sacrifice was necessary," she says, her voice cold. "I've been gathering data. Failing a few missions will seem insignificant if I'm right."

"But why this way? Why not talk to The Continuum? Work together?"

"They used to be open-minded. When they started out, they were innovators, but gradually they became entrenched in their thinking, blinded by what they thought they knew. That's why I've been working alone, because it's the only way to push the boundaries. If I told them what I was attempting, they would try and stop me. Even now, they wouldn't believe me . . . but they might believe you."

"What do you mean?"

"If you're willing to try, I hope it will prove to The Continuum that we can beat resistance." Her enthusiasm builds as she talks. "All my efforts have led to this moment. All the testing, learning, gathering data. The change-event missions are all well and good, but why be limited by them? The people in this house are just one example. There could be opportunities all over San Francisco. Think what we could do if we brought more travelers."

"But how do you know that saving them won't negatively impact the future?"

She shakes her head. "Most lives have zero impact on

shaping the future. I've discovered the shadows within the shadows, pockets of antiresistance where we can achieve amazing results. They are just normal people, Joe. In just a few minutes, the quake will hit, and resistance will be lower. This is how Bill saved you. Can you find it in yourself to give them a chance?"

I stare at her, confused. I feel like I might be seeing her for the first time.

Roles have reversed. Suddenly, I'm Aaron on the bridge, and Scarlett is the mad person trying to persuade me she can see the future. I play back our conversation, trying to find the gaps in her story, but some of what she says rings true. I have trusted The Continuum, and although I think they believe that what they've told me is true, what if Scarlett is right and we can help more people?

I think about rules, what it means to break them. What I had to do to save Amy, what Bill did to save me. I wonder if Scarlett and I are really that different. If she's trying to replicate what Bill did, does that make her wrong?

"Will you try?" she asks.

I imagine the people inside the house. "If this is a trick, I'm never going to forgive you."

"I know."

We face each other, Scarlett's expression intense. "It's five p.m.," she says. "We don't have long. Resistance will weaken and fail just before the quake, giving you a brief window to get in and do what you can. I've studied all the news, survivor testimonials, and subsequent investigations. The building collapses, but you will have enough time to get them out. You *can* save them."

My watch vibrates, and the display begins to flicker.

Change Event.

Followed by three corrupted but recognizable words. They flash across the screen.

Waypoint
Unknown
Error

The waypoint needle spins and snaps to an abrupt stop, pointing directly at the house. Then the screen goes blank.

"A few minutes after the quake, you will head back to the present," Scarlett says. "Tell The Continuum what happened here. Explain what I'm trying to do." She frowns, deep in thought. "I hope they will understand, and that then we can talk."

There's no more time to think. I feel swept along, but also suddenly focused.

The world takes a breath, just like it did when I was looking down on Candlestick Park. The calm before the storm. I'm overwhelmed by a sudden feeling of lightness. I stumble forward, adapting to the easing of negative pressure.

"You feel that?" Scarlett asks.

I nod, taking another step.

"Resistance is weakening," she says.

I cross the street, knowing that a massive earthquake is about to strike and raze this building to its foundations. Yet I'm calm. I feel hope, the familiar tug of potential change.

Attraction guides me. The apartment is saturated in color. Time wants this. Possibilities light up in my brain like a fireworks show.

If Scarlett's right, then our missions won't be restricted to change events.

We could do more.

A lot more.

30

The apartment has no doorbell. Do I knock? Then what? Ask how many people are in the house? Order them outside? I twist the door handle. It's locked, of course. I consider trying to find the rear of the building, see if a back door has been left open. I glance across the street. Scarlett stands there, watching me. Waiting.

I knock hard and wait.

Nothing.

Each passing second has weight, inertia that builds.

I'm not sure why, but I try the door again, and this time there's a click, as though someone just unlocked it from the inside. The door eases open. I stare at it in disbelief, wondering if time is helping me. My nerves jangle as I enter the apartment.

A narrow hallway leads to a spacious open-plan living room. I don't see anyone. The décor is an amalgamation of all the American sitcoms from my youth, a homely and welcoming assault of beige and brown. Dark wood furniture. Leather sofas covered in patterned blankets. Wicker chairs. A beanbag. There's a stone fireplace, and in the corner, an entertainment system with a rack of vinyl. The TV is tuned to the baseball game. The players warm up on the field, and the commentators are well-prepared, excited for a World Series that stretches reassuringly ahead of them. They remind their audience at home that the game will start soon. They are wrong about that. Any minute now, we're going to be rocking and rolling.

Muffled music draws me toward a half-open door. Good smells: butter, popcorn, and fried onions. Slowly, I enter the kitchen. Like the lounge, it's big and busy. A stained glass Tiffany lamp hangs above an island, its surface covered in mustard-yellow tiles. A curvaceous Black woman with a shock of frizzy white hair stands with her back to me, an apron tied around her ample waist. She's preparing food. I see burger buns and bags of snacks and a lidded pan on the stove. The woman turns slightly, still doesn't see me. She's shaping ground meat into patties and wipes her gnarly hands on a towel.

As gently as I can, I say, "Please don't be alarmed."

I may as well have said, *Hi, I'm an axe murderer!*

She spins to face me, her dark eyes wide. She's old, maybe seventy, with soft, delicate features. Her face is lined with age, and those creases deepen now in shock and fear. Her mouth forms a perfect O. She screams and backs away from me.

I raise my hands in a defensive gesture. "It's OK, I'm not going to hurt you."

She clutches at her apron, considers the knife on the island, but then appears to think better of it. Her worried eyes move around the room, planning her escape. Maybe that would be good? I could just scare her out of the house. "What do you want? Money?" Her voice is thin, trembling with fear.

"I'm not going to hurt you," I say calmly, "but you need to get out of the house. There's going to be an earthquake." The words are easy, resistance wonderfully absent.

She frowns. "An earthquake? How could you possibly know that?"

"It's going to happen any minute now. Please, just come with me; get out of the house."

Her eyes flash over my shoulder, back toward the living room.

"Is anyone else in the house?" I ask.

"No," she says quickly, "just me and Higgins."

"Higgins?"

"My dog," she says. "He's in the yard."

Through the window I see a small patch of grass surrounded by a fence. There's a swing, a bench, and a white mongrel with wiry hair.

Higgins begins to bark.

A cloud of birds fills the sky.

I've seen this before.

When I turn back to the woman, she's tapping a telephone handset. Its cord stretches across the kitchen. "I'm calling the police!" she cries, her tone high and melodious.

The clock on the wall reads 5:03 p.m. "Please, we need to get out. I'm begging you, just follow me into the yard."

She shakes her head, causing her large, hooped earrings to rattle against the handset. "Earthquake!" She laughs shakily. "Not today, it's the World Series for goodness' sake." Her eyes remain fixed on me. "Hello? Police? There's an intruder in my house." She pauses, and her face drops. "Hello?"

A pregnant silence.

The corn begins to pop in the pan, staccato and percussive. It's joined by the distant sound of two boulders being rubbed together, a low rumbling vibration that builds like an approaching train, pulsing and rhythmic. The woman's confused expression turns into abject horror. It's too late, but I think she believes me now. The room starts to sway.

Popcorn. Burgers. A swing.

"Where are they?" I bellow at her.

She looks horrified.

"I can get them out!"

"Upstairs," she cries.

"Who?"

"My grandson and his friend. Help them, please!"

Higgins runs into the kitchen, whimpering. Two kids, a granny, and a dog. Inside the house. *Nice work, Joe.*

History repeats itself in the living room. The familiar TV broadcast playing out like a horror movie: *I tell you what, I think we're having an earth—*

Static.

The quake becomes a gentle rocking, and although I know better, I feel a flicker of hope. Maybe it won't be too bad? But then the house lets out a sorrowful moan, and the tremor takes hold. The Tiffany lamp sways violently from side to side. The room convulses to the deafening sound of thunder, the reverberation intensifies, and all hell breaks loose.

Books explode from shelves. Cupboard doors slam open and shut. Glass jars and appliances dance their way off the counters. I'm thrown against a wall, then jostled back toward the living room door. The woman falls to her knees, grabs her dog, and crawls beneath a table in the corner of the kitchen, fast as a well-trained soldier. Her desperate gaze seeks me out, gesturing, pleading for me to find the kids. The tiles on the island pop and jump like a hundred mousetraps triggered in unison. In an ear-splitting burst, the middle of the kitchen floor yawns open. The dark stone mouth swallows the island with shocking efficiency.

The house is one almighty, heaving riot, the chaos all-consuming. I was expecting this, but I can't think, can't move. The floor vibrates with such jarring ferocity that I'm convinced my bones are going to shatter. A high-pitched, splintering crack is the only warning I get that the ceiling is about to come down. I stagger back into the living room, coughing and clamoring. The woman's muffled screams are lost as the kitchen compresses, devoured in a slow-motion hand clap.

The barrage continues. I whirl around and stagger across the living room. My feet crunch over debris. Jolts lift me into the air. The walls separate from the floor, mirrors smash, books and framed photographs leap and spin around like excited birds. Nature roars, as though the earth itself is claiming victory over our futile attempts to build on its surface. I dive over the sofa, stumble, slip, and somehow reach the hallway. I'm at the foot of the stairs now, but they are twisted and warped like a fun house.

Time seems to stop. For a fleeting breath, I feel separated from the heaving power being unleashed on San Francisco. What am I doing? The woman and her dog are probably dead. The front door is right there. In just a few seconds, I could be outside. I have a choice: run away or go deeper still. It isn't really a choice, though. I'm afraid, but what scares me the most is making it through this and knowing I didn't try and save the kids trapped upstairs.

I'm running on instincts and adrenaline now. I lunge, clearing the first two steps in one go. Plaster falls from the ceiling like snow. I don't know which way is up, clambering on my hands and knees, willing myself to keep going. My hands are bleeding. The sharp, stinging pain helps me focus. When I reach the top of the stairs, bookshelves tumble, their contents spinning as though flung by an angry poltergeist. I'm coughing and hacking but can't hear a thing above the thundering growl of the quake. Wheeling around, I'm drawn to a door with a poster of the Incredible Hulk. Angry text shouts, *Hulk smash!* Staggering over, I push it open. My mind clambers to soak in as many details as it can: mental photographs, details that may matter. An old TV, circular dials. A Commodore 64 computer, a joystick and cassette tapes scattered over the floor. A bulb swaying like a pendulum, its shade lost. Walls covered in posters, baseball players, the words *The Dynamic Duo*, the San Francisco Giants logo.

A single window moves in a sickening circular motion. Through it I see the street below. The ground appears liquefied. In the distance is a park, open space, safety. Opposite, an auto repair shop. A car drives past. A rolling wave causes a telephone pole to collapse. It comes down in a crackling explosion of sparks and crushes the car, right down the middle, lifting the front wheels from the road. The window shatters into a shower of glass that joins the rest of the debris rippling over the floor.

That's when I see them, two kids wearing baseball outfits, huddled in the corner beside a bed. One is white with shiny blond hair and eyes wide as saucers. The other is Black, presumably the grandson of the woman I met downstairs. He holds his friend as though that might stop the world from rattling. His eyes are pinched shut.

The room leans worryingly, like a ship in a storm. I call out to them, my throat dry as gravel. They both look at me, shocked, petrified. I stumble forward, steadying myself against the edge of the bed frame, hand outstretched. "Come on," I yell, "let's go!"

They cower, shaking their heads, and squirm their way under the bed. Toys, marbles, debris, and cassette tapes skitter and jump like electrocuted frogs. Wood splinters as a portion of the wall disappears. Through the impossible gap, I see the buildings across the street, smacking into each other like dominoes. I'm falling back, the roller-coaster ride becomes a freight train, and I lose all sense of space. I'm slammed against a wall, a dull stabbing pain in my left side. *My* eyes are closed now.

A strong wind like a dust-filled cough lifts me off my feet.

Miraculously, I land on my front and slide, crashing through the doorway. My hands grip something solid. I spin and look up. The Hulk has broken free of his hinges and is heading in my direction, the door and the wall closing in on me.

The green figure bares his teeth, snarling, *Hulk smash!*

The pieces of the house are no longer where they should be. My confusion is absolute. Somehow, I get my feet and lunge back toward the top of the stairs, my only thought now of survival. The stairs crack and split, dangerous spears protruding like jagged yellow teeth. The ground beneath me gives way in a croaking moan. I attempt to launch myself back onto solid ground but feel nothing below me. My instincts are sharp as a knife. I cover my face and curl into a ball. The house envelops me and folds in on itself, like a pop-up card. Together we drop, convulsing, collapsing inward. I fall into a dark tunnel that blots out all light.

Darkness. Cramped. Pinched tight. The quake stops abruptly. Its absence, shocking and absolute. Fifteen seconds of hell, followed by an awful silence that whistles in my ears.

My awareness slides away, and for a while there is nothing.

Then a dull, throbbing pain pulls me back. My lungs burn. Each breath brings searing pain that radiates from my center. I'm jammed into a narrow space. My right arm is trapped, but my left is free enough to wipe at my face, to pick the thick wet dust from my nostrils. I take shallow breaths.

I'm alive, at least.

The house creaks and moans. The hissing and rattling of dust, working its way through the maze of debris, is worrying. I'm cocooned by a blanket of rubble. My lower half is pinned beneath a cold, solid mass. My right leg feels wet and hot. Shooting pains work their way over my calf and thigh, along with the fierce burn of numerous cuts and bruises, maybe even broken bones. Luckily, adrenaline and shock are doing an excellent job of masking the worst of it, for now.

Trapped in this dark cave, my fear returns, accentuated by the sour odor of gas. News reports showed buildings on fire. Surely, after what I went through in Paris, time wouldn't be so mean as to burn me alive now, would it?

I fight back tears because they won't do me any good. I cough and splutter, panic tightening my chest. Fire may be the least of my worries. There isn't enough air. I've spent the last few minutes wishing time would slow down. Now I want it to hurry up, to feel the reassuring chill of brain freeze. I just want to go home. I call out for help, asking if anyone can hear me. Nothing but the silent mass of the house upon me.

After a couple of minutes, I think I hear a faint whining. Higgins, the dog? I call out. A voice calls back, muffled and flattened, impossible to ascertain any words. I tell them we will be OK. I receive no reply. All I can do is wait, but for what?

My answer arrives a few minutes later.

The ground buzzes and trembles in bursts of rhythmic energy. Aftershocks. I feel the weight on my legs shift. I cry out, trying to wriggle free. There's a pop and a gush of air like someone just opened a can. Debris gives way. It's followed by a pressure that builds and builds. I grit my teeth in a rictus of pain and growl, "No, please, no," but I'm alone.

Only I can hear the fresh cracking and popping. Only I know that it isn't the house. An impossible weight is on me, and the pain sharpens, intensifying into a piercing white light.

It forms a tunnel that stretches out before me, and then that terrible pressure dissipates.

The pain leaves me.

I think I'm dying.

At least I saved Aaron Pennington on the bridge. He was

my real mission. Images and snapshots fill my mind, the colors intense, the details so sharp they hurt. Amy by the lake, shivering in the rain. Lightning flashing overhead. Alexia kissing me on Leckhampton Hill. Running to the finish line on sports day. My dad's hand on my shoulder, proud of me. Playing keyboard in my band.

I'm seeing all of this, feeling it . . . My life flashing before my eyes.

What a wonderful cliché.

And then I'm surrounded by the sudden, overwhelming expanse of an open room. Fresh air. Light blinding me. My ears are clogged, still whistling, but someone is screaming. Alexia kneels beside me.

"I'm alive?" I ask her, a genuine question.

"Yes!" Her eyes well up, and in a shuddering voice, she says, "But don't move, just stay where you are."

"OK," I reply, my voice a faint rasp.

But moving isn't an option. Something is very wrong with me.

The last thing I hear is Alexia shouting at Kristin to call an ambulance.

PART 7

31

A faceless figure rolls a hefty broadcast camera toward me. I'm in an old-fashioned TV studio, the lights hot and bright, the audience a silent wall of black. A man is seated next to me, wearing a smart suit. His skin is tanned, hair jet-black. I recognize him as one of the sports presenters from ABC. He grins at me, his teeth incredibly white. "All set?"

I swallow and begin to panic. All set for what? I'm not prepared for this. No one told me anything about a live television appearance!

A shadowy figure nearby says, "And we're live in, five, four . . ." His fingers continue the countdown in silence. A red bulb on top of the camera lights up. The man next to me eyeballs the lens and smiles. "Hello, everyone. I'm Al Michaels. Welcome back." His voice is smooth and confident. "Well . . . the Battle of the Bay has been fought, and of course, in the end, there can be only one winner." He turns to me, his expression thoughtful. "Joe, what did you think of the result?"

My panic builds. The red light on the camera glows brightly. A trickle of sweat runs down my back.

Al Michaels frowns. "Let me put it this way. Do you think it was a fair outcome?"

"I don't know yet . . . I'm not sure what's going on."

He lets out a short, kind laugh. "OK, why don't we take a look at the replay?"

A screen appears to my left. A video clip, taken from a helicopter swooping over the Golden Gate Bridge, begins to play. The camera zooms in, and I see a familiar scene. Two figures, standing alone in the middle of the iconic structure. One of them is Aaron Pennington and the other is me.

"Why are you showing me this?" I no longer care that I'm on live TV.

Ever the professional, Al Michaels ignores me. "For the folks at home, this is just the first inning. In this replay, we can see our very own Joc Bridgeman." He turns to me with an expression of concerned pity. "It's clear you do your best, but you're no match for the inevitable."

The video feed sharpens, zooms in further. My hands are raised, and Aaron Pennington is backing away, shaking his head.

I don't remember this.

A burst of fresh panic washes over me as Aaron climbs over the railing, pauses for a second, and then jumps. His body falls like a rag doll. I cover my mouth and look away from the screen.

In a jovial voice, Al Michaels says, "Yeah, you kind of fumbled the ball there, allowing time to stage a comeback. Nothing you could have done, really."

Forcing myself to look at the screen, I see myself alone on the bridge. "No, that's not right. I saved him. He didn't jump."

The audience ripples with cruel laughter. I feel the terrible weight of their observation, of their judgment.

"Well, perhaps we should agree to disagree," Al Michaels says. "Let's focus on something positive, shall we? They're calling you the hero of Divisadero Street. Those kids you rescued, that was quite a feat. What you did took a lot of courage. Can you talk us through it? What was going through your mind as you entered the building?"

I'm feeling nauseous. The world is all back to front. I tell him he's wrong. "I didn't save them. The quake hit; there was nothing I could do."

He leans back in his chair. Like the audience, he's judging me. "I feel it's only right that we get our facts straight. I don't think you are a hero. I think you had a chance to save them, but you chose to stay at home eating popcorn. Isn't that, right?"

More snickering from the dark mass, fake, like the canned laughter of a mediocre sitcom.

I've had enough of this. I try and stand, but I'm glued to my seat.

"Coming up after the commercial break, we'll dig into this story more," Al Michaels says, "and I hope, uncover the truth."

Jazz music fills the studio. The red light goes off. The cameraman says, "And . . . we're out." The lights come up, and I see the crew. It's The Continuum: Iris, Felix, Kyoko, Gabrielle. They stand motionless, glaring at me.

I'm being observed. My fate considered.

Again, I try to move but my legs won't work. They're broken.

No, it's worse than that . . . but I can't remember why.

When the man beside me speaks, his voice is no longer his own. It's higher than before and oddly familiar. "We got you," he says, "didn't we?"

My head turns slowly.

Al Michaels plunges his fingers into his neck, pulling at the skin. I wince, expecting blood, but his face is a rubber mask. It pops off. Scarlett is underneath, her purple lips stretched back in a fixed grin, eyes sparkling and wild. She leans forward, as though she's about to whisper to me.

"Fooled you!" she shouts, so loud that the lights in the studio shatter.

My eyes flash open. I'm soaked in sweat, surrounded by darkness. I flail around, pain digging into my side like a hot poker. A red button glows nearby. I press it, and I'm instantly bathed in a warm, reassuring light. The room is clinical. Machinery beeps. The relief of waking is replaced by a sinking ball of realization. I remember where I am.

It's 4 a.m. Not a great time to be awake, bad thoughts, dark outside. Dark inside.

A shadow appears at my door. A man whose name I know but can't remember asks, "Are you OK, Mr. Bridgeman?"

I tell him I am, the taste of fear still fizzing on my tongue.

"You just call me if you need anything."

I assure him I will. He leaves, and slowly the confusing nightmare fades into the background. I'm on strong drugs, but I've never had dreams like this. I focus on my breathing, let my heart rate steady.

It's been five days since I returned from San Francisco. Significant chunks of my memory were missing, so Kristin and Alexia filled me in. An ambulance took me to one hospital, then another. I had various MRIs and CT scans, the results of which eventually brought me here: Nuffield Hospital in Cheltenham, a specialist unit for people with spinal injuries, or SCIs, as they insist on calling them. I had emergency surgery. Now, the focus is on damage and swelling reduction.

I stare down at my legs, the back of my eyes burning. I've stopped trying to wriggle my toes.

As in my dream, the world feels all back to front. Hundreds of conversations, thousands of tears. Two questions dominate.

Me: Will I walk again?

Everyone else: How did this happen?

The answers to both are vague and uncertain. How can I possibly explain my horrendous injuries when I was found in a luxury hotel room? The truth is, I can't. I tell people I was stupid, that I was crushed, that it was an accident.

A kind, well-dressed consultant, Mr. Thorpe, told me I sustained multiple injuries, broken bones, internal bleeding. A few specifics stand out, like one of those automatically generated word clouds.

Mid to lower thoracic spinal cord.

Possible paralysis. Waist-down.

Rehabilitation. Therapy.

Counseling. Depression. Anxiety.

"Am I paralyzed?" I asked, my voice sounding like it came from afar.

"That's uncertain." His voice calm, his delivery measured. "We will know more soon."

"What happens now?"

"It will be tough, but with rehabilitation and hard work, you may be able to walk again."

Anger bubbled up in me. What did this man know? He's young, healthy. He can walk out of here and go home, forget about all this. I gritted my teeth and told him, "I will walk out of here within a month, guaranteed."

He offered me a kind, supportive smile. "It's good to set goals."

I've been bombarded with love from all sides. Love I don't deserve. It's going to drown me. My throat tightens as I think back over all the visits and difficult conversations. A sickening mix of empathy, pity, and positivity. My parents were angry, with me, with the world. It's fair enough; they didn't ask for this. They wanted the truth. I told them I fell from a hotel balcony, said it was an accident. They didn't believe me, but they didn't push it. They just cried. We all did. I begged them not to tell Amy. They said they would have to, eventually. I'm dreading talking to her because she knows that I didn't have to do this, that it was my choice.

Vinny phoned, told me that he was sorry about getting angry, said he will always be my friend. It's amazing what a near-death experience does to the trivial crap. When I last saw him, Vinny said he's going to come over with a record deck and some albums so we can listen to the Beatles.

I told him that would be all good, but right now, nothing interests me.

Tears come, and I let them. I sleep. This time there are no dreams.

When I wake, it's morning. Time is like this now, untrustworthy. Alexia sits next to me, holding my hand. She's been here every day. Each visit brings more pain. She smiles. It takes all my will not to cry again.

"How are you feeling?" she asks.

I want to scream, to rage, to cry and tell her that I'm never going to walk again, but I don't, of course. We talk . . . well, she does. She asks questions, tells me about her day. If she stops talking, the silence builds to a deafening crescendo.

She tells me that she isn't going anywhere, but she feels like a boat, already drifting.

She kisses me, tells me again that she's *here*.

I thank her, but we're done.

There is nothing I can offer her now.

The morning bleeds into the afternoon. I'm alone. Outside, the sky is a flat gray. I watch trees shimmer freely in a gentle breeze. My world has become this room and my thoughts rattle around, sharp and dangerous. My mind gets stuck in loops.

I keep seeing a pedestrian crossing.

Walk, don't walk. Flashing, over and over. I was green. Now I'm red.

Tears come again, and I let them. It hurts too much to keep them in.

This is how it will be now. People must come to me because I can't go to them. I am here, and yet I'm gone. I'm being cared for by good, decent people who wash and feed me, help me go to the bathroom. I'm incredibly lucky to have them. I know that.

But I feel cursed. Cursed, because I tried.

My phone rings. It's Iris, calling from a future I can't be a part of anymore. So far, I've ignored her calls. Kristin spoke to her a couple of times, filling Iris in on what she knew. I stare at my phone. A regular call. No VR today. I suppose that makes sense. Iris's hologram would blow the minds of every staff member here. The other option would be deep VR, sending my consciousness into the future. Once there, my reality in the present would melt away, for me, along with the restrictions of this mangled and broken body. Perhaps Iris knows as well as I do that if I could walk around in a virtual world, I might never come back to the real one.

I accept the call.

"I'm so terribly sorry, Joseph," Iris says. Everyone is sorry. I can't stand it. "What happened?" I open my mouth, but where do I start? It still doesn't feel real. "If it's too difficult, we can wait."

Now or later, it makes no difference.

I tell her what I can: completing the change event, capturing Scarlett's signature. I'm relieved when Iris acknowledges the success of the mission. Aaron Pennington went on to live a long, fulfilling life.

"The tracker worked," Iris tells me. "The next time Scarlett travels, we will know."

"That's good," I say. *I hope it was worth it.*

"Did you see her?"

The line is quiet for a few seconds, both of us breathing. Does Iris know the answer to that question already? Probably. I've seen Downstream. I know The Continuum has incredible ways of visualizing and analyzing time. What else does she know? Does she know what Bill was doing when he saved me in London? Does she know that Felix and I discussed Scarlett, that Felix was onto her? I'm struggling to remember who knows what. There are too many secrets. Maybe it's time for a little more transparency.

"When Bill saved me in London, he broke some rules," I explain. "Somehow, Scarlett found out, and she's been trying to replicate whatever it was he achieved."

"Beating resistance," Iris says.

I frown. "You knew about this?"

"I had my suspicions. Scarlett always felt we could do more."

"She was using some device," I continue. "She found an area in San Francisco where resistance was weak, a building. She told me that only I could change the outcome and save the people inside." My chest tightens, my anger simmering again. "Why did she do this to me, Iris? Did she know I was going to get hurt? Was it deliberate?"

"Honestly, I don't know. But what she said about not being able to change the past is true. It was a constant frustration for her." She breathes thoughtfully. "What happened to you is terrible, but did Scarlett mean to hurt you? I don't think so, but she put you in danger, and for that, I will never forgive her."

"She hoped I would come back, that my success would prove something to you, open lines of communication."

"All she has proved is that she's reckless."

"So what's next?" I ask.

Iris answers without hesitation. "We stop Scarlett and ensure this never happens again."

A long silence passes between us. The void of time feels fragile. What I'm about to ask will affect the rest of my life. Am I ready to know the answer? I'm not sure, but I'm going to ask anyway.

I swallow, lips dry. "Iris, can my injuries be undone?"

She must have anticipated this question, because she answers quickly, her voice calm. "You were injured while on an active mission. I'm very sorry, but we can't alter this."

I grip the phone. "We're time travelers, Iris. Surely, there's a way." The desperation in my voice scares me. "Can't you send someone back to warn me?"

When she speaks, her voice is filled with empathy. "I'm sorry, Joseph, but the change event has closed, the past is now written in time and cannot be undone."

"But . . . if that's true, how did Bill save me in London?"

"We don't know. I don't think we ever will, but you must believe me, if there was anything I could do to stop you from getting injured, I would do it."

"I know," I say. I expected this, but it still leaves me feeling numb.

We talk for a while longer. Iris picks through the rubble of my memories, wanting to know every detail of what Scarlett said to me. She tells me that Felix is giving me some space but would like to talk soon. He's focusing on the Future Change Index, which despite my efforts is still in a steep decline. Seems it's not just my future that's broken.

Iris says all the right things, tells me that it will be a process of adjustment, that I will get through this. I tell her I know, but it's a lie. The only way this is going to be OK is with me walking again.

I obsess over the San Francisco earthquake, researching on my iPad. Aaron Pennington lived a long and meaningful life. There are numerous accounts, some going into graphic detail of what he achieved on that terrible night, incredible stories that focus on the serendipity of a surgeon being on the scene. Aaron Pennington saved people. He was a hero.

I try not to think about the woman, the dog, the kids upstairs. I don't know who they were, and I don't want to. Days go by. People visit. Yet I remain alone, locked in a cell that was once my body.

Iris calls again to check on me. I ask her if there's been any contact from Scarlett. Nothing. I'm not sure what I expected. Perhaps I hoped that when she heard what had happened, she might contact The Continuum, maybe even get in touch with me. She seemed so genuine, and after everything we've been through, I even started to trust her. How am I supposed to feel now? She's been a shadow since my time traveling began. We had one conversation, my only chance to get to know her, and then this. She's the one to blame. And yet here I am, trying to give her the benefit of the doubt. I'm an idiot.

My upper lip curls in disgust as I stare at my useless legs. I play with the sensation, really curling my lip to the left, the natural side. When I try to do the same on the right side, it doesn't move at all. That's what my legs feel like. My brain remembers what to do, but my legs won't play anymore. They can't. I ruined them, let them down. They served me well, and this is how I repaid them.

A war rages inside me. The prize is my soul. I keep telling myself I will get through this, but a voice inside my head disagrees.

"I'm going to walk again," I growl.

But what if you don't? the voice asks, its tone horribly kind and empathetic. *What if this is it for you?*

That makes me think of what older Amy told me when I met her in the future. She said that if her destiny is derailed in my present, and she doesn't travel into the future and trigger the Extrapolation Event, then I must find her and persuade her to jump. What does that mean now?

It takes a week, but I am finally able to look one of my caregivers in the eye. His name is Steve, a good guy. He helps me to the toilet. I thank him. I've been horrible. I want to be better. There's positive talk of a plan, intensive rehabilitation, going home. But all of it has additional caveats, details that my subconscious stores away for when the sun goes down. There will be caregivers looking after me. My house will need "adapting." I don't think I'm going to be able to do this.

Visitors all wear the same positive expression, but they can't hide their sad and worried eyes. Alexia visits again, looking at me like she can see the long road ahead. I think she's trying to convince herself that she has what it takes.

Maybe she does, but love needs light and oxygen, and I'm in the dark with the air running out.

And that's how my mind works now. My mood doesn't swing, it slams into me like a truck. If a glimmer of happiness or potential shows itself, my dark half snarls and bites and scares it away.

And so I take all my anger and fear and focus it on Alexia because we hurt the ones we love. I know what I'm doing, but I can't stop. My soul is a punching bag, and my words are my fists. I tell her that I'm broken, that she has options, her whole life ahead of her. The destruction feels good, the pain raw.

Eventually, Alexia says, "I'm going to go now." She stands, steadies herself. "I know you're angry, and that's OK . . . It's understandable, it's part of the process."

"You should leave me," I say. "I can't be anything to you."

"That isn't your choice!" she snaps, angrily. "It's mine, and I'm not going to let you push me away!"

"You're leaving, though, aren't you?"

She frowns, fighting back tears, and then leaves.

She will get the message eventually. At some point, she'll miss a day, and then the next time, maybe two. And then she won't visit me for a week, and the guilt will form a gap that widens until she can't cross it anymore. And then, if she tries to build a bridge, I will burn it down. It's for her own good. She just doesn't know it yet.

Two days later, panic sets in. Was I right? Has Alexia given up on me? When I see her in the doorway, we both start to cry.

"I'm so sorry," I tell her.

"So am I." She approaches the bed, leans over, and hugs me.

Her warmth brings me home. We hold each other for a while, words unnecessary. My old life, the one with plans and dreams, has gone, yet I am still here, and so is Alexia. She told me this is a process. I know she's right. Life is a process. It never stays the same. Change is inevitable.

How we cope with that change is what defines us.

Eventually, Alexia grabs her bag and pulls out some printed pages. "I did some research. I wanted to understand a little about what you went through, and I found this. You need to see it."

She hands me a printed article featuring a photograph of a young boy called Pablo Constante. He beams at me from a hospital bed. Standing beside him is Aaron Pennington, his expression very different from that of the man I met on the bridge.

"This boy was trapped in a car, losing blood," Alexia explains. "He would have died if it weren't for Aaron."

I stare at the photograph. Two ghosts, alive and well.

I'm not surprised to see a Game Boy in Pablo's hand.

Aaron Pennington saved Pablo and others too. I read about

how an anonymous donation led to the building of a special pediatric wing, Aaron Pennington's dream realized.

"There are some amazing stories," Alexia says. "I know this might be hard for you to see, but I think it might help." She hands me another page, a news article that shows the collapsed Cypress Freeway, its supporting columns splayed out and twisted like a crushed snake. There is talk of survivors, bravery, miracles. A caption details the death toll. Seventy people in the Bay Area. It's horrible, but I remember Kristin telling me in the hotel room that it was seventy-four.

Alexia swims in my vision. My voice trembles with emotion. "Aaron made a difference. He saved the lives of four people. It wasn't all for nothing."

"Your actions did so much good, you must try and remember that." She wipes away her own tears. "I wanted to read this to you as well." She pulls out a page. "I found an interview with Aaron. A reporter gained his trust, got him to open up a little about his experiences. Can I read it to you?"

I tell her she can.

She pops her glasses on the end of her nose and finds her spot. "Here it is . . . This is the reporter, interviewing him:

I ask Aaron what he thinks of being labeled a hero. He considers the question thoughtfully and tells me, 'I can understand why people might say that, but I'm no hero. It wasn't just me. I saw amazing bravery that night. I'm just glad I was able to help. It was an honor, actually.' I can tell there's more on his mind. I ask if he would be willing to share it. He says he's never spoken about it but thinks maybe it's time he did. He says, 'I was at a crossroads in my life, had a decision to make. It haunts me to think I could have turned left instead of right.' I ask him what he means. 'A stranger helped me out of a bad situation. His kindness showed me that I had a lot to live for. He set me on

my path. Little did I know how soon I would be called upon.'
I ask him what it was the stranger said. He smiles and tells me
that it will always remain between the two of them. He leans
in, his expression serious, yet open and warm. 'What matters
is that my hope and purpose were renewed. I realized at that
moment that I had a lot to be thankful for. None of us knows
what lies just around the corner.'"

Alexia squeezes my hand. "What you did was amazing, Joe."

"Aaron was a good man."

"And he was able to help and save those people, thanks to you."

We go on to talk, properly, for the first time since I came
back. The honesty finally fills enough of my mind to silence
the darkness. Of course, I know it's temporary, but I'm overwhelmed by my feelings for this amazing woman.

"Kristin wants to visit," Alexia tells me. "Would that be OK?"

"Soon, yes."

Hours go by, eventually Alexia needs to go, but she tells me
she'll be back tomorrow.

I tell her that I'm looking forward to it, and I'm surprised
to discover that's true.

She leaves, but a few seconds later, she's back.

"Did you forget something?" I ask.

"No, you have a visitor, says he's a friend of yours."

"Bill," I say without thinking.

She shakes her head. "Felix. I wanted to check you're up
to it."

Instinctively, my hand moves to my silver hunter. Felix isn't
a time traveler. As far as I know, the only way that he could contact me in person is virtually, using ICARUS.

"He's here, in the waiting room," Alexia says. "Should I
send him in?"

I nod. She blows me a kiss and turns away. I've learned to

trust my instincts, even though they don't care about my feelings. They just show up, whether I like it or not. They are screaming at me now, certain of two things.

First: that was the last time I'm going to see Alexia.

Second: for some reason, that's good.

32

Felix walks in and pauses a few feet from me, his lean features shadowed in the mellow overhead lights. It's dark outside, the wind howls, rain whips and lashes the windows. Felix's chest rises and falls as he studies the room. I press a button, and my bed adjusts, bending my useless legs slightly, raising me. Eventually, he looks at me, his lips creasing into a ghost of a smile that fades immediately. It's a familiar gesture. Pity. Empathy. Honorable and decent, of course, but painful to see.

"I'm very sorry to see you like this," he says.

His coat is beaded with droplets of rain, his wet hair pushed back over his head. He seems very much here, in my present. "This isn't VR."

"No. I traveled here, alone."

"You're able to travel now?"

"Yes . . . and more . . ." He steps forward, his eyes alive with secrets. "I have so much to tell you."

"Have a seat," I tell him.

"Thank you," he replies but remains standing. He's wearing contemporary clothes, looks like he belongs here. "I *knew*

Bill was hiding something. I studied the Romano mission, cross-referenced it to Paris and your recent mission in San Francisco. It was driving me crazy, but I knew I was onto him." A frenetic energy fizzes around Felix. I imagine the droplets of water on his jacket turning to steam. He draws a breath, holds my gaze. "That's when I found it. Bill's archive. Deleted, of course, but I was able to recover just enough. He unlocked secrets that have eluded me since the beginning of The Continuum, Joe." He smiles to himself, but when he looks at me, his excited expression fades. He glances at my legs, frowning. "I'm sorry. I was determined not to get too excited, yet here I am, babbling on when you're in this . . . situation."

Situation. It sounds so temporary. "It's OK, Felix. I'm listening."

He continues, words pouring out of him like a dam just broke. "Bill knew it was dangerous, that it could be used against us, but he didn't live to see the *potential*. If he had, I think he might have felt differently."

"The potential of what?"

"Bill discovered a way to reinsert a traveler into a change event. It's how he saved you. Scarlett somehow learned what he did—we think via a leak at The Continuum—and she's been experimenting, trying to replicate his achievement in London, but also trying to test the boundaries. That's what she was doing with Nils in Paris. Taking Bill's research further." He pauses with the faint flicker of a smile. "I haven't stopped, Joseph. You need to know that. After I talked to you, I was determined to undo the damage Scarlett was wreaking on our work, our people, the Index. I've joined all the dots, and now we can use this knowledge to give you another chance." He looks around the room, gestures at my ruined legs. "We can undo . . . all of this."

A sudden sense of hope burns through me, its intensity

dangerous, intoxicating. "Felix . . . I'm slowly adjusting to this. Be careful what you promise."

"I understand," he says, "but I'm confident that what I have planned will work. Your mission in London failed. You died, and yet Bill figured out how to reinsert himself into a closed change event, alter the outcome, and beat resistance. Scarlett's attempt to replicate that sent Nils into the void. Now, we take all that research and knowledge, and we perfect the process. We change it all."

"Iris was clear," I say. "My fate was sealed when the change event ended. You can't save me."

"You're right," he says, eyes shimmering. "You're going to save yourself."

I stare at him. "What do you mean?"

"Using a unique form of duplication. Bill managed it. Scarlett was attempting the same when she sent Nils into the void. But she was missing a crucial step in Bill's process."

He takes an object from his jacket and holds it in the palm of his hand, ensuring I can see it clearly. It's a concave lozenge, about an inch in diameter, its surface glossy and smooth. I see movement within the glassy shell, tiny glimmering shapes like stars through the lens of a telescope.

"What is it?" I ask him, transfixed.

"A way to split time," he says, admiring the shell. "It's how Bill saved you. I'm convinced of that now. Based on the principles of the multiverse, this will split the timeline, allowing you to reenter a change event." He hands it to me, cool to the touch, heavy and solid.

The dream in which I saw myself in a mirror comes rushing back to me. Was it really a dream, or was it a viewing or perhaps a hybrid of the two? How could I have foreseen an event that hadn't happened yet? Premonitions are Amy's gift, not mine. Then again, time is relative in that regard. If my future lies in the past, then perhaps I can see the occasional glimpse of what might be.

"This changes the entire game," Felix says, drawing me from my thoughts. "Completed change events are no longer closed. We have opportunities to go back, do more, alter the outcome or find pockets of new potential where resistance is weaker."

"Wait . . . Are you saying Scarlett was telling the truth?"

"I question her motives, but she was on the right track. Re-insertion causes a weakening of resistance in certain locations. It makes sense of her actions. Scarlett was always searching for ways to do more, to bend the rules."

"You just said I'm going to save *myself*, but I can't move, Felix. How am I supposed to do anything?" I still can't bring myself to say the word *paralyzed*.

"Here's where it gets complicated," he says, as if it were straightforward so far. "When we split the San Francisco time-line, we create two versions of you."

I reluctantly tear my eyes from the device. "Two of me . . . That's happened before, right? When Gabrielle and I met ourselves in Paris."

He shakes his head. "That's different. You were revisiting a moment in time that you had already been to, *before* the change event was complete. This process splices a closed event and inserts two versions of you. In order to achieve this, I must travel back to you before your final jump to 1989."

Surprisingly, I'm following so far. My body may be broken, but when it comes to time travel, I'm no longer a newbie. "So it won't be me doing this, it will be a previous version of me from my own past?"

"Exactly."

I think of my clone in my dream, staring back at me. I was consumed with fear. Now, I *want* him to steal this life, and I hope he erases it for good. "What about Aaron Pennington, the man I saved on the bridge?"

Felix considers this. "I know you completed the mission. How did you do? Are there any details you would change?"

I think it through. "We shouldn't change it. He didn't jump."

"Good. OK. There will be two versions of you. Both of you will remember this conversation. I will offset your landing location. Upon arrival, one of you should go to the bridge and allow the mission to play out exactly as it did before. This leaves the other to focus on Scarlett and the people in the house. Once Aaron is saved, all you have to do is ensure that neither of you enters the house. Then you will both safely return to the present."

Visions of myself, spliced and stuck back together like Play-Doh, leave me queasy.

"When you say we will return to the present, you mean both of us?" I ask nervously.

"No, you will be merged again. Time likes things to be neat and tidy."

"Right." I look down at my legs. "And this won't happen?"

He nods, his eyes alight. "You will be back to normal."

Normal. I want to cry, but my conscience is screaming. The time splitter suddenly feels very cold.

"What is it?" Felix asks. "I thought you would be pleased."

"I am," I tell him. "I'm sorry. I really appreciate what you're trying to do for me, but what about the people in the house?"

His brow narrows. Slowly, he rubs a hand across his stubbled chin and shakes his head. "I just knew you'd want to try and save them."

"Is there a way?"

"Yes, possibly, but you don't have to do this, Joe."

Pain pinches my heart. I see the house collapsing, the woman's face, the kids cowering in the bedroom. Their innocence is just strong enough to beat my fear. Felix wasn't there. I can't really expect him to understand. "Look, you were just telling me about beating resistance, that we could do more. If there's a way to save them, I have to try."

Felix finally sits down, his features clearer under the lights. He looks exhausted. I imagine him working day and night beneath Greystone House. He eyeballs me, his expression all stony concern. "Only do this if you're absolutely certain."

"I am," I reply immediately. "Now, tell me how this works."

Felix talks me through the plan. He will go back to before I jumped and give me the time splitter. Once I'm in 1989, I will be able to enter the void and even use time dilation to my advantage. It's complicated, but Felix assures me that I will be fully briefed, in the past.

It's odd to think of my fate lying in the hands of a previous version of myself. If he succeeds, I will be erased. Good, I think, my pointless legs tingling with phantom pain. There's an irony, of course. When I saved Amy, I replaced a previous version of me. There was nothing wrong with him.

Time-travel guilt: it's the worst. It goes on and on, hits you from all directions. But how can I say no? If there's a chance, it's worth a shot, isn't it?

"What's the worst that could happen?" I hold up a hand. "Actually, don't answer that. The worst scenario is that I die, right?"

"You're not going to die." Felix is doing his best. The fact there is a chance at all means I owe him a lot. "There is one thing," he says. "For now, we must keep this plan between us."

"Felix . . . I'm not sure that's a good idea."

He fixes me with a steely gaze. "We have discovered a way to make The Continuum infinitely more effective, but if anyone knew what we were doing, they would try and stop us."

This reminds me of my conversation with Bill. Both of them

are dabbling in the darker side of time travel. He looks at me with a determined expression on his face. Am I about to trust my history to him? I guess I am. It's strange, though. Felix is intense, passionate, and smart, but I've never felt like I've truly seen him. His work drives him, the science, the possibilities, but I can only hope that he isn't blinded by this, that he is considering the human cost. That he's considering me.

Felix smiles. "You told me that Bill was worried about this falling into the wrong hands . . . Well, it's in *our* hands, and we can use it for good. If we can prove this works, and the Change Index lights up green across the board, do you really think Iris will care *then?*"

I think back on my various interactions with Bill. I see the shield mounted on his wall.

Respect the Past
Protect the Future
Trust in the Great Unfolding

His memory comforts me, but he was so adamant that what he discovered must never be used again. Bill was trying to save me, but was that selfish? Like discovering the cure to a disease and then only giving it to a loved one? I think of Iris, so sure that my fate was permanently woven into the fabric of time. I could think about this for weeks. It won't make any difference. It doesn't matter what anyone says, and that's the truth, because if there is a way that I can walk again *and* save those people, then there isn't a choice. My decision is made. I just hope I don't regret it.

"I'm in," I tell Felix. "What happens now?"

"I'm going to use previous data to make my calculations. It's the safest way. To find you, I need to know a good time and location that I can visit, before your final jump to San Francisco."

"OK, there are plenty, I guess."

"Not so fast. For this to work, I need to find you *after* you bonded with the focus object. I need a solid time and location *between* your first and second jumps."

I think that through. I bonded with the Game Boy, landed at Candlestick Park, returned to the hotel room . . . "This might be a problem. I only had fifteen minutes between jumps."

"That's tight," Felix says, standing and pacing the room. His concerned expression shifts. It's clear he has no intention of failing. "I need to brief you without altering your departure in any way. We don't want to change anything unnecessarily or introduce new variables that might alter your jump. Think carefully. Were you alone at any point? A quiet place that we could meet?"

My arrival at the hotel with Alexia plays through my mind at double speed. Entering Kristin's apartment, our conversations . . . I primed the object, traveled, and came back. What then?

Then I remember. "I called Iris, using ICARUS."

"That's good, that gives me a solid reference. Were you alone before or after?"

"I was with Alexia and Kristin," I say. "I asked them to do some research, and then a few minutes later, I went to the bathroom." I shrug. "Will that do?"

He arches an eyebrow.

"To wash my face!" I clarify. "You know, gather my thoughts. It would be the only chance to talk to me without changing anything. Can you be that precise?"

Felix smiles. "I'm going to use Downstream for the calculations. It will be perfect. Now tell me everything that happened in San Francisco. Spare no details, however small. I will need to brief you, and ensure that you avoid the same mistakes, don't get injured, *and* save the people in the house."

The wind and rain lash at the window as I recount my doomed attempt to save the family. Felix wants to know what Scarlett said, what she was planning. I tell him about the woman in the kitchen, how it collapsed, the kids, the stairs. And then finally, precise details of my location before I jumped, exactly when and where Felix will find me in the past.

"I think that's all of it," I tell him. "What are you going to do now?"

"Plot the coordinates into Downstream and then travel back to you. Once San Francisco is locked down and you are safe, I'm going after Scarlett. Thanks to you, we have a way to track her whereabouts. I will talk to her, see if we can work together."

"That's good. I think that's what she wants."

He nods. "We'll see. People say things, but it's what they do that matters."

He's right about that. I don't know Felix that well, don't know if I can trust him, but the truth is, he came back for me. Does he have ulterior motives? Gabrielle once described Felix as a man of mystery. She's right. He's impossible to read, but facts are facts. He's here, and he's willing to help me out of this dreadful situation.

"Thank you, Felix. For coming back and trying to fix this. It means a lot."

"You would do the same for me."

He's right.

Felix leaves me with a renewed sense of hope. Hope that I might walk again, that the people I tried to save will live, that our plan won't mess the past up even more. I close my eyes and listen to the rain, wondering what it might feel like to be removed from existence. Rewritten. Healed. I think of the Joe I once replaced. Same deal, different set of circumstances. Perhaps there are endless versions of me. The good, the bad, and the broken. None of us knowing how this all works.

———————

Two weeks earlier. The Savoy Hotel. Room 612.

The bathroom is massive. Black-and-white marble tiles on every surface. A roll top bath, huge walk-in shower, and a double sink unit, big as a breakfast bar. I lock the door behind me, splash water on my face, and let out a jagged breath. Fear sets my muscles twitching, my own little aftershocks. The man in the mirror looks afraid, already beaten.

"Listen," I tell him. "You're going to be OK." Suddenly, I'm not alone. Felix is standing behind me. His gaze locks onto mine. He appears calm, resolute, like he was expecting this.

"Jesus!" I hiss at him. "What are you doing here?"

"I've just come from your future. You and I agreed on this course of action." He fixes me with a determined stare. "You must trust me now, Joe. We don't have long."

I dry my face and force myself to breathe. So many questions. As far as I know, Felix isn't a traveler. What changed? There's a tap on the door, three knocks. "Just checking." Alexia's voice. "You OK in there?"

"I'm fine," I call back. "Be out in a minute."

Felix launches straight in. "You complete the mission successfully, you save a man from committing suicide."

"If I succeed, then why have you come back?"

"You try and help people trapped inside a building, but you get hurt, Joe."

"How badly?"

"It doesn't work out well, but that's why I came back. We can change it."

"That's not enough," I say, shaking my head. "I need specifics. What happens to me?"

Felix doesn't speak for a beat, genuinely considering my question and how best to answer it. When he does speak, I understand why his expression was so pained. "You were crushed, your spine damaged. I'm sorry, but you are paralyzed, Joe. The doctors don't think you will ever walk again. Even with our technology in the future, there's nothing we can do. I discussed this with you, the idea of coming back and talking to you before you jump, and you agreed that I should come back and tell you all of this. You have a chance not only to complete the mission, but also to save these people and, with extra knowledge of what you're heading into, undo your paralysis."

I draw in a breath. "And you know all of this because I told you?"

"Yes, but this time you can save them *and* avoid being trapped inside the house."

I'm racing to keep up, the possibilities and questions building, but right now, my priority is my impending travel. I stare at Felix, seeing a future in his eyes that I don't want to imagine. "Why would I try and beat resistance?"

"You meet Scarlett."

"In San Francisco?"

"Yes, and she persuades you to try and save the people in the house."

"But that's impossible. Resistance would stop me."

"Scarlett took Bill's research, and she found a way to alter time that was previously resistant to change, to beat the observer effect."

"You're telling me that Scarlett is responsible for my injuries?"

He sighs. "There is a lot we don't know, but you told me you didn't think she meant to harm you. We want to try and work with her, but the top priority is getting you back safely."

"Tell me about the people in the house. What do I need to know?"

Felix takes me through a detailed account of meeting Scarlett and my interactions inside the house. It warps my brain and chills my bones. Then, he holds up a metallic band that looks a bit like a wristwatch. Instead of a timepiece though, there is a glassy lozenge filled with dark, alien light. "This is a time splitter. Press it at the point of travel and there will be two of you when you land. Put it on your wrist."

I take it from him, slip it over my hand and shudder. It's cold to the touch, but my reaction is an emotional one. Two of me. A clone.

Felix says, "When you're in the past, press the splitter again and you will have three seconds before you enter the void."

"The void," I murmur, envisioning windows and zoetropes. "Like Nils trying to escape the opera house."

"Exactly. This is what Scarlett was trying to achieve in Paris. What Bill and Scarlett did enabled this chance, but now *we* have control. You will enter the void and have options linked to various key moments. Choose your entry and exit points wisely, and get out of the building before it collapses. If you need to, you will be able to drag others into the void with you." I consider this, the possibility of moving people around like chess pieces. It could be useful, if a little crazy. "And if you press the splitter accidentally, just press it again to cancel."

A few seconds pass, precious time dripping away. My mind

is buzzing but I can't help wondering who else knows about Felix's plan. "I just talked to Iris. Does she know about this?"

He doesn't answer immediately.

"Why don't you want to tell them?"

"I was afraid that if I did, they would stop me."

Secrets and lies lurk in the shadows. Felix has an agenda, and he's pushing it. There's a niggling deep in my belly that tells me to be wary of Felix, but I have my own agenda. Save the family and get my life back. They say love is blind. Sometimes, it's the same with trust.

"One final thing," Felix says. "You told me that when Bill saved you, he seemed to move at incredible speed. You described it as a red blur." I nod. "The reentry causes a secondary phenomenon, time dilation, like you experienced when you fired the lantern in Paris. Time will appear to move slower after you exit the void, giving you increased speed, relatively speaking. Be aware though, time catches up to you after a few seconds."

"Felix, this is a lot to take in."

"I know, I'm sorry, but you were so close before, and now you have these extra tools. You can do this, Joe. Save these people and put the FCI back to where it should be." His infectious optimism combats my fear.

"How many doorways will there be?" I ask.

"We have no way of knowing, but once each is used, it will close for good."

"I remember; it was the same for Nils."

I've traveled through a zoetrope myself when I was saving Amy. The Continuum had no control over them, so they developed the watches to bring stability and avoid dangerous return trips. Now Felix is removing that stability. What choice do I have?

"I'll do my best," I assure him.

Felix checks the time on a wrist-mounted device that isn't like the pocket watches most travelers have. "I will be here a little longer."

"OK, I should go and prepare."

"Good luck, Joe."

A kind of understating passes between us. Rules are being broken, but the reasons feel justified. "Thank you . . . for coming back, I mean."

There is more to say: about Scarlett, Bill, the dangers. I want to ask Felix how and why he has started traveling, but as always, time is pouring away, fast. I leave him in the bathroom, which feels weird, knowing that he won't walk out.

When I enter the living room, I'm convinced that Kristin and Alexia will ask who I was talking to, but they're huddled around an iPad, watching live coverage of the 1989 World Series. The feed cuts out just as the commentator realizes they're experiencing an earthquake. It's like a Hollywood disaster movie. Déjà vu washes through me. I'm living through my own past. I know I've done this before, but I don't remember it.

Alexia pauses the broadcast. "Sorry."

"It's fine," I assure her. "We don't have long. Tell me as much as you can."

They talk me through the disaster. The upper deck of the Oakland Bay Bridge fell onto the one below. Kristin describes the Cypress Freeway, tells me in a somber voice that most of the casualties occurred there. Noted. We check the map and complete my plan, which only I know is way more complicated than the first time I did this.

Alexia reaches for my hand. I warn her not to touch me, normal time-travel protocols, but I'm also aware of the time splitter. I have no idea what would happen if I was holding her hand when I pressed it, and I have no intention of finding out.

"This is so strange, Joe," Alexia says, "What you can do, I mean."

"You're not wrong," I tell her, and then laugh because just when I think I'm getting my head around what's possible, someone breaks the rules, and it's all up in the air again. I fold my right hand over my left wrist, the metallic surface of the splitter cold to the touch.

Alexia looks at me, concerned. "I heard what Iris said. Don't risk your own life."

"I won't," I tell her, knowing that I did, that I messed it all up.

Not this time.

"Come back safe," she says, feeling almost cross. "I mean it."

I feel stretched. My heart is here with Alexia, my body pulled toward the past, my mind in the future, on a version of my life that took a darker turn. The thought of being caught in the quake, being crushed, makes me shudder.

"Do you need to touch the focus object again?" Alexia asks.

I shake my head. "We were bonded when we first touched."

Alexis smiles, but it fades quickly. My skin shimmers. I'm on my way. As I feel the familiar weightlessness of time travel, I slide my thumb over the time splitter and depress the button. It sinks with a satisfying click.

A gentle buzz on my wrist counts down, and the room fades into darkness. Sudden and brilliant pain makes me scream, soundless in an empty void. A tugging, tearing sensation like being ripped in two. And then the world splits down the middle, and I'm no longer alone. The pain recedes. I'm here, and so is he. Unaware of me, but close. We travel back to 1989. We both have a mission. And if we get this right, we can save them all.

33

I'm on an embankment. Ahead, the outline of the Golden Gate Bridge cuts against a solid, vibrant blue sky. My feeling of disembodiment fades. I am whole, I am real, and I am here *twice*.

Twenty feet below me, on a road leading to the bridge, is my twin.

My mind does a little flip-flop. Watching yourself, seeing how you move, how others see you, is a wholly unnerving experience. This isn't the first time I've seen myself when time traveling, but it feels . . . different. This isn't a rerun. I'm not here to observe what I did before. The man down there is me. We are the same. He knows what I know, will remember Felix visiting us just before the jump. He knows as well as I do that there's a man on the bridge who needs saving. And he knows what's at stake for us, personally.

My clone shields his eyes, looking for me.

When he sees me, we both shudder. What do you call this? The self-observer effect?

For just a few seconds, it feels like it's just me and him,

but then other people arrive in the area, joining our scene like extras in a movie.

We both stare at the bridge. I check my silver hunter. Other Joe does the same.

It's 3:45 p.m. The quake hits at 5:04. Plenty of time.

I make my way down to him. The jogger does a double take as he passes.

Other Joe and I smile awkwardly. "Right," we say in unison. I'm struck by a fierce sense of ownership over my body. What if we had to fight for our place in the world? Who would win? We're literally the same. I banish these thoughts. They are not going to help me achieve my goal.

"Should we flip a coin?" Other Joe asks.

"Maybe," I say.

He holds up his hand, eyebrows raised. It takes me a second to realize why. He doesn't have a time splitter on his wrist. It's the one detail that differentiates us.

Turns out we don't need a coin. I'm the one with the splitter. So I guess *I'm* in charge.

Our watches buzz. *Calibrating* becomes *Change Event*. And then they buzz again. A new alert: *Wake Scan, Signal Acquired.*

As expected, Scarlett's signal, 3.4 km away.

Other Joe glances at the bridge. "What's the plan?"

"You take the change event," I tell him. "I'll go after Scarlett. When you're done on the bridge, come and meet me at the house."

He licks his lips, looks a little scared. It's strange to see myself like this. I want to tell him it will be OK, but he's mirroring my expression. Both of us worried, afraid we might fail. Our fear is a constant force, no matter what the timeline. Something to work on when I get home. We draw a breath and then wish each other luck. The action is so perfectly synchronized that an observer would think we had practiced it for hours.

He jogs away. I watch him for a few seconds, scrambling up a bank toward the head of the bridge. I feel like I've drawn the short straw here. We both know that he will succeed, that he saves the man on the bridge. I'm heading into an almighty mess.

Time to move. Yes, entering a house during a quake is dangerous, but thanks to Felix—and in a freaky way, myself—I know enough to put it right.

In the distance I hear children playing, see a picnic area nearby. Felix told me to steal a bike from a nearby park, said I did this before. It's strange to have been briefed on choices I haven't made yet, but also feel them appearing in my head as ideas. My watch buzzes. I check the display. The red light is illuminated, my final jump warning. I expected it, of course, but it still sends my heart rate up a few beats per minute. As I select a bike from a rack of them, I pause. What if I steal the same one as I did before? Will that create a stolen bike paradox?

No, I don't think so. Felix explained that this isn't a rerun of a previous jump. I'm not overlayed. This is totally different, a rewrite. Still, to be safe, I choose a woman's bike.

Ensuring I wasn't spotted, I cycle far enough away and then pull over to check that I'm heading roughly in Scarlett's direction. The map offers only rudimentary guidance, but it does the job. As I cycle the wide, sun-dappled streets, it feels good to have the wind on my face, to be moving. I'm unfit, so my legs howl and complain, but after what Felix told me, I have a fresh appreciation of the wonder of movement.

As I join Lincoln Boulevard and reach a steady climb, I work back through everything Felix told me, a detailed moment-by-moment description of what I'm heading into: a residential building, an old woman in the kitchen, her grandson and his friend upstairs. Felix told me the kitchen fell in, how I tried to save the kids, the stairs collapsing. I pedal harder, sweat beading on my brow, my lungs burning. *It's not going to play out like that this time.*

I'm confused about Scarlett, though. Felix seemed so open-minded about her. Did he believe what she told me? After what she has done, does he really think she's innocent? There is another side to this. She could easily have been testing theories again, risking *my* life this time, instead of Nils's. Maybe it was my turn to be her guinea pig. A flash of concern washes over me. When Felix offered me the chance to undo my injuries, there was something in the way he waited, allowing me to step into the silence and ask about saving the people in the house. He even said it: he *knew* that I couldn't abandon them. Does it mean anything? Maybe, but I'm also aware that I sound paranoid. There is no point worrying about it now. In time, it will all become apparent.

I reach the brow of a hill, check my watch, and smile.

Mission Complete.

Other Joe did it!

It's 4:10 p.m. The first part of the plan is done. Now it's my turn.

As I sweep downhill, my elation doesn't last. I tried to follow the map, but still manage to get lost. I hit roadblocks, a couple of complete dead ends, residential clusters of houses that all look the same. Felix didn't mention getting lost the first time around. I begin to panic. I can feel resistance, heavy in the air. Is time trying to stop me? Is this a form of recalibration?

A horrible certainty sinks into my bones.

Time isn't going to allow this change. It knows I'm here, and it knows how this movie ends. My fate is sealed. Gritting my teeth, I cycle hard, pushing these thoughts from my mind with each rotation of the pedals. Finally, I reach a residential area in the recognizable version of San Francisco that I've seen in movies. Resistance is everywhere, my head throbbing with it, but I stay focused and keep moving. Scarlett's signal is close. Signage tells me this is the Marina District. I join Divisadero Street. I pass cafés and office buildings, a park, a welcoming and comparatively safe expanse of grass. I check the time: 4:32 p.m. At least thirty minutes until the show.

I pull over to the side of the street and scan the area. The buildings are taller here. One stands out, glowing with potential: a four-story apartment block, painted cream, with pretty bay windows and numerous front doors. Classic San Francisco.

And that's when I see her. Scarlett stands on the curb, facing the building. She looks different than the last time I saw her in Paris, where she seemed refined, even elegant. Here, she's like a punk-rock chick, purple hair, her skin pale even in the warm sunlight, wearing a hoodie and baggy jeans.

Wherever she goes, she blends in. Scarlett is a chameleon.

A potent sense of déjà vu hits me. My mind spins with it. I *know* that all of this has happened before. My thoughts feel intertwined with time, as though this is code and my destiny is written into the data.

Scarlett spots me and raises a hand. She appears calm, like she's expecting me.

More déjà vu, crashing like waves now.

"You don't seem surprised to see me," I say.

Scarlett purses her dark-purple lips. "I figured you'd have a way of tracking me," she says. "How did your mission go?"

"This has happened before. I got hurt, and it was your fault."

That gets her attention. She studies me, her catlike eyes narrowing. "What are you talking about?"

I gesture toward the building. "Your plans. Weakened

resistance. Saving the family inside. You told me all of this. You told me only I could change it, and you sent me in there. I nearly died."

"Wait . . . This was your final jump, there's no way you could . . ." Her eyes widen. "You figured out how to split the timeline?"

I take a step toward her. "Listen to me. The stuff you're messing with is dangerous, you need to stop."

She shakes her head. "No, you need to listen to me, there are people in there, they need—"

"I know!" I shout back. "That's why I'm here. I'm going to help them, and when I'm done you talk to The Continuum."

She ignores me, her confidence replaced by curiosity. "How did you do it?"

"As if I would tell you," I shoot back. "You're the reason I'm in this mess."

There is a lot more to say, but that's as far as we get because just then Other Joe turns up. He's riding the bike that I *knew* he would choose.

Man, I'm good.

Scarlett looks between the two of us, catching up with proceedings.

This is the point where I take a sledgehammer to the previous timeline.

Other Joe acknowledges Scarlett, but his focus is on me. I'm the one with the time splitter. I'm the one who decides how this plays out. "You go upstairs and get the kids down from the bedroom," I say to my clone. "I'll deal with the grandmother in the kitchen."

He bobs his head. "You're thinking, if we can get the kids downstairs, and she sees them, then we just walk out the front door, right?"

"It's a plan," I tell him. "In and out before the quake really gets going."

He looks impressed, which is a little unnerving. "We go in together," I tell him.

Scarlett stares at us both. Perhaps now she understands the power she's playing with.

"What's that?" she asks, pointing at my wrist.

"It's how I undo the mess you made." I glare at her. "You sent me in there, and I ended up paralyzed."

"I'm sorry."

"Don't be sorry," I warn her, "just stop what you're doing and talk to The Continuum."

Other Joe checks his watch, looks up at me. "It's time."

34

"Felix said it would be open," Other Joe says. "Try it again."

He's a bit annoying, keeps stating the facts like we don't know *the same things*. I try the door handle a second time, and it clicks open.

Perhaps time is on our side.

We enter the apartment. Other Joe heads upstairs. I walk quickly through an open-plan living room toward the kitchen. The smell of warm butter and fried onion guides me, and there, exactly as described, standing with her back to me, is a curvaceous Black woman with a shock of frizzy white hair, preparing food. She turns slightly but doesn't notice me.

"Excuse me," I say.

She whirls around, her dark eyes wide with shock. She's old, maybe seventy, her delicate features creased and deepened with fear. "Who are you?" she gasps. "What do you want?"

I've thought about this, had a chance to plan. I look her straight in the eye, and say confidently, "I'm an off-duty fireman. An earthquake is about to hit, any minute now. My brother is upstairs getting the kids."

"The kids," she says, her voice wavering.

"Yes, we need to get you all out." The clock on the wall reads 5:02. I run back into the living room and call loudly, "Joe, how are you doing up there?"

"They won't come down!" he calls back.

"Well . . . make them!"

When I walk back into the kitchen, the woman has a telephone in one hand—its thick cable stretching across the kitchen—and a knife in the other. She looks between the two, probably trying to figure out how she's going to dial. She glares at me, pushes the knife forward, her hand trembling.

My shouting sounded aggressive, untrustworthy. I am royally messing this up. *Again.*

A dog begins to bark.

Through a window I see a small patch of grass surrounded by a fence. There's a swing, a bench, and a white mongrel with wiry hair. Felix told me his name: Higgins.

A cloud of birds fills the sky.

I've seen this before.

The corn starts popping in the pan, a percussive rhythm that builds in intensity. In the distance, a deep rumble like an approaching train announces the end of normality. The woman's expression changes. She believes me now. Shame it's too late. The earthquake has arrived.

This is it. For stability, I grip my left wrist with my right thumb and depress the time splitter. The button sinks with a satisfying click. The display lights up.

Three: The room begins to sway. I hear the familiar TV broadcast. "I tell you what, I think we are having an earth—"

Two: A gentle rocking motion is followed by a sorrowful moan as the tremor takes hold. The Tiffany lamp sways violently. The room convulses.

One: The reverberation intensifies, but just as all hell is about to break loose, I am plucked from reality and thrown into the eerie silence of the void.

When I first entered this place, I thought my mind had constructed it, a way to visualize time travel. Now I know it's real, that it exists outside of the realms we can comprehend. No time, no sense of space, just a vast and endless ocean of nothing.

My body has a silvery sheen, translucent and iridescent. I walk silently, like a ghost drifting in moonlight, no texture, no sense of connection. All sensory input is offline. Light alone can break this dark spell, but there is none.

Where are the doorways?

I'm unsure if time is passing. It's hard to remain focused with a complete lack of sensory input. I'm vaguely aware that I could lose myself in here—Nils almost did—so my relief is huge when I see a series of faint, blurred shapes appear, shimmering columns of light barely visible against the cloak of darkness. Colors dance within the shapes, pale at first, but then deepening into rich, oily hues.

Moments in time.

They take form around me, sharpening their edges, arranging themselves in an orderly fashion until I see a gallery of animated doorways rotating slowly around me. Seven in total. Each one leads to a key moment. I study them in turn, soaking in the details.

An auto repair shop and a road, showered in sparks.

The living room I just walked through, shaking violently.

The kid's bedroom, posters on the walls: *Hulk smash!*

The yard, a swing, a bench, and Higgins, the dog.

Stairs collapsing in on themselves, like a flower blooming in reverse.

The apartment building, seen from across the street, col-lapsed and distorted.

And finally, a fire truck against a pink-and-gray sky. Strob-ing lights, people gathered.

Some of these scenes are clearly after the quake, others are during. My priority is to get the kids out, so I figure I should just go straight to the bedroom and work it out from there. It seems like the obvious choice, but I need to be careful. Once I travel through a doorway, it closes for good. I can't waste a single one. If I need them, then the order I use them could be critical. The doorways spin around me, slowly enough to allow entry. I walk, absorbing their rhythm, and after the third rotation, I feel confident enough to step into the bedroom.

The absence of physical sensation heightens the impact as I cross between realities. The assault is immediate. Feelings, sounds, temperature all come back in a howling rush of energy.

But time dilation now orchestrates the earthquake in slow motion, so utterly mesmerizing that it almost distracts me from the two boys cowering on the floor. Other Joe leans over them.

The world may have slowed, but I can move at normal speed.

Tremendous jolts of power punch the floor, compressing the air. The energy ripples through my body, the intensity pow-erful but manageable because I can shift my weight and adapt with it. The sound of the quake comes in muffled, almighty booms, followed by deep and throaty cracks, like an ancient glacier creaking deep within the earth.

I turn to Other Joe but realize that there's no point talking to him. At this speed, I would probably sound like a chipmunk. I turn my attention to the kids. What do I do? I could try and drag them downstairs, but I will be moving at lightning-fast speed. I could hurt them. A hissing sound seems to twist the speedometer of time, followed by an earsplitting crack. Dust particles begin to move more freely in the air, and toys that were almost frozen in place start to leap in graceful arcs.

Time is catching up to me, the dilation nearly over. Felix warned me about this, how my window of opportunity would be small. The grandmother is in the kitchen, where the ceiling will collapse soon. I still believe that if I can get them all together, I can get them out. A plan forms in my mind, numerous threads joining together.

Other Joe steadies himself, his movements are slow and exaggerated. His eyes find me. They widen, and his lips ease back in an expression of shocked surprise.

Another gust of wind, a powerful kick from below, and time shifts up another gear. The dilation feels like a fraying rope, unwinding fast now. No time to think. I press the time splitter, grab the kids firmly around their wrists, and watch the countdown. The room dances. The kids slowly look up at me, and in a snap, the bedroom is gone.

I'm back in the void.

But I'm not alone.

I've dragged them with me, just as Felix said I could. I wasn't sure of the rules when we got here, though. Would they be frozen in time, or dilated in some way? Turns out, it's neither. They are synced with me and can move normally. They gaze up at the rotating windows, confused but fascinated.

"What's going on?" one of them asks.

"Where are we?" the other says, his voice wavering and echoless in the void.

It was a risk dragging them here, physically and mentally, but I can worry about that later. What do I say to them now? From the posters on the bedroom wall, I know they are into comics and superheroes, so I channel my inner Vinny.

"It's a magical place, a way to travel quickly around your

house," I explain, speaking clearly and confidently. "I'm going to get you out."

I take in the doorways. As expected, the bedroom is now a black-and-white memento frozen in time. One portal down, six left. I discard three of them easily: the collapsing stairs, the house, and the fire truck, all clearly after the quake. My three options are the auto repair shop, the yard, or the living room.

Living room it is.

My plan is to draw the grandmother out of the kitchen and get the four of us, along with Other Joe, out of the front door. For me, minutes have passed. In reality, it's been mere seconds.

"There's Grandma!"

"I see her," I assure the boy, catching a glimpse of her through the doorway into the kitchen. The ceiling hasn't come down yet. Felix told me that it happened not long after the quake started, though, so when I land, I need to move quickly.

"Walk with me now," I tell the boys. "Head toward the living room."

As firmly as I dare, I drag them, not allowing them time to panic. Remarkably, they don't. They're brave kids, and I'm the adult, so they trust me. The doorways rotate around us, faster than the first time I was here. "Keep your eye on that one," I tell them, pointing out our next stop. "When we go through, stay close to me. I will get you all out. Ready?"

They both nod, staring wide-eyed at the doorway.

Man, they are going to have some stories to tell.

"Count with me!" I shout.

They do, and together, we step back into the maelstrom. The living room is alive, the power of the quake unleashed in a slow-motion ballet of chaos. The kids move slowly again, and I realize their speed matches that of their environment. I'm the only one displaced.

OK, what's next?

Through the kitchen door, I see the grandmother cowering beneath a table. Her face slowly creases in confusion when she sees me, then her eyes widen when she sees I'm with the kids. She clambers onto her hands and knees, reaching out. In an almighty upheaval, the floor groans open, sending a shower of dust and chunks of stone into the air. I'm already running. By the time I reach the kitchen, the floor has split into a deep crevasse that consumes the island. The woman is up but sliding. I dart to my right, lunge, and pull her toward me. We somehow find our footing. I don't have time to be careful anymore; the ceiling is coming down, popping, and cracking in a dreadful cacophony of destruction. The room is a blur. I spin and lunge back toward the living room, pulling the woman with me. My muscles howl. Time is accelerating too, its savage motion snapping at my heels. By the time we reach the kids, real time is almost upon us. The woman grabs one of them, I snag the other, and we head toward the front door. With a sonic boom, time catches up with itself. Other Joe careens down the stairs, sees us, takes hold of the woman. The whole room shifts and bucks. One of the kids slips. I grab his collar, pull him up, and he recovers. The five of us move in unison, a spooky, lumbering circus act. We reach the hallway, and a wall of air punches us from behind, ejecting us from the house in a cloud of debris.

We tumble into the street, from chaos to mayhem. The full force of the quake is everywhere. My eyeballs feel like they're being shaken, but through the blurred madness, I see the grandmother cradling her grandson and his friend. Other Joe is on his hands and knees.

We are battered and bruised, but we made it.

We're outside. We're alive.

And then, just as before, the quake stops abruptly, like a

truck juddering to a halt. The sudden lack of movement brings a shocking, unnerving kind of peace. The air feels alive, yet oppressive. My body aches, and my skin tingles with cuts and bruises waiting to tell me they hurt.

The silence is deafening.

I turn and look at the house, still standing, but only just. I get to my feet, coughing. There were still five doorways left, but I guess I didn't need to use them.

Then I see the grandmother's face, and I know something's wrong. "Higgins," she murmurs. "Where is he?"

She calls the dog, panic building in her voice. The kids do the same, heading back toward the house. I look at Other Joe. We don't need words. We both know we need to save Higgins.

"I'll go," Other Joe says.

I hold up my left arm, the one with the time splitter. He nods, tells me to be careful. I click the button and head back into the void.

The bedroom and living room are grayed out. Five doorways remain, rotating faster now. I discard anything after the quake, which leaves two doors: the collapsing stairs and the comparative safety of the yard. The swing and the bench are there, but this time, no dog. I swear Higgins was there before.

Then it clicks: the doorways *update*.

The locations and moments may be fixed in time, but my actions can alter the details of the scene. I consider this for a minute, knowing that time isn't passing in the void. If I land in the yard, what do I do then? This could be my easiest jump yet. Grab Higgins and drag us both to one of the locations after the quake. Right?

I set my feet, lean forward, and attempt to relax. The doorway of the yard passes every second or so, but the rotation is tricky. I lock in and start my run, leaping through perfectly.

I land on the grass, which is rippling like water. The quake is well underway, thundering in a slow-motion growl. Clouds of dust hang in the air like mist. The building sways, slowly but violently. Higgins is nowhere to be seen. The back door is ajar. I hear him barking. He's inside the house!

The quake jostles me left and right as I sprint to the door. The kitchen is a mess: the floor has caved in, the island is gone. Appliances float through the air, falling jars explode like ice. Higgins cowers under the kitchen table. The ceiling beams groan, splinter, and crack. I lurch forward, diving like a goalkeeper toward the dog.

I'm moving at double speed, but my superpower is short-lived. Time begins to accelerate, as though someone is pushing the ceiling from above, trying to crush us. The dog scampers away, but I reach out and grab his collar. He turns as though to bite but changes his mind. I hug him like a bear and press the time splitter. It starts its countdown. The table legs shatter. I maneuver us into the ever-decreasing space. The poor dog's claws skitter on the uneven ground. The table and floor form a mouth that closes on me with increasing speed. I hold my hands up defensively. "No, please, no!" I cry. Dust and debris fill my vision.

Time catches up, and there is only darkness.

The void.

For once, its cold silence is a welcome relief. I laugh. Higgins licks my face, his tail wagging.

What the hell this poor dog makes of all this is anyone's guess. I kneel beside him, scratching his ears, keeping hold of his collar. I don't want to think about him wandering off in here.

Three doorways are now gray. Four remain.

The auto repair shop.

The collapsing stairs.

The apartment building after the quake.

The fire truck at sunset.

I consider my options. I have two safe exits: the apartment

and the fire truck. I could drag us to the end of the story, and we would be safe. So why don't I do it? Call it intuition. There must be a reason that time has offered the stairs and the auto repair shop.

I study the repair shop as it passes. A telephone pole falls in a shower of sparks, looping every few seconds. Beyond the doorway is a fully dimensional world. I walk forward, leaning my head to the side, trying to see a new angle through the portal.

As I get nearer, I feel the deep rumble of the quake, hear the fizzing explosion of the power cables snapping, and spot what I couldn't see before. A car in the road, the shadow of the telephone pole falling to where the car will soon be. I have a chance to save the driver of that car from a potentially horrendous death. But how?

I peer down at Higgins. His tail wags. He nudges my shins. Taking him back to this roadside nightmare risks his life all over again. Frying pan into the fire. When we land, I won't be able to keep hold of him, but we will at least be outside. I decide it's worth the risk. Luckily, he isn't a big dog. I place my hands under his belly and lift. He licks my cheek, and I time my jump.

We emerge into a scene of time-dilated chaos. The auto repair shop is moving in a slow, circular motion. The car and telephone pole are destined for each other. The concrete road ripples. Still holding Higgins, I run over the liquified earth. I place Higgins on the ground, and he walks away in a slow-motion saunter. He seems to know where he's going, and I hope I've made the right choice.

I focus back on the car and see the driver, a woman. She can't see what's about to happen. Why the hell did she carry on driving during a quake? I suppose she panicked, didn't know what to do. It's easy to forget, with all this crazy time dilation, that the quake lasts only fifteen seconds. The ground kicks and heaves. The telephone pole cracks and begins to fall, its electrical wires sparking like fireworks, painting slow bright lines across the sky.

What am I supposed to do? I can't push it. It's too heavy, even in this strange, slow-mo world. I run into the center of the road, the car now heading directly for me. I imagine what the woman has just seen, a red blur like the one I saw when Bill saved me in the church. I remain perfectly still, hoping my image will sharpen with enough time for her to see me and swerve, avoiding not only me but her date with a falling telephone pole. My hand hovers over the splitter. I must wait, but time is accelerating, making it appear to me as though the woman is deliberately speeding up. I see her clearly now, with a man beside her. Shadows in the back of the car. A family.

A burst of déjà vu hits me, and I have no idea why.

Sounds, feelings, the impact of the quake—everything is rushing to catch up to me. The quake's dull thuds turn into pounding drums. Sparks skitter and dance across the tarmac. The woman sees me, her eyes widening.

Now!

I press the splitter. The seconds can't come quick enough. She grabs the wheel with both hands, yanking it hard. The car veers to the left, and the pole falls in a shower of excited embers. She's going to miss me, but the pole is lined up to hammer me into the road like a nail. I leap back. The car misses me by an inch, the pole touches my outstretched hand, and then I'm back in the void.

I let out a triumphant cry, my heart feels like it's going to burst out of my chest. Surely, that must be it. A wonderful cold silence wraps around me as I stare up at the doorways. Three remain.

The collapsing stairs.

The apartment building after the quake.

The fire truck at sunset.

Two offer a safe exit. I can take my pick. I choose the apartment building after the quake. The doorways are spinning quickly now. I take my time to ensure a clean entry. As I arrive,

I see the entire street collapse, buildings falling into each other like dominoes, accentuated by time's acceleration as I watch. The sound intensifies, booming explosions sharpen, the speed of each impact increasing.

And then . . . it's over.

Time locks onto me again. The quake has done its worst, and I have done my best. But was it enough?

I ache all over, but I still feel the first nibble of brain freeze against the back of my skull. I will be traveling back to the present soon. I see the grandmother and the kids, crying joyously as Higgins careens around the corner, his tongue flapping.

"Thank goodness," the grandmother says, spotting me. "There you are!"

I walk over to them smiling, but it doesn't last long.

Everyone is here. Except one of us.

"Where am I?" I ask. "I mean, where's my brother?"

The grandmother looks horrified. "I thought you were him . . . He went back inside!"

"What?" I stare at the wrecked building. "Why would he do that?"

Tears well in her eyes. "He thought he saw you, said he couldn't leave you in there."

I grit my teeth, staring at what's left of the house. What happens if I travel back and leave Other Joe crushed inside the building? Felix said that we will merge when we travel back to the present. After everything I've been through, that is *not* going to be our fate. I'm going to save him.

I walk toward the building. The family calls out, telling me it isn't safe. I press the time splitter, hunker down, and push my way through what's left of the front door.

Inside the void, the doorways rotate at a nauseating speed. Five are gray, as though turned to stone. Two remain. The fire truck is clearly too late, so the stairs are my only option. And that's when I see him, Other Joe, running up the stairs, still holding the detached railing, as they split apart like the mouth of a monster.

I was right about the doorways updating. These moments aren't recorded snapshots, they are live windows into an active world that can be altered. Other Joe was inside the house searching for me when it caved in.

I time my run carefully, leap through the doorway, and slide to a halt at the foot of the stairs.

The house is a blurred explosion. The stairs skew horribly, twisting and writhing. Plaster from the ceiling is thick in the air like flakes of snow. The pathway to Other Joe is a snarling mass of splintered wood. He's falling backward, reaching into the air. There's a sudden shift in the ground, a powerful exhalation. The house is about to swallow us whole.

Knowing that a three-second countdown will be too long by the time I reach him, I press the time splitter and stride forward, dashing to my left and launching onto one of the only remaining intact stairs. Once there, I reassess, squeeze against the wall, and then leap to my right, pushing debris away as I move through the air.

I glance behind me. My previous foothold is already gone. The ground falls away, but I'm nearly there. With a final push, I launch myself, debris and shattered wood scratching against my skin. I make contact with Other Joe and pull him toward me. Now we are both falling, the world cocooning us in a narrow, airless coffin.

We were weightless, but now our mass begins to accelerate. I hear him cry out, the oscillation of time increasing the pitch. I close my eyes, and the last sound I hear is the deafening roar of the quake and the final, sorrowful moan of a dying house.

The two of us crash into the void together, coughing and gasping.

That turns into laughter.

And then, we just lie there, enjoying the glorious silence.

Eventually, Other Joe says, "I was trying to save you."

"I know. We're OK now."

He rubs the back of his neck and looks around at the vast empty expanse of the void. "What happens if we travel, you know . . . in here?"

"I don't want to know."

We approach the final doorway: the fire truck, strobing lights, a gathering of people beneath a fading pink sky. Safety.

Other Joe takes my hand. I smile at him. We are brothers, after all.

"Your lead," he says.

"No, it's your turn."

He squeezes my hand, and we leave the void for the last time.

We arrive on the street, identical twins covered in dust and debris, holding hands. We brush ourselves off. People tend to each other's immediate needs. Firemen tackle a fierce blaze nearby. The apartment building has been reduced to rubble. The quake is long gone, and so is Scarlett, I presume. Other Joe and I stand and soak in the scene, laughing occasionally, nervous energy washing through us like the occasional aftershock that pulses beneath our feet.

A policeman shouts, "Prepare for days without power, people. There will be aftershocks. Stockpile food and water."

"Thank you," Other Joe says.

I arch an eyebrow and smirk. "You would do the same for me."

We laugh, identically. It feels creepy, but what's even weirder is the thought that we're about to become one again.

He is me. I am him. But who is going to remember what?

He nudges me and points to a film crew that has set up

hastily in the street. They're interviewing the family we saved. Higgins weaves around their feet. The kids are gesticulating and talking about impossible miracles and the two brothers who save them. They call us heroes.

Brain freeze, cold as an ice pack, works its way over my shoulders and spine.

Other Joe and I turn away, our work done.

We walk the streets, where hundreds, maybe thousands of people have gathered. They work with their bare hands, meticulously sifting through rubble, some in suits and ties, searching for survivors. Other Joe tells me about Aaron Pennington. It's a horrible situation, but it's good to think of him out there now, doing what he was born to do. A huge black cloud of smoke rises over the marina. The streets are gouged with huge cracks. The air is chalky with concrete dust from the crumbling buildings.

There are heroes all over San Francisco tonight. People struggle to establish some semblance of order while working tirelessly to help others. I'm overcome by the numerous acts of kindness, decency, and love. At one point, I see a girl in a hoodie and think it's Scarlett. She's part of a relay of people digging through the rubble. Someone calls out to her and hands her a bucket. An ambulance pulls up, blocking my view. Was it her? It's unlikely, but I guess I'll never know.

I see a man, his eyes empty, face covered in patches of wet dust, being comforted by a stranger. Twenty or so people pass us carrying a fire hose, shouting, organized, helping one another. It makes me wonder what it would take for the whole world to act like this.

Regardless, it gives me hope.

Hope that Gabrielle, in her darker moments, is wrong.

Hope that we aren't beyond saving.

Hope that the future is worth protecting.

35

The streets of San Francisco are replaced by Kristin's hotel room. Other Joe and I have become one again. I'm now able to recall the mission from both perspectives, and for reasons beyond my understanding, that shared history feels completely natural.

Shadows still lurk in the back of my mind. Vague memories of a third Joe, the one who was horribly injured. Although initially intense, these thoughts immediately begin to fade, like a person shouting from the carriage of a passing train.

"Are you OK?" Alexia asks.

Memories swirl around me. "I'm all right."

She frowns. "Are you sure?"

I take a step toward her and smile. "I wasn't, but I'm all right now. Ask me again, another time."

Kristin makes tea, and I take a moment to pay my respects to this timeline. I am no longer badly injured. The future feels lighter. *Thank you, Felix, for coming back for me.* I glance down at my wrist. The time splitter has gone. I'm glad. I don't ever want to do that again.

Alexia and Kristin look at me expectantly. They want to

know everything, but for now, perhaps for the sake of my own sanity, I keep things simple. I skip the bit about there being two of me because really, it doesn't change what happened. I talk them through a singular timeline of events, saving Aaron on the bridge, getting the people out of the house, and saving the family in the car from being crushed. Kristin checks the death toll. In a somber tone, she tells me that sixty-three people lost their lives.

A vague memory surfaces, perhaps one of Other Joe's; it's hard to distinguish which are mine. I recall Kristin telling me the death toll was seventy-four. "Eleven people." I tell them, "We saved eleven people."

We are silent for a few seconds as that realization sinks in. I wish I could have saved more, but I did what I could. They want details and when their questions are finally answered, Kristin says, "It's over now, isn't it? Extempero, I mean."

"I think so," I reply. "Without objects, Emil can't travel. He can't do any harm."

I explain that I need to talk to The Continuum. Alexia kisses me on the cheek and tells me that they will be in the hotel bar, that I should join them when I'm done.

"You deserve it," Kristin says. "You're a hero."

I don't feel like a hero. I feel like I cheated my way out of my injuries. Maybe I've just been programmed, by the shared memories of *Other Joe* experiences, to expect the worst.

Alexia and Kristin leave, and I lock the door, place my silver hunter on the coffee table, and activate ICARUS. I request Iris Mendell, and after a short wait, the tendrils of our realities reach across time and join. My physical presence in the hotel room remains, but my consciousness arrives at Greystone House. The future. Iris's office.

It's getting dark outside. Ancient trees sway, shedding their leaves. The last remnants of sunlight cut across a distant loch.

Iris's office is filled with illuminated screens, on which a complex array of charts and data hovers silently. Iris stands at the far end of the room facing a large holographic display. The constellations shimmer, but substantial portions are darkened by red shadows, buried into the projected fabric like tumors.

Iris doesn't acknowledge me.

"Iris," I say, tentatively, hoping that she hasn't realized I'm here but knowing that's not the case.

She swipes a hand over the display, shutting it down, and finally turns. She looks tired. Her icy blue eyes, sunken and shaded, seem to assess me anew, like she's trying to figure out if she can trust the stranger standing before her.

"What is it? What's wrong?"

"How did you do it?" she asks. "How did you beat resistance?"

I choose my words carefully. "Have you spoken to Felix?"

"Felix is missing," she says. Her voice is cold, perhaps deliberately. "Do you know where he might be?"

"He went after Scarlett."

Her eyes widen. "How do you know that?"

"I saw him. He wanted to talk to her."

"You *saw* him? When?"

"He visited me in my present."

"How did he reach you?" Her voice is laced with uncharacteristic suspicion. "Who dragged him there?"

What did I think was going to happen? A straightforward debrief just to discuss and analyze our success?

Iris walks to the window and stares out. "I think it's time you told me what you've done, tell me *everything*."

The lies feel wrapped up like a ball of string. I know that once I start, it will unravel. But I have no choice, so I tell her my story. *All* of it. How Bill saved me in London and believed he had hidden the truth of his impossible achievement. How Scarlett somehow discovered his secrets, believed she could do more, and tried to replicate what Bill had done. How the chain continued, and Felix joined the dots, came back after I was injured, and gave me the time splitter, a second chance, hope.

Through all of this, Iris remains silent, her lips pursed. When I'm done, when I've purged all my secrets, she lets out a long sigh. "Why didn't you talk to me?"

"I couldn't. Felix made me promise."

She shakes her head. "But he knows better than this. He knows these decisions are not ours to make. What was he thinking?"

It's a good question. I'm beginning to wonder that I might never know. "He was excited, Iris. He could see the possibilities. I completed the change event and so much more. I saved innocent people. How can that be bad?"

Her eyes shimmer with anger. "Being a time traveler is hard. Of course, we want to do more, but what happens when we start changing the course of history to match *our* will? Where does it end? Do we try and fix it all?" She points at me. "And who decides who lives and dies . . . *you*, I suppose?"

"Iris, please."

She glowers. "Time is an immune system, Joseph. It was doing an amazing job of healing itself. And now, thanks to you and Bill, Scarlett and Felix, *all* of you breaking the rules, we've introduced variables that may have far-reaching consequences. The Future Change Index is red across the board." Her voice wavers with suppressed anger. "What were you thinking? Why would you change the past like this when I told you it was dangerous?"

Did I think about the repercussions? The honest answer is no. I believed Scarlett, that most people have absolutely no impact on the future. And with some help from Felix, I persuaded myself that I wanted to save the people in that house.

But is that the whole truth? Or did I do it to save myself? "They were innocent, Iris. I couldn't leave them."

"It had already happened, Joseph. It was *written*." Her jaw tightens, and she practically snarls. "*One life*. That's all it takes, you know that. One life can alter the entire course of human history."

I know she's right. We like to think of those amazing individuals who have shaped human history for the better, our greatest thinkers, scientists, activists, and leaders. But there are two sides to that coin. I don't want to think of the people who have darkened the past with their hatred and their warped ideas.

"Surely, what I just did in San Francisco, couldn't have . . . I mean, they were just kids." The truth really does have a certain ring to it, and my words sound flat and unconvincing.

Iris sighs, composing herself, absently brushing the front of her jacket. "You just don't understand," she says, "and perhaps that's my fault. The people you saved . . . their actions, their lives won't necessarily have a negative impact on the future. It isn't as simple as that, but their stolen existences will alter history. Time will spend precious energy recalibrating. We will lose existing opportunities, natural change events that took years to build. What you did, beating resistance, it's like starting again. You save a few but risk the entire future of humankind." She lets out a sour laugh. "It sounds so dramatic, and yet it's true. You, Scarlett, Felix. The three of you have caused irreparable damage, set in motion a chain of events that cannot simply be undone. This is what happens when we don't appreciate the gift that time has offered."

A long silence stretches between us.

"Iris, I think that if we can find Felix, he will make sense of this. He was convinced that beating resistance was a positive discovery, that we could do more *without* causing harm. Where is he?"

When she speaks, her voice is cold, impassive. "We don't know, and we have no way to track him. All our systems have been affected. Downstream is offline. It could be weeks before we can even begin to search for Felix." She exhales loudly. "Devon is working to get our systems up and running—only then can we make a plan. For now, I have bigger problems, travelers who want to know why their missions have disappeared."

Should I have told Iris what was going on? Of course. I may not fully understand the rules, but I knew I was breaking them. But I was blinded by my injuries, willing to do whatever it took to restore my own timeline, to get my health and my life back.

"I need time to process this," Iris says. "I thought that when we lost Bill, we would regroup, perhaps even grow stronger. I was wrong. And now I've lost them both." She sighs. "And we may have just lost the future as well."

EPILOGUE

Alexia has a video she wants me to watch on her iPad. A news report from the Bay Area, 1989. She knows I'm having the odd flashback, but she assures me this one is OK, that it's all after the quake. She explains that the ABC7 crew was uniquely positioned to get the story out to the world. They were all set for full coverage of the World Series, so when the power went out, they sprang into action. Generators, makeshift studios, reporters on the ground, a blimp in the sky. It was the most televised quake in history.

She presses play, and I see a scene I recognize. It's impossible, but I was there.

A grandmother, two kids, and their dog. It's a busy scene: lights, people, debris. "They were identical twins, right down to the shirts on their backs," the grandmother tells a reporter. "The one who saved me said they were firefighters. He *knew* the quake was coming. Somehow he knew." The reporter moves the microphone to the kids, who are practically vibrating with excitement. The kid with blond hair says, "He was like the Flash. He's a superhero! He grabbed us and teleported us or something!" His friend chips in, eyes wide as saucers: "One minute we were in my bedroom, then we're downstairs, then . . . we were outside! He moved *so fast*."

The reporter turns to the camera and gestures across the street. "As you can see, this family's home, in fact, the entire block, collapsed. These kids are right—"

"Mr.?" the second kid says, pulling at the reporter's microphone. The boy frowns, adjusts his baseball cap. "The whole place was shaking, but we didn't imagine this, it was real. He grabbed us, see, and we went through a kind of tunnel. Him and his brother saved us, my granny, and our dog too."

The grandmother nods sagely. "They were sent from a higher place, that's for sure. They saved us all. I just wish I could thank them."

The reporter turns to the camera again, his expression serious. "Who were these mysterious men? Brothers, firemen, perhaps even superheroes. Either way, the impact of their actions is standing right here, living proof that miracles can indeed happen. This is Carl Hodges in the Bay Area for ABC7."

Alexia taps the screen and points. "There you are, look."

Initially I can't see us, but then I spot two men in the distance, walking with their backs to the camera. A little blurred, but obviously twins.

She turns to me earnestly. "You saved them and that family in the car. You can't honestly tell me that was selfish."

"No . . ." I say, still not convinced.

Alexia takes my hand. "I only know what you've told me about resistance. But time didn't stop you. That means something, doesn't it?"

I stare at the iPad, itself a strange portal into the past. "I snuck up on it when it wasn't looking."

She shrugs. "Seems to me, time travel is all about saving people. You saved Amy. Bill saved you. You told me about Lucy

Romano and Philippe Chevalier and the man trapped under the stage in Paris." She points at the iPad. "And now, you've saved all these people too. It's a chain . . . a positive chain."

I hope she's right, that in the end, my quantum chain might make sense. A complicated ball of interwoven threads has unraveled, but is there a way to join them again, to weave and stitch these disparate threads together?

I don't know anymore. I'm not sure of anything.

The weeks pass slowly. I'm a mixed bag of emotions. Knowing I was injured plays heavily on my mind, as does Scarlett. When life goes wrong, we look for answers, reasons, a villain. Is Scarlett the villain in my story? Or was she really trying to help more people?

The Continuum calculates the Future Change Index. At the end of the day, they are interpreting data. Can Downstream really reveal the truth, or just a version of it that The Continuum believes? I worry about Felix too, another decent person who sacrificed himself to help me. I probably shouldn't put all of this on my shoulders. Felix is a founding member of The Continuum. He can make his own choices, but I still feel guilty. If he's in trouble, I'm part of that.

Most of all, though, I worry about *my* motivations. Was I truly acting selflessly when I went back? Or simply rewriting my timeline for my own benefit?

Vinny calls, a welcome distraction. I tell him that I'm sorry for butting in on his business, that he was right, that I should stay out of it.

"No, mate!" he says. "It must have been hard for you to deal with the whole Kassandra thing, but you were right."

"I was?"

"Yeah, Kass was kind of bossing me around. She told me to ditch quiz night *and* Cuban dancing." In a hushed tone, he adds, "I drew the line when she tried to cancel my crochet class."

"Obviously."

"I really want it to work with her, Cash. I want to get to know Charlie, I mean, Charlotte." He pauses, laughs. "No, I mean Charlie! Thing is, I mustn't lose myself in this, and I definitely don't want to lose you, mate."

"You won't, Vinny. I'm here."

He wants to hear all about my latest adventures, of course, and I fill him in as well as I can. Vinny has an inherent ability to grasp complicated time-travel concepts. I've seen his DVD collection. He's basically completed a degree in metaphysical sci-fi.

"It's difficult, this," he says. "It's like when Superman hears thousands of problems all over the world. He can't save them all, and he's Superman! It's the curse of being gifted."

"I hear you, but this is different, Vin. I broke the rules, did things I shouldn't have."

"Maybe so, maybe not. We'll see."

"What do you mean?"

He puts on his best Yoda voice. "Ancient Chinese proverb. Look it up, you will. At first, bad news it seems. Ends up being just fine, supposed to be this way, it was."

I smile, hoping he's right.

The world needs more people like Vinny.

Before he goes, in his normal voice he says, "I've been thinking, we should do something regular together."

"I would like that," I agree. "What did you have in mind?"

"Combining two of my favorite pastimes."

Vinny has so *many*, I can't even begin to guess.

"Food and curry!" he announces. "A curry club. Two

members. I'll do the cooking, or we can take turns. I don't mind, as long as we eat it all. We can review our dishes too, like proper food critics."

"It sounds amazing, mate. I'm totally in."

In the days that follow, my life returns to some semblance of normalcy. The shop, friends, time spent with Alexia. It's good. It's right. But something's missing. I was just beginning to embrace my role at The Continuum, and its absence feels palpable.

Iris doesn't contact me, and I don't want to contact her either. I'm not sure what to say. Gabrielle ignores my texts. Perhaps a stalemate is good. Maybe I need a break. It has been full-on since I was thrown back to London. Sometimes I think I'm like a cat that used up too many lives in too short a time.

Then a most unlikely ally takes pity on me. Kyoko calls occasionally. The conversations are brief, but her support feels like just the kind of help I need.

"Any news on Felix?" I ask her one day.

"No contact, no signal."

"What about Scarlett?"

"The same. Although we did discover how the focus objects' locations were leaked. One of our operatives in location services."

"An inside job."

"Yes," Kyoko replies. "Her name was Heather McKinnon. She was with us for four years. When she figured out that we were onto her, she fled."

"Was she paid by Scarlett?"

"Perhaps, or she may just have been loyal to her. I fear that this could be the beginning, rather than the end."

Lies. Deceit.

Bill's death, Felix's disappearance.

The Future Change Index crashing.

Guilt consumes me. Am I a bad omen for The Continuum? The comparative success of my mission in San Francisco is hard to reconcile. I keep thinking of Iris talking of dominoes falling, how numerous threads of humanity's story converge to form a dark decade, one that I've now helped to realize.

"I didn't mean to make matters worse," I tell Kyoko.

"I know."

"What Scarlett said she was doing, I think Felix believed her. But I'm not sure what's right anymore."

Kyoko's voice remains impassive. "Leave it for a while. Iris is trying to figure out what to do next. It's a process. Trust it. Trust us. My analysis shows that these disparate events may have a pattern. I haven't figured it out yet, but I'm confident I will soon."

"Have you heard from Gabrielle?"

"Give her space too. She will come around."

"And what about Emil Zanak?"

"We are keeping an eye on him. Without access to focus objects, he is no longer a threat. It is my personal view that he is also on a journey. We will leave the door open for him to return to The Continuum and serve as a time traveler, if he so chooses."

"Seriously? You would allow that?"

"If that is his wish. Each and every traveler is rare, unique. Losing just one is a terrible waste. Zanak has made mistakes, but if he learns, if he is willing to make amends, then we must remain willing to compromise. No matter what happens, there is always a way back."

As the days pass, I often think of the people I saved in San Francisco. Each life has power, ripples that travel through time like aftershocks. Amy tells me she's been doing a lot of deep thinking, questioning, and planning. She says she's ready to come home, to start a new chapter, whatever that brings.

I think I might know. My sister has begun her journey home,

the journey that leads her to the future. Her destiny is to become the fourth founding member of The Continuum, and her arrival in 2112 will set Iris, Bill, and Felix on the right track. Amy told me that the Extrapolation Event is formative. Without it, The Continuum could peter out and never reach its potential. What would that mean to my history? Was Amy right when she said someone was deliberately altering the past, threatening that event?

What I'm most worried about is that I could be the one who's messed it all up. What if my action stops Amy from going, since I've sent the Future Change Index into a spin and blackened the Bridgeman name? What could that mean for the Extrapolation Event?

———————

As May gives way to June, I decide it's time to stop moping around. Alexia mentioned that she had always wanted to visit the historical town of Bath, so I booked us into a nice hotel. It feels good to be away from Cheltenham, and even better to be with Alexia. Our relationship is blossoming. It feels natural, as though we've spent our lives waiting and now found each other. We don't want to waste any more time.

I look over the city, its elegant buildings cut into the hillside. Alexia is taking a shower.

Even though I try not to think about it, my mind wanders again. Why did I help those people? Was it altruistic? Is there ever a truly selfless act? I can't help but feel I've cheated time, that it won't forgive me, that I've taken my share of goodwill. There's a version of me, somewhere out there, paralyzed. The guilt continues to pile up. I feel as though I have disrespected many brave and incredible people, people who cannot change their situation and must live with their injuries. I never told Alexia about the paralyzed version of me, and I'm not sure I will.

The shower turns off.

I need to turn off as well. This isn't doing me any good. Life is too short to live in the past, to lay this guilt on myself, but unexpected memories flood my mind. Amy, shivering by a lake that once took her life. Alexia kissing me on Leckhampton Hill. Memories of being a kid, my father proud of me. They feel connected somehow, to an uncertain future in a way I don't yet understand. But as Vinny said, what seems bad now might make sense later. Opportunities to fix the future might yet present themselves.

The bathroom door opens, and Alexia emerges in her robe through a wall of steam. I'm overcome with gratitude for her, for our connection. She smiles. I'm home.

Alexia draws the curtains and tells me we have some time before dinner. Until then, she says, she has plans. She kisses me, takes my hand, and walks me to the bed.

All my worries, confusion, and guilt melt away. The future is waiting, but for now, this moment is all there is.

ACKNOWLEDGMENTS

A huge thank you to you, my readers and listeners for sharing Joe's adventures with me. You bring these stories to life. To Kay, my best friend, my partner, and my muse. Thank you for being there through the good, the bad, and the frustrating. All your hard work, heartfelt prose, enthusiasm, and research (especially for the Tang dynasty portion of the story) make Joe's travels richer and more vivid. This book asked a lot, but every chapter, character motivation, and plot twist benefited from your valuable input. The long days were worth it. Shout-out to my amazing review team for helping launch my books in a flurry of positivity. And to the awesome people on my mailing list and Facebook group for their support and kind words. It's amazing to see our community grow, and the lovely messages I receive telling me that my writing has made a difference and urging me to carry on means a lot.

Thanks, as always, to my fantastic editor, Jason Kirk—@brasswax. You always manage to spot those overlooked seams of gold and inspire me to dig deeper. And finally, thank you to Blackstone for their continued faith in me. Here's hoping we make more cool stuff together.

KEEP IN TOUCH

I have a private Facebook group and really enjoy chatting with my readers. You're welcome to join.

https://www.facebook.com/groups/nickjonesauthor

If email is your thing, you can join my reader group here.
http://NickJonesAuthor.com/SignUp

And you can follow me in the usual places:
Website: http://NickJonesAuthor.com

Facebook: https://www.Facebook.com/AuthorNickJones
Instagram: https://www.instagram.com/authornickjones/
Goodreads: https://Goodreads.com/AuthorNickJones
BookBub: https://BookBub.com/Authors/Nick-Jones
Twitter: https://Twitter.com/AuthorNickJones

You can email me too, if you like, at Nick@NickJonesAuthor.com

I read everything I receive.

AUTHOR'S NOTE

There's a joke that always makes me smile. The past, the present, and the future walk into a bar. It was tense. There would have been a time when just the thought of keeping all these plot-threads and timelines going would have melted my brain and set the Nick Jones "Panic-O-Meter" to max. Not so this time. This book, like all I've worked on, was tough, it pushed me as a writer, it wanted to unravel and fly away, but its multithreaded timeline was also hugely rewarding to create. Jim Butcher said he felt his series hit its stride with the fourth Dresden book. A part of me felt the same. A series feels somehow "proper" when there are four books available, with the promise of more . . .

Again, the key to this story was research and planning. Learning about ancient China and the Sogdian people was a pleasure. And, after the opera house fire in book three, I was keen to explore a different, more natural disaster. The Loma Prieta earthquake was captured on live television and fascinated me immediately. If you're interested, there is a lot to see on YouTube. The quote referenced when Alexia and Kristin watch the YouTube clip after Joe's first jump to San Francisco was from e 3 of the 1989 MLB World Series, originally aired on ɔC on October 17, 1989. The broadcast itself, along with the on-location news reports that followed, make for impactful, compulsive viewing, but are also incredibly sad, of course. I was aware it would require a steady hand to tackle such sensitive material and themes, but also knew instinctively that this event would feature in the finale of *The Quantum Chain*. I hope you feel I've done it justice.

I've received hundreds of emails from readers who tell me they can totally see Joe's adventures on the screen. Well, me too. It's how I do this. The camera rolls in my head and words hit the page. It means that my life will only be truly complete when my stories make their way onto the screen—I'm thinking a TV series, but movies could work too. So, if you know someone who knows someone in the biz who might be able to get the series made, email me at nick@nickjonesauthor.com. If your direct involvement leads to it being optioned (a term used by production companies who want "the option" to make it), I will give you 25 percent of my cut from that initial option payment. Feels like good karma to me.

Nick Jones
The Cotswolds,
England, 2022